Battleborne

Book Two

Wrack and Ruin

By

Dave Willmarth

All characters and events depicted in this novel are entirely fictitious. Any similarity to actual events or persons, living or dead, is purely coincidental.

Chapter 1

Silent as a shadow, the grey dwarf thief moved through the dark alleys of Nogroz, now known as Stormhaven. She was Izgren, second in command of the local Thieves' Guild, with the rank of Adept. Among the Nogroz guild members, only the Master was more skilled in the arts of deception and assassination.

Light-headed from too much blood loss, she stumbled around a corner. The sounds of her pursuers were fading, but she was not yet safe. The cursed dwarves and orcs that had invaded her city were ruthlessly hunting her and her guildmates. Already more than a score had been killed, and at least three captured.

That was her reason for being out of the den. She had hoped to infiltrate the city dungeons and free the three prisoners, one of whom was her own son.

Izgren had gained access to the lowest levels of the keep easily enough. Her people had an entire network of secret tunnels and hidden doors that formed an intricate web across the city. Including one that led from the sewers up into the dungeon via an ancient and rusting ladder. From the bottom dungeon floor she crept up a stairway that was unguarded, no surprise since the invaders thought the only access to the cells was from above. Her scouts had already warned her that half a dozen dwarven sentries guarded the thick iron door that led from the keep's main level down to the two dungeon levels.

She reached her comrades' cells without incident, and had managed to pick two of the locks, freeing her son and one other. She was nearly finished with the third lock when a pair of dwarven guards opened the nearby door. Instantly she hurled a dagger at the closest of the two, the enchanted weapon punching through his steel chest plate and penetrating deep into his shoulder. The second dwarf shouted an alarm even as he drew a short sword and shield and leapt forward to stand between his wounded companion and Izgren.

Her son and his fellow newly freed thief, both novices in the guild, rushed toward the dwarf. Her son shouted, "Finish the lock!" as he clashed with the dwarf, slamming a shoulder into the shield. He paid for his bravery with a deep gash on his arm when the dwarf struck back.

Armed only with a dagger she had handed each of them when she freed them, the two young thieves did their best to parry sword blows and harass the armored dwarf from both sides. Izgren tried to ignore her son's plight and focus on the lock in front of her. In seconds, she defeated the uncomplicated mechanism and stepped aside as their third comrade, a journeyman rank thief she'd mentored nearly five decades earlier, flung the door wide. His hand already out, he accepted a dirk from Izgren and joined the melee. Just as he reached the enemy and managed to slide his blade into the guard's back, four more dwarves descended the stair with weapons ready.

Izgren withdrew a pellet from a pouch on her belt and tossed it toward the stair. "Run!" she shouted at her son, who was now bleeding from several deep cuts. The pellet struck the ground at the dwarves' feet and erupted in a burst of foul-smelling, eye-stinging smoke. She caught a glimpse of her son turning to follow her, then screamed as she saw a sword erupt from his chest, heart's blood coating the blade. A moment later a scream that ended in a gurgle told her that the other novice had perished.

Setting aside her grief, the grey dwarf dashed away from the battle, heading toward the opposite end of the corridor, and the stairway down. If she and the remaining thief could make it through the secret hatch and close it before the dwarves caught up to them, they'd have more than enough time to disappear in the sewers while the dwarves searched for the exit. She had no doubt they'd find it quickly, but even a minute or two would suffice.

The soft footsteps of a trained thief behind her gave her some comfort. At least one of the prisoners would be freed. And her son and his friend would not be tortured for information on the guild.

Just as she reached the bottom step, the unmistakable sounds of several crossbows firing were followed immediately by a grunt behind her. Two bolts whizzed past her to strike the stone floor. She leapt to the side as two more weapons fired, those bolts passing harmlessly. But when she peeked around the edge of the doorway to look up the stairs, she found the journeyman tumbling down the last few steps, a bolt through his throat.

Tossing another smoke pellet, she dashed down the corridor, weaving from side to side in hopes of making herself harder to hit. The dwarves fired, then fired again, shooting blindly through the smoke. One of them got lucky, and a bolt punched into the back of Izgren's knee, causing her to stumble forward. She landed face-down on the stone floor with a grunt, then immediately began to scramble back to her feet. The hatch in the floor was in the second to last cell on the left, only ten or so steps away.

The dwarves had focused on the sound of her fall, and two more bolts went past her head, taking chunks from the wall at the end of the hall. A third slammed into her side, easily penetrating her leather armor. Gritting her teeth to keep from making a sound, she took the final steps to reach the cell door, then threw herself inside. Sliding across the stone floor, she fell partway through the hatch opening before catching herself. Securing both feet on the ladder, she reached up with one hand and pulled the hatch lid closed as she lowered herself through. Already she could hear the pounding of dwarven boots on the stone in the corridor above. It wouldn't take them long to find the hatch once the smoke cleared, her two wounds having left a blood trail on the cell floor.

Grabbing hold of either side of the ladder and nearly passing out from the pain, she removed her feet from the rung and allowed herself to slide down the ten feet or so to the stone platform below. Flakes of rusted iron from the ladder sliced at her hands, a few embedding themselves in her skin, but she ignored the pain. Safely on the ground, she took a moment to yank the bolt from the back of her leg. A quick inspection of the one in her side told her that removing it now would do more damage than leaving it where it was. Izgren quickly produced a health potion and gulped it down. It stopped the bleeding from both wounds, and the hole in her knee began to mend. But when she heard tapping near the hatch above, and quickly started forward through the sewer tunnel, the movement caused the wound around the bolt still in her side to reopen.

She had left the sewers at the very next manhole, knowing that the dwarves would be actively searching them as soon as they found the hatch. Now, several minutes later she was almost at her destination. Almost safe.

The invaders had thoroughly searched the sewers already, seeking her guild's den after her master had ordered the initial attempt on the new king's life. They had discovered a few of the hidden doors that led to weapons and supply caches, even a few tunnels. They'd searched every building, patrolled the rooftops, and encountered several of her people, resulting in loss of lives on both sides. But the one place they hadn't searched was where she was heading now.

A few more staggering steps, her hand holding a thick cloth to her side to keep blood drops from leaving a trail. She rounded a last corner and tripped again, her shoulder slamming against the stone of the outer wall. A quick look to either side, and she located a particular stone, slightly off color in one corner. Pressing the stone three down diagonally to its left, she waited, gasping in pain as a doorway slid silently inward. Not waiting for it to open fully, she stepped inside the wall and touched another stone as she passed. The door slid shut just as silently, and she let herself collapse to the floor with her back against the wall.

Outside, the sound of pounding boots drew closer. She held her breath, tears of pain and sorrow streaming down her cheeks. A moment later the pursuers passed by the hidden door and continued down the alley.

Lightheaded from exertion and blood loss, unable to stand, she simply rolled to her hands and knees. Keeping one hand pressed against the bolt in her side, she crawled onward. If she could make it to her master, he would be able to remove the bolt that she suspected had penetrated her liver, and heal her.

A minute later she detected soft footfalls approaching ahead of her. With a sigh of relief, she allowed herself to fall onto her uninjured side. The pain was enough to make her gasp as she lost consciousness.

*****

The orcs had been marching nonstop for two days and a night. Their War Chief, An'zalor, had threatened to take their heads and mount them on stakes outside the city if they failed to capture the mine that now lay just a mile ahead of them. The mine had belonged to the War Chief, until his dishonorable behavior during the sacred arena trials had forced him to concede it to the Chimera King. Many of their fellow orcs had abandoned the city in the days since, unwilling to follow the disgraced An'zalor.

Some had accompanied the new king of Stormhaven, following the War Chief's cousin Gr'tok in a caravan to Stormhaven to begin a new life. Others had been preparing to leave in large groups, to form independent villages of their own. Until word passed through the city that An'zalor had set an ambush for the defectors and specifically targeted Gr'tok's family. Another dishonorable act.

That night the guards at the eastern gate had been drugged into unconsciousness, and more than two hundred orc families had fled the city. They did not remain together, or use wagons or beasts of burden to carry their belongings, as this would have made them easy to track down and murder. Instead they scattered through the woods on foot, moving fast and changing direction often. Some had plans to meet up in predetermined locations after a month or two. Others simply kept going in search of a new place to settle.

Shortly after the few surviving scouts from the failed ambush of Max's caravan returned with word of his brother's death, An'zalor stormed out of his fortress and shouted for his regular troops to take up arms. He spat and cursed at them, stomping back and forth in front of the barracks building as he waited for the warriors to gear up and get into formation. When the last of the warriors dashed from the barracks, An'zalor grabbed the unfortunate orc by the neck and lifted him into the air.

"Too slow! I have no use for weak or lazy warriors!" With a roar of rage he slammed his victim onto the ground, then stomped on the warrior's head. The others went silent at the sound of the crunching skull.

"The puny toy king has taken over the northern mine." He growled to his troops as he moved back to stand in front of the orderly lines. "You will reclaim it! We are at *war* with Stormhaven!" The troops stomped the ground or slammed weapons against shields as they roared their approval. "Kill anyone you find in or near the mine, and send me their heads to decorate my city walls! You have six days. If you fail me, I will mount *your* heads, and those of your families, on the road to the gate as a reminder of the consequences of failing your War Chief!"

Four hundred orcish warriors promptly marched out the gate on foot, their long and muscled legs allowing them to keep a fast pace. Behind them, other orcs scrambled to load a supply wagon and follow. Far ahead, a score of mounted scouts ranged through the woods and fields, reporting back every few hours.

The warriors had been driven hard, their commander ruthless in his ambition. Gr'tok's former position as lead Commander was up for grabs, and retaking the mine would help him earn that title. The column paused in their march only twice per day, and once in the middle of the night, to rest and eat for an hour. Orcs had tremendous stamina, and the well-trained warriors made the march with little complaint. Though many had lost faith in their War Chief, the opportunity to fight in a real battle outside the arena was a great motivator. All but the very youngest were veterans of many small border skirmishes, but none had been alive long enough to remember the larger pitched battles of the war against the dwarves, elves, and humans.

Now, just a mile from the mine, the Commander had called a halt. The orcs had no need for stealth, believing that they vastly outnumbered the Stormhaven forces. Fires were lit, meat roasted, and ale passed freely among the troops. The sun had set, and they would rest until sunrise, when the attack would begin.

In his tent, Commander Iz'tag studied the map that one of the scouts had just handed to him. The road they were camped next to was clearly marked, as were the surrounding hills, fields and forest. Just to the north was a mining pick symbol indicating the location of the mine.

"How many?" He growled at the scout.

"We can not know for sure, as many remain inside the mine. But from the boot and wagon tracks we've found, we believe as many as two hundred dwarves. And we saw twenty or more of the traitor orc warriors." He paused and pulled out a hand-drawn sketch on tattered parchment. "They've already begun constructing a fortification. There is a thick wooden gate across the entrance to the mine, and a twenty foot high wall that extends in an arc about one hundred feet out. They have not yet installed the gate in that wall, though they were working to assemble it when I left."

"Dwarves and traitors." The leader spat in disgust. "No sign of the king?"

"There were many sets of wagon tracks leaving the mine and heading further north. We believe the caravan continued on several days ago. There are also signs of more recent mounted patrols."

"That explains why the frightened dwarves are scrambling to finish their gate. They must already know we are coming." He stared at the map. The mine was built directly into the side of a cliff. "Tell me about the terrain."

"There is forest surrounding the mine, except for the cliff side. It has been cut back to provide lumber for the wall, and there is now a two hundred foot clear zone along the entire wall. The back side of the mountain behind the mine is not steep, but the cliff face is sheer and extends upward nearly three hundred feet. There is a stream nearby, well outside the walls." The scout paused. "If we had more time, we could simply lay siege and let them die of thirst."

"Time is not a luxury we have." The commander shook his head. "An'zalor gave us six days. We've marched for two, so we have, at most, three days to kill these dwarves and seize the mine. A rider with spare mounts could return to the War Chief in a day and a night if he pushes his animals to their limit." He tapped the mining pick image on the map. "No, we must assault the mine at first light and crush them quickly. When we breach the wall, any survivors will retreat into the mine. In those tight spaces, the cursed dwarves are effective and stalwart fighters. Our numbers will mean little, as only a few of our warriors at a time can face them."

The orc leader tapped one sharpened nail against a lower tusk as he considered his options. "Wake four squads and put them to work felling trees. And dig a few wood kiln pits. By morning I want twenty stout ladders, and as much wood pitch as we can make. We shall see how anxious the dwarves will be to defend burning walls."

*****

Max was enjoying himself. He, Dalia, Smitty, and Dylan had spent half a day exploring the tunnels and caverns near Stormhaven. They'd run into a dozen fights with creatures of the underworld, including a solitary stonetalon, and a nest of rock spiders. The fights with lower level monsters hadn't earned any experience for Max, Dalia, or Smitty. But Dylan had leveled up twice and was close to gaining a third. Dalia informed them that the rock spider meat would be a welcome addition to the menu at the tavern back in Stormhaven.

After a long day with Redmane dealing with the administrative issues of his new kingdom, Max had found Smitty and Dylan in the tavern. The three had gotten roaring drunk while they reminisced about old times, and lost friends. They shared their stories of the time spent in this new world so far, until Smitty had passed out cold and fallen to the floor.

Dalia had found them in the morning, much too early for their liking, and suggested the outing. It was part scouting mission, part group dynamics training, and might have gone on all day. Except that Max received a notification that, though he'd been expecting it, he'd hoped wouldn't happen so soon.

Attention!
The Northern Gold and Silver Mine is under attack!

Quest Received: Defend the Mine!
Repel the invaders and protect your property.
As ruler of Stormhaven and owner of the mine, you may share this quest with any citizens or allies you choose.

Max sighed, calling a halt. "Hold on guys, we need to head back." He waited as Dylan, who had been in the lead as their tank, stopped and turned toward him. "The orcs have just attacked the mine."

Without a word, the others followed him at a jog as they retraced their steps back to the city. When they passed through the gate to the inner keep an hour later, Redmane was waiting for them. Behind him were Gr'tok and thirty or so orc warriors, along with a company of fifty dwarves, all armed and armored.

"How'd you know?" Max asked, coming to a halt and shooting a look over his shoulder at a heavily panting Dylan. Ogres were not made to run long distances, and the poor guy looked about ready to collapse.

"As your Chamberlain, I received the same notification you did." His first minister replied calmly. "As did your other councilors. King Ironhand has already dispatched two mounted companies to support the forces at the mine. I took the liberty of bringing them here and sending them through the portal to the outpost. That puts them several hours closer than they'd be had they left directly from Darkholm."

"Thank you, Redmane. Well done. How long ago did they leave?"

"Not ten minutes ago." The old dwarf replied. "They are mounted on battle boars, and will reach the mine by morning."

"Much faster than we'll get there, I'm afraid." Gr'tok approached, bowing his head to Max. "The battle may be over long before we get there on foot."

Redmane cleared his throat and nodded toward the stables. There stood a large, sturdy dwarven wagon with two boars hitched to the front. "We have made arrangements for your ogre companion to be able to travel more quickly than he would on foot."

"My own chariot!" Dylan pumped a fist into the air. Then looked at his still bare feet and wiggled his toes. "I really appreciate it, Redmane. You da man! Uh, dwarf!"

Max made a few quick decisions. "Alright, my group will ride on the wagon. The rest of you, follow on foot at your best possible speed. Redmane, let's make arrangements for more wagons for next time. In fact, if you can get more today, send them through behind us and they can catch up to the guys on foot." The dwarf nodded his head.

"Arrangements have already been made. Wagons were ordered yesterday, though they were intended for trade, not troop transport. They were scheduled for delivery in three days, but I have sent a request, along with a significant amount of gold, that they be rushed. Hopefully we can send them along in the morning."

"Can't we borrow some of the wagons the orcs brought here?"

Gr'Tok shook his head and pointed at the wagon. "Most of the others were sold to merchants after we arrived, to recoup the gold the families paid for them. Those remaining were sent back to the Way Station to bring back crops, ore from the mine, and whatever game the hunters have brought in."

"Maybe try to borrow some from Darkholm? Offer the owners whatever payment you think is reasonable to compensate them for any lost business, or whatever. If you have to, offer to replace their used wagons with one of the new ones." Max was already walking toward Dylan's wagon.

"We shall do all we can." Redmane replied coolly. Max thought he might have offended the dwarf, but didn't have time to worry about it right then.

"Gr'Tok you guys get there as soon as you can, but don't wear yourselves out. You'll need to have the strength to fight when you arrive." Max waited as the orc Commander nodded.

"We'll be there in two days, tops. Faster if the wagons catch up to us. You just hold on until we get there."

"Yeah, save some o' them orc bastards fer us!" the dwarven Commander, whose name Max didn't know, shouted. He had the grace to look embarrassed when Gr'tok turned toward him. "Erm… present company excepted, o' course."

Max had to grab hold to keep from falling on his butt as Dylan flicked the reins and sent the two boars forward with a lurch. Redmane activated the portal as the ogre turned his team, and a moment later they were inside the portal room at the lowest level of Regin's outpost.

The exit door and corridor were more than wide enough for the wagon to pass through. Dwarves, for beings of short stature, always seemed to build greatly oversized structures. Wide hallways, high ceilings with grand arches. Max chuckled slightly, remembering an old joke about why the natives on King Kong's island built that massive wall to keep him out of their village, then built equally massive doors.

With Dalia navigating, Dylan drove the team down the long corridor to the exit. Max had worried he'd need to break open the door at the end, but apparently the mounted force ahead of them had taken care of it. The stone door with Max's image burned into it lay broken and scattered on the ground outside the tunnel. Max and the others dismounted and moved the larger pieces of debris out of the way to keep from breaking a wheel, and two minutes later they were on the move again.

As they departed, Max could hear the chant of the dwarven companies as they marched alongside the orcs down the corridor far behind.

A quick check of the map on his interface, and Max guessed they would make it in a day if the boars didn't get tired and slow down. He'd take them directly across the old battlefield, confident that he and Dalia could heal them through the damage for the short time it would take to cross.

On his left shoulder, Red appeared as if sitting between the studs of his armor. "So, you're off to take on a whole army yourselves, are ya?"

"Yep. I figure to kill them all single-handed." Max looked sideways at her as he whispered. "These guys are just here to help me loot when it's over."

Red snorted, making a hand gesture that Max assumed was considered rude in leprechaun society. "Just remember, if ya get yourself killed, ya get me killed as well. And I'm too pretty to die."

"Duly noted." Max replied. His feisty little companion was quite lovely, after all. And if he teased her about her looks, her wicked temper might manifest itself. As he considered her tiny form atop his shoulder, a reminder struck him, and he cursed loudly. "Ah, dammit!"

"What?" Everyone in the wagon, including Red, asked in unison.

"I was supposed to have dinner with Josephine tomorrow night."

"Who's Josephine?" Dylan asked.

"Lil tart of a gnome that's lookin to climb Mount Max." Red replied with a snort.

"She's a gnome that runs an inscriptionist shop. Sold me most of the spells that I know." Max replied for Dalia's sake.

Dylan looked Max up and down, then grinned. "Are gnomes a lot taller in this world than I think they are?"

"Ha!" Red stood up on Max's shoulder. "Taller than me, shorter than Dalia."

Dylan didn't say a word, just reached out a fist for Max to bump.

"No way I'm going to make dinner. And I don't know how to get word to her in time."

"Yup. You're totally screwed, boss." Smitty added his two cents. Dalia just looked at the three of them, shaking her head. Though the three Battleborne could see and hear Red, the dwarfess could not. To her the conversation was disjointed and odd.

All the fights and completed quests since the arena had not quite given him enough to level up to twenty. He was short a little more than a hundred thousand experience points. He was looking forward to reaching level twenty, if for no other reason than Red had told him that other people, non-Battleborne people, would then be able to see her. He could stop worrying about appearing to be a madman talking to an imaginary friend.

As they passed through the ancient battleground, Max spoke to Dylan. "This might sting a bit. This place is cursed, and will damage you a little every second. Dalia and I can heal everyone through it." He looked at the dragon bones off in the distance. "That reminds me, I'm going to have to try to bribe Steelbender to make you a dragonscale chest piece." He eyed the massive ogre whose weight was making even the sturdy dwarven wagon creak a bit. "Might take all of the scales I've got left."

He shifted his gaze to Dalia, who was already casting heals on everyone but Max. "If we're not in a hurry on the way back, let's stop here for a day. You and the others can harvest the extra powerful herbs, and I'll search for more dragon bits."

It didn't take long for them to pass beyond the boundaries of the cursed land. The party had weathered the damage without issue. The boars leading the wagons had misbehaved a bit, confused and angered by the damage from seemingly nowhere. Dylan managed to keep them under control mainly with brute strength, deep growls, and threats to make them into pork chops.

Another hour or so further along, they stopped briefly to allow the boars to drink at a stream. They were just getting back underway when two orc scouts on tired-looking mounts came into view. They were moving at a full gallop, and Max waved for them to slow down before their mounts dropped.

As they drew closer, both orcs dismounted, leaving their ja'kang to stand with drooping heads and sprinted over to the wagon. Both thumped fist to chest in salute before the first orc shouted, "Chimera King! A large force of An'zalor's troops is marching northward. Our sergeant sent us to warn you, we believe they are heading for the mine!"

Max nodded. "Thank you for the warning. They have already attacked the mine, and we're on our way there. You should have passed a force of mounted dwarves on the way here?"

"We saw a dust cloud in the distance, sire. But did not pause to investigate. It was moving quickly southward, so we hoped it was allies."

"How many orcs did the War Chief send?" Smitty asked.

"Four hundred." The second scout answered. "They were marching rapidly and without pause when we last saw them."

"Good." Max nodded his head. "Then they'll have been tired when they attacked. Let's hope that the engineers and miners managed to secure some sort of defensive structure before the enemy arrived." He pulled some of the baker's pastries from his inventory, as well as a bottle of Firebelly's Finest. Handing them over to the scouts, he said, "You two wait here. Your mounts need a break, and some food, and I'm betting you do too. There's a stream just behind us, and a column of reinforcements coming. Wait for them at the stream, and guide them to the mine."

The scouts bowed their heads in unison, then saluted. "Thank you, Chimera King."

Dylan flicked the reins and once again got the giant boars moving. Max gritted his teeth, anxious to get to the battle and help defend his people, and frustrated by the lack of a Humvee or a transport chopper to get him there.

Chapter 2

The orc forces stood just inside the tree line, staring with hatred at the dwarves and traitor orcs manning the fortification. Despite their commander's rush, the dwarven engineers had managed to construct and install the gate on the outer wall before they arrived. It wasn't pretty, but it was solid, and functional. On the back side, four massive iron brackets supported three heavy logs that acted as braces to keep the gate closed. The logs extended across the entire back of the gate, and six feet to either side. The brackets themselves were secured to the wall with iron bolts a foot long and as wide as a dwarf's wrist. It took four strong orcs or dwarves at least half a minute to remove the bracing logs to open the gate.

Not that the dwarves had any plans to open it anytime soon.

"Is our surprise ready?" Commander Iz'tag asked his lead scout, who stared up at the sky for a moment.

"Not yet, but soon. We should begin the attack now, to ensure the diversion is successful."

"Agreed. Begin the attack." Iz'tag nodded, crossing his arms. "Send the first hundred."

The scout, who served as the commander's second on this mission, raised a fist holding a single arrow as he roared "Attack!"

Up and down the tree line, three hundred and fifty orcs roared a challenge toward the fortification, slamming weapons together or knocking them against shields. One hundred massive green-skinned brutes charged forward across the open kill zone.

Almost immediately arrows and crossbow bolts began to fly from the ramparts. Orcs with long bows sent long arrows toward their former neighbors and clan mates. Dwarves sent a volley of deadly crossbow bolts through the spaces between logs. Here and there, charging orcs faltered and fell, or staggered from an impact but managed to continue forward.

The distance from the trees to the wall wasn't great, and the orcs covered the two-hundred-foot span quickly. Still, the withering fire from the defenders took down more than thirty of them, and wounded another ten.

Those that reached the wall formed up quickly. Half of them raised shields high above their heads and formed a line along the base of the wall, covering themselves and their comrades who swung massive axes at the wooden palisade with powerful arms.

Unable to hit their targets from above, a dozen dwarves hopped down from the wall and moved to shoot their crossbows through the narrow gaps in the lower part of the wall, aiming for the faces and the sensitive groins of the orc axe and shield wielders. At such close range, they could hardly miss. They shouted and laughed with each other as the orcs on the other side of the wall screamed in pain and rage. And the moment one of the shield bearers took a hit and lowered his shield, the orc archers atop the wall took advantage of the opening and made them pay.

Enraged, several of the axe wielders dropped their weapons and produced spears, jamming them through the same gaps the dwarves had just utilized. Most of the dwarves leapt back, or to one side, to avoid the powerful jabs, but two of their number had been focused on reloading and moved too slow. One took a spear through the gut, the blade severing his spine on its way through. The other took a nasty gash in his side, his ironlike ribs deflecting the blade that had managed to penetrate his chainmail.

The entire wall extended less than three hundred feet from end to end. The hundred orcs who had charged were clustered to the right of the gate, focusing on breaking through the wall. Unable to control themselves, a few more orcs dashed from the tree line, sprinting toward the wall. Archers took down all but one, who leapt high in the air when he reached his brethren. His feet landed atop one of the shields and he thrust with his legs, reaching up with an empty hand to grab the roughly pointed end of a log at the top of the wall. With a roar he used the momentum to pull himself up and over the top, swinging a sword with his free hand.

Encouraged, the commander shouted, "Second wave!" and a moment later another hundred orcs charged forward. One third of these worked in pairs, carrying a makeshift ladder over their shoulders as they ran.

Seeing this, a dwarven sergeant atop the wall shouted, "Ladders! Focus fire on the ladder bearers!"

Those dwarves still atop the wall, along with the orc archers, gladly complied as two dwarves quickly finished off the orc who'd made it over the top. One severed his leg at the knee, the other crushed his thick skull with a war hammer as he fell.

The archers took down nearly half of the ladder bearers as they crossed the kill zone, leaving eight ladders to reach the wall. The moment the heavy wooden constructs hit the wall, orcs with swords and spears began to scramble upward. Many caught arrows to the face or chest as they climbed, the defenders above firing down at nearly point blank range. Those who were struck fell backward onto their climbing comrades, or to one side atop the shield bearers. For half a minute, it was a massacre. But each time a defender had to draw another arrow or reload a crossbow, the climbers got a little closer to the top. Eventually, the dwarven sergeant called for a change in tactics.

"Drop yer crossbows! Time to get dirty!"

All along the section that was being hit, dwarves produced axes and hammers, halberds and even a few daggers. They happily launched themselves at the faces of the orcs as they reached the tops of their ladders. The orc and dwarf defenders farther down the wall continued to fire ranged attacks at the climbers, while those below the rampart still harassed the axe wielders trying to break through.

The fighting was brutal, and the defenders began to lose more lives, at about a rate of one for every ten invaders killed. The rampart became slick with blood, causing melee fighters to slip here and there. Orcs roared in fury at dwarves who shouted insults and challenges. Screams of the dying on both sides echoed off the cliff face.

"There's the smoke signal." The lead scout pointed toward the sky above the fortification.

Iz'tag nodded once, and the scout grabbed his bow. A moment later he sent a flaming arrow high into the sky, signaling the fifty orcs they'd sent on a special pre-dawn mission.

Both orcs leaned forward in anticipation as they waited for the trap to be sprung. It was only a few seconds before a massive boulder the size of a wagon wheel plummeted the three hundred feet from the top of the cliff to smash into the ground just inside the wall. The rock bounced once, slamming into three dwarves and crushing them against the inside of the wall.

As one, the orcs roared their excitement even as shouts of alarm rose inside the wall. Dwarves' gazes flew upward in time to see three more heavy rocks fly from atop the cliff.

The sergeant wasted no time. "We cannot stand against them rocks! Retreat into the mine. Set the fuses!"

Almost as one, the dwarves took a final shot at the orcs in front of them, then leapt from the walls. Their orc companions did the same, growling in fury at having to abandon the wall so quickly. The healthy helped the wounded as they scrambled toward the mine entrance and the open gate there. More rocks tumbled down, but the watchful defenders were mostly able to avoid them.

Behind them, orc invaders were topping the ladders unopposed and leaping to follow their foes, cutting a few down from behind. A rear guard of dwarves turned and equipped shields, moving backward steadily as they engaged the orcs, giving the others time to reach the mine. Immediately another volley of crossbow bolts and arrows slammed into the attackers facing the rear guard, knocking many of them down. The dwarves continued their orderly retreat, covered by their brethren, losing two more before they were through the gate.

A forest of spears and halberds massacred the closest orc invaders directly in front of the gate, pushing them back for long enough to close it. Unlike the palisade and its gate, this one was made of wood *and* iron. Ten feet wide and twelve tall, the massive door sported two dozen sharp spikes that protruded a foot out from its face. Several orcs who'd been rushing forward as the gate closed were impaled on those spikes, a few of them mortally wounded. Others braced themselves and held back, resisting the pressure of other orcs rushing up behind. They didn't fare much better, though, as a score of crossbow bolts flew through openings in the gate and mowed them down as well.

At the same time, several of the orcs in the area between the gate and the outer wall fell to friendly fire. They'd moved in so quickly that the orcs atop the cliff hadn't halted their rain of death fast enough. Half a dozen large rocks crushed orcs as they landed, or slammed into them on the bounce. One rock landed atop another and shattered, injuring a dozen orcs with the sharp shrapnel.

Inside the mine, dwarves formed a shield wall four feet back from the gate. A few orc spears were launched toward the gate, but most clanged off the metal and fell to the ground. Those few that made it through the openings in the door simply struck shields, doing no damage. Dwarven crossbows picked off any orcs who dared to get within ten feet of the gate.

Two healers assisted wounded dwarves and orcs alike in a staging area set up in a side room off the main shaft. Food and water were passed around to the defenders, who hunkered down and prepared themselves for a long fight.

The two forces were at a stalemate. Inside the mine, the sergeant chuckled. They had food, water, and ammunition enough to keep the orcs at bay for a week. And reinforcements were surely on the way.

Outside, Iz'tag strode through the now open main gate, snarling in fury. His surprise had perhaps been too effective. He'd wanted to wound a large number of dwarves, weakening the defending force. Instead he'd frightened them into retreating into the mine, making for a much tougher nut to crack. Frustrated and angry, he kicked the helmed head of a dwarf that had been crushed by a falling boulder. Time was not on his side.

*****

Though Dylan pushed the boars as much as he safely could, the wagon remained slow. By the time they reached the way station where Max had left the orc family in charge, the farmer reported that the mounted dwarven troops had passed through four hours earlier.

Max thanked the orc, taking a moment to check on him and his family as Smitty and Dylan unhitched the boars and traded them for a pair of ja'kang. The carnivorous horse beasts were not as hardy as the boars, but the boars were exhausted. And the horses could manage the wagon for the short trip from the way station to the mine, despite their extreme objections to being harnessed. They resisted mightily until Dalia used her druid magic to calm them enough to accept the harnesses.

There was a brief delay when one of the mounts nipped at Dylan's arm. He reacted by shouting, "Ow! Stupid horse!" and punched it in the head. The blow from the massive ogre fist knocked the creature senseless, requiring them to bring in and hook up a replacement.

Max told the farmer that another force was behind them on foot, and asked that he be prepared with water for the troops, and food if possible. Even if it was just bread. He gave the orc a small sack of gold coins for his trouble, asked him to send scouts to search for any additional approaching orc forces, and they were off.

The group and their wagon covered the five miles to the mine in half an hour. As they drew close to the last bend in the trail before reaching the mine, a dozen dwarves mounted on battle boars emerged from the brush on either side of the road. One took up position directly in front of the wagon and raised an empty hand to signal them to stop.

"Greetings, King Max. I be Captain Skullsmasher." The dwarf bowed slightly atop his mount, which snorted as if in greeting.

"Greetings, Captain Skullsmasher. How are things at the mine? Is the battle already over?"

The dwarf shook his head. "Nay, there still be plenty o' fightin to do. Our people could no' hold the walls, and have retreated into the mine. They be safe enough in there fer now, but there be two hundred or so orcs inside the palisade. We got em surrounded."

A shout from above caused Max and everyone else to look up. High above them Max spotted a group of orcs with their backs to him, fighting. The captain chuckled. "Ah, good. The orc commander thought to get sneaky. Sent some o' his own up around the back o' the hill and onto the clifftop, where they tossed big rocks down on our people. Soon as we saw what they'd done, I sent a hunnert o' me riders up after em. I expect they'll be... yep. There ya go!" He hooted with glee as several of the orcs were pushed over the edge to fall three hundred feet atop their fellow orcs below. A moment later, a dozen more went over, screaming as they fell.

The fighting continued as the group below watched, fascinated. A few more orcs fell over the edge, while more died where they stood atop the cliff. Within two minutes, a line of mounted dwarves appeared at the edge, waving a banner.

"That be the all-clear. I hope them ones that took the fall landed on a few more down here!" the captain seemed downright jovial. There were few things dwarves loved more than battle. Especially a battle they were winning.

"Have you tried speaking with them yet?" Max asked.

"Aye, I shouted a bit at their commander. Told him me friend Orby Steelballs be inside o' that mine. He owes me fifty gold after our last game o' dice. I kindly warned the orc that if he kills old Steelballs before I get me money, I'll be very angry." The dwarf's grin was wide as his fellows chuckled.

Max shook his head. "How about you take me to talk to him? Maybe I can get them to surrender. I know you'd love nothing more than to kill every orc in there, but I'd rather not lose any dwarven lives in the process."

"Aye, o' course ye can try. I'd not sacrifice any o' me lads if ye can prevent it." The captain bowed his head slightly, then turned his mount. "Follow me."

Dylan guided the wagon behind the mounted dwarves as they rounded the bend in the trail and moved through the last of the trees toward the palisade. Looking left and right, Max saw mounted dwarves waiting just inside the shade of the trees.

Abandoning the wagon, Max and company strode forward on foot. Dylan walked next to Max, both of them carrying tall shields. Behind them, Smitty and Dalia were joined by the captain, who chuckled. "Walkin behind these big fellas makes me feel like a wee lad again."

Dalia snorted. "They're not very smart, but good fer stoppin' arrows and spells."

Max ignored the jibe from his friend, focusing on the large orc with red stripes painted across his face that stood atop the wall near the gate. About halfway across the kill zone, he called a halt, then shouted up at the orc commander.

"Hello there. I'm Max, King of Stormhaven, and that's my mine behind you." He raised a hand in a friendly wave. "I must have forgotten to put up a *no trespassing* sign when I was here before. My mistake." Behind him Dalia groaned.

"This mine is once again the property of War Chief An'zalor! Leave this place, toy king. Go back and huddle in your hole in the ground!"

Max took a second to check his UI just to make sure, then called out. "Says here I still own it! My people are inside the mine, you and your people are still out here, just knocking on the door. You're outnumbered, and I'm betting you don't have much food or water." He paused, looking for a reaction on the commander's face. There wasn't one, but the orc behind him with a longbow over his shoulder began to shift nervously.

"You can't win here." Max continued. "All you can do is get your warriors killed. Surrender now, and I'll let you all live."

"We do not surrender! Especially to a mixed breed fool who believes himself a king!"

Max sighed. He was thinking about what to say next when several large rocks crashed to the ground behind the wall. There was a scream that ended abruptly as at least one orc fighter perished. The captain, who had leaned far to his left to peer past Dylan's bulk, clapped his hands. "Me boys up top are gettin' impatient."

Not thrilled with the tactic, especially while he was speaking with the enemy commander, Max asked "Can you get them to stop from here?"

Nodding once, the captain whistled loudly, a shrill three-note signal, then waved up at the troops atop the cliff before making a cutting motion across his own neck. An answering whistle echoed down from above, and he winked at Max. "All done."

Turning back to the wall, Max tried a different tactic. Taking a deep breath, he shouted, "I'm sure many of you witnessed my companions and I fighting in the arena trials. And you also saw your War Chief behave without honor, trying to cheat at the trials, violating your sacred ritual. Why throw away your lives for a coward and tyrant without honor?"

Atop the wall, the scout whispered in his commander's ear. "We are doomed here. We have no

35

hope of capturing the mine now, let alone holding it. We are outnumbered and trapped. Even should we somehow escape and outrun those mounted dwarves all the way back to the city on foot, An'zalor would mount our heads on stakes for failing him."

Iz'tag's body practically vibrated with rage. "You would surrender to this honorless dog?"

The scout shook his head. "I watched him battle in the trials. He fought well, fought with honor. And he is speaking the truth when he says An'zalor defiled the trials with his treachery. If you were not there yourself, I know you have heard others speak of it. Despite the treachery, this Chimera King overcame the challenges and became an Arena Champion."

"NO!" Iz'tag shouted at the top of his lungs, as much to the scout as to Max. "We will fight and die as warriors should! And we will take many of you with us! I will eat your heart, toy king! Then deliver your head-"

Iz'tag never finished that threat, as his own head slowly rolled forward, separating from his body to fall to the ground in front of the gate. A second later the scout shoved the body forward off the wall as well, watching it land near the head. He wiped the commander's blood from his sword with a cloth before sliding it back into a scabbard on his back.

"Chimera King! I am Ag'thorn, and I have just relieved Iz'tag of his command. You are correct, we can not win this battle. There is no honor in needless suicide. I would speak with you to discuss terms." He turned as the sounds of battle rose up behind him. A few scattered orcs who were zealously loyal to their War Chief, or to Iz'tag, tried to battle their way to Ag'thorn. Smarter orcs, who had come to the same realization as the scout, quickly put them down.

Outside the wall, Max guessed what was happening. Though he'd never dealt with serious insubordination during his time in his nation's service, his later career as a private soldier had required him to deal with it more than once. He'd even had to put down an outright mutiny, during which a disgruntled subordinate tried to shoot him in the back. His response then had been just as fast, brutal, and final as the orcs'. "You are welcome to join me here, where it's safe to talk." He motioned for the others in his group to step back a bit, then sat on the stump of a felled tree.

The gate opened a short time later, and the orc scout walked out alone. There were a few angry shouts from within the enclosure, but no more sounds of battle. When the orc drew close, Max got back to his feet. "Thank you for coming to speak with me." He smiled at the orc, being sure to display all his fangs.

"Thank you for the opportunity to choose life." The orc nodded his head in respect.

"I'm sure you are aware that Commander Gr'tok and a few hundred of your people have already joined me as citizens of Stormhaven. I have found them to be honorable, hard-working, and likeable people in the time we've spent together. Should you and your warriors be willing to swear an oath of allegiance, I would be proud to have two hundred more skilled and honorable warriors."

"And if we do not wish to join you?" Ag'thorn asked, his voice a deep growl of suspicion.

"Then I would require each of you to swear an oath never to take up arms against me or mine, and allow you to walk away from here." Max paused. "But from what I know of your War Chief, he will not welcome you back in defeat."

The orc nodded. "He has promised to mount our heads on stakes should we fail. There is no returning to the clan for us, that is true. But to live among dwarven dogs…" His voice faded as he surveyed the mounted force of dwarves in front of him.

"Not just dwarves, Ag'thorn. Other orcs, kobolds, gnomes, trolls, ogres, and eventually all races, light or dark. Except grey dwarves, cuz screw those little bastards." The orc chuckled at that. "Stormhaven will be a truly free city that welcomes any who are willing to live in cooperation with the other races. We will grow bigger, and stronger, and eventually I intend to take your city from An'zalor. You could have a hand in running it when that time comes."

Ag'thorn looked over his shoulder at the orcs lining the top of the palisade. "I am willing to join you. I saw you fight with honor, Chimera King. I believe that *you believe* what you say, though I wonder if you have the strength to accomplish your goal."

"Then add your strength to mine. We have a better chance to accomplish it together." Max held out a hand.

Ag'thorn shook his head, his hands remaining at his side. "I will speak with my warriors first. Some will wish to strike out on their own, I think, rather than join you."

Max retracted his hand. "I'll give you an hour. If it helps, let them know they don't have to continue to serve as warriors, or live underground. They can become farmers or crafters, or merchants. We are a new kingdom, and are in need of all of those people, and more." He turned to walk away, then stopped and turned back. "Do you have wounded inside that need healing?"

The orc shook his head. "None would accept it now. Should we become allies, that is another story. I will return in one hour." He turned and strode back toward the gate.

Max shook his head. "Honor and pride are both good things, but these guys take them a bit far."

*****

Max spent the hour in the shade of the forest with his group and Skullsmasher. Max asked him to send mounted scouts out in a wide circle to help him map the area. He also asked that two riders be sent back to the way station to halt the reinforcements there. No point in having them march all the way to the mine for no reason. The troops he had here already could handle the orcs if they decided to fight. He was especially sure of this since Skullsmasher had informed him that it was standard practice for dwarven engineers to booby trap fortifications before abandoning them.

"If I know old Steelballs, he's set explosives or flammables near them walls, and has a fuse ready to light inside that mine with him. One lil spark, and any orcs who survive the blast won't have the walls to hide behind."

The hour hadn't quite passed when the gate opened again, and Ag'thorn walked out. A long stream of orcs followed behind. Max strode forward to meet him halfway even as the entire mounted dwarven force urged their boars out into the open, ready to charge should it be necessary.

When they met in the middle of the open ground, Ag'thorn took a knee. The other orcs did the same. "We have decided to join you, Chimera King."

"All of you?" Smitty asked from just behind Max. When Ag'thorn nodded, Smitty added, "Right on, orc bros! Good call!"

"We have one concern, Chimera King." The scout added, still on one knee. "Many of us have families still in An'zalor's city. If the time comes that we must fight him there…"

Max understood. "I would not ask you to kill your own blood. I hope to take his city from him in personal combat, rather than a siege and large scale battle. But regardless, you and your warriors have my word. And should your families choose to join you and swear the same oath you're about to, they would be welcome as well."

"Then we are ready."

"Right. The oath." Max realized he didn't have an oath ready for them. Smitty stepped forward and winked at him.

"I got this, boss." He took a deep breath and puffed out his chest. "Repeat after me…" he then proceeded to speak an oath that was partly a modified version of one they'd both taken as newly minted soldiers, and part some kind of geeky Dungeons & Dragons wizard's binding or something. Max had to admit, the wording was simple and effective, and not too onerous on the warriors. They agreed to obey Max, to defend him, his nation, and its people, and to act with honor in all things. That last bit might become a problem at some point, but Max figured they could tweak it soon enough. As the orcs repeated the last words, Max saw the swirling lights and felt the binding between them take effect. At the same time, Max and all of his group leveled up, along with most of the allied Darkholm dwarves, and the folks inside the mine, though Max couldn't see them to know.

Quest Completed: Defend the Mine!
Your citizens and allied troops defeated the invading force.
Two hundred and eight enemy troops were killed, and you personally secured the surrender of the remaining force.

Reward: Experience – 250,000; Increased
Reputation with Darkholm Dwarves.
Bonus Reward! For convincing conquered enemy
troops to
surrender and join your cause: Experience –
150,000; Diplomacy +1

The experience was enough to raise Max to level twenty, but he mentally waved away the rest of his notifications until he could find some place to be alone and speak with Red. He didn't want her suddenly appearing here in front of everyone without explanation. "Welcome to Stormhaven!" He motioned for all of them to rise. "Our first order of business is to assist any wounded. And Captain, please go let our people know it's safe to come out of the mine."

Skullsmasher immediately stomped toward the gate, the orcs making room for him as he shouted, "*Steelballs! Where's me fifty gold? Ye better no' be dead!*" Several of the orcs who'd heard the dwarf's earlier threat to their now-deceased commander laughed as the dwarf passed. Max just shook his head.

To Ag'thorn, Max said, "For now, you are promoted to the rank of Commander. I assume you have no trouble serving under Gr'tok?"

"None at all." The orc smiled. "But you assume I wish to remain in your army."

Max leaned back a bit. "You're right, I did. I know a career soldier when I see one. But if you wish to retire,

I'd ask that you lead these warriors until we get back to Stormhaven City. From there, you can become a...?" Max left the question in the air.

"I will continue to serve as a soldier. Though I am no Commander. I'm a scout, and would remain so."

"Then you'll be our Scout Commander." Max grinned at him. "Never waste the skills of an experienced soldier."

Ag'thorn sighed. "I accept. Thank you, Chimera King."

Max left the orcs to mingle with their new dwarven allies and see to their wounded. As he followed Skullsmasher toward the mine entrance, he saw that Dalia was already within the palisade helping to heal both orcs and dwarves. He grimaced at the sight of mangled and crushed bodies of both races, some still trapped under large stones. When he caught up to his people inside the mine, he was saddened to hear that nine of his people and a dozen of Ironhand's dwarves had been killed in the battle. Spotting Skullsmasher happily hefting a small bag of coins, while standing next to a forlorn looking dwarf, told him that the engineer Steelballs had survived the fight, at least.

The wounded all seen to, Max delegated his corporals to organizing the available troops. He had decided to take a few days and use the manpower on site while he had it handy. The dwarves and orc troops would assist the engineers in improving the fortification around the mine. When Gr'tok and the others arrived at the way station, they'd do the same there. Max wasn't foolish enough to think that An'zalor was through trying to take back the mine. A stone wall, a steel gate at the outer wall, and stout steel doors at the mine entrance would better protect his people. In addition, Max learned that the engineers and miners had been working on a tunnel that would lead to a hidden exit further down the cliff face. The tunnel was not completed, but they assured him that it would be done within a week. This would allow them to escape if cornered, or to launch an attack at their enemy's rear guard if necessary.

More troops would be assigned to digging a well within the mine to provide fresh water in the event of a siege. Still others were put to work digging the foundation for a barracks inside the fortification. Max offered a bonus in the form of gold for any of the new orc citizens who wished to stay and guard the mine. More than one hundred of them promptly volunteered, not anxious to live underground in Stormhaven City.

With everyone's immediate plans established, Max found himself an unused side chamber a bit deeper into the mine and sat down. Extending his legs and leaning back against the wall, he pulled up his notifications. The moment he did, Red popped up on his shoulder.

Level Up! You are now a Level 20 Chimera Sovereign.
You have earned three free attribute points.

"Ya be level twenty! Wooo!" She did a brief jig on his shoulder. "I gotta admit, when we first met, I had my

44

doubts either of us would live this long! O'course, without my help, your lanky butt would be a pile of monster poo somewhere in the forest by now…"

Max gave her a sidelong glance. He was tempted to argue, but decided he just wasn't in the mood. Instead he asked, "You mentioned a while back that when I reached level twenty, you'd be able to remain visible all the time. Does that mean others, besides Smitty and Dylan, will be able to see you as well?"

"Well…" the little redhead looked down at her feet.

"Well, what? Spill it, Red."

"Well, I suppose I could make it so that others could see me all the time. But I sort of enjoy bein invisible." She looked up briefly to gauge his response, then quickly added, "And bein visible all the time would take a lot o' power. I'd have to rest quite often."

Max smirked at his leprechaun companion. "How about for now you just introduce yourself to a select few. Starting with Dalia."

"Agreed!" Red clapped her hands and spun around. "Now, where are ya goin' to assign your free points?" Max pulled up his character sheet and studied it briefly. When he'd leveled up to nineteen, he'd put all three of his free points into *Agility*. Since then, he'd gotten a huge boost to several of his attributes. He was momentarily confused, until he remembered the scepter that Regin had given him as a reward for bringing him the head of An'zalor's champion and brother. It gave him boosts even when stored in his inventory. Thinking of the scepter reminded him that it gave him the ability to generate a morale boost among his people once per day. An ability he hadn't used yet. Resolving to start using it first thing in the morning, he refocused on his stat sheet. He'd gotten plus ten to both *Intelligence* and *Wisdom*, plus eight to *Endurance*, and plus four to *Luck* from the scepter. With his already high *Constitution* and troll regeneration keeping him mostly healthy, Max decided to put two points into *Strength*, and one into *Agility*. Finished with the assignments, he closed his character sheet and got to his feet, intending to find Dahlia and arrange an introduction.

Maximilian Storm	Health: 2,700/2,700
Race: Chimera; Level 20	Mana: 1000/1000
Battleborne, Sovereign	Exp: 308,000/2,500,000
Endurance: 25 (33)	Intelligence: 33 (43)
Strength: 38	Wisdom: 33 (43)
Constitution: 45	Dexterity: 15 (17)
Agility: 24 (26)	Luck: 16 (23)

Chapter 3

Max found Dalia resting on a pallet in the healer's room just off the main mine shaft. She'd helped to heal the wounded from the battle, and drained her mana in the process. Since there was no longer an urgent need, she didn't waste a mana potion, choosing instead to rest quietly while her mana recharged.

He plopped himself down on the floor next to her, wondering the best way to start the conversation. He suspected that during their time together Dalia had caught him speaking to Red more than once. How did he explain to a companion who might think he was crazy, but liked and accepted him anyway, that he wasn't actually talking to an imaginary friend?

Red, in her typical fashion, saved him the trouble.

The little redheaded leprechaun appeared out of nowhere, standing on Dalia's chest. She gave a little wave and said "Hello there! I'm Red!"

"Gah!" The dwarfess practically jumped out of her skin, swiping at the tiny figure, who simply floated out of the way. "Max! Get it!"

Max sighed, shaking his head sorrowfully. "If only I could, Dalia. It seems I'm stuck with her. That's Red, my... guide?" He looked at Red, who nodded, floating over to his shoulder. "We're soulbound companions. She helps me navigate this world, and gives me endless shit at the same time."

"You love me, and you know it!" Red stuck her tongue out at him before crossing her arms and turning her back. Which left her facing Dalia again.

"I have been with Max since he arrived on this world, though you haven't been able to see me. Now that we've both grown more powerful, I'm able to make myself visible to others for short periods." She waved again. "Nice to finally meet you in person. I've wanted to thank you, for being a good friend to him."

"Err… nice ta meet you too, Red." The dwarf didn't sound at all sure that it was.

"I'm sorry she surprised you like that. It seems to be her nature to misbehave in mostly harmless ways, and it does get annoying." He glared at Red, who pretended not to see. "Just so you know, Smitty and Dylan can see her, too. We think it's a Battleborne thing. But no one else has seen her yet. We'd like to keep her a secret, if possible."

"O'course." Dalia nodded, still eyeing the redhead somewhat suspiciously. "It's your secret to hold as ye wish." She looked from Max to Red and back. "So… what do you do? Are you a… combat…fairy?"

Max snorted, then laughed aloud, enjoying the mental image of Red flying into battle with a tiny wand or sword. Red shot him a finger and a nasty look. "I'm Max's guide. I help him understand the rules and possibilities of this world. The world he came from is very different. There was almost no magic left, and they relied on technology to accomplish many of their everyday tasks.

Fancy machines that did their heavy lifting, and most o' their thinking, for them."

Max nodded. "Though I hate to admit it, Red has been extremely helpful to me."

"Alright then, that be good enough for me." Dalia gave the leprechaun a hesitant smile.

Red leapt off of Max's shoulder and floated over to Dalia's. She pretended to sit, though she still had no physical form. "It'll be good to have another woman to talk to! Max absolutely refuses to gossip, or do anything fun, really."

Dalia looked nervous again, but Max tuned out the rest of the conversation. The two of them would get along, or they wouldn't. He decided to find his corporals and see how things were going.

Just outside the mine he found Dylan surrounded by dwarves who were all speaking to him at once. The ogre was attempting to make eye contact and respond to all of them, which resulted in him constantly spinning. Max was tempted to just watch and see if he'd get dizzy and fall.

"Corporal!" Max called out, raising a hand as he stepped forward to save his friend. "Is there a problem?"

"No problem, boss. These guys are all looking for me to help them out, is all." Dylan indicated the dwarves, who looked like bulky infants compared to the ten foot tall ogre.

"Aye." Steelballs nodded his head. "This big hunk o' muscle could speed up our construction o' the stone wall by a good bit. He can lift two or three times the weight o' any dwarf or orc."

"No!" Another dwarf shouted. "We need him on the lumber crew. Put an axe in each hand and he'll fell trees like a scythe through wheat. And he could pull a sled full o' logs all on his own."

The four dwarves that surrounded Dylan all began to argue again, each of them trying to claim him for one task or another. Max cleared his throat loudly, getting their attention again.

"Gentlemen. I know Dylan here looks like a big dumb ugly piece of meat, but he's a valued member of my party. He's a veteran of scores of battles, an expert tactician, and apparently very popular with the ogre ladies. Please treat him with some respect."

"I'm a really good dancer, too." Dylan added, breaking into his best version of the robot, then shifted into the running man, which caused the ground to shake. The dwarves all backed off and eyed him warily.

Max barely managed to contain his laughter. "Yes. Any of you need dance lessons, Dylan is your man." Dylan switched to some kind of free-form gyration that made Max snort. "In the meantime, I'm afraid I need him to come with me."

The dwarves bowed their heads briefly and moved off as Max motioned for Dylan to follow him. "You seen Smitty, dancing boy? Also… the robot?"

"Hey, I gotta be me, boss!" the ogre grinned down at him. "Smitty was headed out to talk to the new orcs. He's appointed himself their official liaison, since he's an orc himself."

"Fair enough. Those orcs are going to need some time to get used to working with dwarves anyway. How are things going?"

"Well, I got this terrible itch right on my taint. I don't know if something bit me, or I got a sliver from the wagon, or-"

"Not what I meant, corporal." Max interrupted. "So very not what I meant."

"Oh, right. Sorry boss. The engineers already had a plan to improve the wall, even have blueprints drawn. They've got scouts out searching for the best spot to quarry stone. No shortage of it around here, they tell me, but they would prefer a place that's uphill from the mine, to make it easier to move large blocks from there to here."

"Especially if they can't just hook *you* to a sled and let you pull them." Max chuckled.

"I don't mind workin, boss. Truly. Hard work helps me build up my *Strength* and *Endurance* stats, and if I can be useful at the same time, I'm up for it."

"Good to know. But you choose where you want to help, and when. Don't let those dwarves bully you into servitude."

"No worries, boss. There's Smitty." Dylan pointed to where the other corporal was speaking to Ag'thorn and three other orcs. When Max approached, all but Smitty saluted with fist to chest.

"Hiya boss." Smitty raised a hand in greeting. "I was just getting a report from these scouts. There's no sign of another force coming from the orc city, but Ag'thorn says they were originally given six days to take the mine and report back. So their war chief may still be waiting for word for another few days."

"Well, with travel time, that gives us at least four, maybe five days to beef up the fortification before more troops arrive." Dylan added. He was naturally falling back into his old role in their squad. He had been their logistician and sometimes strategist when Max asked for his input. He had a gift for analyzing data and making connections.

"The scouts are also reporting a structure that they spotted to the west of here."

"Occupied?" Max asked. Smitty turned to one of the scouts, who shook his head.

"We do not believe so. The structure was large, but not intact. It appears to be an old ruins. We spotted it from atop the cliff when we were…" He paused and looked to Ag'thorn, who nodded. The orc cleared his throat. "When we were preparing to drop rocks on the dwarves. Time was short, and we did not investigate the ruins. Did not even see them until the sun rose high in the sky. The stone they were made of… it glitters."

"Dude! A whole building made of gold?" Smitty was already looking westward, ready to investigate.

The scout shook his head. "Not gold. It is stone, we could clearly see that much."

"Maybe quartz, or whatever this world's version of it is." Max ventured. "It's worth checking out. How far away is it?"

The scout looked thoughtful for a moment. "Maybe two miles west and slightly north from where we stood atop the cliff."

"Alright, we can walk from here. It'd be difficult to move the wagon through the forest anyway. Smitty, go get Dalia. We're going to check it out. We leave in ten minutes."

"Boss, okay if I grab some gear? Like maybe one of those big axes the orcs had? There's a bunch that were looted from the dead." He looked sheepishly at Ag'thorn for a moment. The orc just shrugged. Looting the dead was a part of life on this world. To the victor went the spoils.

"Yeah, take what you need. When we get back, I'll see about having one of the masters craft better weapons and some armor for you. Start thinking about what you want. Also, how's your skill with a bow? With your size, we could get you one large enough to throw ballistic missile-sized arrows."

"I did some shooting back home as a kid. Can't say I've touched a bow in… ten years at least. But I'll pick it up." Dylan shrugged. "Or maybe a great big crossbow?"

"Either that, or learn some magic attacks. Or all of the above. Just some way for you to do decent ranged damage."

"Magic! I like that idea." Dylan slapped his chest. "I could be the first ogre wizard in our guild!" His enthusiasm died a moment later when he realized he and Smitty might be the only guild members left. Their entire unit had been wiped out in their last fight on Earth, and there was no way to know if any of the others had been given the choice to become Battleborne, or respawned on this world with them.

"Embrace your inner wizard, if that's what you want." Max patted the ogre's shoulder, having to reach up slightly to do so. "Seems like we can be whatever we want to be in this world."

Dylan nodded and strode off to find himself a battle axe. The heavy two-handed axes the orcs had used to try and chop through the palisade would serve as a good off-hand weapon for the ten foot tall tank. He had more than enough muscle to wield it as a dwarf would a short sword or war hammer. Max temporarily amused himself by plotting to have one of the dwarves craft the corporal a massive steel club with spikes on its upper half. He'd enjoy watching the ogre go all Captain Caveman on somebody.

Red appeared on his shoulder, and Max tensed briefly, looking at the nearby orcs. None of them appeared to notice her as she said, "Dalia will be here shortly. She was just finishing some potions she made from the extra pure herbs."

Max turned his back to the orcs, pretending to stare up at the cliff as he mumbled, "Did you hear about the sparkly rocks? Any idea what that is?"

"Yes, and nope." The leprechaun shrugged. "But I recommend you examine the stone closely. Maybe take a swing at it with a mining pick while you're there?"

*****

A little over an hour later the group pushed through a dense wall of brambles and scrub brush to step onto a wide paved stone area. The stones at their feet were each about six feet square, with grass and weeds growing up here and there in the narrow cracks between them. The paved area covered maybe two acres of ground, in the center of which was the ruins they sought.

There was a low stone wall that was mostly still intact. Only about six feet high, it was clearly more decorative than defensive. At that height it wouldn't hold back anything larger than bunny rabbits or drunken squirrels. At the center of the southern wall was an arched opening. There were signs of it having doors at one time, parts of badly rusted hinges still bolted to the stone on either side.

As the group stepped through the archway, Max noted the sparkle within the stone that the scout had reported. It was only visible with the sun striking the stone at a certain angle that reflected the light in his direction. As he moved, different sections of stone sparkled, then went dark. The stone itself was a muted grey with a faint swirl pattern one might expect to see in marble.

Within the wall stood three structures. One large central building with a flat stone roof that remained only partly intact, and two smaller buildings to either side. In between were roughly square patches of overgrown grass, each with a single silver-leafed tree growing in the center. The trees were both squat, maybe twelve or fifteen feet tall, with gnarled branches and wide canopies that reminded Max of oversized bonsai trees. The smaller structures were each little more than a doorway with a short landing inside that led to a descending stairway.

"Those look like mausoleums." Dylan commented, pointing at both of the smaller structures at once.

"Those are *totally* dungeon entrances!" Smitty pumped a fist into the air.

Max had been thinking along the same lines. "Let's check out the big building first. But Smitty, keep an eye on our six, in case something comes out of those doors."

"Roger that, boss."

Max checked the map on his UI. They were technically outside the area he had claimed from An'zalor after the arena trials, so this wasn't his property. If it did turn out to be a dungeon, would they have to clear it for him to be able to claim it for Stormhaven?

He was about to ask Red if she knew, when the sound of metal on stone, followed quickly by an animalistic squeal of pain, echoed out of the building in front of them. Instantly, all of the party had weapons in hand. Dylan moved to the front, shield and axe ready, waiting for Max to give the word to move.

"Alright, careful now. Let's not leap before we look. Dylan, move to the doorway but no further. Tell me what you see."

Dylan complied, halting at the threshold with his tower shield held in front of him. He leaned his head in just far enough to be able to look to the left and right for any hidden dangers, then withdrew it. "Small room with another door at the other end, maybe ten feet away. Room looks clear, same with what I can see of the next one. Floor's covered in dust, looks like some kind of animal track going through the other door. Four legs, big like maybe a large cat, or small bear?" He turned to look back at Max, who nodded and made a hand motion indicating he should move forward. He stepped across the threshold, still with his head on a swivel, and moved quickly forward to block the next doorway with his shield.

Behind him, Max moved in with sword drawn, also checking the corners as he went. Dalia followed, while

Smitty remained just outside with an arrow nocked, watching their backs. "Hold." Max murmured just loud enough for Dylan to hear. He and Dalia spent some time examining the tracks. Not knowing the wildlife of this world beyond the few animals he'd already encountered, Max looked to Dalia.

"Yeah, I dunno. Nothin' I've seen before, though I'd guess it's a cat." Dalia shrugged. "Then again I ain't no hunter or tracker."

"Smitty?" Max called to the archer who was still standing in the outer doorway with his back to them. The orc turned and stepped into the room, crouching down to inspect the tracks, while Max kept an eye on the door.

"Yup. Seen these tracks before, over by the cave where I spawned. But I never ran into the creature that made them. I found a couple of mutilated bunnies near its tracks one time. Just some fur and bones that were left after it fed."

"Alright, next room." Max motioned toward their tank. "Three steps in, and hold."

Dylan nodded and moved forward, Max right behind him. The ogre's third footfall caused one of the stone floor tiles to sink about four inches, making him wobble before regaining his balance. Even as he looked down, two metal bolts slammed into his torso from his left and his right.

"Ugh! It's a trap!" Dylan grunted as he took a step back and then dropped to one knee. The bolt in his left side had deflected off his shield arm, then his ribs, leaving superficial gashes on his arm and side. The one on his right, however, had managed to penetrate between his ribs and deep into one lung. Down on one knee and leaning heavily on his shield, he coughed up a spray of blood.

Max was instantly by his side, using all of his considerable strength to grab the ogre under his arms and pull him back through the door. Dalia cast a heal on Dylan, but shook her head. The wounds on his left side had closed, but not on the right. "Ye need ta remove the bolt."

Max took hold of the six inches of shaft and fletching that were still outside Dylan's body. "This is gonna hurt, corporal." He waited for the ogre to nod, then yanked on the bolt, being careful not to turn it as he pulled. Unfortunately, the bolt had turned on its own after it passed between Dylan's ribs, so that the barbs on the tip caught on those ribs on the way out. The strength of Max's pull caused both ribs to snap as he forced the bolt out, and Dylan screamed in pain.

Dalia instantly cast another heal, and the amount of blood pouring from the wound lessened, then stopped. Dylan lay flat on his back, panting from the pain and holding one massive paw against his side. "Son of a... I don't like this place, boss."

Max patted his corporal on the chest. "Don't blame you." He moved to stand in the doorway, leaving Dalia to finish healing their tank. "I'm shocked that the mechanism for that trap still works. This place looks ancient."

"Could be somebody came and added the traps more recently." Smitty offered.

"I suppose, but for what?" Max was studying the floor. The stone that had triggered the trap had risen back to the same level as the others after Dylan had removed his weight.

"Who cares?" Dylan paused to cough up some residual blood that had pooled in his lung. "Traps means loot. Gimme a minute, boss. I'll be good to go."

Max shook his head. "Not you. You've got no armor yet. Hang tight, and I'll go across." He didn't wait for the others to object, producing his own shield and stepping forward. He purposely stepped on the same stone that had triggered the trap before, testing to see if the trap had reloaded.

It hadn't.

The stone still sank when he stepped on it, but no new bolts emerged to try and kill him. "Well, that's good, at least." He spoke to the others as he surveyed the room. "Alright, shortest distance between two points, and all that." He stepped forward again, making sure to take short steps so that Dalia could follow his footprints without leaping. He kept his shield up on his left side, and kept his eyes to his right and his sword in hand. In his head, he had visions of ninja moves where he'd knock an incoming bolt aside with his blade.

As he crossed the rest of the distance to the next door, his ninja dreams were dashed. Max tripped three more traps. All three left-side bolts were deflected by his shield, while he completely failed to stop any of the right side bolts with fancy sword slashes. The first bolt took him in the shoulder, the second in the thigh. The last one was aimed even lower, striking the side of his right knee.

Behind him, Smitty couldn't help himself. "HA! I used to be an adventurer like you…"

"Finish that sentence and I'll cut off the parts of you that your girl Birona likes best." Max grunted as he yanked the final bolt from his knee. He felt a heal from Dalia, and his troll regeneration was already at work, so the pain was short-lived.

"Roger that." Smitty's tone was clearly disappointed.

"C'mon boss." Dylan grinned at Max as he got to his feet. "How many chances are we ever gonna get to use that in real life?"

"On this world? Probably more than you'd like." Max grumped back. "Follow my footprints in the dust. Step where I stepped."

Dylan did as ordered, followed a few seconds later by Dalia, then Smitty. All three managed to cross without taking any damage. Max waited for them near the rear door, where there was a wide landing formed from a single slab of stone. That doorway opened into a long corridor that stretched easily a hundred feet ahead of them, with three doorways on either side spaced evenly apart.

"Yeah... definitely traps in there." Smitty observed. Dylan shot him a dirty look.

"This is me again." Max stepped forward. The corridor floor had no small tiles. It was instead several long stone slabs that extended ten feet from front to back, and covered the entire width of the corridor floor. Like the rest of the building they'd seen so far, it had no ceiling or roof, but there was no evidence of debris on the ground, either.

"Someone has definitely been here and cleaned this place up." Max observed as he stepped forward. He tested the first floor slab with half his weight, and when it didn't shift, moved forward onto it. The others moved behind him, following a few feet back. When he reached the first door, which was on the left, he went through shield first.

The room appeared to be empty. It was small, maybe six paces long and five wide. Along the opposite wall was a small window opening, too narrow for a person to fit through, but tall enough to let in some light. Not that light was currently a problem in the roofless room.

In one corner was a stone slab built right into the walls at about knee height. Probably a bed. There was no furniture, or even remains of furniture. Just clean but dusty floor.

"Sleeping quarters." Dalia observed from the doorway. Max tended to agree. If this had been a place of worship, or a stronghold of some kind, then there would be spartan living quarters for priests or soldiers. And it made sense they would be located between the outer doors and whatever was in the center of the complex.

The others moved aside to let Max exit the room, and they continued down the hall, checking each of the rooms, which were nearly identical. Outside the fourth room, however, Max spotted something new. A spattering of blood drops on the floor. He squatted down to get a closer look, and Smitty peered over his shoulder.

"Definitely fresh." the orc observed. "But no footprints near it."

Max stood back up, his gaze rising to the walls. After a moment, he turned to Dylan. "Gimme a boost."

The ogre set down his shield and weapon, then cupped his hands and held them out for Max to step into. With almost no effort, he lifted the chimera up until his head and chest were well above the tops of the walls. A quick glance told Max what he'd suspected. "More blood up here. It's running along the tops of the walls."

"Easy for a big cat." Smitty nodded. "Maybe it got hit by one of those bolts, and jumped up there in a panic?"

"Or to avoid more traps." Dylan offered as Max hopped down. He wiped his hands on Smitty's back with a grin. "This thing could be pretty smart."

Max pointed forward down the hall. "It was headed that way. I saw more blood on the wall near the end of the hall." He led the way, briefly checking each of the remaining two rooms as they passed. The end of the hall was a T-intersection, the corridor leading off both left and right. But in both directions it ended after maybe ten feet in ninety degree turns back toward the center of the structure.

Max mumbled, "Okay, left, or-"

"Left!" Both Smitty and Dylan interrupted before he could finish, then fist-bumped. Dalia looked at the two of them with raised eyebrows, then just shrugged, not caring to argue.

Max turned left and followed the hall down and around the corner. Just a few feet further on was a large chamber with a stone pyramid in its center. The structure was made of the same stone as the rest of the building, but here and there were hints of bright color, as if it had been painted at one time.

Sitting upon the topmost level of the pyramid was a large cat. Its fur was black as night, with a slight sheen reflecting in the sunlight. From nose to the base of its tail it was maybe eight feet long. It lay on its right side, its head stretched back as it tried to grab hold of a bolt stuck in its front left shoulder. The moment it noticed Max and the others, it got to its feet a bit unsteadily, crouched low, and growled.

"First miniboss?" Smitty asked.

Dylan shook his head. "I don't think it belongs here any more than we do. We saw the tracks leading in… and it obviously didn't know about the traps. I think it wandered in just before we did."

Max cast *Identify* on the cat.

64

Panthera female
Level 17
Health: 1,490/2,000

"Please, let me." Dalia stepped forward. When Max put a restraining hand on her shoulder, she looked back at him. "Druid, remember?" Nodding once, Max let her go.

"Hey there, big kitty. You're a pretty girl, ain't ya?" She spoke in a soft voice as she took a couple steps up the pyramid. The cat ceased its growling, but otherwise didn't move. Jet black eyes stared at the dwarf that was a third of the cat's size. "I bet that hurts, eh? I could fix that for ya." Dalia took a few more steps up, her hands empty and held out in front of her. "Here, let me show ya." She cast a heal on the cat, and it shivered as the magic moved through it. On reflex, it settled onto its stomach and licked at the bolt still jammed in its shoulder.

Max and the two corporals were tense as Dalia stepped closer to the oversized cat. It took all the restraint Max could muster to sit back and let Dalia risk her life. He would much rather have just killed the cat and moved on.

Dalia continued to speak softly to the panthera, and the cat actually seemed to be listening. It ceased bothering the bolt in its side and stared at the dwarfess, blinking occasionally as she took the last several steps and reached forward. She gently stroked the creature's neck, saying, "That's a good girl. See? I'm not here to hurt you. Don't be frightened by the big scary monster boys behind me.

We're here to help." She moved her hand to the injured shoulder, and paused. "I won't lie to ye. This is gonna hurt. I need to pull that bolt from ye, but I'll heal ye right up as soon as it's out."

The cat stared for a moment longer, gazing directly into Dalia's eyes, then nodded her head once. It was a clear sign of intelligence, and it surprised all three of the Battleborne. Smitty was the first to give it voice.

"Did... the kitty just talk to the dwarf?"

"Looked that way to me." Dylan replied. Max remained silent, considering the implications as Dalia patted the injured shoulder with her left hand and took hold of the bolt shaft with her right.

"Okay pretty lady, here we go. Don't eat my face when I do this..." She quickly yanked the bolt free of the panthera's hide, the cat screaming in pain as the barbed head ripped a wider hole on the way out. "Eaaaasy girl." Dalia cast another heal on the cat. Max did as well, wanting the pain to stop before the cat decided to take a bite out of his healer. The bleeding stopped, but Max was too far away to see the wound through all the dark fur.

Dalia stepped to her left and reached out, petting the cat's neck again, then moving up to scratch one ear. "There we go, girl. That wasn't so bad, was it?" Purring now, the cat head-butted Dalia's chest, nearly knocking her off balance. "Good kitty. I think we're gonna be friends!"

When Max and the others stepped forward, though, the cat bristled. She got to her feet and stepped back

66

slightly, dropping into a crouch and growling at the males. All three stopped where they were, not wanting to aggravate the big cat with Dalia standing right next to it.

"Hold on, fellas. Gimme a minute." She spoke over her shoulder, holding both hands up in front of the panthera's face. "It's okay lady cat. They're friends of mine. Nobody here will hurt you." She gently placed a hand back on the cat's neck and began to scratch. The cat settled back down, tucking its front legs under its chest, and began to purr again.

"Max, got any of that spidorc meat left?" She asked without turning her head.

Max quickly checked his inventory, but there was no spidorc meat. There was, however, still a stack of manticore meat from their fight in the arena. He pulled out a steak-sized chunk of that and held it out. Immediately the cat's nose started twitching. "You want me to bring it to you?"

"Walk slowly, and hold it out in front of you. Speak softly, say something nice to the kitty."

"Sing *Soft Kitty* to it!" Smitty offered, a wide grin fully exposing his tusks. Dylan snorted.

"Not in this lifetime, corporal." Max replied before taking his first slow step forward. "Nice panthera, are you hungry? We killed a nice juicy manticore a while back, and I haven't tasted it yet, but I bet you'd like it..." He rambled on as he moved closer. Dalia continued to scratch the cat's neck, and the purring grew louder.

When Max got within reach of the cat's head, he extended his hand a bit and let the creature sniff the meat. After just a few seconds she opened her mouth, exposing six-inch fangs, gently grabbed hold of one edge and took it from his hand. Moving back a bit, she pinned the meat with one massive paw and began to tear pieces off.

As she ate, Max asked, "Did you bond with her, or something?"

Dalia shook her head. "I tried, but it didn't work. I'm not sure why. I've never bonded an animal companion before, so maybe I missed somethin'."

The cat finished the snack and let out a chuffing sound. A moment later she seemed to shimmer in the sunlight as her body grew smaller. Max blinked a few times, not sure what he was seeing. Five seconds later the giant black cat had transformed into a humanoid.

She rose from her sitting position. "You couldn't bond with me because I'm no simple animal, druid." She stood a little over five feet tall, covered neck to toe in form-fitting black leather armor. There were a dozen small daggers set in a bandolier across her chest, and several more stuck in various sheaths built into her wrists, legs, and boots. Her exposed face was covered in fur, and she retained the ears and whiskers of a panther. She wore fingerless gloves that exposed sharp claws at the end of each digit. "I am Nessa. Panthera beastkin." She bowed her head slightly toward them. "Thank you for healing me, and for the meat."

"You're most welcome." Dalia smiled up at her. Max just nodded.

"I assume you are here seeking the treasure as well?" She half-growled at them, watching carefully as Smitty and Dylan moved forward to join them.

"Treasure?" Smitty perked up.

"We were just exploring." Max cut in. "I am Max, King of Stormhaven, and we recently claimed new territory near here. Our scouts noticed this ruin, and we came to investigate. We know nothing about it, or any treasure."

Nessa growled deep in her throat. "And now I've told you it exists. Well, I suppose I owe you for healing me. You may join me in seeking the treasure, and share it. Though I get a full half share, and the rest of you will have to divide your half among yourselves!"

Dalia cleared her throat. "About the healing. I saw ye trying to grab the bolt with yer mouth. Why didn't ye just transform and pull it out with yer hand?"

Nessa looked uncomfortable. "I... could not. My ability to fully transform is rare among my people, and quite powerful. But there are disadvantages. Like not being able to transform with a foreign object jammed into my shoulder."

"Makes sense." Dylan and Smitty, the two gamers, nodded their heads in unison.

"You have experience with transformation magic?" Nessa raised an eyebrow at them.

69

"Uhm, you could say that." Dylan gave her a big ogre grin. "Smitty and I both used to be human. Max, too."

"Interesting. I sense a tale worth hearing there." Nessa looked them up and down. "Orc and ogre I recognize, but I have never encountered one such as yourself, King Max."

"Neither have I." Max chuckled. "I'm a chimera, a mixture of four races, and I don't know if there are more like me out there anywhere." He changed the topic. "So you came to seek a treasure, and got hit by one of the traps?"

Nessa lowered her gaze in shame. "Yes. I failed to detect the floor triggers. My master would be greatly disappointed in me."

"Your master?" Max asked.

"I am a novice… liberator." She paused slightly before the last word.

"Ha! Liberator. I like that! She's a thief." Smitty grinned at her. "As if the gear didn't give you away. In that outfit you had to be a thief, or a stabby stabby assassin, or both. Can you disarm traps? Cuz I'm a little tired of this place trying to kill us."

Nessa glared at him for a moment, offended by his blunt words. Dylan stepped in to help. "He wasn't making an accusation. Thief is a perfectly acceptable class where we come from. We've got no problem with that. You know, as long as you don't try to steal from us."

Dalia disagreed, her dwarven honor did not allow for stealing. But she held her tongue.

"To answer your rather rude question, yes. I can disarm traps, up to a certain level of complexity. I missed the traps in that earlier room because my perceptions are… different in my full feline form. I depend more on scent and sound in that form, and my thought processes are more feral. I had not suspected that any traps would still be in working order after so many years."

Max looked up at the open ceiling. "We have concluded that someone has made use of this place more recently. You see that the roof is gone, yet there is no debris on the floors?"

Nessa looked up, her eyes wide and mouth open in astonished realization. A second later she looked at her feet again, shaking her head. "Truly, my master would disown me, were she here to witness this. How did I not notice such an obvious incongruity?"

"Don't feel bad." Smitty offered. "Max here used to work counterintel… uhhh… he got paid to notice stuff. In a past life."

"It be commonly known that treasure fever causes even experienced explorers to forget themselves on occasion." Dalia smiled at the beastkin woman.

"Tell us about this treasure." Max said. "And what do you know about these ruins?"

71

Chapter 4

"This place was originally built by a tribe of half-ogres who'd been banished from the ogre lands in the mountain. So long ago that I was not able to find any records of its original construction. It was said that they abandoned it when their chief married an ogre chieftain's daughter and returned his entire tribe to the mountains." She paused to point toward the walls. "They were talented stonemasons, and chose this location because they found the sparkly stone nearby." She looked at Dylan and shrugged. "As good a reason as any, I suppose. Pretty, shiny stone." Dylan just chuckled at her opinion of ogre intelligence.

"In any event, after it had been abandoned, the gnomes eventually moved in. They were led by a gnomish mechamage, who sought a secluded place to research new inventions. He brought his entire clan with him, and they turned this place into a temple dedicated to one of their gnome gods. The clan remained here for centuries, reportedly long past the mechamage's death, until the orcs invaded and massacred the gnomes."

"Orcs, man... what are ya gonna do?" Smitty shook his head in mock sadness.

Nessa looked confused by the comment from the orc for a moment, but continued. "It is rumored that selling their inventions generated mountains of wealth, and that it was hidden here below their temple."

"And you don't think anyone has come and looted this place before you?" Dylan asked.

"The place was not well known, even before the gnomes perished. And no offense to you, sir orc, but the orcs aren't the best at finding hidden doors or rooms when they sack a town, or in this case a temple. They pretty much charge in, kill everything, take whatever isn't nailed down, and move on."

"So how did you find this place?" Dylan pressed. He was thinking this was exactly the kind of situation where talking to an NPC in a game would lead to an epic quest or first-kill dungeon. Smitty caught on, and nodded with approval. He even crossed his fingers behind his back.

Nessa gave him a wary look, then sighed. "I suppose it doesn't matter, as you're already here. I was given a novice quest by my master. I cannot achieve the rank of apprentice until I complete this quest, which was to locate an obscure ruin, defeat any obstacles it presents, and return with its most precious artifacts. It took me six months, and several failed expeditions to already-plundered sites, before I found this place. I only discovered its existence by accident, finding an old bill of sale for a portal pedestal that mentioned delivery from this temple."

"So the gnomes built portals?" Max was now very interested in whatever treasure might be found in this ruined temple.

"Built them, repaired them, improved them, I'm really not sure. As I said, there was almost no information on this place. The delivery receipt showed that it would be delivered to the human city to the south, the one now occupied by the orc clans. It mentioned six days' provisions charged to the client, which I took to mean that the delivery would take three days by wagon, each way. So I estimated what that distance might be, and have been exploring a wide circle approximately three days' travel around that city. This morning, I found this place. I don't know for sure that this is the gnome's temple, but based on the traps I encountered, my confidence is high."

Dalia nodded. "Gnomes do like their traps and gadgets. Even more than dwarves."

Smitty shook his head. "I see a problem with your reasoning, dudette." When she raised an eyebrow at him, he shrugged. "If I were a gnome who could build portals, and I was delivering a portal to a city, and probably installing it… why would I take the long way home? Why not just take the new portal home?"

Nessa's ears went flat and she growled slightly as she answered. "I considered that, orc. Once I knew the temple existed, I spent a month researching the gnomes and any references to this place I could find. As I said, the gnomes were reclusive. I gambled that they would not wish to connect their home portal with every other portal they delivered. Hence the need to travel home the long way."

Smitty nodded. "Okay, I see where you're going with that. Good thinking!" He grinned at the beastkin, taking no offense at her tone.

"I'm so glad you approve." She looked from Smitty to Max. "Now that we've covered all of this, shall we proceed to finish exploring this place?" She motioned to the pyramid they were all standing upon. "This structure has short steps, easily managed by our druid here... I'm sorry, I did not ask your name?"

"I be Dalia, and this is Max, as ye heard. The ogre is Dylan, and that's Smitty." She introduced everyone.

"My pleasure, Dalia. And thank you again for the healing." She bowed her head slightly. "As I was saying, these steps were built to gnomish dimensions, not ogre. Which leads me to believe this was an addition built by the gnomes. I suggest we begin searching here. Look for levers, hidden doors, discolored stones, that sort of thing."

The group split up, spreading out around the base of the pyramid, with Nessa beginning her search at the top. They peered closely at the stone, looking for signs of secret levers, trigger panels to push, or any other oddities that might indicate a hidden opening. After an hour, none of them had discovered anything promising. Finally, Max shook his head and shrugged.

"Maybe it was just a way for their leader to elevate himself above the others."

"That may be, though it seems unlikely." Nessa answered. "From what I know of gnomes, no way would they be able to resist putting a gadget or secret compartment into a structure of this size." She looked toward the door at the rear of the room. "However, I suggest we continue to explore the rest of this building, then move on to the two smaller buildings out front. Since I have you with me to help fend off any monsters that may arise, I shall remain in this form. I'm much more capable of detecting and disarming traps this way."

"Sounds like a plan." Max agreed, the others nodding their heads as well. They gathered at the rear door, and this time Nessa took the lead. She spent a moment examining the door frame and the stone floor just in front of it, making sure there were no traps or trip wires before stepping through.

The door led down another short corridor, in which Nessa identified two different flagstones on the floor that were trap triggers. Marking each with a few drops of water dyed bright red that stood out on the dusty floor, they avoided the traps and moved on.

The next room, the last in the building, Max guessed, was even larger than the previous. All around its outer edge were a series of stalls separated by short three-foot high walls, each facing toward the center of the room. In that center was a decorative fountain that featured a ten foot tall toga-clad ogre female holding a large pitcher in both hands. The pitcher was tilted forward so that water could pour out into the basin below. Just a trickle of water ran out to splash into maybe an inch-deep pool in the basin.

"She's a hottie!" Dylan admired the ogress for a moment, then looked around the open space. "Some kind of market, maybe?" Dylan ventured, looking at the scores of stalls around the room.

"Aye, or a place fer crafting." Dalia added. "Like the apprentice area ye worked in yerself, Max."

Nessa agreed. "I think crafting the more likely option. The gnomes were introverts, recluses. While I'm sure there was some trade and barter between the few residents here, I doubt there was need for a marketplace so large. And the short walls must have been built by the gnomes. They'd only be knee-high for ogres, and would serve no purpose to them. Crafting stations makes more sense."

"Well, there's nothing left here now." Smitty observed. "No craft items, tools, furniture, trash, nothing. Either it all rotted away, or this place has been cleaned by someone since the gnomes were killed off, just like the rest of the building so far."

After a short time spent searching the room, the group agreed to return to the front temple entry and check the two smaller structures. Nessa led the way, carefully checking for undiscovered traps as they moved. When they reached the areas of known traps, she confirmed that the ones they had triggered had not reset. Max waited until they'd passed through the final door and out onto the wide stone area where they'd began before asking the question that had been nagging at him.

"Nessa, if the traps didn't reset after we triggered them, how old does that make them?" He paused to organize his thoughts. "I mean, if the gnomes had built those traps, you would think that random wildlife wandering into the building would have set them off

78

centuries ago. Meaning there wouldn't have been any live traps for us to trigger, right?"

"I agree." Nessa nodded. "These were likely set by whomever has occupied this place more recently." She looked at Dalia, who just shrugged. Dwarves were nearly as good at traps as gnomes were, but they weren't Dalia's specialty.

"The form and construction of these traps would suggest they spent a good deal of time here. I mean, they'd have to have redone the floors to place the triggers, opened up walls to install the mechanisms and bolts, then resealed them..." Dylan rubbed his chin as he spoke. "Even just cleaning up all the debris from the fallen roof sections would have taken a good bit of time and effort, and where did they put it all?"

"All good points." Max motioned toward the smaller structure on the left side. "Maybe some of the answers are in there."

Once again Nessa led the way, carefully examining the floor and walls as they entered and began to descend. She tested each of the stone steps, prodded gently at nicks and cracks in the walls, making their progress very slow. Max and the others didn't complain, happy to trade the delay for the opportunity to not be skewered or blasted by traps.

When they were maybe twenty feet below the surface, there was a groaning, grinding sound in the stone, followed by a loud crack. A second later, an entire section of the stair fell away at their feet, dropping the group into the darkness below. Max was just able to turn himself to see the ground below when he hit hard, his shoulder and hip absorbing most of the impact. He felt a couple of ribs break, and he thought his shoulder had probably dislocated.

The sounds of cracking bones and gasps of pain around him told him that others had landed badly too. Dalia cursed quietly but impressively somewhere off to his right. Max was relieved that she had survived the fall. Instinctively looking upward, his darkvision showed him the jagged opening in the stairs maybe forty feet above them.

Max cast a heal on himself, then turned to do the same for the others. The worst off seemed to be Dylan, who was laying on his belly, his head in a pool of blood, one arm obviously broken and trapped beneath his bulk, and jagged breaks in both shin bones protruding from his skin. It looked as if the ogre had landed atop a large chunk of the stone stairway that had fallen with them.

After allowing his healing magic and troll regeneration to repair him for a moment, Max pushed through the pain and got to his feet. He moved to Dylan, rolling him over as gently as possible. The ogre's forehead was dented in on one side, the wound bleeding profusely. Max cast a heal on his friend, trying to stem the bleeding, then moved to his badly broken legs.

"This is gonna hurt, buddy." He warned, taking hold of Dylan's left leg at the ankle and knee. With a grunt of effort and pain from his still sore ribs, he yanked his hands apart, pulling the broken ends of the leg bones apart, then relaxed and let the leg muscles pull them back together in roughly the appropriate alignment. He quickly did the same for the other leg, worried that Dylan didn't wake up screaming. His head injury could be more severe than Max had hoped.

He took a moment to reset the broken arm as well, then cast another heal on Dylan. By this time, Dalia was on her feet and had already cast heals on Nessa and Smitty, neither of whom were as severely injured as Dylan. She knelt near the ogre's head, taking it into her lap as she cast a spell that glowed a deep green as it seeped into his head.

"His skull be broken, bits puttin' pressure on his brain." She bit her lip, looking up at Max. "I see'd worse, on warriors takin' hammer hits to the noggin. I can heal it, but there be no way o' knowin' if he'll be himself when he wakes."

"Please, do what you can." Max asked quietly. Smitty moved up behind her to peer over her shoulder.

Dalia placed both hands over the crushed area of the ogre's skull, closing her eyes and pressing her lips together as her hands began to glow with a warm green light. After half a minute, the glow faded, and she gasped for breath. Leaning back against Smitty's leg, she looked up at Max. "Best I could do. I think he'll be alright. He'll need to sleep for a bit."

With her hands removed, Max could see that Dylan's skull appeared to have returned to its normal shape. The skin was healed, though there was some obvious bruising. They all relaxed a bit when the ogre began to snore loudly. Dalia produced a blanket from her inventory, folded it over several times, and placed it under his head as she got to her feet. She quickly checked over the others, finding no one else in need of additional heals. Moving to the nearest wall, she took a seat on the floor and leaned her back against the wall. "I could use a lil rest meself."

"Right. Thank you, Dalia. Everybody else, check this room, make sure it's clear. Then we'll all rest and eat." It was obvious from the faint light streaming in through the gap above that it was still daylight outside. But it wouldn't hurt for everyone to rest and replenish themselves while they waited for Dylan to wake up.

Max took in the area around them. They'd fallen through a hole in the ceiling of a natural underground chamber. Water dripped from the edges of the hole above their heads, the drops impacting the stone floor making the only sound other than their own breathing and footsteps. The cavern was roughly round in shape, their landing zone being near one edge. The floor spread out for a hundred feet directly across, the opposite wall curving up to the twenty foot high domed ceiling.

He spotted Smitty standing very still, his hands held out in front of him as he took tentative steps. Once he'd left the faint circle of light from the opening above, the orc had no way to see through the deep darkness. "Hold still Smitty. Can't have you stumbling around blind." Max bent and picked up a handful of loose pebbles. Biting his lower lip hard enough to make it bleed, he sucked on it till he had a good mouthful of blood, which he then spat into his hand. He used his other hand to rub the rocks and sand around, covering them in blood.

Setting the stones in a small pile on the ground, he stepped back and cast *Spark*. The stones flared to life, his blood burning brightly.

Skill Level Up! Your Alchemy skill has increased by +1!

Realizing that the flame wouldn't last long before the blood burned away, Max asked, "Anybody got any firewood?"

Smitty obliged, the scout having wisely been keeping a small supply in his inventory. In less then a minute they had a cheery campfire burning brightly enough to illuminate a large portion of the cavern. The still sleeping ogre grunted once upon feeling the heat from the fire, unconsciously rolling closer to the flame and curling into a fetal position.

"If he wasn't so big n ugly, he'd be cute." Smitty grinned at Max. "Don't tell him I said that." Max mimed a zipping and locking motion in front of his lips.

Nessa appeared from behind the orc, making him jump in surprise. "Shit! Don't sneak up on me like that."

"I was not sneaking, orc." She glared at him. "You were simply speaking too loud to hear me approach." She motioned over her shoulder toward the darkest part of the cavern's opposite wall. "There is a rough opening that way. It leads to a short tunnel and another chamber. Not a natural one, like this."

Max turned in the indicated direction, making out a deeper darkness that was the opening. A quick scan of the rest of the walls showed no others.

Smitty, still annoyed, griped at the beastkin. "I thought you were supposed to be able to detect the traps." He pointed upward. "Seems like you missed a pretty big one."

Nessa growled at him, the sound coming from deep in her chest. "That was no trap, orc. You hear that water dripping? See that stone over there?" She pointed to broken and discolored chunks of stone stairway that were scattered around their landing area. "This was simple rot. The water probably ran down the stairway from above with each storm. It found a small crack or hole, and doing what water naturally does, worked its way down. Over the centuries, it has weakened the stone supporting the stairway above this natural void. I am a thief, not an engineer. My skill is particular to manufactured traps, not natural weaknesses in the stone."

She paused and looked at Dylan, then looked Smitty up and down. "If it were not for the significant weight of yourself, the ogre, and Max here, we might have crossed safely without it collapsing."

"Did you just call me *fat*?" Smitty unconsciously sucked in his gut, which had little to no visible fat, only thick abdominal muscles.

"Muscle weighs more than fat." Nessa informed him matter-of-factly.

Flexing his biceps and striking a pose, Smitty grinned. "That's right, baby! Biggunz!"

Resisting a laugh, Max shook his head. "Right, well here we are, regardless of the cause. Let's grab some food and maybe a little sleep. I'll take first watch. If Dylan isn't awake in four hours, Smitty you have second watch. Then Dalia."

"No watch for me?" Nessa asked.

"No offense, Nessa. But we just met you. I don't think any of us would be comfortable sleeping with just you on watch right now."

"And I should sleep peacefully amidst four strangers?"

"That's up to you." Max smiled at her without showing his fangs. "But I submit that if we'd intended to hurt you, we easily could have before now."

The beastkin just nodded her head slightly and moved to the opposite side of the fire from Dylan. Producing a blanket, she set it on the floor and sat down, crossing her legs. "I shall meditate for a while." she said as she closed her eyes.

*****

Max was just about to wake Smitty when Dylan came around. The ogre snorted a few times, then groaned in pain. One massive hand began to rub his head, and his eyes fluttered.

"Ow." Was all he managed at first. Max snorted.

"Welcome back to the land of the living, corporal. Again."

"What? What happened? Did I die and get rez'd?" Dylan tried to sit up, but quickly changed his mind. Instead he shifted his head so he could see Max.

"No, you didn't die. But you were damn close. Crushed your melon a good bit. Broken arm, legs, probably ribs as well. Dalia healed you."

"Damn. I remember falling, and breaking my legs. I think I passed out right then, don't remember the rest." Dylan rubbed his head again, then his belly. "I'm hungry."

"Ha! Dalia said you'd need to refuel. The healing she did took a lot out of both of you." Max pulled some meat on a stick from his ring. Taking a look at Dylan's bulk, he pulled some more, and then a few more. "Here, eat up. You're a growing boy, after all."

"You know it!" Dylan set all the food on his chest and began to devour it one stick at a time. "Thanks boss."

Max let the others sleep, or meditate in Nessa's case, as Dylan finished his meal and they talked for a bit. He was in no rush to get everyone moving. They appeared to be safe for the moment.

As if reading his mind, Red appeared on his shoulder. "Can't leave ya alone fer five minutes without ya fallin in a deep hole in the ground." She winked at him.

"At least ya had the sense to start a fire and create a campsite safe zone."

"Oh. Right." Max thought back to his first campfire out in the woods when the leprechaun had explained safe zones to him. "Wait, don't we need a tent, or something?"

"Just shelter." Red replied, spreading her arms wide to indicate the cavern. "This counts as shelter."

"Good to know, thank you."

"Who are you talking to?" Nessa's voice drifted across the fire.

"He does that." Dylan replied as Max stammered, flustered at being discovered. He'd already gotten used to everyone in his party knowing about Red, and forgotten about Nessa. "He talks to himself, even answers himself. Not quite right in the head, our Max. But don't worry, he's not dangerous." Dylan looked at Max, seeing the glare he was sending. "I mean, he's totally dangerous. A real hard-core killer. But not to his friends."

Max gathered his wits and took over. "I apologize if I disturbed your meditation, Nessa."

"It is of no consequence. I am well rested." She shrugged, getting to her feet. "That food smelled quite good. Do you have more, perchance?"

"Of course." Max produced a couple of kabobs and handed them to her. "Enjoy."

Nessa sat back down and daintily consumed the bits of meat in a very catlike manner. Smitty and Dalia, both awakened by the conversation, approached and received their share as well, and Max took the opportunity to eat a couple kabobs himself.

Nessa wasn't the only one who was attracted to the smell of the kabobs. Max's elven hearing and Nessa's beastkin ears were the first to detect the sound. "Something's coming." Nessa got to her feet, a dagger already in each hand as she turned to face the only opening in the cavern.

"Several somethings." Max corrected. "Heavy, by the sounds of it."

He'd barely finished speaking when a roar echoed through the opening, followed quickly by a large shadow moving into the cavern. Answering roars from behind it confirmed Max's guess. Max focused his gaze on it, and darkvision showed him a creature he'd never seen or heard of before. The monster was taller than Max, maybe eight feet, and walked on two legs. It had a thick, hairy body with long arms and large hands with sharp claws that nearly scraped the ground as it walked. Its shoulders were wide and powerful looking, supporting a thick neck and oversized head. When it opened its mouth to roar again, Max saw a set of very sharp teeth designed for rending flesh. A second later his *Identify* skill kicked in.

> *Shadow Troll Mutant*
> *Level 20*
> *Health: 2,500/2,500*

"Deep trolls." Dalia whispered, then spat on the stone floor even as she equipped her shield and sword. "This be bad."

"I'm showing they're called shadow trolls." Dylan offered.

"Aye, that be what the gods named 'em. We call 'em deep trolls, cuz we only ever find em deep down in the mountains. They be vicious, and hard to kill. Tough skin, and the same rapid regeneration ability as you have, Max." She looked again at the troll. "This one be larger than I ever heard of."

Three more of the monsters entered the cavern behind the first, which had been stalking toward them. It halted some twenty feet away, unable to enter the safe zone, its gaze focused on the fire, roaring in anger.

"It clearly doesn't like the fire." Max stated the obvious. "Is their blood also flammable like mine?"

"Yep!" Dalia grimaced. "But if ye light one up, get yerself far away. They explode, and the burnin' bits fly everywhere."

"Okay, we can work with that." Max looked at Smitty. "Same plan as with the undead in the arena. Only I'm not getting close this time. Dylan, you're in front. Dalia, you too. Shields up, and get low. Smitty, you and Nessa right behind them. Nessa, when you hear me shout, get low and stay there."

Max produced his bow from inventory and nocked a wooden arrow. Taking careful aim at the stationary troll,

89

he fired. The arrow struck it's cheek, only penetrating a short distance, but knocking the troll backward. Almost immediately, another arrow from Smitty struck its chest, pushing it further off balance. As it teetered backward, Max focused on his arrow and shouted, "*Boom!*"

The others hit the dirt as Max dropped his bow and equipped his shield. He was still crouching down to hide behind it when the arrow exploded. A chunk of the falling troll's face exploded with it, showering the monster and its companions with blood and bits of flesh.

Not needing to be told when, Smitty equipped an arrow wrapped in cloth and cast *Spark* on the tip. The moment it lit, he fired at the lead troll. The arrow struck its shoulder just below the ruined side of its face, and the flaming cloth touched off its blood.

"Get down!" Max shouted, the orc quickly dropping to his knees behind Dylan and his huge shield. There was a high-pitched whistling, followed by the sound of a wet explosion. Flaming bits of troll showered both groups, most bouncing off the shields. But several flew in a high enough arc that they passed over top of the shields and landed on those behind. Nessa gasped in pain as a hairy chunk of troll arm landed on her back. Dalia was hit with a flaming finger, burning her hand when she grabbed it to keep it from damaging her valuable leather armor. Smitty was hit with several burning droplets of blood, but shrugged off the pain while he swiped them away, then shook off what had stuck to his hand.

Max was also hit with a few chunks, his adrenaline pumping as he watched them land on his chainmail-covered back. One chunk lit his long white hair afire, and Max nearly panicked. Having flammable blood, being on fire was a serious threat to him. His mind briefly took him back to the mortar round exploding right in front of him, ending his life on Earth. The flashback caused him to panic. He reached back and grabbed a handful of the burning hair, yanking as hard as he could. He ripped away the burning bit of troll flesh, along with a good bit of his hair, and threw it to the cavern floor. He ignored the pain from both his torn scalp and his burned hand, checking to make sure the other chunks didn't burn through his mail armor. Grabbing an arrow from his quiver, he used the tip to flick the burning pieces off his back. He felt a heal wash over him, and the pain in his scalp eased a bit.

The roars of pain from the trolls brought him back to the battle, his terrified lizard brain giving way to his combat instincts. The lead troll was down, what was left of its body engulfed in flame as it twitched on the floor. The other trolls were liberally coated in burning bits of flesh and blood, and were gyrating around, bumping into each other. But the movements seemed to be caused by fear more than pain. Their tough skin was resisting the flames enough to keep them from exploding like the first troll.

"Okay, that was a bad idea." Max said aloud, unwilling to cast *Boom!* again and risk more flaming shrapnel. "Dylan! Knock them down. Smitty, head shots!" he called out, quickly adding, "No fire!" His mind

91

raced, trying to find a way to kill the enemy without closing to melee range and endangering himself. Arrows would knock them back, but with their regenerative capabilities, only a lucky shot to the brain stem, or maybe the heart, would kill them. Using fire spells might result in more explosions, which was also a hard pass.

At that moment, Nessa appeared behind the troll who was furthest from the group. Her black armor reflecting the light of all the tiny fires on the trolls' bodies, Max saw her grab the troll's chin with one hand, lifting it up and driving a long dagger up under its jaw. She must have penetrated its brain, because the monster instantly went limp, falling to the floor. A blink later, the beastkin had faded from sight again, none of the other trolls even realizing she'd been there as they frantically tried to rid themselves of the flames.

Dylan roared, thumping his shield with his newly acquired axe while using some kind of taunt ability. The remaining trolls focused on him as he advanced toward them. That moment's distraction was all Nessa needed. She appeared behind another of the trolls, this time ramming a dagger into the back of its neck. The blade penetrated the monster's thick skin, the tip sliding between two of its vertebrae. Nessa used both hands to give the hilt a hard twist, causing the blade to turn and flex, separating the two segments of the monster's spine. This troll went limp as well, but the damage wasn't fatal. Its eyes bulged and blinked and it roared in pain as it hit the floor and Nessa spun away. It lay there, unmoving, watching as Dylan the massive ogre approached.

"Dylan, kill that one before it heals itself!" Max called out. The ogre nodded, then used his shield to bash away the one troll that was still upright, knocking it back toward the exit. Raising one massive foot, he stomped down on the immobilized troll's skull. Surprisingly, the thick bone resisted the ogre's weight.

Grunting in surprise, Dylan stepped back and swung his axe, the heavy blade cleanly severing the troll's neck. As the head rolled free, he growled, "Regenerate that!"

Smitty hit the last troll in the chest with an arrow, pushing it back nearly to the cavern exit. Unfortunately, his arrow struck its gut through a burning piece of the first troll, penetrating its thick skin and pushing some of the flaming flesh through with it. "Oh, shit! That one's gonna blow, boss!" He called out.

Thinking quickly, Dylan rushed forward and bashed the troll through the exit opening. "Move to the sides, guys!" He called out as he planted his shield across the opening and ducked down. Max and the others did as he said, rushing to either side until they were out of the line of sight of the burning troll even as the telltale whistling began. A moment later the explosion hit the ogre's shield, knocking him back onto his butt even as a shower of flaming bits passed over his head to land in a fan-shaped arc on the cavern floor.

"Damn. Sorry, guys." Smitty got to his feet and walked over to Dylan, who was laying on his back with his shield on top of him. Several chunks of troll were burning his scalp and forehead. Smitty quickly picked or wiped them off, ignoring the damage to his hands, as Dalia cast heals on both of them.

When both were flame-free and fully healed, Dylan used his shield as a crutch to get to his feet. "Let's not do that again, huh?"

"Right on, dude. That was gnarly." Smitty agreed.

"Yeah, note to self. Don't turn trolls into flaming flesh grenades." Max shook his head, still slightly rattled by the near death experience.

"I did warn ya." Dalia walked over and patted him on the back. "If Battleaxe were here, he'd laugh his fool head off. Then punch ye really hard and say, 'Don't do that again, ye damned fool!'"

Despite the adrenaline and lingering fear in his lizard brain, Max chuckled. "That's exactly what he'd say." He leaned down and gave the dwarfess a brief hug. "Thanks."

Max allowed the others to loot the corpses, not wanting to touch the still burning bodies. He laughed as Dylan looked through the opening at the last exploded troll, not finding a body to loot, then gingerly extended one ogre pinky to touch a crispy eyeball that was stuck to a wall. That apparently did the trick, as the ogre's eyes unfocused to read the loot notification.

"I got three vials of troll blood." He called out. "And its heart."

"Four vials here. And some claws." Nessa added. The others received similar loot, as did Max. In total they received three of the four hearts, a dozen very tough and sharp claws, ten teeth, something called a control crystal, and eleven vials of blood. Max spent a moment wondering about receiving the blood in glass vials, then just wrote it off as a vagary of this new world. Neither Dalia nor Nessa seemed to question it at all.

In fact, Dalia was smiling widely. "Me da would love to have a few o' them vials. If he could distill the blood and use a few drops in a healing potion…"

"Troll healing!" Smitty shouted. "Like, you could drink one before a fight and it would speed up your regeneration for a while?"

"Aye, that be it exactly." She smiled at him.

"Totally!" his wide grin faded suddenly, though. "But, uhm… would it make our blood explosive, too?"

"Ha!" Dalia slapped his butt as she walked past him. "Nay, it'd be too diluted by the potion and yer own blood."

Max shook his head. "If that is possible, why didn't you ask me for some blood? I'd have happily donated some to your father."

The dwarf shook her head, looking embarrassed. "We, ummm… we figgered since yer blood be o' so many different races, the result might be tainted. I mean, unpredictable." She gave him an apologetic look.

Not offended in the least, Max just shrugged. "I see. Well, as I get better at alchemy myself, maybe I'll experiment with that." He looked at his loot notification again, which included the crystal. "What is this control crystal?" There was silence as everyone just shrugged or shook their heads, indicating they didn't know. Eventually Smitty ventured a guess.

"These things were described as mutant trolls. Maybe the crystal has something to do with that? Could the gnomes have used implanted crystals to somehow control creatures?"

"Might explain why they were so close to the surface." Dalia agreed. "We only run across 'em in the deepest mines and caverns."

Max shook his head, thinking. "Only one of them had a control crystal. How long do trolls live? Could it have been alive back when the gnomes were here? Maybe these others were its offspring?"

Nessa cleared her throat. "This is all very fascinating, but I suggest we move on before more trolls show up."

"Right. Let's go." Max motioned to the exit and the short tunnel beyond, where most of the troll bits had burned themselves out. Dalia cast a spell that created a small globe of greenish light to hover above her head. It illuminated the area well enough for Smitty to see clearly for ten feet or so in every direction.

Though they didn't expect traps in the obviously naturally formed tunnel, Nessa still took the lead as they proceeded out of the cavern and began to explore.

Chapter 5

As they stepped into the next cavern, Dalia pushed her light globe outward so that it illuminated a wider area in front of the group, and cast less light directly upon them. Max and the others who could see well in the dark scanned the area, but found no immediate signs of danger.

Leaning close to Max, Smitty whispered loudly enough for everyone else to hear. "Hey, boss. You think if we shoved that control crystal into Dylan, we could like, remote control his dance moves?"

Max snorted as Dylan gave Smitty the stink-eye. "Might be worth it to try."

"You're both just jealous." Dylan shot them the finger. "My moves are epic!"

"That's not what that bartender in Austin called them. What was the phrase she used?" Smitty scratched his chin, pretending to try to remember.

"Peacock with its tail on fire?" Max offered, smiling at both his corporals.

"No, no. That's close but..." Smitty tapped the side of his head. "I know! She said you danced like a penguin with oversized testicles, and its feet tied together!"

Dylan laughed despite himself. "Yeah, that was it. I'm really gonna miss that girl. She was totally into me."

They were all silent for a moment, thoughts of their deaths on Earth and those they'd left behind sobering the mood.

At least until Red appeared on Dylan's shoulder, and asked "What's a penguin?"

Chuckling, the three Battleborne got back to business, searching the cavern with heads on a swivel as they advanced across, while Dylan quietly described a penguin to Red.

They were nearing the center of the space when Nessa hissed at them, signaling for the group to stop. Every head turned toward her as she pointed at an innocent looking rock. One of many strewn across the cavern floor, this one was about the size of a beach ball, with an odd spiral pattern on its surface.

Max and the others took a knee as Nessa moved back beside him. "That rock just moved. Not much, but it moved on its own."

Max took a closer look at the rock, but it didn't move again. Picking up a smaller stone, he tossed it overhand, not putting any power behind it, just hitting the larger rock with enough force to sting whatever it was. They were all surprised when the stone hit its target and there was a metallic clang.

"Ah, damn." Dalia began looking around the room with a frown. "It be an iron slug. And we're surrounded."

"Iron slug?" Max asked as he too surveyed the room. They'd walked past more than a dozen similar sized

99

and shaped rocks on their way across the room already. When he turned back to the one in front of him, he saw slime begin to ooze out from the base of the rock, quickly followed by the fleshy body of a snail.

"Nasty lil buggers. They feed on the minerals in the underground, and be especially partial to iron. Somethin' in their bodies lets 'em process the metal and use it to form the shells ye see here. Hard to break through, as they be several inches thick."

Already the slug he'd hit with the stone was moving in his direction, its head now extended out of the shell, and two eyes on the end of long stalks focused on him. He saw the creature was leaving a trail as it moved unexpectedly quickly toward him.

> *Iron Slug*
> *Level 17*
> *Health: 2,900/2,900*

Smitty saw the same, and complained. "Whoah. Snails are supposed to be slow. This one's movin like it's late for dinner, and it thinks we're the main course."

"And Max rang the dinner bell." Nessa pointed in several directions toward other snails that were now all moving toward the group.

"No booms, Max." Dalia warned. "There'd be shrapnel everywhere. And ye might collapse the ceiling."

"Right." Max agreed. He looked around, figuring they had about ten seconds before the nearest slug reached them. It was a lower level than him, but there were dozens of them approaching, and Dalia had already noted that they were hard to kill.

He was trying to formulate a plan other than 'run away' when Dylan took matters into his own hands. He took two long steps forward and punted the nearest approaching slug. There was a much louder clang, and the snail, which should have flown halfway across the cavern, simply tilted to one side slightly. There was a slight slurping sound as part of its body was pulled out of its slime bed on the floor, then pulled back down. Dylan fell backward on his butt, reaching for his injured foot. "Damn, that hurt! Broke my toes! It was like kicking a train locomotive." He let go of his foot and scrambled back to standing after Dalia healed the damage.

"Don't step in their slime trails." the dwarfess warned. "They be acidic and sticky. Eat yer boots and make ya get stuck if yer unlucky." She was about to warn them about the slugs' attack when several of them reared back their heads then thrust them forward, emitting a short stream of viscous liquid. Everyone managed to dodge the first volley, and Max noted the stone floor begin to bubble and liquify where the streams landed. Dylan caught another incoming spit attack on his shield, and it too began to smoke, though the damage was much slower.

Grabbing his halberd, Max thrust the spiked end at the same slug Dylan had kicked. The pointed end punched through the fleshy head of the monster, clanging as it slammed into the metal shell behind it. Using all the muscle in his arms, Max twisted and ripped the weapon

101

free. There was a spray of slime, a couple drops of which began to burn his hands, and the creature's head drooped to the ground. His troll regeneration began to battle against the acid eating his skin, the pain considerable.

"They're vulnerable to head shots." Max called out. "But don't let them spit on you! And let's move toward the back wall. No good letting them surround us. Dylan, Dalia, shields! Let's make a three-sided box and move through them. Smitty and Nessa, stay in between us." He produced his own shield and formed up with Dylan, holding his at a ninety degree angle to the ogre's. Behind him Dalia did the same. Smitty and Nessa got behind Dylan, and they all began to move toward the wall. Smitty had his epic *Bow of Shootyness* out and was doing his best to skewer snail heads as they moved. Max saw him hit one cleanly between its eye stalks, the arrowhead punching clean through the monster's head. A moment later the shaft melted in half, corroded by the creature's acidic blood.

Max heard glass shattering behind them, and turned to see a broken vial on the stone floor in front of several of the pursuing slugs. Dalia called out, "They do no' like salt. It'll slow em down and eat at their flesh from below. I've only got one more vial on me."

"Save it for when we stop. We can spread it out wider, maybe slow them down enough to kill them all." Max ordered. He was starting to form a plan involving one of the new spells he'd purchased from Josephine at her inscription shop. In the meantime, he needed to get them out of the center of the room alive.

Wincing slightly at the cost, he produced a bottle of Firebelly's from his ring and smashed the neck against the top of his shield before pouring its contents in a wide arc behind them. He produced a second bottle, and a third, throwing them high into the air so that they landed hard and shattered, spraying the liquid wide. He quickly cast *Spark* on the puddles, causing the high-proof liquid to catch fire. Several of the slugs began to emit high-pitched screams as they burned. Others stopped before entering the flames, then turned and began to move around them.

Nessa screamed as a spit attack landed on her back, quickly eating through her leather armor. Some of the acid splashed onto Smitty as well, causing him to flinch and fire an arrow wildly off into the distance to crash against the stone wall. Dalia cast heals on both of them, but the acid continued to eat at their flesh even as the healing spell restored it. Smitty cursed, gritting his teeth against the pain as he drew another arrow and fired. All three of their shields were smoking from multiple spit strikes as they continued forward across the cavern. Dylan was using his axe to smash at a snail that stood directly in their way, but the weapon was just glancing off the metallic shell and doing no damage. Max equipped his halberd again and handed it to the ogre.

"Use it to stab their heads, or lever it underneath and flip them. Once their bodies are off the floor, you should be able to punt them."

Grunting, Dylan took the weapon and went to work. Max watched as he slid the point along the stone floor, jamming it under the slug directly in front of him. He kept

103

pushing, putting his ogre weight behind it, and the shaft eventually levered the creature up and over onto its side. As it spun slowly around to present its back to Dylan, he kicked it to one side, sending it sliding on its metal shell until it crashed into another approaching slug with a clang of metal on metal.

A quick inspection showed Max that the halberd's dwarven steel was already beginning to smoke and pit slightly, as was the haft. "Let's move! Gotta pick up the pace. Dylan, clear the road as best you can, we'll move around the ones you can't push away. Watch your feet!" he followed his own advice, stepping carefully over the slime trail he nearly missed seeing.

A minute, and several painful hits later, they reached an opening at the back wall of the cavern. It was about ten feet wide, too wide for them to hold with just three shields. Desperate, Max put his plan into play. "Grab your canteens. Spread water over the ground in front of us!" He ordered the others, who quickly obliged, all but Smitty who was now growling in pain as he sent arrow after arrow downrange.

Max slammed his shield down so that the bottom edge bit into the stone slightly. "Nessa, come hold this up. Just crouch behind it and keep it standing upright." He motioned for the beastkin to take his spot. She was moving slowly, tears of pain rolling down her furred cheeks as she did what he ordered. Taking pity on her, he produced one of the good healing potions from his ring and handed it to her. "This might help."

Nodding gratefully, she quickly downed the potion with one hand as she crouched behind the shield and used her other hand to hold it upright.

Standing next to Smitty, Max drew his own bow and proceeded to skewer as many of the slugs as he could with arrows. There were less than twenty of them still advancing on the group, and between he and Smitty they managed to kill three more before the first few crawled into the puddle of water from the canteens.

"Everybody step back, make sure you're out of the water!" he ordered, then held out his empty hand. Like *Boom*!, this spell he'd bought from Josephine was another that was created by a member of her family, and had a similarly amusing name. Max pointed toward the slugs already in the puddle and shouted "*Zap*!"

A bolt of lightning shot out from his hand to strike the nearest slug. The creature froze in place as blue sparks shot across the surface of its shell, and its flesh began to smoke. A fraction of a second later, two more of the creatures who were within the conductive puddle froze as well. They didn't take as much damage as the original target, but the shock had caused them to seize up and stop advancing.

"Right on, boss!" Smitty shouted as he put an arrow into one of the stunned slugs. "Fire for effect!"

Grinning at his corporal's enthusiasm, and glad to have an effective weapon, Max did just that. He used *Zap!* again and again, quickly draining his mana as he hit each new slug that reached the puddle. The secondary damage transmitted through the water was building up on the other monsters, and they began to perish.

Those still living managed just a few more spit attacks in between stunning lightning attacks, and Dalia began to run low on mana. "Hurry it up, Max, I be gettin' low!" She grabbed a mana potion and gulped it down.

"Same here!" Max's mana was draining quickly. At level one, the spell ate sixty mana per cast. With a one thousand mana total pool, he was quickly running dry.

Max was about to cast the spell again when the last of the slugs that hadn't reached the puddle hit him with a lucky spit attack. The glob struck a glancing blow to his cheek before splashing past, but it left more than enough of the acid on his face and ear to make him scream. Forgetting the spell completely, he clapped his hand to his face, spreading the acid further and making his hand begin to burn as well. The pain very nearly made him lose consciousness, and his legs collapsed, causing him to land hard on his butt.

Dalia cast a heal on him from behind her shield, but if anything it only increased the pain. Panting, Max closed his eyes and tried to focus. The acid was eating away at his teeth and gums, having already burned a wide hole in his cheek. He could taste the foul slime mixed with the coppery taste of his own blood for just as second before his tongue began to dissolve as well, ratcheting up the pain level a bit more.

A strong arm gripped his bicep and began to lift him back to his feet. "C'mon, boss. You gotta hit em again.

Don't flake out on us now!" Dylan's voice penetrated the pain.

Opening his eyes, Max saw half a dozen of the slugs still living, recovered from his last stun and beginning to move forward again. Taking a deep breath, he cast the spell.

"*Thhhap!*" his mostly eroded tongue would no longer make the z sound, but it seemed that the world's system understood his intent well enough. The lead slug was hit by lightning, the others around it freezing as their muscles seized. Smitty continued to fire arrows, killing three more that Max saw before he made a huge mistake.

Distracted by the pain… Max swallowed.

The mixture of blood and acid burned its way down his throat, causing him to gag at first, then begin coughing up blood. He dropped his bow and gripped his neck with both hands, spreading some of the acid from his hand onto the skin of his neck, making things worse.

"Stop it, boss!" Smitty slammed into him, knocking him onto his back as the orc grabbed both his wrists and began to pull. As strong as the muscular orc was, Max was stronger. He resisted at first, until Smitty's yelling reached a lucid part of his mind. He relaxed and let Smitty pull his hands away, then pin Max's arms to the ground under his knees.

"They're all dead, boss. Here, swallow this." Smitty poured a health potion into Max's mouth, nearly half of it dribbling out through the hole in his cheek before he forced himself to swallow again. The pain eased slightly, but it was also spreading through his chest and into his gut. With a quiet and ragged moan of pain, Max passed out.

*****

Out of mana again after healing Max and the others as much as she could, Dalia began passing out the best healing potions she had. All of them had acid burns that persisted in eating away at armor, flesh, and even bone in some places. Max lay unconscious, having taken the worst of the hits, and Dalia wasn't sure how long he'd survive. Even his troll regeneration might not save him.

Frantically searching her inventory, she looked for something that might neutralize the acid. She'd learned a good bit watching her father the alchemist, and knew of several ingredients that might help... if she was carrying any of them.

"Yes!" She located a vial of powder from a dried mushroom called chalk cap that was a known neutralizer. Grabbing her mortar and pestle, she poured about a third of the powder from the vial into the bowl, then mixed in some of the high-grade healing potion before pouring the now thicker liquid into another vial. Handing the vial to Nessa, she said, "Here, pour this slowly down his throat! Make sure he swallows it all!"

The moment the beastkin took the mixture from her, Dalia went back to work. She poured the rest of the powder into the bowl, then quickly added a few more ingredients and crushed them all together as rapidly as she could. When she was done, she had a bowl filled with a thick ointment that smelled like dirty socks and crotch rot. Dipping a finger into it, she ignored the smell and applied an experimental dab to a wound on her own arm. Instantly the acid began to bubble, but the pain lessened. She watched for maybe ten seconds as the ointment neutralized the acid and her flesh began to heal.

Holding out the bowl, she said "Here, rub a bit o' this wherever ye be burnt! Just a bit! This be all we have." Ignoring her own wounds, she waited for the others to pull dabs of the ointment from the bowl, then crouched next to Max's prone form. She gently applied some of the healing mixture to the edges of his cheek, making sure the acid stopped spreading before moving on. The mixture Nessa had poured down his throat had worked as well, the damage to Max's tongue, throat, and presumably his innards, already beginning to heal.

When she was sure he wasn't dying, Dalia used the last bits of ointment on her own wounds, sighing with relief. With her mana partially recovered, she drained it again casting a single heal on each of them before collapsing, exhausted.

"That sucked. A lot." Dylan plopped down next to her, examining the many burn marks on his shield. "This thing is pretty much useless now." To illustrate his point, he lifted it up and peeked through a wide hole at Dalia, giving her a wink.

"Aye, when we get back we'll get ye some better gear." The dwarfess promised, laying back after checking that there was no acid on the floor behind her.

Off to one side, Smitty whistled quietly. "Damn, Nessa." He looked at her exposed back and shook his head. The acid had burned away armor, fur, and flesh down to her rib bones on one side. The flesh had regrown, but the hair had not. "You should rest a while." He motioned for her to sit as he crossed his legs and sat down himself. "Here, eat some of this." Smitty pulled some leftover roasted spidorc meat from his inventory and handed it to her. "It's uhh… spidorc meat. Sorry, that's all I have. Tastes better than it sounds." He shrugged apologetically.

"Thank you, Smitty." Nessa accepted the food and began to eat quietly. The orc grinned at her use of his name for the first time.

The group rested, eating and drinking and doing their best to repair their damaged gear for half an hour or so before Max woke up. When he did, he bolted up to a sitting position and promptly coughed up massive quantities of blood.

"Gah!" he spit a few times to clear his mouth, and started to wipe it with the back of his hand before remembering the acid and changing his mind. Instead he looked at his hands, seeing that they were fully healed and free of acid slime.

"Let's not do that again." He looked at the others, who were nodding in agreement. "I mean, if we see these things, we run away. Period."

"Roger that, boss. Run from the heavy metal acid snail band. Right on. No argument here."

They gave Max a few minutes to eat and recharge as Smitty and Dylan went to loot the dead slugs. Dalia used some glass vials to collect some of their slime, then did the same with the pool of vomited blood that Max had produced. "Never know when flammable acid vomit might come in handy." she explained as she tucked the vials into her inventory. Only a little creeped out, Max just nodded and took a bite of kabob.

The loot ended up being large quantities of shell metal, an alloy that Dalia said the smiths would be interested in, and three dozen bits of slug meat. Even though Dalia insisted the meat was safe and edible, Max made them dump it. Just the thought of eating one of those things made him want to vomit some more.

With everyone healed up and recharged, Dalia cast another light globe, and the group moved out of the snail cavern into another tunnel. This one was clearly carved by hand from the surrounding stone, with a series of glyphs etched into the walls, bunched in clusters every twenty feet or so. None of them could read the glyphs, though Nessa said they looked gnomish, so they moved on.

The end of the tunnel brought them to a stairwell, with stairs extending both upward and down from their level. Dalia, with her natural dwarven sense of direction and distance underground, speculated that this was the same stair that they'd fallen through earlier, and Nessa volunteered to climb up to confirm it. She faded mostly

111

from sight as she activated one of her stealth abilities, and began to climb.

There was a stone door on that level that Max ordered Dylan to close. "Don't want any other snails or trolls sneaking up on us." When the door was secured, Max sat with his back to it and closed his eyes. A moment later, Red spoke up. "That looked nasty, guys."

"Felt nasty too." Smitty agreed.

"Well, the good news is ya all leveled up!" The leprechaun tried to improve their mood. "Dylan, ya be catchin up fast."

"Yeah. Sweet, sweet xp." Dylan mumbled, much less enthusiastic about leveling than normal.

"Everybody take a few minutes to assign your points. I'm... assuming Red can answer questions if you have them?" Max opened one eye and arched his eyebrow at his guide.

"Aye, I can answer *some* questions for all of ya, it seems." She nodded, taking a seat on Dalia's shoulder and favoring the dwarfess with a smile.

For the next thirty minutes, the other two Battleborne asked many of the same questions Max had asked Red, about things like which stats directly effected which attributes, and what she thought their best build options might be. While she was happy to explain the relationships between attributes, with a little help from Dalia, she said she could not make recommendations.

Nessa returned to tell them that this was indeed the stair they had started on. "There are two more landings between here and where we fell through. Both doors are closed. I checked the stairs carefully, and they appear undamaged. There were no traps that I could see."

"We go up first." Max decided. "No point leaving monsters at our back if we can avoid it." He started up the stairs, the others following along behind. Since Nessa said the stairs were clear, they made good time. Max bypassed the first landing they reached, continuing up to the higher level. With the huge gap in the stairs above, he was reasonably sure nothing would be sneaking down on them from the surface level.

When they reached the landing and the stone exit door, Dylan raised what was left of his shield and waited. Max tried the door, but it was locked. Nessa took over, dropping to one knee and producing a pair of slim metal tools. In less than a minute she nodded and stepped back to make room for Max and the ogre tank. The moment Max worked the lever handle and pushed the door open, the ogre stepped through.

There was a medium length corridor ahead of them, stretching some fifty feet till it dead-ended at a stone wall. On either side of the hall two doors stood open, each pair facing the other. Nessa took the lead again, examining the hall for traps. The dust on the floor showed no signs of passage down the corridor, and they quickly reached the first pair of doors. Dylan raised his shield and stepped in front of the door on the right, while Dalia covered the left. Max and Smitty drew arrows and prepared to shoot over

113

Dalia's head at any monsters in her room. Nessa crouched low and faded from sight.

The room was some kind of workshop or laboratory. Max imagined a mad gnome inventor with wild Einstein hair bustling around between the work bench along the back wall and the heavy steel table in the center. The walls were covered in racks of tools and shelves filled with boxes of seemingly random parts. When Dalia stepped into the room, two overhead lights blinked several times before calming to a steady blueish-white glow. The room was clear of anything living.

"This place has electricity?" Smitty's mouth dropped open as he leaned into the room, his feet remaining in the doorway. "I didn't think that was a thing on this world."

Dalia looked up at him. "Dunno what electricity be, but them lights be mechapowered devices. Gnomes be fond of harnessing mana into storage devices they use to power their machines. Everything from lights to big ol' steam wagons that move on their own."

Max blinked a couple times. "I've seen that the dwarves use steam in Darkholm. Why don't you have steam wagons?"

"Bah! They be loud, slow, and always breakin' down or outright exploding. And if ye hadn't noticed, most dwarves focus on physical attributes. Gnomes be the opposite, so there be hundreds o' them around all the time that can recharge the mana storage. The steam systems we use in the city be powered by nature. Heat from the magma chambers or bled from the forges. Water from underground streams. No mana required."

"Fair enough. Let's keep going." Max nodded toward the door. They quickly explored the other three rooms off the hallway, finding similar workshops in each. In the third room, sitting on a table near the door, Max spotted some familiar-looking stones. Picking one up, he Examined it.

Control Crystal
Level 15
Power charge: 10%

Holding it up for the others to see, he asked, "Would these be worth anything at the marketplace?"

Dalia shook her head. "Not in Darkholm. Not many gnomish gadgets around, and I dunno anyone who would know how to control a creature with one o' them."

Nessa had a different opinion. "If you were to sell them through one of the auction houses, particularly one of the gnomish auctions, they might bring a significant profit." She eyed the box of twenty or so crystals. "These might be the most valuable items we find down here..."

"Which is what your quest says you must bring back to your master." Dylan finished for her.

Max nodded, dropping the crystal back into the box and depositing the whole thing into his inventory. "I'll hold on to them for safekeeping. When we're done here, if we haven't found anything more valuable, I'll give you half of these."

Nessa briefly looked suspicious, but quickly adopted a neutral expression and nodded to indicate her agreement.

Having cleared the four rooms, the group moved back to the stairway and down to the next landing and another locked door. This one also led to a group of workshops, six of them this time. Also free of any monsters, the workshops here featured a wider variety of materials. Two of them appeared to be biological in nature, one filled with dried plants and herbs in jars, pots of soil, and what appeared to be an extensive watering system piped across the ceiling. The other was more gruesome, shelves of jars containing preserved body parts next to bins filled with bones of all shapes and sizes. The tools were all sharp knives and saws, drills and pins.

The last room on that level was quite different. There were few tools, but a vast number of scrolls, papers, and chalk boards on the walls. There were several small scale models of machines, including one that looked to Max like a portal pedestal. "This must have been the gnome's equivalent of an architect or designer's office."

"Aye, and there be a preservation spell cast here, or none o' these papers would be intact." Dalia offered.

"Actually…" Dylan looked out the doorway. "That's probably true of all the rooms we've been in. Otherwise lots of those tools would have rusted, the furniture rotted."

"Cool!" Smitty grinned, his full orc tusks gleaming. "This would be a good place to store snacks. Like spidorc kabobs and those ridiculously big eggs. They'd stay fresh for like, a really long time." While Max and Dylan knew that the corporal was clowning, the two ladies looked at him like he was an idiot. Smitty just shrugged off the looks.

"I wonder… if I were to study these drawings enough, could I learn to make portals?" Max asked, mostly to himself.

"Aye, possibly. If all the information be here." Dalia answered. "But it might take ye years o' study. It'd be faster to bribe a mage who knows the magic to teach it to ya."

"Or simply hire one to create a portal for you when you need it." Nessa added.

Max nodded, accepting their advice. But in his head he wasn't thinking of stable portals installed at fixed locations. He had his eye on personal teleportation magic. The kind that would allow him to move himself, or his group, from place to place in an instant.

"Alright, we'll just leave this here for now. Let's head back down and finish exploring this place."

Chapter 6

The group followed Nessa back down the stairway, passed by the level where they'd battled the trolls and snails, and continued downward. The stairs ended perhaps forty feet deeper underground at a wide landing with a round metal door. The door was at least ten feet in diameter, and was held up by a single massive hinge on its left side. The handle was a spoked wheel that resembled a ship's helm wheel.

"Any chance it's unlocked?" Smitty took a seat on the stairs, leaning his bow against the wall. "I mean, if I had a massive multi-ton door protecting my precious album collection, I'd totally leave it unlocked."

Nessa, still not appreciating the orc's sarcasm, touched the door with one hand. "Unlikely. Had it been left unlocked, the orcs would not have bothered to close it on their way out."

Dylan and Smitty just looked at each other and rolled their eyes. Dylan passed on the obvious jibe and instead asked, "Are you able to unlock it? I mean, there's no keyhole that I can see."

Dalia approached the door as Nessa ran her hands over it, the beastkin closing her eyes and mumbling something as she worked. Dalia took out a small hammer and began to tap at the stone wall to one side of the door. "Might be we could break through the wall if them gnomes didn't think to..." She stopped talking as the sound of the tapping changed. A few more experimental hits, and she shook her head. "Nope. There be a metal plate extendin' through the stone here."

They waited a few minutes while Nessa completed her inspection of the door. Eventually she too shook her head. "The lock is not accessible from this side of the door. It also has a magical component that I do not recognize. There is an active ward spell, and at least one trap that would trigger should we somehow force the door open."

Smitty, who had gotten to his feet and was pacing impatiently, turned and walked to the door, giving Nessa a wink as he passed by her. "We have a secret to opening doors on our... in our homeland." He tripped over his own tongue as he raised a hand. "It's called knocking."

Smitty raised his arm and pounded three times with his large green fist on the metal door. There was a resounding thrum of vibrating metal after each strike. He lowered his arm and waited expectantly as Nessa glared at him. Dalia covered her mouth to hide her grin.

They all stood in silence for maybe half a minute before Smitty shrugged. "It coulda worked..." He mumbled as he stepped back, then nearly jumped out of his skin when a loud, high-pitched voice with a metallic echo filled the room.

"Go away! Damned trolls. There's no food in here!"

"Holy shit, it worked!" Smitty pumped a fist in the air as Max and Dylan searched the ceiling and walls for speakers. "Hey! Uhm, we're not trolls. We're... visitors. Yeah. New neighbors come to say hello."

"Visitors?" the voice repeated. "Neighbors? The only neighbors are hated orcs! Not visitors, intruders!" the statement was followed by cackling laughter that ended quickly. When the voice spoke again, the tone was suspiciously friendly. "It could be visitors. Let them in, yes? Get a good look at them. They'll never suspect a trap!"

The group exchanged incredulous looks as the door's wheel spun briefly, then the door unsealed with a soft pop of released pressure. A metallic and vaguely foul scent pushed through the widening opening at them. When the door had opened fully, the voice continued.

"Enter, *visitors*. Step right in. Lots of interesting stuff in here, yes! Shiny things, tasty treats, gadgets and gizmos galore! Ooh, and secrets, yes! Many yummy secrets to share!"

Max looked at Dylan. "Don't say it..."

"It's a trap!" Smitty happily provided. He grinned like an idiot as Dylan offered him a fist-bump and Max shook his head. The two ladies looked between them.

"Ye seem oddly pleased at the prospect o' this bein a trap." Dalia commented.

Nessa snorted in agreement. "I begin to wonder about this group's sanity."

"Trap? No!" The voice shouted. Then continued in its previous friendly tone. "I mean, welcome, friendly new neighbors. It has been so long since I've spoken to friends. Won't you come in and visit?"

Max sighed with resignation. "Alright, eyes open, shields up. Let's go say hello."

Dylan raised his battered and acid-holed shield and stepped through the doorway, Smitty right behind him with an arrow nocked. Dalia followed with her own shield raised, sword in hand while Nessa crept forward, fading from sight as she moved. Max brought up the rear, his own shield equipped on his left arm with his halberd in his right hand.

The chamber they entered was round, maybe a hundred paces across. Several light fixtures mounted about three feet high around the perimeter wall emitted a soft blue glow. Others were dark, and a few blinked on and off intermittently as if shorting out. There were no other doors that Max could see, and the room appeared empty. As they all searched for the room's occupant, the door slammed shut behind them.

"HA! You fell for my clever trap!" the voice shouted down from above. As all eyes shifted upward, a square section of the ceiling separated from the rest and began to lower itself toward the floor. A moment later cables could be seen attached to each corner of the lowering platform. "You have sealed your fate, invaders! None can defeat me!"

As the platform neared the floor, the group could see a creature standing at its center. At first Max mistook it for a giant spider, but a moment later he realized it only had four legs, and those legs were mechanical. He took a moment to *Identify* it.

MechaMage Super-Destructo Construct
Level 20; Elite
Health: 10,000/10,000

Max heard Smitty chuckle as he too read the creature's name. It was just his style of naming. The construct featured four spiderlike legs with jointed segments that attached to a round metal body about six feet in diameter. Centered in the top of the body was a sort of pilot's seat, with what looked like gun turrets on its left and right sides. Sitting in the pilot's seat was a little mechanical gnome construct with a clear glass skull that protected what looked like a live brain floating in clear fluid.

"Aha! Another foul orc!" the mechanical gnome's head turned toward Smitty, it's eyes flashing with a blue light. "I knew it! Did I not kill enough of your kind when you raided my temple? Have you come back for more?" The platform reached the floor of the chamber, and the construct stepped forward toward the group with much clanking and squealing of rusted metal joints. The nearest shoulder turret shifted to point at Smitty.

Max stepped forward. "Smitty is an orc, yes. But he's not from one of the orc tribes. He's with me. I'm

Max, King of Stormhaven. As we said before, we're your new neighbors. We just came to explore this place..."

"HA!" the gnome spider thing interrupted Max. "A likely story! If you're not with the orcs, then you're a band a thieves!" Just as it finished shouting, the construct's two weapons fired. Twin burst of blue light shot forward, one striking Smitty in the chest and knocking him back a few steps. The other impacted Dylan's shield as he stepped closer to the construct. Another step, and there was a loud clang as he slammed his shield into the nearest leg, impacting a knee joint.

"Stop that! How dare you!" the gnome screeched at the ogre. "Stupid giant orc! I will crush you!" The leg raised up off the floor with a rusty squeal, its sharply pointed foot aimed at Dylan's face, then froze as its joint locked up. Dylan took the opportunity to rush past that leg and slam his massive axe into a second leg, also at the knee joint. The blow didn't do any damage that he could see, but the construct did wobble dangerously.

Max, unwilling to cast *Boom!* at a metal target in an enclosed space, charged forward with his halberd in both hands. He thrust the weapon's sharp spike up toward the gnome construct's face, threatening the fragile-looking glass brain pan.

Immediately both turrets focused on Max and fired. The twin bolts struck his chest, knocking him onto his butt and reducing his health by about ten percent. The impact stunned him for a moment, and the giant spider spun on three legs so that the raised appendage was now pointed at

Max. As he watched, a tiny version of the spider construct emerged from the main body and scuttled down the frozen leg. When it reached the rusty knee joint, it produced a tube of some kind in two tiny robot arms and squeezed a viscous substance out of the tube, directly into the joint before scuttling away.

A moment later, with the screech of metal against metal, the knee joint flexed slightly. Then it reversed and tightened itself. After a couple more strained movements, the lube did its job and loosened the joint. The leg promptly shot out toward Max, who was just getting to his feet. He dodged to his right, stabbing forward with his halberd at the same time. The leg missed him by at least a foot, while his own thrust impacted the mechanical gnome's skull and skittered off. The glass was tougher than it looked.

Two more blasts from the shoulder weapons struck Max, forcing him back and draining another ten percent of his health. He felt a heal from Dalia, but hung back as Dylan stepped between him and the construct. The next thrust of the sharp pointed leg met Dylan's shield with a deep gong. A quick second thrust punched through a hole created by the snail acid and deep into the ogre's forearm. Dylan grunted and yanked his arm free, blood spraying.

"Screw this! Time to cook some brain stew." Max growled as he pointed a hand at the gnome's head. *"Zap!"*

A bolt of lightning energy shot forward, hitting the metal gnome directly in the face. The whole construct froze, seizing up as the power flowed through its metal body. The fluid inside the skull glowed brightly for several seconds.

"What was that!?" The gnome shouted when its body unseized. It shook its metal head, causing the liquid inside to slosh around. "Do it again!" The construct swung back toward Max, and he thought it moved more quickly this time. "Do it again!" the gnome demanded, firing both its weapons at Max's feet.

"Don't do it boss. I think you just charged its batteries or something." Dylan warned, keeping his eyes on the construct as he spoke.

"More! More power!" the spider legs chipped into the stone as it moved closer to Max. "Please! More power!"

Max hesitated. The thing was pleading now, instead of threatening. He let the butt of his halberd rest on the floor as he raised his other hand toward the gnome. "If I give you more power, you promise not to attack us again?"

"Promise? No! No promises. Never promise. I made a promise once. Didn't keep it. Failed to protect my acolytes. They all died. Stupid orcs!" The seemingly insane gnome's eyes and brain fluid flashed blue for a moment. "Give more power!"

"Everybody back away. I'm gonna try something." Max warned. He waited a few seconds as the gnome ranted on about wanting power. When he saw that everyone was clear, he shot the creature with another bolt of lightning.

"Yessss!" the gnome cried out in ecstasy. "Power! It has been so long." It backed away from Max, lowering the threatening leg it had been jabbing at him and the tank. "More? Please?"

"No more, until you promise not to continue this fight. We came here to explore, not to fight."

"More!" two square panels in the gnome's body opened and two small T-Rex style arms extended, looking just like the ones the tiny lube bot had used. The hands at the ends of the arms opened, revealing a lump of shiny metal in each palm. "I will pay! No fighting. More power!" the hands spun at the wrist joints, turning palm down and dumping the metal lumps onto the floor at Max's feet.

Max looked to Dalia, who just shrugged. "That be lightsteel." She nodded toward the lumps of metal, each about the size of an apple. "Rare, and valuable."

Max looked back at the construct, the little gnome pilot leaning forward eagerly in its seat. "Alright, more power." He cast *Zap!* once more, taking a little guilty pleasure in hitting the gnome in the face again.

The eyes and brain glowed more brightly, and this time the glow didn't fade right away. Instead it pulsed softly, much like a heartbeat.

"Thank you, ugly white-haired stupid orc! It has been… a very long time since I have been fully charged." The mechanical gnome bowed its head slightly.

"You're welcome. And I'm no orc. I am a chimera." Max stepped closer, wanting a better look at the mechanical gnome and its floating brain. He kept a wary eye on it as he bent and picked up the lumps of lightsteel. "Again, my name is Max. What's yours?"

"I am the great MechaMage Glitterspindle! Supreme Ruler of this Temple and Holder of over one thousand Holy Patents!"

Nessa appeared next to Max, causing him to flinch slightly. "Glitterspindle? As in the founder of the temple?"

"None other!" the gnome raised one mechanical hand and waved.

"But the accounts I read all said that you died over a thousand years ago.

"Ha! Died? Me? Never! My meat body grew old and weak, yes. But my genius could not be allowed to perish! I created this construct to house my mind in an immortal body! Well, nearly immortal. I could use a tune-up." He paused for a moment, flexing slightly squeaky finger joints. "Now tell me why you have invaded my home."

"We are not invaders. We meant no harm in coming here." Max took over. "We are at war with An'zalor, the war chief who controlled this area. I took the nearby mine and surrounding territory from him, and my scouts noticed your temple. We simply came to explore the ruins made of the strange sparkling stone."

"Ruins? How dare you insult my home!" The weapon turrets once again targeted Max. "Take that back!"

Max raised both hands. "I'm sorry, Glitterspindle. I meant no insult."

"Stupid orcs, bashing and smashing everything in sight! I tried to rebuild when they finally left. Cleaned up the debris, the bodies of my poor acolytes. The ones the orcs didn't haul away for their cook pots!" The lifelike gnome construct lowered its head, even managing a sorrowful look on its face. "I even tried to rebuild, to bring stone from the quarry, but didn't have enough energy remaining. The damned orcs stole my power rods! I have been in power conservation mode for one thousand one hundred eighty three years, two months, and four days!"

At the mention of power rods, Dalia shot a look at Max, who was already thinking the same thing she was. They had recovered three power rods from an orc camp they had looted.

"So, these power rods, they run your construct?" Max ventured a guess.

"What? Yes, my construct. The temple, the lights, the portal, my experiments, all of it!"

"They must hold a lot of power." Max was getting that feeling again, engaging the gnome, expecting a quest for his trouble. By the looks on Smitty and Dylan's faces, they agreed.

"They do store some power, yes." Glitterspindle rubbed his metal chin with a tiny metal finger. "But their main purpose is power conversion. They absorb raw mana, condense and convert it to power my inventions. On their own they slowly absorb whatever ambient mana is available, or a mage can infuse their own mana supply directly through the rods."

Max, who was always thinking, always strategizing, began to see a way to kill several birds with one stone. Or three power rods.

"Glitterspindle, I have a proposal for you." He took a step closer to the construct. "But before I present it, I have a few questions."

The gnome's eyes flashed briefly, then it nodded once. "I will listen." The spider legs shifted, lowering the construct's body until it rested on the floor, then folded themselves in close to the body.

"First, you mentioned a portal. You have a working portal here?"

"Of course I do! Stupid orc! I constructed and sold portal pedestals. It would be foolish not to own one myself."

"I'm not an… you know what, never mind. Could you build more portals?"

The metal gnome shook its head. "I can not. The damned orcs took most of my materials. And in this body…" The gnome raised its two hands, as well as the two short T-Rex arms that had extended from the spider body. "If I still had my acolytes, and materials, we could build you portals."

"Hmmm... " Max pretended to think things over. "Could you teach me, or a few of my people, how to build them?"

"What!? You've come here after my secrets! My Holy Patents! I knew it!"

"No, no. Before coming here I knew nothing about you, or your portals, or any other secrets you may have. I'm just trying to find a way that we might work together. The orcs are on the war path, and their army will be coming to this area very soon to reclaim the mine. If my scouts found you, so will theirs. I propose that we work together." Max paused, seeking the best words.

"Your acolytes are long gone, MechaMage Glitterspindle. Forgive me, but your temple is badly damaged, and your resources depleted, as you said. You are in no condition to fight off another orcish army on your own, even with the additional power I've supplied." He waited for a reply, but the gnome just stared at him with a metallic poker face.

"We share a common enemy in War Chief An'zalor. Join me and my kingdom. Allow me to claim this temple and the territory around it. You can stay here, under my protection. If we can reactivate your portal, my allies and I can provide troops to defend this place within minutes of any attack. In addition, we might be able to find you some new acolytes, and resources. You could repair your construct, or even create a new one, and build portals for us to use as we expand our territory."

"Trickery! It's a trap!" the gnome shouted, making Dylan and Smitty chuckle. "Resources are useless without power! Will you remain here and recharge me every day, oh mighty king? I think not!"

Max shook his head. "No, I have a war to fight. A kingdom to grow. Though I may spend some time here with you, learning about portal magic, if we can make a deal." He reached into his inventory and pulled out the box that contained the gnomish power rods. Keeping it closed and held behind his back, he continued. "But I happen to know where to find a power rod that I believe would suit your purposes."

"Power rod?" The gnome leaned forward again, straining against the edge of its cockpit. "Fine! Bring me a power rod and we have a deal." A notification popped up in Max's vision.

Quest received: Produce the Juice!
Present MechaMage Glitterspindle with a power rod compatible with his constructs.
Reward: *250,000 Exp; Right to claim the temple and surrounding lands;*
Cooperation of MechaMage Glitterspindle.
Increased reputation with Glitterspindle. Increased reputation with Gnomish race.

Max silently congratulated himself. While not the gamer that Smitty, Dylan, and some of his other guys had been, he was quickly learning that pushing what amounted to key NPCs on this world could gain him some significant benefits.

"Easiest quest ever." He grinned at his corporals, who looked confused. They had also received the quest. Max winked at them, then produced the box from behind his back. Holding it up toward the gnome, he opened the box. "Power rods, as agreed."

"Power rods!" The gnome shouted, both hands reaching out toward Max like a small child asking to be picked up. Max handed the box over, and the gnome's eyes glowed as it inspected the rods. "These... these are *MY* power rods. Stolen by the damned orcs!"

At that moment, the quest completed, and both Nessa and Dylan leveled up. A quick check of his interface showed Max that the gnome had awarded three times the stated quest experience, for three rods.

"Yes, we took them from some orcs we killed not long ago." Max confirmed. "I had a feeling they might have come from here."

"I must install these right away! Come, come! We shall visit the heart of the temple!" The construct got back to its feet, and the group followed it back to the lift. Once they were all aboard, the platform began to rise. When it cleared the ceiling, they continued to rise up a square shaft, the sound of rusted gears straining above them. When the lift came to a halt, they followed the construct down a short, square corridor with a ceiling so low that Max and Smitty had to bend low to walk, and Dylan actually had to crawl.

After a short distance, the wall ahead of them slid to one side. Max and the others followed the gnome through into a large chamber with a pedestal in the center. The construct stopped moving, lowering itself down and folding in its legs again. The metal gnome hopped out and, ignoring the pedestal, moved to a panel in the nearby wall. A mumbled command caused the panel to slide open, revealing what looked like an early version of a circuit board from Earth. Glitterspindle cackled with glee as he placed each of the control rods into what Max would have called circuit breakers, the ends of each rod fitting snuggly into metal receptors.

"This is the main control panel." The little metal construct with the glowing brain said as he pushed a big red button. Lights came on around the chamber, and a humming sound from behind the walls became audible. A moment later, several loud screeches and clanks echoed through the structure from somewhere outside the chamber. "Yes, well. Several systems may need some slight maintenance." Glitterspindle mumbled. He motioned toward Max. "Place your hand here, orc, and I will grant you control authorization."

"Still not an orc." Max mumbled to himself as he stepped forward and placed his hand over a flat metal plate indicated by the gnome. The plate glowed blue for several seconds, then faded.

Congratulations! Through combat and diplomacy, you have conquered the MechaMage's Temple! Do you wish to claim ownership of the temple at this time?

Yes/No

Max quickly selected *Yes*, and Glitterspindle's temple became part of Stormhaven. As the gnome mumbled to itself and fiddled with the controls, Max walked over to the pedestal. Equipping the portal control crystal that Regin had given him, he set it in the empty slot at the top of the pedestal's face.

New portal discovered! Would you like to claim this portal on behalf of Stormhaven?
Yes/No

Max wondered why he should have to claim the portal separately, since the structure around it was now his, but he quickly selected *Yes* anyway. Accessing the controls, he left the portal's designation as *MechaMage Temple*, seeing no reason to change it. He authorized the portal to connect to both Stormhaven's and the Outpost's portals, set it to connect with Stormhaven, then tried to activate it. When nothing happened, he turned to the gnome.

"Glitterspindle, the portal's not working."

"Stupid orc! I have only just installed the power rods! It will take several hours for the mana spring to recharge the temple enough to power the portal. Be patient!"

"Yeah, c'mon boss!" Smitty piled on, a wide grin on his face. "Give the little fella a chance to recharge the batteries."

Dylan, however, focused on a different bit of the gnome's statement. "Mana spring?"

"Yes, mana spring!" the gnome turned toward the ogre, leaning backward so that it could glare up at him. "Which of those words did you not understand, giant stupid orc?"

"You know, I could crush you like a soda can, you psychotic little droid." Dylan clenched a fist and showed it to the gnome, who seemed unimpressed.

"I am not familiar with what a mana spring is, Glitterspindle." Max stepped between Dylan and the gnome. "Please, enlighten me."

"I'm busy!" the gnome turned its back on Max and began to fiddle with the control panel again.

Dalia cleared her throat. "I can help ye there. All the world be infused with mana. It be in every livin' thing, every stone, even the air around us. The ambient mana here on the surface o' the world comes from deep within. It pushes outward from the source through earth, through stone, through water. In some places, the path to the surface be easier, and a higher concentration o' mana pushes outward. Those places be called mana springs. Me guess would be that the gnome built his temple here cuz he found one o' them springs. Most dwarven cities be the same. We follow a new mountain's ore as we mine, but if

135

we stumble across a mana spring, that be reason enough to establish a settlement."

"Sweet!" Smitty looked around the room as if he might see the extra mana seeping up from the floor. "Does that mean we regenerate mana faster if we're on top of the spring?"

"Aye, it does. And if ye spend a great deal o' yer time here, yer body will adapt to the higher concentration o' mana, and learn to absorb more of it, faster."

"Right on!" Smitty crossed his legs and dropped to a sitting position. Placing his hands on his knees, he closed his eyes. "Ohhmmm… ohhhmmm…"

"What is he doing?" Dalia asked.

"Meditating." Dylan answered. "In many of the uh… games, on our world, meditation grants focus, allowing you to recharge faster."

Max shrugged. "I want to stay at least long enough to test the portal. If that's going to take a few hours, we might as well make the best of it. Smoke em if ya got em."

He took a seat as well, pulling out the alchemist's kit that Dalia had purchased for him after their orcish arena victory. After setting up the equipment and arranging some ingredients, he used *Spark* to light the tiny burner, and began to work on creating more potions.

Chapter 7

It ended up taking nearly twelve hours before the temple's power reserves were charged enough to activate the portal. Mainly because Glitterspindle kept diverting power to other systems, charging and activating several of his constructs, cackling madly as each one came online.

Smitty volunteered to run back to the mine and update the others. Having a portal so close to the mine and the way station made them much easier to defend, as well as speeding up the transport of ore and supplies back and forth. The crops from the farms would be that much fresher when they reached the city, and the farmers would save days of travel time that could be put to better use.

As he was getting ready to leave, the orc corporal looked around, then down at the lift. "Uhh… boss? How do I get out of here? If I take the lift back down, and go back the way we came, there's still that big gap in the stairs."

Max blinked for a second, looking up from his alchemy workings. "Glitterspindle? Where's the way out?"

"What? Out? Why would you want to go out? Stupid orcs." the metallic gnome didn't even look away from the control panel.

"How about for food? Water? Not all of us are made of metal."

"Oh! Of course. How silly of me. One moment. The lever is right... over... here!" There was a grinding sound, and the back wall of the chamber began to crack open. Two halves of the wall split apart, sliding like barn doors. Sunlight came streaming in, and Max recognized the room that held the pyramid. Walking out into the open, he turned to see that the pyramid itself had split open, and that the portal and control chamber were in fact inside it.

"Well, at least we know what the pyramid's for now." Nessa spoke from behind Max. He flinched again, getting a little tired of the beastkin sneaking up on him.

"Very clever idea." Max gave her a smile he didn't feel. "What are your plans now, Nessa?"

"I must return to my master and complete my quest." She paused, giving him a significant look. When he didn't respond right away, she held out a hand. "The control crystals? We had an agreement."

"Oh!" Max had forgotten. He pulled most of the crystals from his inventory, as well as the box they'd come in, and handed them over. "Here you go. I hope we see you again, Nessa. We worked well together. If you ever find yourself near Stormhaven, please stop and say hello."

"Thank you, I may do that." The woman stowed the box of crystals, then gave a little salute before morphing into the large panther they'd originally met. With a twitch of her tail, she turned and dashed off into the forest, disappearing through the wall of brush that lined the stone courtyard.

Smitty emerged just as she disappeared. "Not one for big goodbyes, eh? I don't blame her. If I spent six months on a quest, I'd want to turn it in right away too." He turned and looked up toward the cliff that stood above the mine. "I'll bring our mounts back with me. Along with a few of the dwarves and orcs, I imagine. They'll want to start planning a road from here to the mine."

Max shook his head. "Not yet. A road would just advertise that this place is here. An'zalor will be sending more troops soon. I'd like to keep this place a surprise if we can. If he commits troops to a siege of the mine, we can use the portal to bring in a force to surround his, pin him against the fortifications. Nessa said the receipt she found was for a portal in the human city, the one An'zalor controls now. So he may have access to a portal of his own, if it's still operable. We don't want him to find this one, and be able to transport in his own troops." He thought about it for a bit, then continued.

"Ask the engineers how hard it would be to extend a tunnel out the back side of the hill. Big enough for wagons of ore and supplies to move through. If we can build a secret mine exit in the woods somewhere near here, we won't need a road."

"Can do, boss." Smitty waved and set off at a jog.

Dalia, who had been peering over the gnome's shoulder as he brought the temple and its constructs back online, walked over to join Max. "That lil fella be a genius. Completely insane, but his gadgets be a real wonder. I'd

139

wager some o' Darkholm's engineers would pay ye well fer a chance to study this place."

Max's first reaction was to tell her that Stormhaven owed Darkholm a debt, and they were welcome to study the gnome and his gadgets for free. But he stopped himself, remembering that he had a small kingdom full of people to look out for. He couldn't afford to be so generous at their expense. "I'm sure we can work something out. Maybe they could perform a service for Stormhaven in return."

"Aye, good thinkin'" Dalia nodded, flashing him a knowing grin. "I'm gonna search the woods around these ruins, see what kind of herbs and other ingredients I might find."

"Not ruins! Stupid orcs." Glitterspindle yelled without even turning away from his work.

"Please take Dylan with you. Just in case there are any unfriendlies out there. Maybe teach him how to harvest the plants while you're at it?"

"Will do!" the dwarfess turned toward the exit and shouted "Hey, big stuff! Come with me!" Dylan didn't hesitate, rising from where he'd been lounging against a wall, picking at his toenails with a dagger's point. With a nod toward Max, he followed the dwarf out the door and across the stone paved area, disappearing into the foliage with her.

*****

Izgren woke to the quiet sounds of stealthy individuals with soft-soled shoes moving about the room. She didn't need to open her eyes to know who was there, or where she was. She recognized the footsteps of every thief or assassin she'd ever trained. And too few of them still lived. From the sounds of things, those who remained were making preparations to leave. The sounds of clothing being stuffed into bags, the clink of metal valuables being tossed into chests, the occasional grunt of a heavy weight being lifted, then the thump of it being set back down.

Opening her eyes, she met the gaze of her master. The ancient grey dwarf was sitting at the foot of the cot she lay on, his legs crossed and his hands working at shaping something out of stone. "Ah, she rejoins the living. For a while there, we were not so sure of that outcome."

Izgren grimaced. Memories of the wounds she had taken led to reliving the loss of her son and his fellow prisoners. "My son and the others are gone. But they died fighting, rather than as caged animals."

"I know, I have seen. I hope you do not mind, but I took a small peek at your memories when we were unsure whether you would survive. We needed to know whether to send others in your place. I'm sorry for your loss."

Like any thief, Izgren was uncomfortable with anyone poking about in her mind. She had more than her share of secrets. But she trusted her master above all others, and just gave a resigned sigh. "You did what was necessary." She took a quick glance around the parts of the room she could see from her position, confirming what her ears had told her. "We're leaving?"

"The hated ones and their kobold lapdogs are scouring the city. Many of our secret places have been discovered, and our losses continue to mount. It is only a matter of time before they discover this place within the wall. You and I will guide the few of our people that remain through the underground to a new home."

Izgren raised her arms, then slowly sat upright on the cot, expecting pain, but experiencing none. She quickly got to her feet and checked over her body, moving and inspecting each limb.

"You are fully healed. I used one of the superior potions to ensure that you'd be well enough to travel. Your bags are packed and already loaded. Take some time to eat a good meal, replenish your body's resources, then we will depart. Time is short, so don't dawdle." The ancient grey dwarf grinned at her, sharing an old joke.

"I'm no longer that flighty girl who joined you so many years ago, master."

"Ah, but I still see that girl when I look at you, little one." He used the affectionate term she hadn't heard from him in at least a century. That in itself made her nervous. Their circumstances must be dire, indeed.

"I can eat while we move. If everyone else is ready, let us depart." She looked around, finding a plate with a couple of sandwiches on stale bread, and a slightly softening apple. Fresh food was difficult to come by, even for thieves. Dropping the sandwiches into her inventory, she grabbed the apple and took a bite. Despite the slightly off taste of the fruit, she smiled at her master and licked her lips. "What is our destination?"

The old master shook his head. "None of my messengers have returned. I don't know if any of the other three guilds will grant us shelter. And with so few of us remaining, we could not fight for the right to claim a territory in any of their cities. So, for now, we will disappear. Find a secure location in the wilds of the underground and establish a temporary base. We will hunt for our food and live like animals while we gather intelligence."

Izgren nodded once, accepting the decision without argument. There were less than twenty of her guildmates remaining, of more than a hundred members from just a few days before. And it was likely they would lose more before they reached their destination. The damned kobolds hunted the tunnels around the city, and though every member of the guild had stealth abilities that made them invisible to the eye, kobolds had excellent hearing and a keen sense of smell.

"I will scout ahead, master, and leave the usual markers where the path is safest."

"Thank you, little one. The rest of us will be safer for it. You are still the most skilled of all my students, even after all this time." He paused to think. "Let us head north, deeper under the mountain ranges. There was an old orc settlement in a cavern near the surface, abandoned long

143

ago when they moved down out of the mountains to fight the humans and elves."

"Gar'doz. I know the place." She nodded once. "And I know the route. It will take three days, maybe longer without pack animals… she raised an eyebrow at the old dwarf, who chuckled.

"No, we do not carry the treasury. It is safely hidden. We travel light this day, only carrying what we need to survive. We'll have to gather food and water along the way. When we have established a base, we can obtain pack beasts and return for the dead king's treasure." Her master got to his feet. "Off with you, then. I shall round up the younglings and those few veterans who remain, and we will be an hour or so behind you." He waved one hand at a pack that sat on the floor under her cot.

With no need to say more, she shouldered the pack, confirmed her remaining knives were in their proper places, took her short sword from the table next to her cot, and sheathed it on her back. A quick nod to her master, some smiles for the others as she crossed the room, and she was on her way.

*****

Max spent some time conversing with Red while he waited on his team members to return. The crazy gnome, who spent a good deal of the time talking to himself, didn't appear at all bothered to see Max doing the same.

"Everybody all up to date on their stats, Red?"

"Yep! I can't see theirs like I can yours, but they each read them out to me, and I've started keeping notes on each o' them. Even Dalia asked a few questions."

"Good. Then let's talk about professions for a minute. I'm leveling my *Alchemy*, making all these potions, and I've noticed that my skill levels up faster when I use the rare ingredients than when I use the others. Why is that?"

"It's not so much the ingredients, it's the potion ye get as the end result. Creating higher quality potions earns ya more experience in your craft, advancing ye faster toward the next level. You could get the same result if ya took your time and worked in a real alchemist's lab, makin' proper use o' the common ingredients to produce high quality potions. In fact, you should stop using the good stuff right now. You're just wastin' it. Wait until ya get back home, and borrow a lab, or build your own. Take your time to create the best potions ye can with common herbs, till ye get no more benefit from them. Then ye can try usin' the better herbs. Though I'd consult with Dalia's da before you do so. He may be able to give ya some intermediate options first. No point in squandering valuable resources to earn levels ya could achieve without 'em."

"Good point. I'll do that." Max nodded. "Maybe I can bribe her father into building me a proper alchemy lab in Stormhaven. Or… shouldn't there already be one there someplace? I mean, didn't the grey dwarves make potions and poisons and such."

145

Red shrugged. "I assume so. We can ask Redmane when we get back."

"What about *Blacksmithing*? What other trades can I learn that'll help me there?"

"Well, the obvious one be *Mining*, which ya've already started to develop. There be related skills like *Leatherworking* for weapon grips and scabbards, *Enchanting* to add power to your creations, *Engraving* to help with the enchantments, and just for decorating the blades or armor ya make..."

Max held up his hands. "Okay, okay. That's probably more than enough for now." He was feeling a little overwhelmed, but excited at the same time. "I'll focus on that list to start with. If I live long enough to master those and move on to new things, great." He thought about how much time he spent with Redmane each day he was in Stormhaven, working through the piles of issues that needed to be dealt with. If he was to spend any time adventuring with his group and leveling everyone up, his crafting time was going to be limited. And it wasn't like his city was going to depend on him to craft their weapons and armor for them. He had citizens and allies who were already master smiths, leatherworkers, alchemists, and such.

Max needed to temper his urge for personal development with the need to think on a larger city/kingdom scale. Time spent on leveling his smithing might be better spent recruiting more allies or establishing new trade agreements. This wasn't one of those

MMORPGs where individual achievement and getting on a leader board was the mark of success. He and his men were a part of this world now, and they were playing for keeps.

"Your ears are smokin'." Red's voice interrupted his reverie.

"What?" Max blinked a few times, looking over at his shoulder, where the leprechaun sat.

"Ya shouldn't think so hard, it can't be good for that pea brain o' yours. You focus on all the sword-swingin' and face-biting, leave the deep thinkin' to me."

"Heh. Alright." Max had the urge to poke her in the belly, see if she was ticklish, but he knew she still had no real substance. "Since you want to do all the heavy brain work, how bout you tell me the best way to level up my *Sovereign* class? I mean, do I conquer new lands? Add more citizens? Earn more taxes? Expand the city and its territory?"

"Aye, all o' those things help. But also the less tangible actions ya take. Make wise decisions that benefit your people, your kingdom. Be aware that they won't always be the same thing. For example, ya may need to raise taxes to help pay for a war. The people may be unhappy, but it would be the right thing for the kingdom. Treat your people fairly and well, even when it might be easier, or more satisfying, to punish those who annoy you. I haven't been showin' ya all the little notifications, but actions like instructing Redmane to get the mages' guild to put up lights in the city for those who'll need them... that

147

earned ya some points toward leveling your class. Not just because it's considered city building, but because ya made the decision out of a desire to help those citizens who would suffer without those lights. And ya made it before any o' them came to ya to complain."

"Cool. Who's a good sovereign? I am!" Max thumbed his chest, grinning at Red, who just rolled her eyes. Becoming more serious, he added, "Do me a favor and tell me if I'm leaning toward a decision that might cause me to lose… uhh… sovereign points? I don't know what to call them."

"That's as good a name as any." Red nodded. "And aye, I'll warn ya, *if ya give me time.*" She gave him a significant look, making Max think back to the first day in his new body, when he dumped a bunch of attribute points in *Constitution* all at once, and paid the price.

"Right. No hasty kingly decisions. I suppose that's what I have the councilors for as well. Talk things out, make the best choices possible." He paused and looked sideways at the leprechaun, who in turn gave him a suspicious look. "Aaaand that makes you one of my ministers! You are officially my Minister of Snark!"

"Shut it, ya big windbag!" She snapped at him. But Max didn't miss the small smile she fought to keep off her face.

*****

Back at Stormhaven, Max spent half of the following day with Redmane, going through the various issues stacked on his desk. The Mages' Guild had agreed to light the city, outside the keep, and the work was already underway. Redmane chuckled as he added a note. "Old Puckerface has agreed to our terms, and will be bringing three o' his apprentices here to provide mage lights in the keep. He's also going to install a few additional security measures that we agreed upon, which are listed here." The old dwarf handed Max the next sheet of paper. He reviewed it quickly, then approved it. The chamberlain had his complete trust in these matters.

"Our merchant councilors have executed several trade agreements, bringing in more than enough food for double our current population for three months, including the two hundred new orcs you've recruited. They spent a bit o' your coin, but not an inappropriate amount." The dwarf handed Max another sheet to review, a summary with several agreements attached behind it. Max spent a little more time on this one, noting that they had purchased a large quantity of the birds that produced the oversized eggs, as well as other livestock meant to sustain his people. There were also significant quantities of grain and seed. Again, he approved it all.

"Last item o' the day. Most o' the goblins have found jobs, either as castle staff or as helpers for the crafters and shopkeepers. Sweeping up, carrying boxes, delivering messages, and such."

"That's good to hear. I have high hopes for those little rascals." Max was sincerely pleased that the formerly starving and fearful goblins were improving their lives in his city. "I'm about to head to Darkholm to speak with Ironhand, let him know about the new portal near the mine. Would you like to join me?"

"Bah!" Redmane shook his head, but smiled good-naturedly. "Got things to do here. Besides, he already knows o' the portal. One o' his engineers sent word through the portal last night to send more troops, miners, and such. Still, ye should share the news in person, just to be polite."

"I'll do just that. I've got a few other stops to make while I'm there." Max paused. "Do we have an alchemy lab here? One I could use? And if not, how hard would it be to set one up?"

"There's an alchemy shop in the town, but Dalia's father already arranged to purchase it. I believe he's there now, settin' things up. As to settin' up a lab here in the palace, it would be simple enough. I'll get a list o' needed equipment from him, then send someone to Darkholm to purchase it all."

"Perfect! I won't bother him in the middle of setting up his shop. My questions can wait a day or two." Max got to his feet. "I'm off to see the king!" he waved at his chamberlain and exited his office. Along the way he picked up Dylan, wanting to get him some better gear. One special thing in particular he had in mind.

As soon as they stepped through the portal, Max led the ogre, who was getting lots of stares from the dwarves they passed, straight to the apprentice level forge area where he'd spent his first days in Darkholm. It only took a moment to locate Master Oakstone, sitting near the same forge at which he'd trained Max in the basics of blacksmithing.

"Master Oakstone! Good to see you again." Max smiled, resisting the urge to bow his head. He didn't think a king bowed to a smith, even a dwarven Master smith.

"King Max! Back fer more lessons, are ye?" The old dwarf greeted him with a smile. "And who's this big fella ya bring'd with ye?" He looked up from his seated position, Dylan's head being a good six feet above his.

Max's voice got quiet. "This is Dylan, a Battleborne like myself, and one of my soldiers on our old world. Dylan, this is Master Oakstone, who was kind enough to teach me how to make a cheese cutter." He grinned as the old dwarf chuckled. "Could we speak… privately?"

"O'course." The dwarf grew serious, looking at the three apprentices who were working nearby. "Go get a meal! Take yer time. Ye got fifteen minutes!" Max rolled his eyes at the gruff old master's orders. When they were alone, Max brought out one of the stone dragon scales from his inventory. He immediately had the old dwarf's undivided attention.

"As you may know, Master Steelbender is making me a few armor pieces from additional scales that I gave him." He waited, and the dwarf nodded, looking slightly jealous. "Well, seeing as he's busy, and you told me that your family were the best at crafting with these scales… I

151

thought you might be willing to craft a chest piece for my extra-large friend here."

Oakstone's eyes widened. He looked from the scale to the ogre, stroking his beard in thought. "That be no easy task, boy. And yer friend be strong enough to wear steel plate n not even feel the weight! Why commit such a valuable resource?" He looked up at Dylan again, "No offense."

"None taken." Dylan, who was as surprised by the request as Oakstone, shook his head.

Max grinned at them both. "Well, you see… we're trying to find a mount for my friend here. He can't ride a wagon in some of the places we'll need to be going, and he's not exactly fleet of foot, if you get my meaning. So I was thinking, assuming we find him an elephant or something to ride, the poor beast will suffer enough without the added weight of steel armor."

"Ha!" both dwarf and ogre laughed together. Dylan added, "Screw you, boss. You wish you were this sexy." for good measure.

Oakstone looked from one to the other, then pulled a knotted length of string from his pocket, followed by a notepad. He set the pad on a workbench, then motioned toward Dylan. "Sit down here, lad. I ain't got no ladder to climb up there n measure ye."

Dylan did as instructed, sitting on the floor with his legs straight out in front of him. Oakstone still had to get on a stool to reach high enough to measure the ogre's shoulders, but in short order the dwarf had taken the necessary measurements and written them down. He took a moment to convert the numbers into a rough sketch, then mumbled to himself as he did some calculations. He even took the scale from Max and measured it carefully, confirming first that they were all roughly the same size, jotting down notes around the sketch.

"It'll take thirty scales, and that's only coverin' the lad's torso and shoulders, not the rest o' his arms."

Max pulled out twenty nine more scales and handed them to the wide-eyed master. "Here you go! How long do you think it'll take you?"

"Bah! This be an art, boy!" The dwarf recovered quickly from his shock, reverting back to his natural gruff attitude. "Ye can't rush an artist! A week, at least. Maybe ten days."

"That should be fine. Please send me a message when you're ready for a fitting?" Max waited for the dwarf to nod, then pulled out ten more scales. "Can I assume this will be sufficient payment?"

"No, lad. That be too much. It be an honor to work with these scales like me da and me grand before him. It might even allow me to level me own smithin' skill, and that be rare for a Master o' my level." Oakstone pushed the stack of scales back toward Max.

"Then, consider it payment for the work, and a bribe. I'd appreciate it if you'd take some time to come to Stormhaven and continue my training?" Max saw Dylan raise a hand next to him, and added, "My training, and Dylan's?"

Oakstone eyed the two tall visitors, then shook his head again. "There be plenty o' dwarves already in yer city that could teach ye what ye need to know at yer low levels."

"True. But none of them have your sparkling personality!" Max winked at the dwarf.

"Bwahaha! Alright, boy. Ye got yerself a bargain. But to even the scales, so to speak, I'll do ye one better. I'll have me clan build ye a private forge and stock it with the tools and supplies ye'll need. Nothin' fancy, mind ye. Just whatever scraps n old bits we've got layin' around. It'll serve ye well enough until ye reach Journeyman."

"Perfect!" Max handed over the scales. "If I'm not there when you arrive, Redmane can coordinate everything with you. We've got to go see King Ironhand now."

"Aye, about yer new portal. Congratulations, by the way. Every engineer in the city, and half the smiths, are dyin' ta see yer metal gnome and his gadgets!"

Max shook his head, unsurprised that word had spread so quickly. "Well, you have a personal invitation to visit anytime you like. I'll warn you, though, Glitterspindle is crazy. Spent something like a thousand years talking to himself."

"Sounds interestin'!" Oakstone waved them away, already stashing away the scales and going back to his sketch.

Max then led Dylan to meet Ironhand, by way of his favorite bakery, with a short stop at the kabob vender's stall, during which they cleaned out the happy dwarf's inventory. Max also purchased several more packets of spices, and traded a few that he'd obtained from the orc city.

They made a quick stop at Fitchstone's shop, where Max introduced Dylan. They spent a few minutes chatting, and the dwarf purchased some of the scrap loot that each of them were carrying. Max did his best to recruit the old dwarf, offering him a prime shop location in Stormhaven. Fitchstone declined, saying he was comfortable where he was. Bidding the dwarf a good day, they continued to the great hall.

Upon arrival, Ironhand waved them forward as he stepped down off his throne and took a seat at one of the long tables, There was no way Dylan could sit at the table, even if the bench might have supported his weight. So he simply sat cross-legged on the floor next to Max.

"I heard about yer new acquisition, and the portal. Congratulations, your highness!" the dwarf gave Max a mock bow.

"Thank you, your majesty." Max bowed his head in return. "At the very least, it'll make the mine and surrounding territory easier to defend."

"Aye, that it will. And it'll mean we get our cut o' the ore from yer mine that much quicker!" Ironhand thumped the table, and a few of the attending elders laughed. The dwarf continued. "We've had nearly a

155

hundred volunteers just this mornin, miners, engineers, even farmers, lookin' to travel to yer new lands. Most are interested in the gnomes' experiments. I told em all that they'd need yer permission to go pokin' around out there."

"More miners and farmers are always welcome." Max replied immediately. "As for the engineers, we could use a few more to help us build the tunnel to the ruins... and I suppose it wouldn't hurt for a dozen or so to explore the ruins and see what they can learn from Mechamage Glitterspindle."

Max thought about it for a second. "Though, such an opportunity shouldn't come for free, right? I mean, we only really appreciate knowledge that we have to struggle for. Master Oakstone taught me that!" He grinned at the dwarven king, who was developing a wide grin of his own, seeing what was coming.

"So, if your engineers assist with whatever's needed at my mine, and agree to help the gnome with some defenses for the temple, they're welcome to, how did you put it? Poke around the ruins for... let's say a month."

"Six months!" Ironhand shouted, thumping the table again as some of the elders leaned forward, curious as to how Max would fare this time.

"My dear king, do you really want your best engineers away from their duties here in the city for six whole months? Six weeks!"

"Who says I'm sending me best?" Ironhand winked at him. "Two months!"

"You've got yourself a deal." Max held out a hand, which Ironhand shook as the elders nodded their approval.

"Well done, Max. Yer learnin'." Ironhand looked proud of him. "Redmane tells me yer city is comin' along nicely."

"Mostly due to his efforts, and those of the other councilors you loaned me. I feel like a monkey being trained to dance for a crowd." Max bowed his head in embarrassment.

"Aye, that be pretty accurate. But don't feel bad, I were the same way once upon a time. When me da passed under the mountain, I were a simple warrior. I wanted nothin' to do with runnin' a kingdom, and thought I had another century or two o' fightin' and adventuring before I'd need ta learn." He let out a long sigh. "Me sire died well, fightin' them cursed greys, but it were too soon. So I had to learn much like yer doin now."

"Thanks for that. And for the teachers." Max bowed his head, sincere this time.

"Oh! I nearly forgot!" Ironhand looked over his shoulder and shouted a name, causing a young dwarf to jump to his feet and dash out a side door. "There be a visitor here, arrived an hour ago askin' fer you. I knew you'd be comin here this morning, so I had em wait."

A moment later, a larger than average orc sporting scars over most of his body emerged from that same side door, led by the nervous young dwarf. The orc approached, then bowed twice, once to each king. "King

Ironhand, thank you again for your hospitality. Chimera King, I have come with a message from my people. Well, some of my people. Are you willing to hear me?"

"Please, sit." Max motioned to an empty place on the bench. "What can I do for you?"

"My name is Or'gral, and I once led the army for An'zalor's predecessor. I retired when my War Chief was displaced by that coward. I watched you and your companions fight in the trials, and you fought with honor. Though I have always hated dwarves, having fought them all my life, your sergeant Battleaxe proved himself a courageous and loyal warrior. He died a good and honorable death." Or'gral saluted with fist to chest, a gesture which all of the dwarves within earshot, including the king, returned.

"I also witnessed the cowardly acts of An'zalor, as did thousands of my people. Were I thirty years younger, I would have challenged him and removed his head that day. Since then, he has grown paranoid and hostile to his own people. His shame, and the public nature of it, eats at his pride. Many of our people have come to me, wishing to leave the city. Some have already set off on their own in the dark of night, to establish new camps in the wilderness. Many others, including myself, wish to join you. We know that An'zalor has declared war upon you, Chimera King, and we wish to help you defeat him."

"How many are we talking about?" Max asked. His mind turned to his discussion just that morning with Redmane about feeding his people.

"Nearly a thousand have come to me so far." Or'gral replied. "But I'm sure thousands more would follow. Warriors, hunters, crafters, farmers, and their families."

Max let out a long, slow exhale. "That's a lot. Your people are, of course, welcome. I think we could accommodate that first thousand right now, with a little extra effort. But my city is small, and our food supplies are limited. With your thousand people, especially the farmers and hunters, we might be able to grow our reserves enough to accept more in a few months..."

The orc nodded, unsurprised. "That is as we expected. My people and I will be coming with only what we can store in our inventories, or carry on our backs. It is impossible to leave the city with wagons at this point, as An'zalor has closed the gates. Any caught emigrating are forced to fight in the trials. Another perversion of the holy rights that the coward shall have to answer for."

Ironhand asked, "Just out o' curiosity, how many o' yer people inhabit the city?"

Or'gral looked thoughtful for a moment. "Several clans have gathered together over the years. I would estimate thirty thousand, maybe slightly more. Though, I believe what you're asking is how many warriors would An'zalor be able to muster?" He grinned at Ironhand, who nodded. "With the losses he has already sustained at the hands of the Chimera King and your forces, An'zalor has maybe six thousand warriors in his standing army. With another two thousand retirees and others that could be called into service."

One of the elders whistled. Max, who was used to battles on Earth involving tens of thousands of troops on either side, gathered that on this world that was a significant force.

"However." The orc held up one finger. "If I know my people, half of that number might refuse to fight for the coward. Of the thousand who wish to come with me now, nearly two hundred would be defectors from the army. Many of them I trained myself as younglings."

Max grinned at this, his mind whirling. Psychological warfare was something for which he was well trained. If he could get half of his enemy's army to desert, or even better, turn and fight against him... "You and your thousand are welcome, Or'gral. You'll need to swear oaths of loyalty to Stormhaven, of course. Can you get them to the northern mine? Or do you need some assistance?"

"We can get there." The scarred veteran orc assured him. "We will need to take a roundabout path, and cover our tracks. Expect us in... a week."

"We'll be ready and waiting for your arrival." Max promised.

Once the orc had been escorted out, and Max had concluded his business with Ironhand, he and Dylan excused themselves. As they left the great hall, he looked at his corporal. "Were you serious about learning magic?"

"Totally serious, boss." The ogre nodded his head.

"In that case, come with me. I have to go apologize to a certain lady gnome for missing our dinner date. While we're there, we'll see what she has for you."

Chapter 8

With the improvements to the mine and the ruins underway, his city growing in the capable hands of his councilors, and his lands reasonably protected for the moment, Max decided to focus on leveling up his group.

The following morning they headed out into the tunnels and caverns surrounding Stormhaven. To begin with, they followed the same path they'd taken previously, hoping to quickly push past the mostly cleared areas near the city, into less explored places where they might find higher level monsters to fight.

The kobolds, after raiding and completely depleting his wine cellar, had happily moved out into the tunnels to hunt any grey dwarves who'd fled the battle. In the process, they'd eliminated dozens of wandering monsters, which they added to their cookpots. Alongside any grey dwarves they captured, who were cooked alive. Karma was a bitch.

As a result, in just a few hours Max, Dalia, Red, Smitty, and Dylan had moved five miles out from the city. Monsters were becoming more numerous, and harder to kill. They'd just defeated a level twenty four rock spider, and Max called for a rest while Smitty butchered the monster. Dalia had informed them that rock spider legs were even more tasty than spidorc meat. Also, the venom sack of a monster that size contained enough venom to make several batches of poison and cure potions.

Smitty finished up his harvest, gaining two stacks, or forty pieces of rock spider leg meat, along with the mandibles and claws. Despite their name, the huge spiders weren't covered in a hard exoskeleton. Instead, their tough skin was hairy, much like a tarantula. The short hairs acted as sensory organs, helping the spider to locate its prey by detecting the minute air fluctuations caused by motion. Creatures of the deep, dark underground lived in a harsh environment, and had developed many ways to survive.

As the group got to their feet and prepared to move on, one of those creatures made its move. Smitty, who was in the rear of the group as usual, let out a pained grunt as something struck him from behind. Stunned, his hand went numb, causing him to drop his bow. Even as it clattered on the stone floor of the tunnel they were marching through, the others turned to see him drop to his knees.

Behind him, one hand raised to deliver a killing blow to the back of Smitty's neck, stood a familiar monster.

Stonetalon
Level 25
Health: 2,800/2,800

Much like the creature Max had observed during his time in limbo reviewing possible race choices, this monster was intimidating. Seven feet tall, it was rail thin with corded muscle and sharp claws. Hairless, its eyes glowed slightly red, even in the greenish light of Dalia's floating globe. Its skin was a dull, mottled black, much the same

163

pigment as the surrounding stone, and seemed to absorb the light rather than reflect it. The monster flexed its raised claw once, then swung downward, intending to rip into and remove Smitty's spine.

Max roared at the stonetalon, distracting it slightly as its claws descended. Smitty's life was saved by the combination of that distraction, and the fact that his still stunned body tipped and fell forward, causing the swiping claws to miss him by several inches. Unfortunately for him, his arms could not move to break his fall, so he impacted the floor face first, his nose crunching as his tusks scraped the stone.

Max leapt forward, some primal reaction to the creature that shared part of his bloodline causing him to bare his fangs in challenge. The stonetalon responded in kind, forgetting about Smitty and grappling with Max. It tried to clutch Max to its chest, craning its neck forward in an attempt to savage his neck with its own, more prominent fangs. The claws of both its hands dug at the chainmail on Max's back, unable to penetrate the dwarven steel.

Though they were of similar size, Max's troll blood and attribute investments made him much bulkier and stronger than the full-blood stonetalon. He placed his left hand under its chin and shoved it away from him, forcing its head to tilt backward and its neck to stretch. With his right hand, he punched it in the throat with as much strength as he could manage with his limited leverage.

The stonetalon released him, both hands moving to grasp its wounded throat, wheezing for air as it took a step back. Max was about to hit it again when Dylan let out a roar behind him. Spinning around, he saw another Stonetalon smash against the tank's new shield. They'd replaced his old one from the armory, and gotten him some decent leather armor as well, including an oversized pair of leather boots with steel toes. Leather wasn't ideal for a tank, but it was the best they could manage in his size on short notice.

Dylan thrust his shield forward, pushing the stonetalon back. This one was even larger than the first, and based on her physical features, was clearly female. She stood maybe eight feet tall, with a narrower waist than the male, and small but obvious breasts. She raised her head and let out a long howl, which surprised Max. The previous stonetalons they'd fought before the orcs attacked the mine hadn't made a sound louder than a growl.

"She be callin' fer help." Dalia called out. "Must be mating season. It be rare to find more than one or two together at a time."

Checking to make sure the first monster was still down, Max roared at the female and sprinted toward her. His instincts to rend and tear a competing stonetalon left him no room to think of drawing his sword, or any weapon. His fingers curled slightly, claws out and already reaching for the female as he moved forward.

Hearing Max's roar, the female straightened her posture and turned toward him. Blinking as if confused by what she saw, her arms dropped slightly, and her head tilted to one side as she sniffed the air. She heard a stonetalon male, but her eyes and nose told her the creature rushing toward her was *not* a stonetalon.

The confusion cost her, as Max reached out and grabbed hold of her neck, spinning to his left, using his bulk and momentum to pull her off balance even as his claws dug into her flesh. She gagged and whined for a moment before the sound was cut off by Max's sharp thumbnail penetrating her throat. A moment later her head and shoulder were slammed into the tunnel wall.

The impact would have snapped the neck of a lesser creature, but stonetalons had extremely strong bones. Still, the blow stunned the monster, causing her legs to go limp, forcing Max to either support her full weight, or let her drop. He chose the latter, letting her body fall to the tunnel floor. Right next to him, Dylan stepped forward and stomped on her neck, his blow sufficient to snap the spine and finish her.

Smitty, meanwhile, was back on his feet and approaching the first stonetalon with his sword drawn. The monster was on its hands and knees, retching and desperately gasping for air. The orc scout wasted no time, raising his sword overhead and bringing it down to cleanly sever the stonetalon's neck.

"Friggin thing jumped me from behind!" Smitty kicked the head hard enough to make it bounce off the tunnel wall and roll a distance away. "Thanks for the save, boss."

Dylan, bending down to loot the female, cleared his throat. "Uh, as rear guard, ain't it kinda your *one job* to watch behind us for ambushes just like that?" He grinned at his friend.

"Kiss my sexy green ass." Dylan shot him a finger before kicking the headless corpse to loot it.

"Speaking of sexy…" Dylan turned to Max. "That female looked like she was diggin' your vibe for a second there. Right before you went all rage-monster on her, I mean. That was brutal, boss."

Max, his blood just beginning to cool, nodded his head. "Yeah. Not sure what happened there. I literally wanted to eat their faces. Must be a racial thing. Competition for food or mates, or something. I didn't even have time to think about it."

"Probably a good thing." Smitty injected. "If you had given her a chance to get warm for your form, boss, she might have gone all praying mantis on you. Bitten your head off during the nookie dance."

Dylan laughed as Max rolled his eyes, and Red and Dalia asked in unison. "What's a praying mantis?"

Smitty shook his head. "Damn. What I wouldn't give for a smartphone and a web connection. There's so much I could teach you two." Both the dwarfess and the leprechaun just looked more confused.

"Explain later." Max shook his head. "She called for reinforcements, remember? We might have more of these things incoming. Form up, let's move." He paused, grinning at Smitty. "Head on a swivel, yes?"

"Aaargh! I got our six, boss." Smitty retrieved his bow, watching the tunnel behind him as he did so. They got back into formation, and began moving forward, Smitty grumbling quietly in the back. "Ya let one lil stealth monster sneak up on ya…"

They followed that tunnel for another five minutes before reaching an intersection. Not having seen or heard more of the monsters didn't reassure them any. The creatures were, as Smitty had pointed out, built for stealth.

Dylan paused at the branching of two tunnels. The one they were in continued on straight ahead, sloping slightly downward. The other veered off to the right and upward. "Uh, I know the rule is 'always go left'… but what do you do when there's only straight, or right?"

Max looked at Dalia, one eyebrow raised.

"We're about six miles north n slightly west o' the city, and a hundred paces deeper. This tunnel heads roughly northwest, that one northeast. So basically north either way. Question is, do ye wanna go up, or down?"

"If we've been going roughly north all this time, then we're deeper under the mountain range, right?" Max pulled up his map to confirm. Unfortunately, it didn't show the surface map that he expected. Instead it showed a mostly blank area with just the series of tunnels they'd advanced through clearly marked. All it showed of the two branches ahead of him were the few hundred feet that he could see from where he stood.

Looking at Dylan, he asked, "How far into the mountains was your ogre village?"

Dylan shook his head. "Not sure, boss. I can't access that part of my map right now. It was a lot of up and down, then a lot of searching in random directions until I found the dwarves' city. If I had to guess... maybe thirty miles as the crow flies?"

Max sighed. "No point in trying to get there from down here then. Without knowing where we're going, or whether these tunnels could even take us in that direction, we might be down here for weeks and not find a route there. When the time comes to visit them, it'd be faster to get you back to the surface and retrace your steps."

"We're already pretty deep below ground, even without the mountain peaks above us." Dalia added. "Remember, Stormhaven be well below the level o' Darkholm to begin with. All the tunnels we took while fightin' the greys went deeper under the mountain." She nodded her head toward the straight branch that sloped downward. "The deeper we go, the bigger and badder the beasties will be."

Max nodded, thinking aloud. "Those last two monsters were level twenty five. That's probably as nasty as we want to see on this trip. Dylan, what level are you now?"

"Nineteen, boss. Maybe a dozen kills or so away from twenty."

Max, Smitty, and Dalia were all over level twenty, and Dylan was catching up. And while they pretty easily handled two higher level stonetalons, if they were to encounter a larger group of monsters, like they did with the trolls and snails in the ruins, he wasn't confident in their ability to survive without losses.

"Alright, let's head upward. Maybe we'll find another route to the surface." He pointed toward the rightward branch, and Dylan set out, shield and axe at the ready.

*****

An uneventful hour later, the group paused for a short break. They'd reached a mid-sized natural cavern, which spread out below the ledge they sat upon. Though the tunnel they'd chosen had steadily, if slowly, climbed upward, Dalia informed them that they were still well below the surface. In unfamiliar territory, she had no way to tell if they would emerge in a valley, or partway up the face of a mountain. As they'd walked, she explained to them what she knew of the geography in their area.

"First, ye should know that Stormhaven sits below a mountain, but not the same mountain that Darkholm occupies. In fact, there be a wide valley between 'em. That valley be where Darkholm's few farmers grow their crops, on farms established a thousand years ago, when it were vital to protect our crops from the orcs. There be forts and smaller outposts ringing the valley, and a network o' traps set at each o' the passes. Any army that tried to break through would get buried under thousands o' tons o' falling stone."

"Good to know." Max tried to picture the valley, thinking back to his few minutes atop the ridge of the outpost. "And the mountain above Stormhaven?"

"One of those in the second ridge, as ye move north. Among the smallest o' the mountains in that ridge." Dalia replied.

"Don't worry, boss." Smitty piped up from behind. "You know what they say. It ain't the size of the mountain, it's the... uhh... motion of the... yeah. Sorry. I got nothin." The orc shrugged as Dylan chuckled up front. Max couldn't help a small grin himself.

Shaking her head, Dalia continued. "The legends of my people say that each mountain has a heart. Opinions vary on its form, some claiming each heart is a gem, others a chamber, still others that the heart be a living form, like an earth elemental. The heart gives the mountain its power, causes it to grow taller, resisting the outside elements that wear it down. At the same time, the heart generates the life's blood of the mountain, in the form of veins." She paused, watching Max's face. When his eyes widened a bit, she smiled. "Ye guessed it. Veins o' stone, or metal ore. Younger, weaker mountains be filled with simple copper, agates, or quartz, while older more powerful mountains grow gold, diamonds, even mithril."

"That's actually pretty interesting." Dylan commented. "We should look for the heart of your mountain, boss."

171

Dalia coughed, seeming slightly embarrassed. "That be why I brought up this topic, Max. Our people have long thought that your mountain was once much larger and richer than it be now. But long ago, the first grey dwarf king, Nogroz, found and removed the heart o' that mountain. The greys weren't always so different than me own folk. We were cousins that lived in peace, traded between our cities across the continent. But Nogroz, he craved power above all things. He stole the heart o' his mountain and used it in some arcane ritual taught to him by a lich. The ritual was supposed to grant him eternal life, along with great power."

"I can see where this is heading." Smitty mumbled from the back. "Can you say epic quest chain?"

Dalia ignored him. "He used the heart, performed the ritual. The magic drained some part o' each of his people, corrupting their souls. And rather than grant eternal life to Nogroz himself, it devoured his soul, granting its power, and all the power stolen from his people, to the lich. The grey dwarves rose up, stormed the keep and killed the lich's undead body. But they were never able to locate the lich's phylactery to destroy its soul. Nor did they ever find the stolen heart o' the mountain. In their shame, Nogroz's people isolated themselves. The evil influence of the lich's spell was passed on from generation to generation, some say getting stronger with each new babe. Eventually many o' the clans left the city to find new homes, murdering or enslaving any that got in their way. Or so the legend goes."

Max asked, "How long ago was this?".

Dalia's eyes squinted slightly as she tried to remember. "I'm not rightly sure? At least two hundred generations back, likely more. Ironhand, or maybe Redmane, could tell ye more."

Dylan did some quick math. "Two hundred generations, so about four thousand years ago?"

"What? No, no." Dalia shook her head. "Ye be thinkin' in human terms. Few self-respectin' dwarves would settle down and make babies at the age o' twenty. They still be considered babes themselves at that age. No... a dwarven generation be fifty years or so. Meanin' Nogroz lived ten thousand years ago, at least."

"And for those ten thousand years, the mountain has been missing its heart. So the weather outside has been wearing it down, while the other mountains continued to grow." Max guessed. "And... the mines we have are just pulling out whatever was already there before the heart was taken?"

"Aye, if the legends be true, then that would be accurate." Dalia nodded.

Dylan stopped and turned toward the others, holding up his hands in a halting motion. "Please boss, allow me?" When Max just nodded, the ogre turned to Dalia. "And if we were to locate the heart of the mountain and return it to... wherever it belongs? Would that start the mountain growing again?"

"I dunno. Maybe?" Dalia shrugged, looking thoughtful.

Instantly they all blinked and unfocused their eyes as a quest notification popped up.

Epic Quest Received: Hard Hearted, Part I
Find and retrieve the heart of the mountain stolen by Nogroz.
Reward: 1,000,000 experience; 1,000 gold; access to quest Hard Hearted Part II

"I knew it! Epic quest chain!" Smitty pumped a fist in the air, following it up with a couple of hip thrusts for good measure. "This is awesome!"

Dylan agreed. "A million xp would put me over level twenty. Sweet!"

Now, sitting on the ledge looking down at the cavern below, Max was considering the best way to pursue that quest.

"If the heart of the mountain was used in the ritual, and Nogroz was killed during the ritual, and the other dwarves didn't find the heart…" He looked around, seeing that his mumbling had garnered everyone's attention. "Then it seems to me the lich must have taken the heart?"

"Or it was destroyed during the ritual." Dalia offered.

Red, sitting atop her left shoulder, shook her tiny head. "Ya wouldn't be havin' the quest if there were no heart to find."

Dylan ventured, "Maybe the greys lied about not finding the heart?"

"What for? If they had it, wouldn't they return it to its proper home, so that their mines would be more productive?" Smitty paused, then seemingly changed his mind. "Unless… were they maybe hoping to use it to reverse the spell that changed them all?"

Max tapped his chin. "Good points. I was thinking as we've been walking that we should try and find the ritual site. But if the heart had been just left laying there, someone obviously would have grabbed it back then.

Dalia, looking a little self-conscious, raised one hand. "I might have an idea where to start lookin'." She glanced at Max, who nodded for her to continue. "Remember, back then the greys were not so different than us. Dwarves, I mean." She blushed slightly. "It be our tradition to bury our kings and heroes with their weapons, armor, and most valuable possessions. So it may be that they buried the heart with Nogroz."

"And left it alone all this time?" Red's tone was doubtful.

"No dwarf would dare disturb the tomb o' their king!" Dalia nearly shouted. "Even the dirty greys wouldn't sink that low!" Realizing what she'd done, she covered her mouth and looked around quickly. Making loud noises in the underground was a foolish move.

Max reached out and patted her knee gently, a calming gesture. "And if the heart is indeed buried with

175

Nogroz? How will you feel about us raiding his tomb for it?"

Her eyes widened. Max saw the conflicted look on her face as she considered her answer. Eventually, she replied. "He weren't me own king. And by all accounts, he was unworthy o' the title, at least at the end. Even so, I'd not disturb his tomb without grave need." She sighed, her shoulders drooping. "But I think even King Ironhand would agree that restoring the heart o' the mountain be a cause worthy of such an intrusion. And clearly, the gods agree, havin' seen fit to give us this quest. If the heart be entombed with Nogroz, we should take it."

"Then it's settled." Max got to his feet, stowing away his canteen. "When we get back to Stormhaven city, we'll start looking for his tomb. As good a place as any to start. In the meantime, I see one exit to this cavern." He pointed downward and to the left. "Over in that wall. Let's make our way down and search the place before we leave here."

The others made themselves ready, and Max began to pick his way down the cavern wall below the ledge. The tunnel and cavern both being natural, there was no handy ramp or stairway leading down. He got down on his belly and slid his legs over the edge, slowly lowering himself down until his right foot found a small ledge. Putting some weight on it, he was just trying to decide whether to trust it with his full weight when Dylan spoke up.

"Uhm, boss?"

Looking up at the ogre, Max grunted. "What?"

"You know when we were at the little gnome lady's shop? And you were talking about spells and stuff?"

"Little busy right now, corporal." Max was feeling around with his left foot, looking for another foothold.

"Right, boss. It's just that, I'm pretty sure I heard you mention a levitation spell? Seems like that would be a lot easier, and faster, way to get down from here."

"Shit." Max cursed under his breath. He wasn't the gamer that his corporals both were, and still didn't have the mindset of using magic in everyday life. Quickly pulling himself back up onto the ledge and dusting himself off, he nodded at the ogre. "You're absolutely right. Like Dalia said earlier, I'm still thinking in human terms. You guys gotta help me remember when magic might be our best option. At least until I get my shit together."

All of the others nodded, and Max looked to Dylan again. "Since it was your idea, you get to go first. I feel I should tell you, I've really only used this spell on others as a way to kill them. Fling them way up in the air n let them fall…" As he finished speaking he cast the spell on his corporal, then quickly made a sideways motion with his hand, pushing the now floating ogre out into open air.

Dylan cussed quietly and struggled a bit, waving his arms and legs wildly, much to Smitty's amusement. "What do you call those dance moves?"

Max directed him downward, slowing his descent near the cavern floor and canceling the spell when he was less than a foot off the ground. Dylan stumbled slightly

177

upon landing, but kept his feet. One by one, Max sent the others down, then cast the spell on himself. As he drifted down to the others, he commented, "This is pretty damned handy. Remind me to get this spell for you guys too."

The cavern floor was mostly level, with a few stalagmites rising up here and there, corresponding stalactites above them. Near the center was a lumpy mound, roughly circular in shape, that rose up maybe twenty feet or so above floor level. Some parts were higher than others, and the stone was a much darker color than the walls or ceiling. Max thought it looked almost like a magma bubble had risen up through the floor, then hardened, leaving a mound of volcanic stone. Most of it was rounded, smooth-looking stone, but there was a spiraling ridge of jagged edges that wound from the floor up to the top. A pressure fracture, maybe? Out loud, he asked Dalia.

"Okay dwarf lady. Is that... what do you call the really hard volcanic stone? Obsidian! Is that a great big pile of obsidian? And does that mean this mountain was a volcano?"

Dalia shook her head. "No evidence o' there bein a volcano here. The tunnels woulda been more round, like lava tubes. This whole ridge be dormant, as far as I know, unless ye dig deep to reach for a magma flow for power generation." She approached the mound as she spoke, taking out the same hammer she'd used to tap the wall outside Glitterspindle's vault door.

"So maybe that's what this is? Somebody dug a deep hole here, hit a magma flow, and it bubbled up to the surface?"

Shaking her head but not speaking, Dalia put her ear close to the mound and tapped it with her hammer. After just a couple taps, she gasped and backed away, a look of terror on her face. Covering her mouth with her hammer hand, she used the other to motion the party back. Clearly seeing her attempt to move quietly, the others took the hint and stayed silent as they too stepped back several paces.

Dalia moved right past them, her eyes wide and frightened, and didn't stop until she had stepped behind a large stalagmite. When the others had joined her, she removed her hand from mouth and opened it to whisper an explanation.

Before she got her first word out, a massive voice echoed through the chamber, causing the others to hunch down in surprise, and Dalia to nearly wet herself.

"Hiding will do you no good, little dwarf. I can hear your terrified heart pounding in your chest! Who dares to enter my domain and disturb my rest? Step forward and present yourselves like proper guests!"

Clearly shaken, Dalia looked at Max and visibly gulped. When she had cleared the lump in her throat enough to speak, she whispered. "It be a dragon."

"Well, shit." Smitty pretty much summed it up for all of them.

Chapter 9

"Come now, little morsels. Step forward and
present yourselves so that I may choose which of you will
have the honor of being first. I have not eaten meat in... let
me see... eleven hundred years or so."

Red appeared on Max's shoulder, a determined look
on her face. "You lot do get yourselves into the most
interestin' trouble. Let me handle this. Follow me." She
floated off Max's shoulder and out from behind the stone
pillar of the stalagmite. The others followed, Dylan first,
followed by Dalia, Max, and Smitty.

"Greetings, ancient one. I request parlay, under the
laws of the First Magic." She called out. Max, surprised by
her action and her words, looked from her to the dragon.

The creature had raised its head, and was slowly
unfurling its long body. What Max had thought to be a
magma mound was simply an obsidian dragon curled up
with its tail around its head. Centuries of dirt and moss had
covered it, smoothing out the rough edges and hiding its
scales. The sharp edges he'd guessed were a pressure
fracture were actually the dragon's spinal ridges, obsidian
blades protruding from its back in a long line from the back
of its head to the end of its tail. Bright yellow eyes with
vertical slit pupils gazed at them, and a palpable wave of
pressure accompanied the attention. Max felt the urge to
bow, to flee, and to whimper, all at the same time.

"First Magic? Parlay? Who are you to…" The dragon paused, tilting its head slightly to one side as it gazed at Red. "A fae? A… leprechaun, if I recall correctly. Well, this *is* an unusual day." He shifted his gaze to the others one by one, focusing for a moment longer on Max. "A chimera, as well. And one marked by more than one of the Elders. Most interesting…"

The dragon pushed itself up onto its feet, shaking its body much like a dog fresh out of the rain, sending a cloud of dust and debris throughout the chamber. The party members blinked and covered their mouths, all except for Red, whom the dust just drifted right through.

Max couldn't help but take an involuntary step back as the dragon's massive head suddenly pushed forward, emerging from the dust cloud just a few feet from his own face. "I see troll, and elf, human, and… one of the scentless ones." The dragon sniffed at him, not seeming to be bothered by the dust it inhaled.

"S-stonetalon." Max offered, barely able to find his voice. The dragon's head was twice the size of Max's entire body. If it so desired, it could probably swallow Dylan's ogre body whole. The fine scales of its face reflected the dust-muted light from Dalia's globe. It's eyes flashed, pulsing with a golden light that bathed Max, making him feel like he was being x-rayed.

"Chimeras are rare. I do not recall ever meeting one with your particular combination of bloodlines. And you are Battleborne, which explains at least the mark of

181

Odin upon you." The dragon sniffed again, and turned toward the others. *"Three* Battleborne?"

Dylan, taking a deep breath, stepped forward. "We were brothers in arms in our previous lives, great dragon. Max there was our commander."

"Silence, flea!" the dragon swung its head and breathed on Dylan, a black mist surrounding him. The ogre cried out in fear, but the sound was choked off. A moment later, the party's tank was encased in an obsidian prism in the vague shape of an ogre. "Speak when spoken to, or not at all!"

"You forget yourself, dragon!" Red practically screamed at him. "I have invoked the ancient rite of parlay, and you attack one of my party? Release him!"

"I have not agreed to your parlay as yet, leprechaun! And do not presume to dictate terms to me!" The dragon reared back its neck, its head rising to a height of thirty feet or so, glaring down at the party. Then it let out a long breath, visibly calming. "Still, you are an interesting group. I will honor your request for parlay." He lowered his head once again and sent a puff of air at Dylan, causing the obsidian shell around him to dissolve almost instantly. The ogre heaved in a gasping breath as he fell to his knees.

"By the laws of the First Magic, I welcome you, fae. You and your party have one hour of grace in which to speak. When that hour has passed, I shall decide your fate." The dragon raised a foreclaw and made a surprisingly complicated gesture with its four digits. The creature shifted, as did the cavern around them.

Max blinked and looked around, the rough stone walls and floor were shifting, moving closer and becoming straighter, smoother. In seconds, the party found themselves standing in a carpeted hall with a throne at one end. Tapestries lined the walls, and a massive fireplace burned brightly to one side. In front of the fireplace were several plush leather chairs, a side table next to each of them. The dragon himself had shrunk to a humanoid form, taller than Dylan, with the same impressive aura the dragon projected in its natural form. He was dressed like a king, all in black cloth with silver stitching, a black leather belt with a silver buckle, and a sword at his hip with an ornate pommel and guard. Max was able to recognize the metal as mithril.

"Please, sit and be comfortable." The dragon waved toward the chairs, taking the one nearest the fire. Max and the others hesitated a moment, still trying to adjust to the rapid changes. Dalia was first to move, taking a deep breath and moving to hop up into one of the dragon-sized chairs. She missed the first try, and blushed.

"My apologies." The dragon waved a humanoid hand, and each of the chairs shifted, sizing themselves for their occupants. Dalia's chair shrank and lowered itself, while Dylan's chair widened and deepened slightly to accommodate his bulk. A tiny bright green chair that appeared to be made of vines appeared atop the table next to Max, and Red took a seat as well. Max was surprised to notice the vines shifting slightly as she sat, meaning she had some physical interaction with them.

The dragon chuckled. "This is a place of magic, chimera. Your guide is as solid here as you or I." Max bowed his head in acknowledgement, having no idea how to respond. Once again, Red stepped up for the group.

"Thank you, Ancient One. And I apologize for my tone a few moments ago. I have grown quite fond of these companions, and was concerned for Dylan's mortal existence."

"I too must apologize, little fae. Having slept so long, and been so rudely and recently awakened, I acted rashly. Your companion was in no mortal danger. In fact, I believe he'll find he has been… improved by the experience." The dragon raised an eyebrow at Dylan, who opened his mouth to answer, then shut it again. The dragon chuckled. "You learn quickly, for an ogre. You may speak."

"He's right." Dylan replied, his eyes clearly on his interface. "I received a permanent buff called *Obsidian Skin*. It gave me plus ten percent each to *Constitution* and *Strength*, and increased resistance to fire and piercing damage." He looked over at the dragon, who had leaned back in his chair and crossed his legs. "Thank you for that."

"You are welcome, Battleborne." He nodded slightly. "Now tell me, leprechaun who for some reason does not use her family name, why have you disturbed my rest?"

"That was not our intention, oh great and powerful dragon." Red began. Max thought she was laying it on a bit thickly, but the dragon seemed to enjoy the flattery. "We were simply exploring, and stumbled upon your resting place. We did not realize you were… you. No offense, but we mistook you for a magma formation. At least, until Dalia-"

"Had the audacity to strike my scales with her tiny hammer?" The dragon interrupted, turning his gaze to the dwarfess, who did her best to disappear into her chair. He chuckled, waving a dismissive hand. "You meant no harm or disrespect, little one. I take no offense. In truth, your intrusion has presented me with a most interesting diversion. I cannot remember a more intriguing meal in recent millennia." He grinned, showing a mouthful of sharp fangs, not putting Dalia at ease in the slightest.

Max blinked a few times, an idea coming to him. He reached into his inventory and produced some of his favorite vendor's spiced kabobs. "Great dragon, you must be hungry after sleeping so long. I have only been on this world a short time, but this is my favorite of all the foods I've tried so far. Please, accept these as a humble apology for disturbing you." He held out the kabobs.

The dragon sniffed once, a curious look appearing on his face. He did not reach out, simply held his hand open, and the food drifted from Max's hand to his own. Another sniff, and he took a bite. The entire party watched as he chewed thoughtfully, then swallowed. "Quite tasty, actually. The combination of seasonings is… interesting, if simple." He took another bite, then another, finishing the handful of kabobs while the others watched. "I am a master chef myself, you know." He blew on his hand and the empty sticks disappeared. "In fact, I am a master of many professions. When one lives for an eternity, one must find ways to pass the time, other than sleeping." He looked at Smitty, who maintained a pokerface. "The last meal I cooked was orc pot pie. Blasted vermin were everywhere, swarming through the mountains, infesting the area. In fact..." He turned his head back to Max and sniffed again.

"Just before I settled down for my nap, my cousin had gotten fed up with the annoying orcs, and gone to teach them a lesson. You have his scent on you, chimera. I did not notice it before, underneath the odor of the Elders upon you. The scent of that dwarf tinkerer Regin is strong." He shook his head as if to clear his sense. "Where did you encounter my cousin? And how did you survive the experience? Compared to me, he is downright antisocial."

Max cleared his throat, afraid to answer, and afraid not to. "If your cousin was a stone dragon, I'm sorry, I'm afraid he's dead." He waited for a reaction for the dragon, who just raised an eyebrow and motioned with a hand for him to continue. "A few days after I arrived on this world, I came across an ancient battlefield, where I found the bones of a stone dragon. I was told later that the battle happened over a thousand years ago. The dragon battled an army of orcs, and was brought down. From the evidence I saw, he took at least several hundred of them with him."

"I see." The dragon sighed. "But that does not explain why his scent is so strong upon you. I take it you did more than just stroll through an ancient battleground?"

This time both eyebrows raised, and the dragon's stare was a clear warning not to attempt a lie.

"I did not. I gathered some of the remains, hoping to use them as crafting materials." Max gulped visibly, then decided to just lay it all out. "Some scales, a few bone slivers, a few sections of vertebrae, and-"

"And his heart." The dragon finished for him. He held out one hand, palm up, an obvious demand. Max produced the dragon stone from his inventory, and once again it drifted out of his hand. The dragon examined the stone, turning it slowly around, then closed his eyes for a long moment. "Yes, I see it. The fool took on ten thousand orcs. They may be insignificant little pests, but in such numbers, and with time to prepare, they can be dangerous. They waited for him to get close, then shredded his wings with ballistae and water magic." He opened one eye and looked at Max. "You misjudged his prowess. Of the ten thousand, only four thousand stood at the end of the battle. They removed his head and dragged it home as a trophy."

To Max's utter surprise, the dragon tossed the stone back to him. "My cousin left a brood behind when he died. The eggs have surely hatched by now. I will contact his mate and inform her of his fate. When the little ones have grown strong enough, they will reclaim their sire's head. As for the rest... I sense your fear, and it is unfounded. I will not punish you for wishing to make use of his remains. Your intentions are good, and you acted without malice. That is the way of our race. When we fall, our parts become the seeds of great weapons and powerful magical artifacts."

Relieved, Max decided he needed to say something else. "Great dragon, I am a newly crowned king of a nearby kingdom, one that includes the land on which your cousin fell. My friends and I are on a quest to take the head of the current orc war chief, and when I accomplish this task, I intend to take his city. I have found that many of the orcs living there are kind, honorable beings, and have even recruited several hundred of them to join me as citizens of Stormhaven." He paused for a breath, trying to find the best way to present his case. In his head were visions of himself ruling the city, only to be attacked by angry young dragons.

"Should I find your cousin's head in the city, it would be my honor to return it to lay with the rest of his bones, and create a shrine to honor him."

The dragon stared at him for several seconds, then began to chuckle. A moment later the chuckle turned to a full fledged laugh. "And there would be no need for his offspring to lay waste to the city and those inside?"

Max bowed his head. "Those orcs had nothing to do with a battle that happened so long ago. And, yes, I would prefer to conquer the city and have it remain intact."

"Interesting. I can see that you yourself have killed a large number of orcs. The scepter you carry is in fact a reward for doing so. Yet you would spare their lives, at the risk of offending a dragon." He leaned forward, putting his elbows on his knees. "I think I like you, chimera!"

"My name is Maximilian Storm, great one. Please, call me Max." He motioned to Dalia. "This is Dalia, the druid, our healer. The orc is Smitty, and Dylan is the ogre. As he said, both served under my command in our previous incarnations. And this feisty leprechaun is Red." He smiled at her.

"Red, is it?" The dragon actually winked at her. "You fae, always reluctant to share your true names. Not that I blame you, in your case. That knowledge would grant great power over you, your magic, and your people. I see you are soulbound to Max here. You are his guide? Another unusual turn of events. Rare is the Battleborne who is gifted a guide. I myself have only ever met three." The dragon burped, then thumped one fist to his chest.

"What other delicacies might you be carrying?" He looked at Max, who immediately dug into his inventory and produced several pastries. "You may call me Lysbane. It is a name that primitive humans gave me long ago. I believe it means *Light's Bane*. My true name is long, and impossible for you to pronounce." He took the pastries and sniffed at them, then took a bite.

"Amusing taste. But I crave meat." Lysbane hinted.

Max thought for a moment. "I have... manticore meat. But it is uncooked.

"Manticore? That will do nicely!" the dragon got to his feet and waved a hand. The massive fireplace widened, the hearth extending outward. In a moment the fire itself had moved out into the space between the chairs, and now there was an ornate metal grill positioned over top of the flames. Next to them was a wooden worktable, atop which stood several pots and pans, a set of chefs' knives, and an extensive spice rack. The dragon, now wearing a summoned white apron over his black attire and a chef's hat tilted rakishly to one side, turned to look over his shoulder at Max. "Don't just sit there, bring me the manticore meat! We have a meal to prepare!"

*****

When the party all received the notification that the hour of amnesty granted under the rite of parlay had expired, they were gathered around a table, enjoying a fine meal of manticore steaks, spiced baked potatoes, freshly baked dark bread, and some berries that Dalia had found in the woods near the temple ruins. Each of them froze at the notification, fearful gazes moving instantly to the dragon at the head of the table.

"Ha! Fear not, little ones. You are safe enough. I find I value your company more than I would enjoy the slight snack your combined corpses would provide."

The party relaxed, Smitty biting down on the forkful of potatoes that had frozen just inches from his open mouth. Red, having transferred her tiny vine chair to the center of the table, slapped a knee as she laughed. "Ya shoulda seen the looks on all yer faces!" Lysbane smiled widely, showing his mouthful of sharp fangs.

"What?" Dalia asked after swallowing her bite of steak.

"First magic, rites of parlay… you mortals are sooo easy!" Red winked at the dragon, who did laugh this time.

"Our host wasn't going to eat you lot. He spoke to me while Dalia was tappy-tappin on his hide, and though he was a bit grumpy about you disturbin' his nap, he was more curious than angry. I suggested the whole 'rite of parlay' bit, a very old joke. And you all bought it!" Red giggled, snorting as she bent over, holding her belly with both hands.

"Dammit, Red!" Max grumped at her, sorely tempted to reach out and flick her temporarily solid body out of that tiny chair.

"Please, do not be angry, Max. I have so few opportunities for a little innocent fun." Lysbane's smile did not fade in the slightest. "No true harm was done, after all. And we've had some fun, haven't we?"

Max took a deep breath. Lysbane had recruited them all to help prepare the meal. He'd given them a new recipe for manticore steaks, and leveled up their cooking skill several times. During the prep, Lysbane had told them a story about a dragon who posed as a grumpy old wizard and lived among mortals, adventuring with them. All of them had forgotten for a short while that their lives were in danger.

"Fair enough, you got us. Well played." Max offered the dragon and the leprechaun a semi-sincere smile. Dylan just shook his head, while Smitty actually laughed.

"That was an epic setup, little dudette. I was totally sure we were gonna end up as dragon grindage."

"If by grindage you mean food, you should know that we dragons rarely eat adventurers. First, you don't taste all that good. And peeling you out of your armor is tedious. Not worth the effort, really." Lysbane grinned at the orc. "However, these morsels have reminded my stomach that it has not been filled for quite some time. I must leave you all and go hunt for more substantial fare. I thank you for the company, and the tasty offerings." He stood and waved his hand, and all of them felt a tingle. "I name you all friend. Should you encounter other dragons, they will sense my mark upon you. That is no guarantee of their behavior, but every little bit helps, no?"

"Thank you, Lysbane." Red stood up and bowed deeply, and the others quickly did the same. Another wave of the dragon's hand, and their surroundings morphed back into the original cavern, and he returned to dragon form.

"Before I forget, you have a deal regarding my cousin's thick head." All of their interfaces flashed up a new quest notification.

Quest Received: Head Hunters
Find the stone dragon's severed head
and return it to the Brightwood grave site.
Reward: ??

"I will hold off on seeking out my cousin's mate and informing her of his fate. It has been a thousand years, what is one or two more? And since you've provided such an entertaining interlude, what favor might I do for you?

Keep it small, Max. I'll not be turning over my horde or smashing an enemy city for you."

Max grinned, trying to think quickly. "Umm... is there any chance you know of Nogroz, the dead king of the grey dwarves? He stole the heart from the mountain my new kingdom occupies, and we'd like to find out where it might be."

Lysbane's eyes narrowed, and he snorted. "Yes, I remember. We dragons are attuned to our elements, and many of us felt the anguish of the mountain when that wicked little mite ripped the heart from it. I would gladly assist you in returning the heart to its rightful owner." Lysbane closed his eyes for a moment. "Seems I remember there was a lich involved. Tricked the little shit into surrendering his soul along with the mountain's. I cannot sense the undead, at least not from a great distance. But I can sense the dwarven horde that was buried with Nogroz" he grinned. "Dragons excel at locating treasure. Here, let me mark it for you."

Max's interface ding'd, and the map appeared, a glowing golden triangle appearing not far from his city. "Thank you, Lysbane! That will save us a great deal of time." He started to offer a hand to shake, then nervously withdrew it. "After this wonderful dinner, I'd be happy to host you for another at our home. It is the city formerly known as Nogroz. You are welcome anytime, though please... uhm, arrive in your human form? A dragon suddenly appearing at the gate might cause a stir."

"I know the place. Spent some time there before Nogroz cursed his people. They used to make a tasty mushroom sauce that they poured over nearly everything. Overdid it if you ask me." The dragon pointed a foreclaw at the opening across the cavern, the one the party did not arrive through. "Alright, I'm off to hunt. That passage will take you to the surface, if that is your goal. Otherwise, I assume you can find your way back the way you came? Wonderful. It has been a pleasure to meet you all, and I wish you good luck!"

Max and the others all received a buff.

Luck of the Firstborn.
A powerful being of an elder race has bestowed a blessing upon you.
Your Luck attribute has been permanently increased by +5

Lysbane twitched his tail, and a massive portal appeared inside the cavern. Through the portal Max and the others could see a wide expanse of rolling hills and green fields, covered in a massive herd of some sort of large shaggy beast that resembled a buffalo. The dragon launched himself through the portal, spreading his wings and soaring into the clear blue sky as the portal closed behind him.

"Well, shall we proceed to the surface?" Max started walking toward the cavern's exit.

"Just like that?" Smitty stood still, looking at the spot where the portal had just closed. "Boss, I think we need to take a moment to appreciate that we totally just hung out and became bestest buds with a friggin dragon! I mean, it coulda just turned us into paste, or shiny black statues like Dylan there, and gone back to dreaming of dragon hotties."

Dalia nodded in agreement, not seeming all that steady on her feet. Max realized that he was feeling a bit of an adrenaline hangover himself. "Alright, let's chill for a few minutes. But not too long. That meal gave us some pretty tasty buffs, but they're only good for eight hours. No point in wasting them."

*****

Three hours later Dylan blinked rapidly, covering his eyes to block the bright light of the sun. He'd just stepped out onto a ledge at the end of the tunnel they'd been following since leaving Lysbane's lair. The others emerged behind him, making various noises from the stabbing pain of sunlight in their eyes after so long in the dark.

The ledge was halfway up the side of a tall mountain. Max's map told him they were facing west, and the sun was low in the sky, shining right in their faces. Once his eyes fully adjusted, Max could see the ocean several miles off in the distance.

"Nice view." Dylan commented, taking in the mountain range and the green valley below. Where to, boss?"

Max was consulting his map. They were well north and west of Stormhaven and the outpost. Closer to the ocean than he had been so far. The mountain they stood upon was part of a chain that ran directly toward the ocean, a series of valleys down below that were separated by lower ridges and passes. The one directly below them was mostly forested, with a small lake maybe a mile across near one end. The area around the lake was clear meadow and sandy beach. "Since we're here, let's go explore that valley. It looks peaceful enough, and if nobody has claimed it, we'll make it part of Stormhaven."

"Good plan." Dylan looked down along the edge of the ledge for a minute, then stepped over to one side. "There's a path here. Looks mostly clear, like someone has used it quite a bit." He didn't wait for orders, simply stepped down onto the path as he equipped his shield and held it facing outward toward the drop-off. The others followed quietly.

Halfway down the descent, Max heard a sound that immediately took him back to his first visit to the outpost. Looking up, he scanned the sky, then instinctively ducked down, hissing for the others to do the same.

Circling high above was what he suspected was the very same bird that had nearly taken him from the top of the ridge that day. The ridge wasn't that far away, as the roc flies...

Roc Female
Level 20
Health: 5,000/5,000

The gigantic bird wasn't nearly as terrifying as it had seemed before, now that Max was a much higher level, and had friends with him. Still, he didn't want any of them to be plucked from the mountainside and potentially dropped to their deaths. He had no doubt that the oversized predator with a twenty foot wingspan had the strength to lift even their ogre tank.

"Stay still, all of you." Max whispered loudly enough for them to hear. "Let's hope that thing is triggered by motion, and not our body heat, or something." He watched with the others as the roc banked to the left out over the valley, making a lazy circle that brought her directly over their heads for a moment. All of them breathed a sigh of relief as she continued on, riding a thermal that pushed up the mountain face, and disappeared over the ridge opposite theirs. Still, Max kept them in place for several minutes, making sure she didn't circle back around. When they stood back up and got moving, Dylan set a faster pace than before.

The trail reached the bottom of the rocky slope, transitioning into a well-worn dirt path that turned more sharply downslope and led into the forest. The party continued to follow their tank as he ducked a few low branches and scanned to their left and right. A hundred yards or so into the woods, the trail ended at an intersection. The perpendicular trail extended east and west from their position, and Dylan waited silently for Max to make the call.

"The lake is west. As is the ocean. When I first got here, I had an idea about walking out till I reached the ocean, then following the shoreline until I found a port or a fishing village. We might as well try that out."

Dylan obediently turned west and followed the much wider path. This one was at least eight feet wide, and there was faded evidence of wagon tracks visible.

"So much for this place being uninhabited, boss." Smitty called from the back. "Looks like if you want this valley, we'll have to conquer it!" His enthusiasm was evident in his tone.

"How bout we find whomever lives here and try talking to them before we kill them all and drink from their skulls?" Max flashed the orc a grin, and got a thumbs-up in reply.

"Drink from what?" Dalia looked disturbed.

"Oh, sorry." Smitty shrugged. "It's a figure of speech. From a popular story about a bloodthirsty barbarian from our world. Max didn't mean it literally."

"Your world is a strange and violent place, I think." Dalia ventured as she walked behind Dylan. "I'm not sure I'd like it there."

"Well, there's no magic, for one thing." Dylan added. "So no magic healing. We depended on drugs, kind of like your potions, though not nearly as effective, and more mundane methods like bandages, surgeries, and stitches."

"That sounds horrible. Did many of your people die in battle?"

All three of the former soldiers went silent. After a few steps, Dylan lowered his head and mumbled. "Too many. Way too many."

Dalia, sensing that she'd struck a nerve, changed the subject. "Speaking of potions, there are lots of useful herbs and ingredients in this forest. I've seen half a dozen already. And though this place doesn't have the same magic boost as the battleground, these plants are mature and untouched. So the potency should be quite high. Do you mind if we pause now and again to harvest some of them?"

"Not at all!" Max smiled at her. "Can't hurt any of us to improve our flower picking skills. And good ingredients are never a waste of time. As your king, I declare the rest of the day to be flower day!"

"Uh, boss?" Smitty called out from the rear. "Before you start pulling weeds n such, maybe check with these folks and make sure it's okay?"

They all turned toward Smitty at their rear, and Max stepped toward him. Off in the distance, maybe a quarter mile down the trail, they could just barely make out a pair of large boars pulling a wagon. Two beings sat atop the wagon, seemingly chatting with each other.

"Do we take cover?" Dylan asked, glancing at the trees and brush on either side of the wide trail, not seeing anything that would easily hide his ogre bulk.

"I don't think so." Max shook his head. " They don't seem aggressive, and there are only two of them. Let's just wait for them to catch up, and introduce ourselves.

Chapter 10

It turned out there were many more than two of them. Behind the loaded wagon walked another dozen individuals, well armed and armored. Each of them, including the drivers, stood on average about six feet tall, with wide shoulders, thick muscles, and dark eyes. Their skin colors varied from pasty white to a slightly greenish hue. Some sported dwarf-like thick beards and moustaches, others were cleanshaven. All of them sported a set of lower jaw tusks, though some were more pronounced than others.

Fortunately for Max and company, though the new arrivals quickly spread out from behind the wagon and bared their weapons, they did not take immediate aggressive action. Their leader, one of the two drivers, stopped the wagon a dozen or so paces from Max, then stood and called out. "Who're ye and why d'ya be blockin' our path?"

Max held up a hand in greeting. "My name is Max Storm, King of the newly formed Stormhaven. My friends and I certainly don't intend to block your path. We are simply exploring, and came across this valley. We were on our way to the lake, and spotted you approaching. I thought it only polite to wait and say hello."

There were some dark murmurs among the gathered fighters, and the one up top spat over the edge of the wagon. "A likely story. A king, you say? Just wanderin' around out here in our valley? More likely scoutin' fer an invasion!"

Max shrugged. "I admit, upon first seeing the valley from above, I had hopes of claiming it for Stormhaven. It's a beautiful place, and peaceful. But that was before I knew you folks owned it. I've no interest in war, my friend. I already have one with An'zalor the orc and his army, I don't need another."

"Ye be at war with the orcs?" This came from a young looking fighter with bright red hair and beard standing near the wagon's front wheel. He held a two-handed war hammer like he knew how to use it. "Ye got an orc in yer party with ya."

"I am at war, with some orcs. Not all orcs. In fact, some of An'zalor's people have left his city and joined me as citizens of mine. Several hundred of them so far. As for Smitty, I trust with him my life."

There were more grumblings among the soldiers, and Max waited several long seconds before interrupting. "Might I ask your name?"

The leader grimaced, but obliged. "I be An'dro Pickstone, leader o' this convoy and elder o' the Blooded Clan." He stood slightly taller than the others, and his shoulders were wide enough to pull the wagon on his own if he chose.

"Glad to meet you, An'dro Pickstone. Any chance your Blooded Clan is looking for trade partners? My city, and my kingdom, are growing quickly, and we need to purchase supplies of nearly every kind to keep up."

Pickstone leaned back slightly, surprised. "Ye... would trade with us?"

"Is there some reason I shouldn't?" Max smiled up at him, showing his fangs inadvertently. Grips tightened on weapons all around him.

"Most won't even speak to us, let alone trade." Pickstone had seen Max's fangs as well as any. "Some kind o' mixed breed, are ya?"

"I am. In fact, I'm a chimera, a being of four bloodlines in equal parts. Is that a problem for you?" Max thought he understood what was happening, and took another good look at the fighters in front of him. He flashed back to a conversation he'd had with Battleaxe the day they'd met.

Pickstone stared at him for a moment, then sat down. "Ha! Lads, King Max here wants ta know if we have a problem with his bloodlines!" There were a few laughs, some whistles, and grunts. Some of the fighters even lowered their weapons and smiled.

"No, King Max. We here o' the Blooded all be like yerself. Though, not with such exotic blood as yer own. All of us be part dwarf, part orc, with varying degrees of either. Descendants o' those who were shamed into exile after the wars, and those who've been born of mixed blood since. The sons n daughters of slaves, rape victims, and perverts, most claim. Commonly known as *dworcs*, we call ourselves Blooded for the names we're called; half-blooded, mixed-blooded, weak-blooded. Despised by orcs and dwarves alike, we isolate ourselves up here and avoid them all." His tone was bitter, and he spat again when he was through.

"I see. That is… unfortunate." Max could hear the pain in his voice, and wasn't sure how to answer. Dalia took the initiative and stepped forward.

"Me name's Dalia, born and raised in Darkholm, though now I be a citizen of Stormhaven. I've heard tales o' ye dworcs since I were a wee lass, and I freely admit that most were not kind in nature. Though none I've ever heard speak o' ye held any malice toward ya, nor do they blame ye for the circumstances of yer birth. It were more… distrust of orcs in general, and suspicion o' yer orc blood." She held out a hand to indicate Max. "Since I've been with Max here, I've learned much about orcs. I've learned they be mostly honorable and loyal, honest and friendly enough, despite our long-held grievances. With a few exceptions, o' course."

The others had gone quiet as she spoke, some nodding their heads as if in agreement. Though when she mentioned the honor of orcs, several growled. Max assumed that dworcs were most often created when orc males had their way with dwarven females, as he had trouble imagining a dwarf going after a female orc. Then again, one never knew…

Max decided to step in. "Pickstone, I have declared Stormhaven to be open to all races, except grey dwarves, from whom we took the kingdom. As of now, living in my city or my lands are orcs, dwarves, ogres, goblins, a leprechaun, gnomes, kobolds, and one crazy guy made mostly of metal. Dworcs, if you do not mind that term, would be just as welcome as any others."

"Dworcs be what we are, and none o' us take offense at the word." The young redhead spoke up. Be you offended when called a chimera?"

"Generally, no." Max smiled at him, purposely showing his fangs this time. "Though a few have managed to make it sound like an insult. Most of them are dead, now."

"Ha!" Pickstone slapped a knee. "I think we'll be getting' along just fine, King Max. If ye've no where urgent ta be, walk along with us. We've a village near the lake, and ye can spend the night." He motioned over his shoulder with his thumb. "We've just finished a honey harvest, and we can talk about what ye might trade for some o' the delicious mead we'll be makin'."

Chapter 11

Max and company fell in with the Blooded Clan, walking behind the wagon, at the rear of the fighters. Dalia made an effort to mingle and speak a bit with those nearest the back of the group, asking a few questions and doing her best to improve relations between dworcs and dwarves.

They'd made it more than halfway across the valley when the sun disappeared behind the mountains, sending the valley into a grey twilight. The air cooled, and the sounds of night creatures began to filter through the trees. The moon was not yet risen, but sunlight still reflected off a few of the clouds that floated higher than the mountain peaks. Max was using his elven hearing to monitor Dalia's progress, when he detected something that caused his blood to stir. It was a good distance away yet, but he heard a definite sound of something large crashing through the brush upslope and downwind of them.

Drawing his bow, he whistled at Pickstone. "Something big coming up from behind us." He warned his party as he began to jog to catch up to the wagon. As soon as he reached it, he called out. "I can hear something crashing through the trees above us, and slightly behind. It's getting closer, and moving fast."

Pickstone and the rest of his clan all turned their heads in the indicated direction, some tilting to one side as if to hear better. The elder had just opened his mouth to ask a question when a tremendous roar echoed down through the forest.

"Shit!" Pickstone cursed loudly. Immediately all the dworcs had weapons in hand, several drawing shields and moving a few steps toward the sounds. The wagon stopped, and three of the Blooded hopped up onto the bed, readying crossbows. "It be old Cantankerous! He must have scented our honey."

Turning his back to the wagon, Max raised his bow and asked, "Cantankerous?".

"That be what we call him. An overgrown cave bear, as mean n angry as any creature alive. Bigger'n this wagon from nose to tail, with claws of iron that'll rip ye in half if yer not careful." Pickstone's eyes searched the trees as he spoke. The crashing sounds were now close enough for everyone to hear. "He has a taste fer honey, but not the stings o' the giant bees who make it. He likely sniffed us on the wind as we passed, and figures on an easy meal."

"Giant bees?" Smitty asked, his bow in hand as he moved next to Max. Dalia stood next to him, while Dylan moved to take up a spot at the center of the line of shield-bearers.

"Aye. That be part o' why we chose to settle in this valley. Everything here grows faster and bigger than be normal. The bees grow to the size o' miss Dalia there, and got barbed stingers as long as me forearm. Impossible to get out without cuttin' em free, or rippin' big holes in yer hide. Which is why Cantankerous, though he be several times bigger than yer average bear, is hesitant to try n steal their honey. He don't have hands to cut out the barbs, or smokers to calm the bees, like we do"

"So we just rang the dinner bell for a giant, angry, hungry bear with a sweet tooth." Smitty summarized. "Anything else we need to know?"

"His roar can stun ye, if yer not careful. Best to stuff somethin in yer ears right quick. And if he knocks ye down, play dead. If ye struggle, he'll finish what he started. Just go limp and lay still, we'll pull him away. Once he's focused on us, run as fast as ye can."

"Good to know." Smitty nodded once at the elder. Dalia was already handing him some kind of waxy substance to press into his ears. She helped herself, then passed some to Max, who in turn offered it to Pickstone, who shook his head. He and his clan had already plugged their ears with something that resembled cotton balls. Clearly, they'd fought this monster before.

Max trotted forward and made sure Dylan's surprisingly small ogre ears were plugged, then took up position behind and to the left of the ogre, where he could clearly see the treetops shivering a good distance behind them. It wasn't long before the gigantic bear appeared as a shadow emerging from the trees and pausing on the road. Its head rose into the air, sniffing for a moment, before it let loose another roar and bounded down the track toward them.

> *Cave Bear Alpha*
> *Level 30*
> *Health: 10,000/10,000*

It was a higher level than Max or his people, and Max hadn't bothered to check Pickstone or his fighters' levels. The bear had a massive health pool, nearly four times Max's own, and he had a feeling it was going to do some damage before they could bring it down.

When it came within a hundred yards, Max and Smitty both loosed arrows. Max's arrow sunk into the bear's shoulder, barely causing any reaction other than a grunt. Smitty had used one of his new abilities to enchant his, causing the arrowhead to explode a second after impact. The arrow struck the top of the bear's head, digging a furrow in its fur and hide as it bounced off. The enchantment went off as the arrow passed just above its back, startling the bear into stumbling to one side as it looked over its shoulder.

Both took the opportunity to launch a second arrow as it stumbled, then began to pick up speed again. When it reached fifty yards, the dworcs with crossbows fired. The cave bear roared in pain, but continued forward seemingly unphased. The blood from Smitty's first shot ran down between its eyes and dripped from its muzzle, making the monstrous thing seem just that much more terrifying.

Dylan, who was about half the size of the charging bear, raised his shield and stepped forward, shouting one of his favorite insults. "Your mother was a hamster!" At the same time, he used one of his tank abilities that turned the insult into a taunt. As Smitty shouted something about elderberries from behind, the bear focused on Dylan, who charged forward.

The action did not go as Dylan had planned. His charge should have allowed him to stun the bear on impact. Instead, the giant ursine attacker lowered its head and slammed into Dylan's shield, denting the metal, knocking the ogre clean off his feet and sending him rolling backward into the line of shields, his health bar down to thirty percent. The dworcs were battle savvy enough to open a hole and let him pass before locking their shields together. They began to chant in unison, and their shields glowed a soft blue in the deepening twilight.

Though the bear wasn't stunned by Dylan's charge, it was slowed considerably. Much of its momentum was lost when it bashed into the line of shields. The tanks grunted, their feet digging in as its weight pressed them back, causing the line to bow, but not break. Short swords stabbed out to puncture the thick hide of its neck and legs. Hammers struck at its knees, hoping to pop a joint. One ambitious tank landed an overhead hammer blow directly onto the bear's skull as it took hold of the top of his shield with its jaws.

The hammer struck with a resounding thwack, but the bear just shook his head violently, pulling the dworc off his feet as his shield was yanked to the side. His arm instantly broken, the tank dropped his hammer and tried to free his shield arm. But before he could manage it, the bear lowered his head until the dworc touched ground, then used a treestump-sized forepaw to pin him down, ironlike claws digging into his chest. In a split second the bear let loose of the shield and lowered his massive jaw over the screaming tank's head. A hideous crunch abruptly ended the screams.

Not finished, the bear repeated its tactic, shaking the dwarf's corpse left and right so violently that it knocked down the tanks that had stood on either side of their dead comrade. He then dropped his first kill, raised up onto its hind legs for a moment, then slammed both front feet onto the body of the downed dworc to its right. The sickening crack of ribs and sternum could be heard over the sounds of battle.

With a roar of anger, Dylan charged back through the open hole, dented shield held high and war axe already swinging for the bear's head. Max, Smitty, and the crossbow wielders all put arrows and bolts into its exposed belly before Dylan blocked their line of sight and reengaged the monster. This time he applied a little strategy, rather than just brute force. Standing upright, the bear was easily half again as tall as the ogre, and at least twice his bulk. Before it could use its advantage against him, he raised his shield up sideways and thrust upward, knocking its forepaws up and away at the same time that he drove his heavy axe's blade into its chest.

Leaving the axe where it was, Dylan spun to his left as he took a single backward step, guiding the increasing weight of the bear's head and front legs off to his side, thus avoiding being pinned or crushed.

One of the brave dworc tanks shot forward, slamming his own shield into the rear blade of the axe, driving the front blade an inch or two deeper. Both he and Dylan could hear when it impacted bone and stopped dead.

211

The bear completed its fall, managing to swat the smaller tank aside with one paw, leaving his face a mess of blood and exposed bone. Ignoring the axe embedded in its chest, it pushed forward into the dworc line, which was still struggling to reform and reconnect their shields. Two more tanks were knocked down as it charged over them, then turned to swat at the back of another.

Less than twenty seconds since first contact, and so far it was a massacre. Max had considered both *Boom!* and *Zap!* while firing arrow after arrow into the beast, but either might have created collateral damage he didn't want. He quickly tried to *Levitate* the massive monster, but its bulk was too great for his current spell level.

Dylan roared again, taunting the cave bear as he stood his ground, well in front of the tanks and off to one side of the road. The bear turned instantly, blood spraying from dozens of wounds as it spun toward the ogre. Having equipped his halberd, Dylan banged it against the dented shield and spit a glob of blood onto the ground. His health bar was back up to half, thanks to Dalia's healing efforts, but it was clear the initial impact had done some internal damage.

The bear picked up some speed as it charged, and Dylan calmly hunched behind his shield as he shouted more insults. When the bear was maybe four steps away, Dylan jammed the butt end of his halberd into the dirt at his feet, then tilted it forward so that the pointed end slammed right into the charging bear's body. He'd been aiming for its heart, for a spot right next to his still-stuck axe. But he'd judged the timing wrong, and the blade slid into the monster's neck right where it met the shoulder.

Still, it did the job. The bear's momentum was stopped dead, its body pushing upward as the blade sank deeper, several muscle and an artery before scraping against bone. The shaft of the sturdy weapon bent, then broke under the strain, and the bear fell forward onto Dylan.

One paw hit the top of his shield, dragging it downward, even the ogre's prodigious strength not up to resisting the weight. The other paw raked at Dylan's right side as it fell, and the jaws closed on his right shoulder. The badly wounded bear still had plenty of strength in its jaws. Eight-inch long fangs crunched through his chainmail and the layers below, shattering his collarbone and causing blood to spurt. Dylan roared in pain, his body being twisted as his left arm was pinned under the shield and his right arm went numb. He was bleeding badly, and the bear was completely covering him, preventing Dalia from being able to see him to cast heals. Without the use of either hand, he couldn't produce a healing potion from his inventory.

The bear continued to savage his shoulder, wrench its head back and forth with all the strength it could muster. The other tanks had all charged forward, stabbing and pounding at the monster's head and neck. Dalia and Max both charged around to where they could see their tank's head, casting simultaneous heals on him once, then again, bringing him back from the brink of death.

And still the bear kept tearing at him.

Desperate, Max drew his sword and leapt at the bear's head, driving the point through its eye and deep into its brain. With a final shudder, the monster died.

Without pause the dworcs went to work, grabbing handfuls of the bear's fur and pulling it toward one side, rolling the massive weight off of Dylan's body. The ogre heaved a deep breath of relief, having found it difficult to breathe with the heavy weight pinning him down. Dalia fed him a healing potion, then set another on his chest as she moved to help with the wounded dworcs.

Five of the company were beyond help, but she managed to save the one with the shredded face, and a couple of others who were less than mortally wounded. The one's face would bear horrible scars for the rest of his life, but he seemed to just shake it off. Several of his comrades took a good look, then patted his arm or slapped him on the back in congratulations.

The entire party, except for Pickstone, who turned out to be level 40, gained at least one level. Dylan got two, and Max made a mental note to ask Red about the experience distribution from fights like this. Max hadn't thought to group up with the dworcs before the fight, so the monster was killed by two separate groups, assuming they'd created one of their own.

The loot was better than average, though Red informed him that the cave bear wasn't technically an elite level monster. It was, however, very old, overgrown, and powerful. Max received thirty pieces of cave bear meat, two foreclaws that were each as long as his hand from palm to the tip of his middle finger, and three teeth. Smitty, Dalia, and Dylan received similar, with Dylan also receiving its heart. Picklet received a gold ring, which turned out to be a storage ring that had been lost along with one of the clan's elders years earlier. It had been one of only two storage rings the clan had possessed, and Pickstone was thrilled to get it back. And now they had an answer to the question of what had happened to their elder and his party.

While Dylan recovered, the dworcs went to work harvesting the corpse. They removed its hide, the fur seeming large enough to carpet an entire room once it was laid out in the grass. They removed its head, and Pickstone asked for permission to keep it so that they could mount it in the village.

"We've lost more'n a few to this beastie over the years. An old enemy, and worthy o' many a tale at the tavern! The wee ones fathered by them we lost today will be able to look up at the skull with pride!"

"Of course it's all yours." Max answered immediately. "I'm glad we could help you defeat this beast, though I suspect we're the ones responsible for it catching up to you. If you hadn't stop to speak with us…"

"Nonsense! This wagon be slow as the honey in them barrels. Old Cantankerous woulda just caught up to us later. Better here than within sight o' the village, where wee ones might've been hurt. Or worse."

Max nodded his head, appreciating the sentiment if not quite believing it. A quick look around showed him that the dworcs were ready to continue, having stored their dead in the recovered storage ring, retrieved the loot and any lost gear, and harvested the corpse down to a few scattered bones that were too broken to be of use. One of them walked up to Dylan with the business half of his broken halberd, holding it up. "Would ye be wantin' this back, then?"

"Dylan shook his head. "No, thank you. I'll grab a replacement when we get home."

"Mind if I be keepin it?" The dworc grabbed the haft near the broken end and give it a few experimental swings and jabs off to one side. "It be a good length for a shield battle now."

"May it strike fear in the hearts of your enemies." Dylan grinned down at the warrior, who grinned back through a bushy black beard before nodding once and walking back to his place behind the wagon.

*****

Darkness had truly fallen, and several fires were lit in braziers atop the stone wall by the time the group reached the clan's village. Max and the others hung back just inside the gates, allowing the others to report on the battle and their losses. Runners were sent to fetch a couple of families that weren't there when the wagon arrived.

Max did his best not to intrude upon the grief of the villagers. From the size of the place, there was a not a large population. If he had to guess, maybe a hundred or more souls in the clan. Losing five warriors was a heavy blow. He and his group took seats and leaned against the interior of the wall, waiting patiently for Pickstone and the other to remember them.

Eventually, the redheaded dworc who'd spoken up when they first met came jogging over. "If ye please, me da invites ye to the tavern for food n drink. We'll be celebratin' the victory, and honoring our dead."

Max and the others got to their feet and followed. Dalia asked, "You be Pickstone's son?"

"Aye. Ye can call me Picklet. Everyone else has since I were a wee one."

"Ye fought well in the battle, Picklet. And I see'd ye pull one o' the wounded right out from under the beast's belly. Yer father should be proud o' ye."

"Was him that trained me to fight. Me, and most o' the others here." Picklet stopped at the tavern door, motioning for Dalia to step in first. "There be an empty table for ye, King Max. And ye others." He looked up at Dylan apologetically. "I'm afraid ye'll have sit on the floor."

"I'm used to it." the ogre grinned at him.

Inside there was indeed an empty table, right in the center of the tavern's main room. When Max and the others began to step through the opening the locals made

217

for them in the crowded room, there was a rousing applause and cheering, led by Pickstone himself. When they'd taken their seats and the room had settled a bit, the elder raised a mug.

"To King Maximilian, and his heroes of Stormhaven! Without them, might be none of us returned home this night, and old Cantankerous would be back in his cave with a belly full o' honey!"

The crowd roared their approval, Max and company raised the pints of mead placed in front of them, and the celebration commenced. Pickstone and a few of the others told the story of their meeting with Max, and the subsequent battle. Already the enthusiastic and slightly inebriated warriors were embellishing the truth a bit. Max was pretty sure the bear hadn't breathed fire or farted lightning. A fight broke out when one of the warriors swore that his comrade with the shredded face had gotten it when he was struck in the face by the bear's nutsack. A nightmare common enough among tanks who have to fight oversized monsters.

After his first pint was consumed in a single gulp, a helpful bartender began to bring Dylan his mead in a bucket, which he happily drained while holding the bucket with one hand, his pinky sticking out like he was drinking tea, much to the approval and laughter of the crowd. Inevitably, he nearly cleared the room, inviting everyone outside where he had some space to demonstrate his dance moves. When the dworcs began emulating him, Smitty laughed so hard he cried, and lamented the lack of cameras on this new world.

Red sat atop Max's shoulder, visible only to the Stormhaven party, and giggled like a schoolgirl along with Smitty. Dalia had elected to remain inside, deep in conversation with Picklet, and missed the whole show.

After a while, when sufficient refreshment had been consumed, and the battle had been retold twice, the clan gathered in an open courtyard behind the tavern. The bodies of the fallen were brought out on stretchers, their bodies covered in grey cloths so that their families might be spared a look at their injuries. Each stretcher was carried by four dworcs, with a fifth leading them, chanting a funeral song as they went.

Max thought the song was beautiful. Low, and slow, with a rhythm very close to his own heartbeat. The words escaped him, but their meaning was clear, and he wasn't surprised to find Dylan wiping a tear from his eye.

When the stretchers were placed in a row upon a pyre, Pickstone spoke a few words about each of the fallen, and how they met their end. With each described death, the crowd roared in approval, shaking the buildings around them as they raised weapons or fists into the air. Both dwarves and orcs considered a death in battle to be an honor, and these warriors were celebrated as much as they were mourned.

The eulogies presented, Pickstone nodded at his son, who picked up a torch and lit it, then pushed it deep into the center of the pyre. In moments the whole structure was blazing, and the dworcs resumed their sad song as the bodies were consumed.

219

Surprisingly, as the crowd began to disperse, many of the dworcs approached Max and company, quietly and earnestly presenting them with small gifts. A carved bit of bone for Smitty, a small woven blanket for Dalia, a drinking horn for Max. Dylan was presented a leather necklace with one of the bear's massive claws set between two of its teeth. When he looked confused, Pickstone leaned close and whispered. "Ye damn near got yerself killed savin' me boys and I. If ye hadn't taken them hurts upon yerself, distracted the beastie when it broke our line... well, that necklace is a small way of thankin' ye."

For the first time ever, Max saw Dylan at a lack for words. The ogre just nodded his head and sniffed.

The celebration over, Max and the others were each given a room above the tavern, which featured beds long enough for all but Dylan, who just moved his mattress to the floor and stretched out comfortably.

Max was drifting off to sleep, pleasantly buzzed despite his troll regeneration, when Red spoke from atop his chest. "Ye need to help these people, Max."

"What do you mean?"

"I mean, in case ya didn't notice, they nearly beggared themselves to throw ya that party tonight. Did ya not notice that half of them weren't eatin'? And most only had a drink or two while that big lug of an ogre downed the mead by the gallon? They've had a rough life here, Max. I'm betting they've only just been getting' by. And today they lost five o' their own."

Max had sat up, causing Red to float away from him as he tried to recall what he'd seen in the tavern. He had a sinking feeling in his stomach, and guilt crept up on him. "I didn't notice any of that. I'm sorry."

"It'll be easy enough to fix, dummy. In the mornin' when ye go downstairs, give everyone ya see a kabob or a pastry, or both. Give all the bear meat you n the others received to the tavernkeeper. And when Pickstone arrives, ya make a big deal o' the mead. Tell him loudly so that all can hear that it's the best thing you've ever tasted, and ask to buy as much as he'll let ya take. Then pay him about ten times what it's worth. Pay him in gold, weapons, trade goods, whatever he wants most. It'll take em a few days to turn that honey into drink, so you and the others hang around here and help. Hunt, fish, sharpen swords, whatever needs doin." She crossed her arms and glared at him. "If ye don't, I'll never forgive ya!"

"You don't need to push me, Red." Max grumped at her. "I'd be happy to do all of that, and whatever else I can do to help them."

"Good! They've had a tough break from birth, shunned by both sides o' their heritage. I know ye need to build up yer kingdom and such, but don't ya be doin' at their expense. They'll be so anxious to trade that they'd offer up their firstborn if they thought you'd take em."

Max tilted his head, thinking. "That might be a good idea. Maybe I'll just ask them to join Stormhaven. We can make this an outpost, open a trade route through the underground…"

221

"Nope." Red interrupted him.

"No?" Max was confused.

"Would ye have them disturbin' Lysbane every time they traipsed back n forth underground? The only route we know of goes right through his home. What you do is get that crazy metal gnome to build ya a portal to place here. Or bribe the old wizard with some more Firebelly's." her judgmental glare somehow intensified.

Max chuckled. "As you say, Minister Red." He gave her a mock bow before laying back down. It'll be good to help these folks. I'm sure the others will agree."

*****

Morning came earlier than Max would have liked, the sunlight breaking over the mountains and directly into his window. The birdsong outside sounded particularly loud, as did the sounds of wood being chopped and iron being hammered at the smithy. He felt like a lazy teenager, having overslept while others were out there working.

Rolling out of bed, he took a drink of water from the pitcher on the nightstand. It was cool and refreshing, and he used another mouthful to wash the fuzz out of his mouth. Taking a moment to check himself in the mirror, he left his room and banged on the others' doors. As it turned out, he was the last one up, the other rooms already empty.

He made his way downstairs and did as Red had instructed. There were maybe thirty locals sitting at the tables in the common room, all of them eating some kind of porridge for their breakfast. Max began passing out pastries and kabobs, sending a few runners out to bring the rest of the locals in for breakfast. "This is the least I can do after the wonderful celebration last night."

While those who'd received food were munching, he quietly gathered the bear meat from the others and stepped into the kitchen, where the innkeeper was preparing more gruel. With a small bow of his head, he placed nearly a hundred chunks of the meat on the work counter and left the room.

"King Max!" Pickstone called out and raised a hand as he entered the room. "Hope ye slept well?"

"I did. And for much too long. I feel like a layabout." He saw some new faces and handed out more kabobs and pastries. "A little sample of my favorite snacks, in hopes of enticing you and your people into trading with us. That mead you served last night, it was… wonderful!" Max enthused, being careful to smile as widely as he could without baring his fangs. "I simply must take some back to Stormhaven with me!"

Pickstone stared at him for a moment, and Max worried that he'd overplayed his hand. But the elder nodded once, clearly making up his mind about something, and replied. "We can brew maybe ten barrels worth with the honey we have now. It'll take a couple of days. And if ye can wait a week, we can gather another load and make more."

"I can certainly wait on the first batch, but I'm afraid an additional week is too long. I must get back to Stormhaven and make sure the city hasn't burned down, or been overrun with drunken kobolds." Max grinned. "Maybe we can arrange a regular trade? Let's talk about what you'd be willing to trade for, and see if we can agree on a price. I'll warn you, though. My councilors have been helping me train my barter skill. As much as I love your fancy drink, and I'm sure my people would too, I can't bankrupt my kingdom over it!"

"Ha! Don't ye worry. We'll work somethin' out." Pickstone sat at one of the tables and took a bite of the kabob. His eyes widened, and he licked his lips. "Fer starters, we'll be needin' the recipe for whatever this is! And the spices. Me wife would make me sleep in the barn if she gets a taste o' this and..." He paused, looking over his shoulder, eyes wide and hunching slightly as a female dworc in a baker's apron strode in. "Sssshh! There she be in all her glory!"

Max grinned, making a show of bowing to Mrs. Pickstone and offering her a kabob with one flourishing hand, a pastry with the other. "Please, ma'am, sit and enjoy these samples. I was just speaking with Elder Pickstone here about trading him a few recipes..."

Max followed the rest of Red's demands over the next two days, he and his people helping out around the village. Dylan hooked himself to a plow and dragged it through the earth, tilling a new field just outside the wall. While there were still wolves and others predators in the valley, the death of the massive cave bear removed a lot of the threat to the villagers. Dalia gathered herbs from the forest with Smitty as an escort and trainee. Smitty also did a little hunting while Dalia and Max used those local herbs to make some health and stamina potions, which they gifted to the clan. They weren't the best of potions, since the ingredients were just above average, but each health potion would restore one thousand health points, which might save one of the warriors in a fight. And Max increased his *Alchemy* skill level by +2.

Pickstone negotiated like a dwarf, thinking he was getting the best of Max, and proud of it. For their ten barrels of mead, he secured five times more gold than Max would have paid for a similar quantity of Firebelly's Finest. Initially the dwarcs didn't want to accept gold, as they had nowhere to use it. They bartered goods and services amongst themselves, and did not venture into cities or towns to trade. It took a while, but Max convinced them to come and trade in Stormhaven and Darkholm, on his word that they would not be attacked or otherwise abused. Then he reminded Pickstone that gold was much easier to carry compared to barrels of mead or hides or other goods, and had a definite value that fluctuated less than barter items. It was also more easily divisible – one could not easily trade a tenth of a barrel of mead for an item that was only worth that much.

Over a dinner of bear stew the evening before they were to leave, Max made his final pitch. "Pickstone, I like you and your clan. You're good, honest, hardworking people, and I've been thinking you'd make a wonderful additional to Stormhaven's population. It would mean protection for you, regular trade between this village and our allied cities, and I believe some acceptance from the dwarves and orcs."

"What makes ye think we crave acceptance?" Pickstone bristled a bit.

"I think everyone craves acceptance of one kind or another. I can't pretend to know how you feel. And maybe I'm wrong and acceptance of your ancestor races means nothing to you. But if you join me, and become more prosperous, and that acceptance just happens to spread as a consequence, would that be such a bad thing?"

Pickstone glared at him a moment, then shrugged. "I suppose yer right about that. I don't see how it could hurt us. But we don't want a bunch o' strangers traipsin' around our valley. We like it as it is, nice and quiet."

Max pulled out his last arrow. "If you make yourselves citizens, and this valley part of my kingdom, I'll have a portal installed here. We can limit who comes and goes by only connecting it to Stormhaven's portal, over which I have complete control, and you would be named Governor of this valley. You run the place day to day, with your fellow elders in whatever structure you see fit. You can use the portal to call for help if you need it, or even as a means of escape if you are overrun for some reason. And of course, for trade. From Stormhaven you can reach Darkholm, or our new mine and farms to the south. Eventually I hope to connect with more cities and kingdoms.

Several of the dworcs in the common room had been listening in, at first just leaning closer from their nearby tables, but eventually giving up all pretense and just gathering around Max and the elder. Two more elders had pushed through the crowd, and now took seats. It was Max's understanding that there were five elders on the village council.

One of the others, a female with rough hands from working in her carpentry shop, thumped the table. "I think it be a good idea. But we'll be needin' some time to discuss this, amongst the elders as well as the rest. I been watchin you the last couple days, King Max, and I believe ye to be honorable. Few kings I ever heard of would pitch in the way ye have here. But we Blooded isolated ourselves fer good reason, and need to be sure o' what we want before we rejoin yer world."

The other elders at the table nodded their agreement. Pickstone said, "Leave us to discuss this, and we'll let ye know in the mornin' before ye depart fer home."

Max and his band retired to their rooms for the evening, and Max lay awake for a long while, listening to the sounds of arguing from downstairs. He thought he'd made a pretty solid, logical case for the Blooded to join him, but he might have underestimated the depth of fear and mistrust the clan members held in their hearts.

Chapter 12

Morning came, and Max joined the others for breakfast in the common room. It was a simple meal, scrambled eggs and bacon, but it tasted great. Having learned how lean the village resources were, all of them ate sparingly, even Dylan. They would be on the road shortly, and could supplement the meal with rations from their bags as they walked.

Pickstone and the elders met them outside, standing in front of a stack of mead barrels. "Here be your shipment, as agreed, Max!" the proud dworcs beamed at their visitors. "As fine as any in the land, I'll wager!"

"It is truly delicious." Max agreed, returning the smile. "You're all going to make me very popular back home!" He waited as there was some cheering and applause. Dylan and Smitty stepped forward to deposit the barrels in their inventories as Max produced the heavy bag of gold they'd agreed upon. "This much gold could buy you another wagon, a couple boars to pull it, and a great deal of food to get you through the winter. Plus some other items you might need."

"Bah, food we can grow, or hunt. The boars we breed be bigger'n what we could buy, and there be no shortage o' lumber fer buildin' wagons. What we need is steel for tools n weapons, sturdy cloth, and other such items we can't produce ourselves."

Max nodded, leaving the details of what the Blooded desired up to them. "And have you reached a decision about my offer?"

"We have not." Pickstone shook his head. "Instead, we be havin a counteroffer to put before ye." He held out a hand and Picklet stood forward. "Would ye be willin' to take me son back with ye? He can do our tradin' well enough, return in ten days with our purchases, and report on how he's treated in yer city."

"Picklet is most welcome to join us on the trip, as are any of your people. He'll be under my personal protection. I myself may not be able to return in ten days, as I don't know what is happening back in Stormhaven right now. But he will be protected until he's returned safely to you." Max remembered something else Dalia had said. "On the subject of returning with goods... do you know of a route to the south out of the mountains? One that you could navigate a wagon through? Our path here led us through a dragon's lair, and while he was friendly enough to us, I don't wish to disturb him again if we can help it."

This caused a great deal of commotion within the crowd. Eventually, the elders quieted everyone. Picklet spoke up, "Aye, there be a trail. I'll show it to ye if ye'll swear to hold it secret, regardless o' whether we join yer kingdom or not."

All of the party swore themselves to secrecy regarding the hidden path, the familiar light swirl of the gods taking note surrounding each of them, including Red, though none of the locals could see her.

Picklet was handed the sack of gold and the storage ring, and they set off. Their hike around the end of the lake was quiet, most of them lost in their own thoughts. The only sound other than footsteps was a quiet conversation between Dalia and Picklet, who walked closely side by side and barely spoke above a whisper.

Max found himself gazing at the lake, wishing for a fishing pole and a few spare days. He made a note to buy himself a pole if such a thing existed in this world, or create one if it didn't. Since fishhooks were included in the dwarven pack that Regin had first gifted him, he suspected he could find one in Darkholm. Then the next time he found himself by a serene lake, he'd try his luck.

It was late afternoon when Picklet led them up an incline on the far side and far end of the valley. Max saw nothing more than what looked like a small game trail winding its way up toward the rockier part of the rise. When they'd reached the very edge of the tree line, Picklet left the trail and disappeared behind a fallen slab of stone that leaned against the rock face at a precarious angle. When the others followed, they were surprised to see a smooth stone ramp about six feet wide leading into a cave.

Smitty shook his head. "I could have passed here a hundred times and not noticed this."

"Says a lot about your scout abilities, doesn't it?" Dylan grinned at him, causing Red to titter on Dalia's shoulder, where she often rode these days.

"Remind me… how far back did that teddy bear fling your oversized arse?" Smitty smiled at the ogre. "I thought tanks were supposed to pick a spot and hold it."

Dylan kicked at the dirt, still sore about being bested by the bear, and mumbled something about trying to stop a freight train. Smitty just grinned and moved on after the others as they entered the cave. Which turned out to be a tunnel leading southward through the mountain. Max could barely make out a tiny pinprick of light at the far end.

The tunnel was more than wide enough for a wagon to pass through at this end, and Picklet assured them it was the same all the way through. The ceiling was high enough that Dylan could walk upright without bumping or scraping his head, which he was grateful for.

The tunnel turned out to be nearly two and half miles long, and about an hour after entering, they paused at the exit to adjust their eyes to the sunlight. Before them lay another valley, this one much smaller than the Blooded's valley, and narrower. Picklet glanced at the position of the sun, which was now low over the peaks to the west, and suggested, "I know of a good spot to camp down below. We can get started again in the mornin'. There be a narrow pass through the next and final ridge, then we descend to the old road on the other side.

Partway down the slope, Max looked back to see that the trees hid the tunnel on this side nearly as well as the rock had done at the other end.

True to his word, Picklet led them to a small clearing on the valley floor. Ancient trees rose high above, their canopy covering all but the center of the clearing, where a ring of bowling ball-sized stones surrounded an overgrown fire pit. It only took a few moments to pull the weeds and clear out the pit while Smitty and Dylan gathered some firewood. After sharing a quiet meal and spending a little time listening Dalia tell Picklet about the markets in Darkholm, the group set out bedrolls and camped under the stars. Max took watch, needing less sleep than the others due to his high *Endurance*. He sat there watching over his companions, thinking he was glad that he hadn't seen anything resembling mosquitos on this world, yet.

There was some rustlings in the brush during the night, though Dylan's snoring easily scared off most of the nightlife. Max assumed this valley had some kind of alpha predator of its own, but whatever it was, it didn't make itself known. Keeping a wary eye on things anyway, Max spent the hours trying to organize his plans in his head. There were so many things he needed to take care of, and even with the assistance of his councilors, he was feeling overwhelmed.

His merchants seemed to have a handle on the food supply, at least as long as his coin held out. Based on conversations with Redmane, and his own calculations, the money from the captured bank should hold out for a year or more. But Max knew from experience that a year went by quickly. And who knew what emergencies might arise? He needed to solidify a steady income stream for his kingdom. The gold and silver mine near the temple would help, as would the farms he planned to establish near the

Brightwood, where the remainder of the dragon's mana might produce higher crop yields and better quality.

In the long term, he could potentially sell portal pedestals created by Glitterspindle, assuming the old gnome wasn't too far gone to recreate them. But in the immediate future he wanted any portals that could be manufactured for his own use. The Blooded's village wasn't the only location he wanted instant access to. He'd need to find out from the gnome what materials were needed, and determine the cost of portal production.

If he could locate the tomb of Nogroz, as his quest demanded, it was possible there was a significant amount of loot buried there, as well. He'd wrestle with the ethics of taking that loot if and when they got there. He could eventually profit from taking An'zalor's city from him, but that might be years down the road. And there were mines in the underground that he'd inherited with the city. The dwarves and kobolds were working them steadily, but other than the diamonds, the profits were minimal. Mainly they were a good source of crafting material, and a way to employ a hundred or so citizens. There were more dragon bits and high-grade crafting ingredients to gather from in and around Brightwood, and some of those could bring in a decent profit. But again, he wanted to reserve most of that for his kingdom's and his own personal use.

Max had read in one of his favorite gamer books somewhere that a player had nearly broken the game economy by inventing an in-game cheat version of cigarettes, something that the game company had forbidden. Maybe he could do something similar? Figure out a useful tool from Earth that didn't exist here yet. He'd have to ask Redmane whether there were such things as patents on this world.

There were other things on his to-do backlog as well. He held soul stones in his inventory for the elite guards he'd fought during the battle for the city. He fully intended to have someone revive those guards so that he could make use of them.

Max needed to spend more time leveling up his crafting skills. Particularly his Blacksmithing, Weaponscrafting, and Alchemy skills. When they returned to the city, he promised to spend some time with Dalia's father, hopefully in his own newly built lab. And he'd make arrangements to spend a day or two with Master Oakstone at the keep's forge. While he could afford, for now, to have the various master smiths in Darkholm create epic armor and weapons for him and his party, he eventually wanted to be able to do it himself. He was still a low level noob as smithing, but thanks to Dalia's coaching and his own practice, he was nearing the apprentice level alchemist. The usefulness of potions in this world couldn't be overstated. And with his access to prime ingredients, he should be able to level up that skill more quickly than most.

He had just started to walk a circuit around the camp, keeping his back to the fire so that his eyes didn't need to adjust to the darkness surrounding them, when a louder than normal sound caught his attention. The snapping of a stick, probably as it was stepped upon, maybe fifty yards out in the woods, back in the direction they had come from. Max drew his bow from his inventory and nocked an arrow, using his monster heritage darksight combined with his improved elven vision to scan between the trees in the direction of the sound. It could simply have been a deer, or a bear, but he didn't think so.

When the night birds in the trees went silent a moment later, he was sure. Bending to pick up a small rock, he turned and tossed it at Dylan's head. The object struck the ogre's cheek, causing him to wake with a grunt and a sputter. The experienced soldier's eyes immediately found Max, who put a finger to his lips, then pointed out into the woods. A couple quick hand signals later, and Dylan nodded.

Max advanced into the forest, bow at the ready, moving as quietly as he could. Which wasn't saying much. Despite his elven and stonetalon heritage, he still hadn't gotten the hang of moving stealthily through a forest. Behind him, Dylan quietly woke the others with nudges and whispers. Smitty was already on his feet and moving out into the forest to flank whatever was out there, moving much more quietly than Max. The others were equipping weapons and spreading out behind the fire, Dylan watching their backs as the dwarf and the dworc watched Max disappear behind a large tree.

Aware that he wasn't fooling anyone, Max gave up on the idea of stealth, stood still, and simply spoke into the night. "Whoever you are, show yourself." He might as well make himself as much of a distraction as possible, to make it easier for Smitty to circle around unnoticed.

His ears picked up a sharp intake of breath ahead of him and slightly to his right. Raising his bow, he spoke again. "You have five seconds to show yourself before I start shooting."

Almost immediately, a small figure emerged from behind a tree. Only about three feet tall, Max initially mistook it for a goblin. When it emerged into a small pool of moonlight, he got a better look, and lowered his bow? "What are you doing here?"

"I… I am sorry, great King Max!" a small dworc child stepped closer, hands in the air in front of her. "I only wanted to see your city! And you did say that any of my people were welcome to join you…"

Smitty stepped out of the woods behind the girl, causing her to jump and emit a small scream before she recognized him. He wasted no time, scooping her up and carrying her over one shoulder as he walked toward Max. Both of them returned to the campfire, where Smitty set down the now tearful child. She stood there, back straight and shoulders back, acting defiant even as she wiped tears from her cheeks.

As soon as Picklet got a look at her, he growled, "Teeglin, what are you doing here?"

The girl spun to face him, scowling. "King Max said anyone was welcome! When I heard that, I ran to get my things, but by the time I returned, you had already left. I tracked you across the valley, but lost your trail among the rocks. It took me a little while to find the tunnel entrance and catch up."

"You should be back at the village." Picklet sighed. "I assume the elders do not know you've followed us?" When the little girl looked guilty and shook her head, he stepped forward and knelt down in front of her. "It's dangerous out in the wilds at night. What were you thinking, child?"

"By the time it got dark, I was already at the tunnel!" She protested. "It would not have been any safer to go back than to keep following you."

"She's got a point there." Smitty smiled at the brave child. "Got guts, too."

Ignoring him, Picklet asked, "But why follow us now?"

"Why not?" Her eyes dropped to focus on her feet. "There's nothing for me in the village anymore. Everyone kept staring at me and shaking their heads... I... didn't like it."

Picklet looked up at Max and the others. "Her father was one of those lost in our fight with the bear. Her mother died in childbirth." He shook his head. "It happens much too often among the Blooded. Our races were not meant to breed together, and complications often arise."

Max's heart went out to the little orphan. From her appearance, she was clearly more dwarf than orc. Guessing she was maybe ten years old, her small stature and pale skin, combined with tusks that were understated compared to most of the villagers, told him that her mother likely leaned even further toward their dwarf heritage.

He too got down on a knee, capturing the girl's attention. "You understand that what you did was wrong? Besides the danger to yourself, your village is probably worried sick about you. They may even be out searching the valley at night, trying to find you."

She shook her head. "No, they won't. Even if they noticed I'm gone, we have strict rules. They will wait until morning to search for me." Max gave Picklet a quick glance, one eyebrow raised in question. The dworc nodded, confirming the girl's words.

"The valley has always been a dangerous place. Even more so at night. We stay inside the walls when the sun is down, and any caught outside in the dark know that they are on their own until morning."

"Survival of the fittest." Dylan mumbled from where he sat by the fire.

"Indeed." Picklet agreed. "There are no weaklings among the Blooded. The weak are challenged, until they become strong, or perish. It is our way."

After fighting old Cantankerous, Max couldn't say that he blamed them for their way of life. Though it may seem harsh on its surface, he understood the need. Any weak link in a time of trouble might spell the deaths of others, even the whole village.

"I can fight!" Teeglin declared, a dagger appearing in her right hand, just inches from Max's face. She bared her tiny, rounded tusks and narrowed her eyes in what she imagined to be a battle visage. To Max she just looked adorable.

Humoring her, he fell onto his backside, feigning fear as he widened his eyes and held up his hands. "Whoa! Careful there, little warrior. No need to cut my nose off!"

She instantly lowered the weapon, putting both hands behind her back. "Sorry." She mumbled. "But it's true. I can fight better than any of the younglings! Take me with you, and I can be your bodyguard! Make sure nobody sneaks up on you like I just did!" She stuck her chin out, eyes blazing.

"Ha!" Smitty grinned at the little girl. When he saw that his laughter hurt her feelings, he added, "I like it, boss. Tiny ninja bodyguard! Every king should have one!"

Beaming now, the girl looked from Smitty back to Max, hope shining in her eyes.

Max shook his head. "Well, we can't very well take the time to escort you back, and I'm certainly not going to send you home on your own. Technically, I did say anyone was welcome to join us. So I suppose we'll bring you along with us to Stormhaven." He smiled as she hopped up and down with excitement. "But for now, go curl up by the fire. You've been up all night, and we have a busy day tomorrow."

The girl nodded her head, and Dalia motioned for Teeglin to take a spot next to her own bedroll. In just a minute she was situated and stretched out between a

239

protective Dalia and Picklet, smiling happily as she rested her head and closed her eyes.

*****

The group let the youngling sleep well past dawn, quietly going about camp business, feeding the fire and cooking breakfast, then packing up their gear as they waited for her. Smitty left to see what game he might find, while Dalia and Max spent an hour making more potions, and Dylan kept watch. Picklet quietly told them about Teeglin's parents. Her mother had indeed favored her dwarven heritage, and had been a leatherworker before she passed. Her father was a warrior, and a veteran of many battles. When he was at home, he worked as a mason, improving the walls and homes within the village.

Max and the others also learned more about the clan. There were nearly a dozen orphans that were raised by the entire village. Each of them was fostered in a family home, and as soon as they were old and strong enough, were given odd jobs to perform. At age twelve, they were apprenticed to one of the crafters, or went to live in the barracks to train as warriors. The clan remained small due to a higher than normal mortality rate at birth, for both mother and child. Combined with losses to local predators, occasional lethal personal conflicts, and the usual infections and diseases, the clan was left with small hope of growth.

Dalia, who seemed exceptionally interested in the genetic aspect of their woes, asked in a whisper, "Would it

240

help ye to add some fresh bloodlines? Like pureblood dwarves or orcs?"

Picklet flinched at the word pureblood, but quickly shook it off. "It be hard to say. Me da believes that the answer lay in further diluting our blood. Y'see…" He paused and blushed slightly as he looked at Dalia. "The main problem be that dwarven females, as tough as they be, were not meant to birth orc babies. The strain on them be… significant. And the delivery be dangerous. Orc babies be nearly twice the size of dwarf babes at birth."

Now it was Dalia's turn to wince. She nodded her understanding. "So new orc blood might make things harder on those with more dwarflike bodies. What about new dwarf blood?"

Again, Picklet shook his head. "We just don't know."

"I'm going to marry King Max and have chimera babies." A sleepy Teeglin announced as she got up from her bedroll. "I will be Queen Teeglin, and we will have many little princes and princesses!"

"Hush, child!" Picklet scolded, while Dylan and Dalia laughed.

Max did his best to keep a serious face for her. "Well, while you are quite lovely, little one… I'm afraid I'm a bit too old for you." He stuck out his bottom lip, trying to look sad.

Determined, Teeglin just shook her head as she sat down and accepted a kabob from a smiling Dalia. "You'll see, I'll grow up fast! And I'll be the best warrior in your kingdom. You won't find a better queen than me!"

"Well, how could I resist a beauty like you who is also a great warrior?" Max grinned, patting her on the head, much to her annoyance. "Let's see what happens in fifteen years or so."

Quickly changing the subject, Picklet growled at the girl. "Eat quickly, and pack up your things. The rest of us have been up since dawn. We have much ground to cover today, and you have very short legs!"

Grunting in indignation, the girl chomped down on the end of the kabob closest to her fingers, cleaning the entire stick off in one bite. Speaking around the mouthful of meat, she said, "I'll keep up!" as she got to her feet and stomped over to her bedroll. By the time she was done chewing and swallowing the mouthful, her bedroll was packed up, and she stood ready with a small bow in one hand and a quiver of arrows at her belt.

Once again Picklet led the way, heading southward across the remainder of the valley.

The remainder of their trip went more quickly than Max expected. True to her word, Teeglin kept up, though Picklet set a slightly slower pace than the day before. Smitty and Dylan bracketed the child as they walked, educating her on the fine art of knock knock jokes. She was enchanted, as was Dalia, both of them giggling at the most ridiculous of jokes the two soldiers could conceive. Walking behind them, Max just shook his head.

They crossed over the pass through the final mountain ridge, finding themselves looking down over the same vast forest where Max had appeared on this new world. According to his map, they were west of the outpost be several miles. He took over the lead position and continued south through the trees until they reached the road. From there, it was a simple matter to follow the overgrown stone path back to where the hidden outpost entrance was.

As they got closer, he told them the story of his first encounter with the goblins, and his attempt to secure the door. They all laughed when they reached the doorway with his likeness burned into the stone. "Looks just like you!" Teeglin giggled.

Max looked over the stone, searching for a particular mark. He'd had a report from Redmane that a few of his dwarven engineers had taken the time to repair the door's locking mechanism and hinges, leaving a mark that would tell him where to press on the stone to open the door. When he finally found the mark, he snorted.

They'd placed it in the middle of his drawing, right on his nose.

He pressed his thumb against the nose, and to his surprise, a blue glow infused the likeness of his face, the eyes glowing especially brightly. "Nice touch." Smitty observed. "Likely to scare away any goblins that stumble across this place and have the guts to touch your face."

A moment later there was an audible click, and the door swung inward without a sound. Max let the others pass through, not needing his direction to follow a long, straight tunnel. When they'd all passed inside, he set a hand to the door, expecting to have to put some muscle into closing the heavy stone slab. Instead, it moved easily, no harder to move than a standard wood door on Earth. When it closed, there was only a soft snick as the lock reengaged.

There was a similar lock on the door at the other end of the tunnel. Asking Dalia to move her light globe close to the door, he pointed it out to all of them. It was a subtle symbol, almost like a cattle brand, a half circle with a wavy line across it. "We're going to use this symbol for such things across our kingdom. Now you'll know what to look for."

A few minutes later they all stood in the teleport arrival zone within the inner keep of Stormhaven. Teeglin looked around in wonder, eyes wide and mouth open, hugging her arms tight across her chest. Picklet was less obvious, but still impressed. Neither of them had ever been in a city, both having been born in their village. Just as they were staring at the dozens of orcs and dwarves in view, they were receiving stares in return. Some of them hostile.

In moments, Redmane appeared to welcome them back. "Redmane, I'd like you to meet Picklet and Teeglin, of the Blooded clan. New friends of ours." Max called out loudly enough for everyone in the courtyard and on the walls to hear. Several of those who'd been staring quickly returned to their business.

The white-haired old chamberlain hesitated for a moment upon noticing their obviously mixed heritage. But being a dwarf of culture and poise, he quickly recovered. "Welcome to Stormhaven, new friends from the Blooded clan. I was told tales of the Blooded as a child, but thought them to be just made up stories. It is a pleasure to meet you." He gave the dworcs a polite smile.

"Dylan, Smitty, can I trust you to show them around without getting into any trouble?" He raised an eyebrow at his corporals. Before they could answer, Dalia stepped forward.

"No, ye can't. These two are trouble incarnate. I'll go along to make sure everyone behaves." She took Teeglin's hand and led her toward the gate that would take them into the city proper. "Let's do a bit o' shoppin' before dinner."

Max saw Redmane look toward one of the guard captains and give a brief nod. The captain returned the gesture, gave a whistle and a hand gesture, and four dwarven guards peeled off from their posts and following behind Dalia and party. "Just in case their heritage should cause a reaction." Redmane whispered to Max.

"Thank you, Redmane." Max felt he should have thought of that himself. "So, before I share what we found on our little adventure, is there anything urgent I need to attend to immediately?"

"A patrol of orc guards tried to execute a goblin they caught stealing from the butcher's shop on the main square. Another patrol stopped them, and the goblin is in a cell awaiting your return. As king, you must preside over such matters. At least until you appoint someone to oversee these things."

"Dammit." Max cursed softly as he followed Redmane into the keep and then into his study. There he sat behind his desk, once again covered with the three familiar stacks of reports, only taller this time. "Alright, arrange a trial for in the morning. Get the patrol who found him, and the butcher, to attend. I assume the little fella is being treated humanely?"

"Of course, Max. He has a comfortable cot, and three meals each day. He's living better in that cell than he did before coming to Stormhaven."

"Good. Thank you. Unless I say otherwise, let's assume that all prisoners are treated humanely. I don't exactly want them to feel comfortable down there, but I also don't want them starved or abused."

"I assumed as much." Redmane took a small pad from his inventory, along with a short pencil. "I noticed you arrived via portal, rather than on foot. Would you like to fill me in on the pertinent details of your trip?"

Max grinned at his advisor. "Well, let's see... We walked through some tunnels, killed some stuff. Met a dragon, didn't kill him, or get eaten ourselves. Discovered a valley full of dworcs, helped them kill a massive monster cave bear, made some new friends, drank a lot of mead... oh! Here." Max pulled one of the small kegs of mead from his inventory. "For your personal stock. I think this is going to be very popular around here."

Being a dwarf, Redmane naturally had a tap and mugs in his own inventory. The two of them tipped the keg on its side right there on Max's desk, and Max held it while Redmane tapped it. Max filled in the details of the story, emphasizing how much he wanted to help the Blooded, as they shared a mug of the ale.

"This be damned good." Redmane nodded his approval as he refilled his mug. "Ye know ye way overpaid for it, but I do understand why ye did it. Fer now, because of its rarity, the dworcs'll be able to get a good price per keg. But ye'll need to let em know that won't always be the case. The novelty will wear off eventually, and the price will drop."

"Hopefully by then they'll have been able to purchase most of what they need." Max agreed. "And I'm still keeping my fingers crossed that they'll join us as citizens."

"Speakin' o' citizens, yours need ya to make some decisions, Max." Redmane gestured toward the piles atop his desk. "Shall we start with the most urgent, as usual?"

Max sighed, sitting forward in his comfortable chair, placing his elbows on the desk. "Might as well." The first report on the top of the pile related to the kobolds. A group of nearly two hundred of them who had been hunting down stray grey dwarves in the region around the city had submitted a request. Max read through it, chuckling a bit, then smiling. "They want to become citizens?"

"Aye, as ye can see, they think you bring good luck. They've been fattening themselves on grey dwarf stew, eatin' better than they have fer years."

"They do know that they'll run out of greys to catch and eat soon, right?"

"Aye, they do. I've had no reports of any greys in two days now. But they believe you'll find somethin' else for them to eat, somethin' interestin' to do."

"No pressure." Max shook his head. "Alright, let's make them citizens. I have an idea on what they can help with when they're done hunting greys. Are you familiar with the story of King Nogroz...?"

Chapter 13

Max spent the rest of the day with Redmane, working through the stacks of issues. He learned that Dalia's father had finished setting up his own shop in town, and had set up a full alchemy lab for Max within the keep. Master Oakstone, true to his promise, had fully equipped a personal smithy for Max as well. Redmane informed him that Oakstone would return in two days for a private lesson.

There had been a minor flood of engineers applying to visit Glitterspindle's temple and 'interview' the artificial gnome. Not all of the applicants had been dwarves, either. Several gnomes were offering significant bribes to be the first to gain access to the temple. Max had Redmane invite those gnomes for an audience. He had questions to ask them. In addition, he requested that Redmane hire someone to find out as much as they could on the gnomes' backgrounds. Based on the size of the bribes offered, they were a little to anxious to get there first for his comfort. Besides, several of the dwarven engineers who'd been at the mine already had visited the temple.

The goblins, all but the little thief, had been adjusting well. Several were on track to become apprentices and learn trades. A party of kobolds, who considered the goblins their lesser cousins, had volunteered to take twenty of the goblins out hunting with them. The little fellas had been power leveled, and encouraged to put their points into intelligence and strength. As a result, they were beginning to think for themselves, much to the dismay of Ugnok. Max made a note to give the goblin shaman a title of some sort, to ease the blow to his pride. Maybe level him up and send him out as an ambassador to other goblin tribes. He grinned to himself, picturing a level twenty Ugnok, with an honor guard of orcs, walking into a goblin village.

The mines were all producing at close to peak capacity. Working for a percentage of the haul was a good motivator for the miners. Redmane even presented Max with a small pouch of diamonds harvested over the previous week. Max left it with him to be deposited in the treasury. The fortification around the mine near the temple was now complete, a thirty foot stone wall with a well inside, and a second well within the mine itself. Which also had a solid iron gate at the entrance. The way station near the mine now had a palisade, with the house, barn, corrals, well, smokehouse with escape tunnel, and a new barracks for the scouts and guards, all within the enclosure. It was currently constructed of wood posts, but the foundations for a stone wall had been laid, and construction was proceeding. Several farmers had begun plowing fields, temporarily living at the way station or the mine while they constructed homes for themselves.

A small clan of minotaurs had requested permission to become citizens and take up residence in Max's new lands near the way station. Redman informed Max that their representatives were being hosted in the keep, awaiting a meeting with him. Max scheduled it for first thing in the morning. In addition, a gnome merchant had arrived at the gates two days earlier, his caravan escorted by grey dwarves. Max's guards immediately captured and executed the guards, turning their corpses over to the kobolds. They put the gnome under house arrest at the tavern, and confiscated all three wagons worth of goods. The gnome had claimed he owned a warehouse in the city, and had significant funds on deposit in the local bank. Redmane handed Max the paperwork the gnome had presented as proof.

"I'm afraid the warehouse was cleared out long ago, the contents either consumed or sold. His bank records appear to be in order. He had just over one thousand gold on deposit."

"And what was in his wagons?"

Redmane cleared his throat. "This is where the problem begins. Two of the wagons carried supplies, mostly meat and grains, some common enchanted items, a small quantity of mithril ore." He paused for a moment, looking at Max. "The third wagon contained a dozen kobold slaves."

"Ah, shit." Max thumped his desk.

"Exactly. The kobolds are naturally quite incensed, and are demanding the gnome's head. The gnome is demanding protection from the kobolds, and the return of his goods and funds."

"And he just rode right up to the gates with this load of slaves?" Max asked in disbelief. "He didn't notice the dwarves and orcs on the walls?"

"He had been traveling the underground for some time, using his guards to find and capture wandering kobolds. Apparently, though he received the notification that you had taken control of the city, he assumed you were a grey dwarf like Agnor. He further assumed that the guards on the wall were mercenaries, hired to compensate for losses when you took the city."

"So this gnome is not very smart." Max sighed. "I can't very well just kill him and keep his stuff, as much as I might want to. As far as he knew, he was coming to a city where slavery was legal." Max paused for a moment. "On my world, slavery is not just unethical, it is considered a crime in most places. Is it the same here?"

Redmane shook his head, a sad look on his face. "Unfortunately, no. Slavery is common among all the dark races, and even some o' the light. We dwarves do not keep slaves, though we do allow for indentured servants. They are treated as employees, with limits to how hard they be worked, and requirements that they be well fed, housed, and not abused."

Max thought it over. "Alright, I'm not ready to tackle that whole issue all at once right now. So here's what we'll do. Give the gnome back his wagons and cargo, minus the kobolds if they haven't already been set free. Give him his gold from the bank, and have him sign receipts for all of it, then banish him from my kingdom and escort him out the of the city. If he doesn't have drivers, have someone drive his wagons through the gates for him, then close the gates on their way back in. If he can get himself home without the kobolds getting their payback, good for him. Either way, whatever happens, I can't be called a thief or an unjust executioner." After a moment's thought, he added, "And make sure the news of what happens is spread far and wide. Our neighbors need to know that slavery will not be tolerated here. Post some signs outside the gates. Any slaves brought into the city, or found on my lands, will be freed. By whatever means necessary."

Redmane nodded. "An elegant solution, Max. I'll be sure that the kobolds know they owe you such a juicy gift. We'll likely have that thousand gold back by morning if you are willing to sell them some mead."

Max just nodded, already wanting to move on. The choice was a distasteful one, but necessary. His tirade got him thinking about his plan to revive the souls of Agnor's elite guards. Would forcing them to serve him be just another form of slavery? He decided to get Redmane's opinion on it. Once he'd framed the question, the old dwarf was silent for a while, considering.

"I admit, the thought never occurred to me." He finally answered, speaking slowly. "On the one hand, it weren't you that killed them and captured their souls. They were doomed to serve long ago. On the other hand, I don't have enough knowledge o' soul magic to know if they still think fer themselves, or if their... personalities? If their personalities still exist within them, or they're just mindless constructs powered by the captured souls that be capable o' followin' simple orders like *guard* or *kill*."

Max nodded along as the dwarf spoke. "We need to find someone who knows about this magic. Maybe... if their souls can still think for themselves, maybe we revive them and give them a choice. They can remain alive and serve as guards, or we can destroy their gems and set them free." He paused again. "Shit. We don't even know if destroying the gems does set them free. What if that just banishes them to a void, or some other existence that's even worse?"

Their conversation was interrupted by the crash of his study's door as an excited Teeglin burst in, followed by a blushing and apologetic Dalia.

"King Max! This city is amazing! I want to live here forever! There's a market, and shops with glass windows, and right outside the inner gate there's a bakery that makes such yummy treats! She rushed across the room, around his desk, and launched herself into his lap, nearly tipping him over in his chair. "When I'm queen, we're going to have make that baker our royal chef, and eat pastries every day!"

Chuckling, Redmane said, "Eating pastries every day is a good way to get big and fat, like Dylan."

The little girl threw him a scornful look. "Don't call Dylan fat! He can't help it if he was born an ogre. Not all of us are perfect when we're born!"

Realizing he was speaking to a dworc, and feeling chastened, the old dwarf bowed his head. "My apologies... lady Teeglin. I meant no insult."

"He's right." Max defended his chamberlain. "Eating pastries all day will make you round as a battle boar! And you mind your manners when you speak to an elder. First, you interrupted an important meeting, barging in here without permission. Then you scolded my chamberlain, who works very hard to run this place for me."

Not ready to give up on her anger, the girl grumped. "This place wouldn't be so hard to run. There's hardly anybody here. It's not like he has to do anything himself, he can just boss people around all day." She crossed her arms and threw both of them a defiant look.

"Oh, really?" Max got an idea. "Well, since you think it's so easy… you'll just have to try it for yourself! Starting first thing in the morning, you will be Master Redmane's assistant. You will observe what he does, run errands for him, and learn what it takes to run this place."

Redmane opened his mouth ot object, but Max shook his head slightly. Teeglin was a little slower. "What? Why?"

"Didn't you say you wanted to be queen of this place someday? Seems to me that a queen should know exactly how to run her own city, shouldn't she? Learn the proper way to boss people around all day?"

That did it. The angry look turned thoughtful, then excited. "Yep! Okay Master Redmane, you can teach me."

"So kind of you to consent, little one." The dwarf replied dryly.

"Good! Now, apologize to Redmane for interrupting our meeting. And from now on, you knock before entering someone else's room, yes?"

"I'm sorry, sir." Teeglin lowered her eyes, her hands fidgeting. "And I promise to knock from now on."

"Apology accepted. Now, you will report to my office at seventh bell tomorrow morning, ready to work. That means with breakfast already in your belly. If you have trouble finding it, anyone in the keep can show you where it is. Don't be late. No excuses!"

The girl nodded her head emphatically, launching herself from Max's lap over the desk. She hit the ground running, grabbing ahold of Dalia's hand on her way out. "I'll find her a room close to me own." Dalia managed before being dragged through the door.

Redmane chuckled. "She's quite spirited."

"She wasn't exactly raised by wolves, but she never knew her mother, and her father was a warrior. I have no idea how much education she's had, or training in etiquette. I'm sorry for springing her on you like that. If you prefer, I'll find something else for her to do."

"No, it might be interestin' to see what she's capable of. And what better ambassador for the dworcs than a cute lil fireball of a lass. Seein' her at my side might help our people, both dwarves and orcs, accept the dworcs more easily. It'll be good to have a runner, save some o' the wear and tear on these old legs."

*****

256

Max had breakfast in the keep's small dining room at six bells. Dylan and Smitty joined him, both soldiers used to early mornings. They were halfway through their meal when Teeglin and Dalia joined them. Max heard Dalia explaining to the little girl about the bell system for keeping time. The still-sleepy Teeglin yawned as she nodded her understanding.

"Assistant Chamberlain Teeglin, good morning." Max greeted her with a smile. "Grab some grub, you need to be in Redmane's office in about half an hour." She nodded her head, loading a plate of with eggs and sausage from a side table. They took seats, and Dalia poured her a glass of juice.

"Are you excited about your new job?" Dylan asked.

"I don't like Redmane. He called you fat." She grumped, taking her glass and downing several big gulps of juice. When she set it down, she had a red juice moustache on her upper lip.

Dylan patted his belly. "Well, I'm sure he didn't mean it as an insult to me. Redmane is a good man. Dwarf. You should listen to what he has to teach you. His job involves every little thing that happens around here. Think of all the juicy secrets you'll learn!"

"And keep to yourself, right? Everything you learn while you're with Master Redmane is a secret." Max admonished.

Teeglin gave a solemn nod, taking the responsibility seriously. "I promise." Her eyes widened when a swirl of lights surrounded her, binding her to her promise.

"Now the gods have taken note o' yer promise." Dalia warned, her tone serious. "Ye be sure n keep that promise, or you'll feel the wrath o' the gods themselves. This be no small thing, girl."

Max put a reassuring hand on the now frightened child's shoulder. "You'll be okay. Just remember to think before you speak. And as a general rule, don't talk about what you hear to anyone but Redmane or the folks in this room."

The girl finished her meal quietly, deep in thought. The others made small talk until she was through. She got up, put her plate and utensils back on the side table, and left the room without speaking. Since she turned in the general direction of Redmane's office, which was only a short distance away, Max just let her go.

"Redmane will give her a bunch of fetch quests and such. She'll be able to level up, earn a few coins, and learn about this place. It'll be good for her." Max said to no one in particular. The two corporals just grunted their agreement as they ate.

"What are you guys up to today?" Max changed the subject.

"Goin to see me da at his new shop." Dalia volunteered. "Any messages ya want me to deliver?"

"Ask him if he has time to visit my lab this afternoon? It's not a command, if he's busy, we can do it another time. Also, ask him if he knows of a reputable summoner that we can consult on the soul stones I looted from Agnor's elites. In fact, all of you ask around and see if you can find one. I understand they're pretty rare."

"Will do, boss." Smitty said as all three nodded. "I'm heading out to see if I can find a trainer for my Scout class. Maybe get them to teach me some things. Thought I'd start with your new Scout Commander out at the mine."

Dylan chimed in. "And I'm headed over to Darkholm to see Master Oakstone. He said to return for a fitting. Hasn't quite been a week, but I also want to talk to him about a weapon. My axe is okay, but…"

"Good idea. You need some gold?"

"I have some, boss. And if it's not enough, I'll tell him to put it on your tab." The ogre winked at him.

"He's supposed to be here tomorrow for a smithing lesson. You can tell him I'll pay him then."

With that, the others got up to begin their days. Max headed to main hall where he was going to have to conduct the trial of the little goblin thief. He wasn't looking forward to that at all.

On his way down the main corridor, he peeked into the open door of Redmane's office, where he saw Teeglin sitting in front of the chamberlain's desk, leaning forward to look at a parchment. The dwarf was observing her as she read aloud from the text. From what Max could hear, she was doing well. He smiled to himself as kept moving, then turned into the great hall.

Servants were setting up a few dozen chairs behind a pair of tables that faced the throne. Max didn't like the idea of sitting in the throne while conducting this trial, so he asked that another table and chair be brought out and set directly in front of the other two. Sort of like a judge's bench. He would be setting a precedent today, one that would impact all future trials in his kingdom. As an afterthought, he had two more chairs set alongside his table, for Redmane and Teeglin to observe.

When the time for the trial approached, citizens began to filter into the room and take seats. Ugnok appeared, along with half a dozen other goblins from the tribe. He approached Max, who had taken a seat at his table and was looking through some of his interface tabs.

The goblin cleared his throat, and bowed. "Mighty King Max. Ugnok sorry about thief. Max want, I take his head now. No need to waste time for trial."

"Thank you, Ugnok. And no, do not take his head. In my kingdom, criminals get a trial. And the punishment will fit the crime. Petty theft will not require his death."

The shaman nodded, seeming happy that one of his tribe wasn't about to be killed.

"While you're here, since we have a few moments, I wanted to talk to you about something. I could use your help, if you're willing?"

"Whatever King Max need, Ugnok do." He nodded decisively.

"Well, you know some of the other goblin tribes in the forest, yes?"

"In forest, under mountain, many tribes." Ugnok confirmed.

"I would like to make you my official ambassador to the goblin tribes. Your job would be to journey to their camps and see if you can convince them to join us. We could use another tribe or three around here."

Ugnok's brows knitted together, and he thumped his staff on the floor. "King Max no happy with Ugnok tribe?"

"Yes, I'm very happy with Ugnok's tribe. You have shown me that goblins make valuable citizens. I'm told you're working very hard, and making yourselves useful. In fact, I'm so happy with Ugnok's goblins, I think we need more."

Ugnok puffed out his chest, grinning widely. "Ugnok do this thing for King Max. Bring back good goblins." He paused, raising one eyebrow. "You want Ugnok kill chiefs and shamans first?" He looked hopeful at the prospect.

"Only if they attack you, Ugnok. Try to convince them. I'll send some guards with you, so you shouldn't be in danger. And you can take along some gifts to help convince them."

"Ugnok not need guards! Stronger than any chief or shaman already. Kill them easy!"

Max took a moment to *Identify* the shaman, seeing that he was level fifteen, up from the level five he'd been when Max first met him. He must have joined the kobolds for some power leveling. "I see you have become much stronger! I'm proud of you, Ugnok. And yes, you could probably kill all the goblins in a tribe by yourself. But that's not why I'm sending the guards with you. I am sending them as a show of great power. So that no goblins dare to attack you. Remember, I want them to join us, not to die in a foolish attack on my ambassador."

"Ugnok understand." the goblin flashed a toothy grin at Max. "I go tomorrow?"

"That's fine. I'll arrange for Redmane to send you to the outpost in the morning. You can find your way from there, yes?"

"Yes." Ugnok turned to see that the accused goblin was being led into the hall. "King Max no kill?"

"No kill." Max assured the shaman, who moved to take a seat with the other goblins. It occurred to Max that he also couldn't be too easy on the little thief, or he'd have a crime wave of goblin thieves.

A few minutes later the eighth bell rang, and Max indicated that the doors should be closed. The accused was seated at one of the tables next to a dwarf wearing a silk vest and spectacles. At the other table was seated another dwarf in more casual clothes. The chairs behind them were nearly filled with dwarfs, orcs, and Ugnok's small group of goblins.

"Let us begin." Max thumped the table with his fist, not having a gavel. The lone dwarf stood up to speak. "Prosecutor Garlan, Majesty, on behalf o' the kingdom. The accused, a goblin by the name of Drig, was arrested for theft. A guard patrol witnessed him stealing meat out back o' the butcher's shop."

"No steal!" Drig shouted. "Drig work for meat!" The spectacled dwarf put a hand on the goblin's shoulder and pressed him into his seat, leaning closer to whisper harshly to his client. When the goblin slumped in his chair, the dwarf got to his feet. "Barrister Throm for the defense, Majesty. My apologies on behalf of my client. He claims to be innocent of the charges."

"So I heard." Max tried not to grin at the dwarf's discomfort. Max himself had learned quickly that the little goblins were difficult to control. "Please, Prosecutor Garlan, present the case against Drig."

"The kingdom calls guard sergeant An'dag." The dwarf turned and nodded toward one of the orcs in the audience. A battle-scarred specimen in patched armor, Max recognized him from the first convoy that had accompanied him from the orc city. The orc moved to stand in front of the prosecutor's table, and Max motioned for another chair to brought. He should have thought of that earlier. When the orc was seated, Garlan began.

"Please tell the court what you witnessed three nights ago behind the butcher's shop."

"We were patrolling the area around the market square, when one of my guards spotted a shadow in the alley next to the butcher's. Thinkin' it might one of those damned grey thieves, we rushed down the alley, where we spotted this little rat." He paused and pointed to the goblin, "He was taking a sausage link from a box of meat on the back stoop, stuffing it in his greedy little mouth."

Max frowned at the orc. "You will refrain from name-calling or insults while in this court, sergeant. Refer to the defendant by name, or race, or simply call him the defendant."

The sergeant bowed his head slightly. "Yes, Majesty."

"And what action did you take upon witnessing this act?" Garlan asked.

"We grabbed the little… goblin, and pinned him down. I was about to remove his head for the crime of theft, but another patrol joined us. The dwarf sergeant shouted at me to stop, so I did." The orc sounded angry over the interruption of the execution. "The goblin was placed under arrest, and taken to a cell in the lower level."

"Thank you, sergeant. You may step down." Garlan stepped forward and placed a sheet of parchment on Max's desk. "A copy of the guard's report on this incident, Majesty."

Max quickly scanned the report, not seeing any new information other than the names of the guards involved. "Anything else, Prosecutor Garlan?"

"That is our entire case, Majesty." The dwarf bowed, then took a seat.

"Barrister Throm?" Max looked to the defense table.

"Majesty, I must apologize. I was only this morning brought here from Darkholm to act as goblin Drig's barrister. In the short time I was able to consult with my client, he has maintained that the box of meat was in fact his, payment for services rendered to the butcher. Further, he was taking that meat home to his family, who he is afraid have not eaten since he was arrested. He requests that the meat be returned to them after your Majesty takes his head." The dwarf coughed into his fist. "His words, Majesty. In any case, I have not had the opportunity to interview the butcher in question, so I would like to call him as my first witness."

A dwarf in the audience stood up and walked forward, taking a seat in the witness chair. Throm asked, "Are you Brilon, the butcher behind whose shop my client was arrested?"

"I be Brilon, aye. And I can save ye some time. Had them guards asked me, I'd have told 'em that the wee goblin were tellin' the truth. He worked in me shop all day, haulin' boxes and cleanin' up. I give'd him a box o' scraps n leftovers to take home."

Drig leapt up from his chair. "See! Drig no steal! Tell truth!" He growled and bared his fangs at Throm, who tried to put him back in his seat. It took a moment, but

265

the goblin obeyed. Throm shook his head, adjusted his vest and spectacles, then turned to Max.

"Based on this testimony, Majesty, I move that all charges be dropped."

Max turned to look at Garlan, who stood. "No objection, Majesty."

Max looked around the room. "Is sergeant… Orin, who halted the execution present? If so, please stand. Sergeant An'dag, you stand as well." When both guards were standing, Max continued. "Sergeant Orin. You are to be commended for halting what would have been a murder committed by my kingdom. For that, I award you a bonus of fifty gold, and my thanks. Sergeant An'dag, listen to me very carefully. You are not empowered to conduct executions on my behalf unless directly ordered to do so by myself or Chamberlain Redmane. This goes for all of my guards! Anyone committing a crime is to be arrested and detained for trial. If a suspect resists, you will use appropriate force to defend yourselves, but nothing more. Is that clear?"

Both sergeants and all the guards in attendance bowed their heads. "Clear, Majesty."

"Further, both of you sergeants will receive a reprimand for failing to question butcher Brilon. A simple questioning to confirm the crime would have saved all of us a lot of trouble." Max looked at the orc sergeant. "It is clear to me that your dislike of goblins shaded your judgement in this matter. Would you have tried to summarily execute a dwarf or a fellow orc?"

An'dag hung his head, shaking it, unable to meet Max's angry gaze, "No, Majesty."

"I thought as much. I have made it clear to everyone from the beginning that Stormhaven is to be an open city. We will have residents and visitors of many races, light and dark, as we grow. All of you need to be able to set aside your grievances and preconceived notions regarding other races. I understand it will take time, and will not be easy. But we *can not* have another incident like this, where a citizen is presumed guilty, and nearly killed, based solely on being a goblin. Let this be a warning to everyone. If such an incident happens again, there will be dire consequences for those involved." Max bared his fangs and let the last sentence come out with a growl. "Drig, please stand."

Max waited for the little goblin to hop off his chair again. His head barely cleared the top of the table in front of him.

"Drig, on behalf of my guards, and myself, I apologize to you. I'm glad you found a good job working for Brilon." He looked at Garlan. "Can I assume the box of meat was preserved as evidence?" When the dwarf nodded and produced the box from his inventory, Max nodded toward the goblin. The box was passed over to him. "I return your payment from the butcher, and award you ten gold coins as compensation for the time you've been falsely imprisoned."

The little goblin, tightly hugging the box of meat, gasped in amazement when he heard ten gold. "S'okay, King Max. Drig thanks you!"

Max smiled at the little guy, then sought out the butcher. "Brilon, as a reward for the kindness you've shown our little friend here, and your no-nonsense testimony that saved us all some time today, I award you fifty gold as well. Can I assume that you will continue to employ Drig going forward?"

"O'course, Majesty. And thank ye. He be a hard worker, and learnin' fast."

"In that case, this young lady," He indicated Teeglin, sitting next to Redmane. "will be bringing you a parchment with my favorite recipe for meat on a stick. If you can teach Drig to properly cook that recipe, then I will use your shop as my personal supplier of travel victuals here in the city. I like to take several dozen portions with me when I hit the road."

"We'll start today, Majesty. Right after young Drig takes that meat to his family."

"Wonderful! Now, unless anyone else has something to add?" Max scanned the room, but saw no one interested in speaking. "This court is adjourned. Please clear the room, as I have some visitors to meet with."

Max remained at his table as the room emptied, nodding to Redmane who in turn whispered to Teeglin. The little girl hopped up and dashed out a side door exit.

Spotting Captain Rockbreaker among those leaving, Max called out to him. "Captain, please remain a moment."

Rockbreaker turned and walked back to stand in front of Max's table, saluting with fist to chest. "Majesty!"

"Relax, sit. And knock off the majesty stuff when it's just us chickens here." Max waited for the dwarf to take a seat. "I need your help with this. I'd like you to write the reprimands for the two sergeants. Give them and their units some real shit duty for the next week or so, to press my point. The more they bitch about it to their fellow guards, the better. And spread the word as emphatically as you can. I won't tolerate another incident like this. Next time, I will demand blood."

"Understood, Max. I don't like it any more than you do. It be hard not to look at orcs n goblins as enemies, but not that hard. I'll make sure the word gets passed around. This coulda been a serious stain upon our honor."

"Thank you, Rockbreaker." Max motioned that he had permission to leave. Rockbreaker stood and saluted again, grinning as he did so, then left the hall.

"Well done, Max." Redmane offered when they were alone. The chamberlain motioned to a servant, and suddenly a dozen more appeared, gathering up chairs and removing them. "Might I suggest you retire to the throne? It is only proper when receiving visitors at court."

Max snorted. "Court? Really? Does this have to be a formal function?"

Redmane chuckled, familiar with Max's aversion to formality. "You are the king here, Max, and you can decide how formal an event should be. However, you are about to welcome several minotaurs. If you have not met one up close, they are all generally at least a foot taller than you. It is... difficult to project authority when looking up at your audience."

"Ah, gotcha. See, it's the little things like that where I rely so heavily on your judgement, Redmane. Thank you." Max got to his feet and stepped up the two steps of the dais before taking a seat on the throne.

The last of the tables was being set near a side wall when Teeglin arrived through the main doors with six minotaurs walking behind her. "Here they are!" She called out happily, causing Redmane to sigh and shake his head in resignation. Max just pretended not to notice the lack of protocol.

Redmane took over, motioning for the girl to stand behind him at the bottom of the dais. "Your Majesty, may I present Barlon, Elder of the Thunderhoof Clan, who has requested an audience."

Max smiled without showing his fangs. "Welcome, Elder Barlon and members of the Thunderhoof Clan. I hope your stay here in Stormhaven has been a comfortable one?"

Barlon bowed at the waist, immediately followed by his followers. "It has indeed, Your Majesty. And thank you for taking the time to meet with us. It is an honor."

"Of course. You are, in fact, my first official visitors! Now, what was it you wished to discuss?"

"My clan and I request your permission to join your kingdom, become citizens of Stormhaven, Majesty." The elder bowed again, just his head this time. "Our home has become... inhospitable, of late. We seek to settle in new lands, and have heard that you welcome all races here."

"Inhospitable?" Max was curious as to what might drive away an entire clan of minotaurs.

"We lived in the mountains, not far from here. Three days' walk overland. Our village has stood for nearly four hundred years, and though we are not a prosperous clan, we were comfortable. Until recently, that is. We have been... invaded, Majesty. Undead creatures have attacked our village, slaughtered our livestock. Those things we can handle. But they have also fouled our water supply, a stream that runs down the mountain from above. They have piled corpses in the water upstream of the village, contaminating it. We tried several times to clear it, removing the corpses and burning them, but more appear in other places within a day or two. Many of my people were sickened by the fouled water, and three of our children died, only to have their corpses rise as undead."

Alarms went off in Max's head. Everything he knew of undead was based either on Earth movies and TV, or the fight he'd had with the necromancer in the orc arena. That fight had showed him that zombies were basically unthinking drudges that moved as commanded, not intelligent creatures that might band together to repeatedly foul a water supply. Which meant that someone was likely controlling them.

"That sounds like odd behavior for a bunch of zombies." Max looked to Redmane, who nodded. "And I don't like the idea of a pack of undead wandering about so near our home. This bears investigating, as soon as possible." He looked at the elder minotaur. Would one of your people be willing to guide me back there in the near future?"

"I'll take you there myself, Majesty." Barlon agreed.

"Thank you. In the meantime, you and your clan are absolutely welcome to join us. Were you thinking of a particular place you'd like to settle? And how many of you are there?"

"There are sixty of us, including children, Majesty. And we were hoping to settle in the lands near the base of the mountains. Some of us have family and friends in other settlements within the mountains, and would like to be close enough to visit them occasionally."

"Are you... farmers? Crafters? What kind of land would best suit you?"

"We do have a few farmers among us. I myself am an enchanter. We have hunters, miners, crafters of most trades, and of course all of us train as warriors, a tradition of our people."

Max nodded, thinking furiously. Having several dozen massive warriors wanting to live in the buffer zone between his city and the orcs was a real opportunity. "I can think of several appropriate places in my newly acquired lands south of the ridge line. There is a way station already constructed not five miles from a mine we captured from the orcs. There are several newly established farms nearby. Your people could take up residence there while you scout locations. There's also a temple ruins that we are repairing using stone from a nearby quarry, if you have masons in need of temporary work. Or you're welcome to remain here in the city if you prefer."

"Thank you, Majesty. My clan is camped in a nearby cavern for now. This way station sounds like an improvement, and a chance to get back out under the open sky. How many days' walk is it from here?"

Max grinned. "Less than one! Once you've gathered your people here and taken the oath that Redmane will administer, he'll send you through a portal that'll drop you at the temple. From there it is a six mile walk to the way station. You may even be able to borrow a wagon or two at the mine to help you transport gear and your little ones. I must warn you, the existence of that temple is not to be shared with anyone. Also, I am at war with An'zalor and his orc army. That way station, the mine, and the temple may come under attack at any time. Please consider that before you choose. There are areas of forest further north that would be safer for your clan."

Chapter 14

For the next several days, Max remained in Stormhaven City. Part of each day was spent being a king, handling the day to day issues that his councilors brought to his attention. They handled the vast majority of decisions themselves, but a few were passed up to Max for his review. He would then either make a decision himself, or pass it back down for them to use their best judgement. Max didn't pretend to know how things should be run, or that he knew as much as the professionals that had been loaned to him by Ironhand and the other clan leaders. Instead, he did his best to learn from them.

The rest of his time he spent crafting. Dalia's father visited Max in his new fully equipped lab within the palace. The old dwarf bowed his head when Max entered the lab. "Yer Majesty, it be an honor to meet ya. I be Norin, Dalia's papa."

"The pleasure is mine, Norin." Max grinned at the dwarf. "Your daughter has saved my life more times than I can count. And not just with her magic. The alchemy skills she learned from you have worked miracles for us and our people. I would be honored if you would share some of your knowledge with me, as well."

"Ha! From the way she tells it, ye saved her behind just as many times. And the rare quality ingredients ye brought us... well, in just three days at me own shop I've managed to increase me *Alchemist* skill level twice! Fer that alone, I'd happily teach ye."

The two of them got to work, chatting about Dalia and Max's adventures as the elder dwarf showed Max the proper way to use all of his new equipment. Max soon discovered that what Dalia had claimed out in the wilds was true. Working in a full lab with proper equipment, using a stable and easily adjustable heat source, taking the time to properly prepare all of your ingredients, all of it made for much more potent results. His very first batch of healing potions using standard quality ingredients were his best by far. They healed two hundred and fifty points immediately, and another four hundred over thirty seconds.

To demonstrate the power of the Brightwood enhanced ingredients, Norin followed the same procedure he'd just shown Max, using the very same equipment, same herbs, only at the rare quality. The end result was a brightly glowing purple potion that granted one thousand health points instantly, and another one thousand over thirty seconds. In addition, while Max's batch had produced six vials of potion, the same quantity of the rare quality herbs produced eight.

When Norin held up the first vial for Max to *Examine*, he said "Each of these would sell in my shop for twenty gold. King Ironhand's quartermasters would buy 'em for fifteen gold each, in lots of one hundred. If I were to use all the rare quality herbs me daughter brought me, I could produce nearly one thousand o' these potions. That'd earn me enough gold to retire with just a week's work, even sellin' em at the king's discount."

Max was beginning to fully realize the value of the Brightwood and its surrounding land. If just a day's worth

275

of harvesting one small area's herbs could produce such a fortune… And the herbs that Norin was speaking of were just Dalia's one third portion of what they had gathered. Max remembered something just then. "Master Norin, if you can earn that much from the herbs you have, what would you pay for an equal amount of the same herbs? I am still holding Battleaxe's share of what we gathered, as well as my own. I'll be holding onto my share, but if you'd be willing to purchase his…"

Norin's face, which had be alight a few seconds earlier at the prospect of more herbs, fell. "Aye, Battleaxe. He were a friend o' mine, yaknow. And me girl told me how he sacrificed his own life to save hers, and yours." He shook his head. "I owe me old friend a great debt. To answer yer question, under normal circumstances, assuming I had the funds, I'd pay ye maybe three thousand gold fer those herbs." Max nodded, thinking that sounded like a fair price.

"But… seein' as it be fer Battleaxe, and since I don't yet have such funds, especially after openin' a shop here in Stormhaven, I have a different offer." This got Max's attention. "I know ye give'd his family a bag o' gold from yer arena winnings. That were right kind of ye. And another three thousand gold would certainly be appreciated by his family." The old dwarf began to grin as he spoke. "But I'm thinkin' I can help all three of us at the same time. I'll keep me daughter's share o' the ingredients, use em to level up me own skill, rather than waste 'em on health potions. We'll take Battleaxe's share, and I'll help ya level yer skill, until we can turn it all into these potions.

Sell most o' those to the quartermasters, to help heal the old scout's fellow soldiers. The rest I'll sell in me own shop at the higher price. It'll take some time, but the five thousand ye already give'd them will hold them for years. When we're done, you'll have grown yer *Alchemist* level, as will I. We'll use our time to turn the three thousand gold worth of ingredients into ten thousand gold fer Battleaxe's family, and I'll earn enough to leave some gold fer me girl when I go."

"You have a deal!" Max shook the old dwarf's hand, being careful not to squeeze it too hard in his excitement. He was still getting used to the economy of this world, and a lot of his recent transactions had been on a kingdom level of spending, but he was pretty sure that ten thousand gold, in addition to the five thousand he'd already given them, would secure Battleaxe's family for a generation or two.

"Alright." Norin rubbed his hands together, then checked the inventory of ingredients arrayed before them. "With what we have here o' the common ingredients, ye can work for a full day or so. With me here watchin' over ye, it should get ye a dozen or so skill points before yer done. In the meantime, I'll send Dalia out to gather more ingredients near Brightwood. Not the rare quality, but uncommon ones that'll help ye level up even more. In the meantime, I'll cook up some batches of the good stuff!"

Max cooked batch after batch of health potions using the common ingredients, the quality of his results slowly but steadily increasing under the master's supervision. He got pointers on better ways to grind the

277

herbs in the mortar, Norin tweaking his wrist movements while holding the pestle. He learned to judge the heat of the flame by its color, and how to make the small adjustments that would make the ingredients heat more evenly, thus improving the process.

Unlike out in the wilds, where he often poured out his experiments to free up vials for the next batch, every potion Max made went into the kingdom's storage. Even the early versions were good enough to help save lives during a battle. And by the time he finished early the following morning, his healing potions had maxed out at five hundred instant health points, and five hundred over thirty seconds. The system still classified them as common healing potions, but they were right on the edge of reaching uncommon.

Leaving Norin to continue cooking up the good stuff, Max went to the small dining hall to grab some breakfast. Master Oakstone was due to arrive, and it was time for him to work on his smithing. It would be another couple days before Dalia returned with the intermediate quality herbs, and hopefully more of the rare ones as well. He'd sent Smitty along as escort, and Picklet had volunteered as well. The battlefield was on his way home, after all. The dworc had spent his gold wisely, with the help of one of Max's merchant councilors, and was ready to head back to his valley with the goods. Max had sold him one of Stormhaven's orc wagons for the princely sum of one gold, and made sure that he was taking back several one hundred slot storage rings. Max saw signs that the dwarfess and the dworc were developing more than a casual friendship, and he found himself hoping that would play a part in convincing the dworcs to join him.

Entering the small dining hall, he found Oakstone sitting there with Redmane and Steelbender. "Ah, Max!" Oakstone called out, raising a hand in greeting. "Ready to begin working with iron?"

"Ready, and excited!" Max grinned at the dwarves as he swung by the side table to grab a plate and dish up some food. "Master Steelbender, are you here to watch and laugh at a poor novice?"

"Ha! As amusing as that might be, I'm here on business. Yer scale armor be nearly complete, and yer swords be ready." The master smith pulled out a beautiful two handed sword as Max approached their table. Max immediately set down his plate and reached for the weapon. It was longer than the blade Steelbender had loaned him, with a single wide fuller down the center from the hilt to about eight inches short of the point. Inside the fuller were several engraved runes, and it glowed faintly when Max held it. Below the wickedly curved and pointed guard, the crimson leather grip was long enough for two hands, and wider than normal to fit Max's hands. The pommel was round, with a smoky onyx mounted in the center, and a steel knob at the bottom for cracking skulls. As Max hefted it, it felt light in his hands. Max *Examined* the blade.

> *Storm Reaver*
> *Item Quality: Unique, Epic*
> *Attributes: Intelligence +5; Wisdom +5; Agility +4*

Enchantment: Sovereign's Stand
This blade was crafted for King Maximilian Storm by the Dwarven Master Steelbender, to protect his life, the lives of his people, and to instill fear in the hearts of his enemies.

Sovereign's Stand: *When wielding Storm Reaver, King Storm can activate this enchantment, boosting the strength, constitution, and health regeneration of his people by 10%. At the same time, enemies will suffer a hit to morale, and a 10% strength debuff. Effect will last 1 hour. Cooldown: 24hrs; Area of effect: 500ft radius.*

"Master Steelbender, this is…" Max was at a loss for words. "This is incredible. I cannot thank you enough."

"Aye, that be quite the powerful enchantment." Oakstone agreed, sounding a little jealous as he inspected the sword himself. "Not one I recall ever hearin' about before."

Steelbender grinned. "Ye might say inspiration struck me. I had planned a simple sharpness enchantment that would cause yer foes to bleed a good bit when ye sliced 'em. The center o' the blade be dwarven steel, but the outer layers be mithril, which holds enchantments well. The night before I planned to enchant the blade, Regin came to me in a dream. He slapped the back o' me head and said "What master worth his salt would waste a mithril blade on a sharpness enchantment?" He shook his head, rubbing the back of it with one hand. "Knocked some

280

sense into me, then suggested this enchantment. When I finished the blade, it leveled up me *Enchanting* skill by five points!"

Now it was Oakstone's turn to shake his head. "A gift directly from Regin himself. Bein' a friend o' yours has its benefits, Max." Max was barely paying attention, busy adoring his new weapon.

"I brought Battleborne Smitty's blade too." Steelbender said, looking toward the door as if expecting Smitty.

"I'm sorry, he's out helping Dalia gather some herbs." Max apologized. He pulled three of his best health potions from his inventory and handed one to each of the dwarves. "I'm working on leveling up my alchemy skill. Just finished these a little while ago." The three dwarves made approving noises over the quality of the potions. "We'll be making a thousand potions for Ironhand's army, each with a total of two thousand points of healing. The proceeds from that sale will go to Battleaxe's family." He paused to look at Steelbender. "I can deliver the sword when he returns, if you like. Though it might be more fun for you to present it personally."

"Aye, both of ye come to visit when ye have time. I should have yer chest pieces ready in a few more days. Ye can try them on so we can make any needed adjustments." With that, the old dwarf nodded his head, grabbed a couple pastries from the side table, and headed out.

Max and Oakstone followed Redmane to the private smithy, Max having never been there himself. They took a moment to familiarize themselves with the surroundings, then got to work. As Oakstone had promised, he began instructing Max on how to forge with iron.

They didn't make weapons out of iron, because it was both heavier and softer than steel. But lots of tools and everyday items, from horse and boar shoes to fireplace pokers to door hinges were forged from iron. As with copper, Max learned the proper temperature to heat the metal to make it most workable, how far and how fast he could bend it without it breaking, and how much stress it could take once it cooled. He learned how to add elements that Oakstone showed him in order to prevent the iron from rusting for a thousand years or more. A secret the dwarves had discovered that humans on Earth never had.

By the end of the long day, Max had increased his Blacksmithing skill level by four points. He'd created hundreds of nails, a dozen hinges with the pins and the screws to go with them, and for his final test, an ornate door knocker that had required him to twist, bend, fold, and chisel the iron to match the drawing Oakstone provided.

Oakstone examined the knocker, turning it over and running a thumb across a few decorative details. "It be fit to hang on a woodshed door, mebbe a goblin's quarters, I suppose." He glanced sideways at Max, a grin forming under his beard. "It'll do. Next lesson, I'll teach ye how to make iron into steel."

And so it went for another several days. Half of each spent running the kingdom, then a half day of potion making, alternating with a half day of blacksmithing. Dalia arrived with the better quality herbs, and Max began cranking out uncommon quality healing potions. Oakstone spent half a day showing Max the secret of making dwarven steel, then told him to practice it for a week, making knives, simple swords, whatever struck his fancy. At the end of that week, Oakstone would return with Dylan's dragonscale chest piece, and examine Max's work.

When the ninth day since they'd left the dworcs' village arrived, Max couldn't justify making the trip himself. There were too many other things happening within Stormhaven for him to be out of touch for several days. Instead he sent Dalia and Smitty out to try and convince the Blooded to join him. They went mounted, taking the portal to the outpost first, which enabled them to ride through the first valley and into the dworc territory in less than a day. Max hoped to have see them back a day or two later, with good news.

In the meantime, he needed to check on the mine, temple, and way station. Or'gral and his thousand orc defectors had arrived at the mine days earlier. Max took the portal to the temple, where he found a whole herd of dwarves puttering around, most of them pestering Glitterspindle with questions. Grabbing one of the engineers, he asked, "How goes the secret tunnel from the mine?"

"What" The distracted engineer fiddled with a large instrument he'd been trying to use to measure the metal gnome's head. "Oh, King Max! Aye, the tunnel be underway. Another week or so, and it'll be complete.

Them orcs ye sent been helpin' us dig, three full shifts, nonstop. It'd take another week at least without their help."

Max released the dwarf to go back to torturing the mechamage, leaving the temple and jogging through the woods until he reached the mine. He took a moment to appreciate the new stone wall surrounding the mine complex. Thirty feet high and as smooth as ice on the outside. Several dozen orcs with bows walked the ramparts at the top, a few of them saluted Max as he jogged past them toward the gate. Walking inside, he found Gr'tok speaking with Or'gral and several other orcs. As he approached, he noticed rows of tents set up within the open space inside the wall. Orc families had small fires built in front of every third tent, orc children helping with chores or running about at play.

"King Max!" Gr'tok raised a fist to chest in salute, followed immediately by the other orcs standing with him. "We were just discussing logistics."

"For the relocation to the city?"

"Yes, in part." Or'gral replied. "Though the majority of us do not wish to reside in the city. There is much work to be done here, and we can be of help. The mine, the farms, and the repairs to the temple, we can assist you with all of them. And the warriors among us are happy to help defend these places against that coward, An'zalor."

Max looked at the small tent city. "And where will we house everyone? You can't live in tents for long."

We will build a pair of barracks buildings at the way station, after we have extended the wall there to accommodate them. Some will live here temporarily, inside the mine, in the side chambers off the main shaft. Others will live in the temple, once we have repaired the roof. And some three hundred of us, mostly crafters and merchants, will return with you and Gr'tok to Stormhaven city. We have been working with the dwarven engineers on expansion plans. We won't just be building housing for the thousand who came with me, but for thousands more who wait to join us."

Gr'tok added, "The secret tunnel is nearly complete. Our people have been laboring to get it done as quickly as possible, with the help of the dwarves, of course. Our plan is to turn the way station into a fortified town that can hold out against an attack by at least a medium sized force of An'zalor's warriors. We need only hold them long enough for reinforcements to arrive through the portal and smash them against our walls. Should our scouts report the approach of a larger force than we can handle, we can evacuate to the mine. And, if necessary, through the mine to the portal at the temple."

Max shook his head. "You guys decided this all on your own?"

"Nothing is decided, King Max." Gr'tok bowed his head. "We have simply made plans, which we are presenting to you for approval. If you disapprove of any aspect, we will make other plans."

Max chuckled. As a soldier on Earth, he had done the same to several officers above him. They were left with the option to either approve his plans, or take the time to come up with a better one. And the plans the orcs were making were already in line with his own, just on a much faster timeline. But with a thousand eager new citizens that needed housing and feeding, as well as protecting, he had no choice but to agree. "Sounds good to me! Well done, gentlemen." Max thought about his other potential new recruits, and asked questions.

"Have any of you spotted a bunch of minotaurs roaming around the forest or the fields?" When several of the orcs nodded in the affirmative, he followed up with, "Do you know where they are now? And whether they've chosen a location?"

"They are at the way station." Or'gral replied. "Or rather, they were this morning. I believe they plan to join us in building it up into a town."

"Wonderful! Now, I have a serious question for all of you, and I want you to be honest with your answers. Have you heard of the Blooded clan?"

Gr'tok and a few of the older orcs present nodded their heads. The others just gave Max blank stares. Gr'tok answered, "The dworcs, the mixed breeds. Half orc, half dwarf. Unfortunate souls who are outcast from both societies."

"Maybe not anymore." Max shook his head. "I ran into them several days back, and have been trying to

286

convince them to join us as well. But I need to know...
will your people have a problem with that?"

Or'gral stepped forward and stood next to Max, his
gaze meeting those of every orc present one at a time. As
he stared at them, he spoke. "None here will object to their
presence, Majesty. Their heritage is no fault of their own,
and we do not hold it against them. If anything, it is our
own feelings of shame, the shame of our ancestors who
dishonorably assaulted dwarven prisoners, that gives us
discomfort in their presence."

Max watched as orc after orc nodded their
agreement. Some more readily than others, but it was
unanimous, all the same. Max assumed this gathering to be
the leaders of the larger group, and would have to depend
on them to enforce this attitude.

"Thank you, Or'gral, and all of you. The dworcs
are good people, who have been surviving, but not thriving,
mostly due to their isolation. I'd like to help them
reintegrate into both dwarven and orc society. With your
help, that task will be easier to accomplish."

"Speaking of making tasks easier..." Or'gral
produced several scrolls from his inventory and handed
them to Max. "One of the orcs I convinced to come with
me was the old War Chief's enchanter. These are scrolls of
communication. They are simple devices, allowing a link
to be established for up to five minutes. They transmit
voices only, but are quite useful. With these, we can report
any attacks to you immediately, and you can let us know

when reinforcements are arriving, so that we may coordinate our counterattacks."

Max remembered looting a few of these scrolls in the orc scout camp he and the dwarves had wiped out. But he didn't think this was the best time or place to mention that. "They would indeed be useful, thank you. Tell me, does this enchanter know of other communication enchantments?"

"He is a Master Enchanter, and quite old." Or'gral shrugged. "We can certainly ask him."

Max was constantly surprised by the orcs in general. Earth's fiction had mostly portrayed them as savage brutes with limited intelligence and crude weapons, living for battle and slaughter. The orcs he'd observed in their city, and since then, were just the same as humans or dwarves. They had their share of brutes, of course, An'zalor being a prime example. But they had crafters, shopkeepers and farmers, stooped elders who sat with toddlers on their knees telling fairy tales. He was constantly telling folks on this world that they needed to accept other races, at least within the confines of Stormhaven. It was time he worked on ignoring his own preconceptions as well.

*****

Lagrass looked out from the alley where he'd hidden behind a pile of broken crates and trash. Someone from the tavern he was leaning against had tossed a bucket of rotted vegetables and food scraps onto the heap, and the sun had ripened it so that the stench was nearly unbearable. But until the city guards moved on, he dared not move. Twice they'd walked by the mouth of the alley already, stopping to peer into the shadows a moment before moving on. The smell discouraged them from investigating more closely, so he figured he should be grateful for that.

Another pair of guards appeared, their shadows stretching down the alley ahead of them. "Maybe he's down there." One of them suggested.

The other sniffed, shook his head. "Feel free to go check. Whatever that is, I don't want to be cleaning it off my boots all night. I've got a date with Lucinda after our shift."

"You do not." The second guard peered down the alley, leaning forward as if tempted to step in. "Lucinda wouldn't give you the time of day if you were covered in gold and suddenly declared the old king's heir!"

His partner snorted. "Shows what you know. Lucinda has taken a liking to me. She says I'm funny."

"Funny looking, maybe. Take heed my friend. That woman will empty your pockets and leave you crying in that refuse heap over there." He pointed directly at Lagrass, making the man cringe. He held his breath as the banter continued, the two guards turning and moving on down the street. When he could no longer hear the voices, he let the breath out. Which meant he needed to inhale that horrible stench again.

After ten minutes, when no more guards appeared, he extricated himself from the rubbish and did his best to wipe off the various bits that had stuck to his clothes, which were hopelessly stained with this world's equivalent of dumpster juice. The seat of his pants was soaked through, and even as he distanced himself from his hiding spot, the wind at his back told him the stench was going to follow him wherever he went.

Reaching the end of the alley farthest from the street, he faced a ten foot high brick wall that stretched from building to building and effectively blocked the alley. Lagrass took a few steps back, then rushed forward and leapt as high as he could, gripping the top of the wall with his fingers and pulling himself upward. Having not eaten for two days, he was weaker than he'd like, and barely made the climb. Once atop the wall, he sat there panting for a few minutes, reflecting on his time in this world, and how he'd gotten here.

He'd died on earth. Or, more accurately, been killed. Lagrass had been sitting in his office, gloating over the demise of Storm and his unit. It was a simple matter of passing along some unconfirmed and, to him, blatantly false intel. He'd known it was a trap, the clumsy attempt at a fake leak apparent from the first moment he'd seen it. But he was sick of Storm and his squad, the so-called elite operators. Always swaggering around their operating base, thinking they were better than everyone.

Better than Lagrass himself.

They never showed him any respect. He was just some desk jockey to them, not worth inviting for a drink after a successful mission. He didn't think Storm even knew his name. So he'd sent them into an ambush, a literal meat grinder, and done his best not to smile in front of the others as they listened to the massacre on the comms. Good riddance.

He was smiling to himself, remembering that moment as he signed the after action report, when his door was kicked open. A haggard and bloody operator in torn gear staggered into the room, growling. "Lagrass you piece of shit!" Behind him in the hallway there was shouting, and two figures appeared in the doorway, reaching for the man he now recognized as corporal Blake. Lagrass froze, his mind taking a few seconds to absorb the fact that a dead man was stomping toward him. "You killed us, you sonofabitch. Killed us all. I know what you did, traitor!"

Before Lagrass could even open his mouth, Blake raised a .45 and shot him in the gut. The loud retort in the small room made him jump, then the searing pain in his belly made him scream. There was another report, then another, and pain blossomed in his groin, then knee. His hands already moving to his belly wound, he tried to look down to assess his injuries, but he head was pushed back violently, slamming into the back of his chair as a final round slammed into his face. He felt his teeth shatter along with his jaw, his mind going into overload from the pain of his multiple wounds before everything went black.

He didn't see Blake drop his weapon, his shrapnel-ridden arm and hand too weak to hold it any longer. Nor did he see the two soldiers behind Blake grab him as his legs gave out. Lagrass died a moment later in his cushioned leather office chair, followed less than a minute later by Blake, the last man of Storm's massacred unit, who bled out from his multiple wounds on the hallway floor, even as two medics tried to save him.

The next thing Lagrass knew, a voice was speaking to him. A male voice that echoed with power. He couldn't see anything, or feel the pain of his wounds, for which he was thankful.

"Do you wish to live?" The voice came from nowhere and everywhere at once.

"I'm hurt. Badly hurt. My face…" Lagrass could recall being shot in the face, and the groin. Even if a woman would talk to a disfigured mess like he would be, he suspected the damage to his manhood would negate any interest.

"Your former existence has ended, your body expired. I am offering you a chance to live again. A new life, in a new body."

"Like, reincarnation? Are you… god?" Lagrass was suddenly terrified. He'd committed uncountable sins, including the recent murders of Storm and his squad.

"I am a god, yes. Though not the one you're referring to. I have taken note of your actions, of the clever way you disposed of your unsuspecting comrades to gain power and respect. I can make use of one such as yourself. So I offer you a new life, on a new world, where you will serve my purposes. Do you agree?"

Confused and overwhelmed, Lagrass stammered. "W-wait. A new world? What world? Like, Mar or Saturn or something?"

"Which world does not concern you. You have a choice. Perish now, and have your life force absorbed into your Earth, or serve me in a new life. Choose now."

A coward at heart, Lagrass had no real choice. "I want to live."

A moment later he found himself in a room filled with grey mist. He blinked his eyes, and a different, female voice echoed through the mist around him. "You must choose a race." Several boxes appeared in front of him, each a life-sized being of various builds and races.

"This… is like one of those games. The one Storm's guys were always blathering about." Not having played more than a few games of this type himself as a kid, he looked at the selection of unfamiliar and beastly looking ogres and orcs, goblins and trolls. The moment his eyes settled on a representation of a human, he seized on it. "Human! I choose to be human!"

The other boxes disappeared, and the human avatar moved front and center. Lagrass had sighed with relief. The voice spoke to him again, telling him that he'd been marked by Loki, and thus would receive a special gift. Then the mist had faded to blackness again, and Lagrass had next awakened in a tavern cellar, surrounded by casks, crates, cobwebs and rats.

Aggressive rats. Almost immediately one of them charged from behind a nearby crate and took a bite out of his ankle! Lagrass shouted in fear and pain, swatting at the rodent with his hand, knocking it away briefly as a red minus three drifted across his field of vision. The rat recovered quickly and charged forward again. Desperate, Lagrass grabbed hold of a broken chair leg and smashed at the wicked little predator as hard and fast as he could. His first blow missed, but the second swing stunned the rat. His next several swings smashed it to a pulp as he growled and shouted at it.

No sooner was the rat dead than he received several notifications on his interface. He paused, breathing hard, to read them. One was an experience notification, another was telling him he'd learned a *Blunt Weapon* skill. He didn't get to the third, as another rat had emerged from cover to bite him on the ass.

That was how he had entered this new world. Sitting atop the wall, he looked down to see a rat scurrying along the ground below, and spat at it. "Friggin rats. I hate rats."

Chapter 15

Max toured the mine, then the way station, which had already grown larger than the last time he'd seen it. The orc farmer and his family greeted him happily, inviting him to stay the night in their home, kicking one of the boys out of his room. The farmer's wife, whose name neither Max nor Red knew, bowed her head to Max when her husband went to take care of something.

"I admit, I was scared when we first agreed to stay here." She spoke softly. "But the patrols have kept a tight watch on the area between here and An'zalor's city, and with all these hundreds of people here, the new wall… thank you, Chimera King. We could not have asked for a better new start than this."

"I'm very happy that it has worked out for you." Max replied, and meant it. He'd been concerned about their safety as well.

The initial wall was already completed, and crews were digging foundations for a second, much larger wall two hundred yards out from the first. The newly enclosed area would provide enough room not only for housing and some protected fields, but for crafters shops and a tavern or two. A new stable and corral were being constructed, the original one not large enough to accommodate the nearly one hundred ja'kang now housed at the way station. If Max's people wanted to, they could field a significant mounted force against any attacking foes. Though most of the mounts were used in rotation for the scout patrols.

Max and the others were suspicious that An'zalor had not sent another force. It was true that he'd already lost roughly four hundred and fifty troops to Max in battle, about half of those killed, the others actually joining Max. Another few hundred were among those who had left the city with Max, or defected on their own and joined Stormhaven. So while the war chief was losing resources, Max was gaining. Still, Max would not have guessed that An'zalor would bide his time this long. Gr'Tok and Or'gral were nervous as well, doubling the scout patrols and having them range nearly all the way to the city.

Another pleasant development Max found at the way station was the minotaur clan. They had set up their large communal tents just outside the first wall on the north side. Already about half their number had pitched in to help build the outer wall, while others were busily constructing a pair of longhouses as more permanent shelter for the clan. Max greeted them warmly, and Gr'Tok administered their oaths. After a short meeting with the orc and dwarven leadership, and a consultation of the maps, a one mile square section of the forest north of the growing town was assigned to the clan. They were given rights to cut the lumber and/or farm as they saw fit. In addition, Max granted them a section of the land between the inner and outer walls, approximately one tenth of the land area there, to create housing, businesses, warehouses, whatever they needed.

He was introduced to their master enchanter, and spent some time sitting with the elder minotaur who, even sitting down, was a foot and a half taller than Max, not counting his horns. After introductions were made, Max asked for something he'd greatly desired since his first trip to the orc city began. "I was hoping you could create a more… stabile and flexible communication device? We have the scrolls, which are great, but they are quite limited. In my…" Max paused, catching himself. He was about to say that in his world they had radios. Instead he went with, "In my dreams, we are all united, this town with the mine, with the outpost and the palace, in a network of instant communication. Something like a ring, or a necklace, that would allow me, for example, to contact you from wherever I happen to be, then contact Gr'Tok a moment later, then Glitterspindle at the temple."

The old enchanter, who name was Erdun, nodded his head. "I could create such an enchantment. It would require multiple… rings if that is your desired device, to be crafted at once, all included within the same enchantment in order to create the connections you desire."

Max's heart skipped a beat. "What do you need?"

"I'm not sure yet. I shall have to experiment a bit, test some materials. I do not know if metal would hold this enchantment better, or a gem of some kind."

Max immediately withdrew some of the gems he'd looted in his time on the new world. He handed the enchanter several emeralds and rubies, then produced a couple of small diamonds from the necromancer's ring. As an afterthought, he searched that ring as well as his own inventory, and found a few ounces of mithril, the most enchantment-friendly metal he was aware of. The minotaur's eyes widened at such a casual display of wealth and trust as Max handed them all over to him.

"I will get to work immediately, Majesty." the minotaur bowed his head.

*****

The following morning Max departed through the temple portal with the orcs who were going to take up residence in Stormhaven city. Redmane was there as usual, along with the guard captains and several other councilors, all of whom helped direct the newcomers. Erdun was among them, as was his daughter, both of whom carried humongous and heavy looking packs on their backs. Max asked Redmane to arrange a shop for the enchanter somewhere close to the palace, his first year's rent to be free in return for his work on Max's magical radio network. Max couldn't emphasize enough the importance of real time long distance communication.

He sent a message to both Dylan and Smitty, directing them to Erdun's shop to receive whatever training they could. Dylan had an interest in the profession, while Smitty was always looking for new enchantments for the arrows gifted to him by Regin.

The rest of the morning was spent with Redmane, working through the ever-renewing pile of reports on his desk. The first was an agreement with the mages' guild for him to sign. They agreed to magically light the city streets, and maintain the lights for ten years, in return for the deed to a building of sufficient size to house a guild branch. Max signed it without hesitation, as well as invoice for

Spellbinder and his mages, who were already in the process of lighting the palace, as well as installing some magical security measures. Max gulped when he saw the invoice amount, but Redmane assured him that the old dwarven mage had given them a good price. "I believe he is fond o' you, Max."

"More like he is fond of how often he receives bottles of Firebelly's from me." Max grumped halfheartedly before handing the signed invoice to his chamberlain.

Later in the morning, Max came across a page that made him pause. It was a crude stick drawing, featuring several figures, one of which wore a crown. Holding it up for Redmane to see, he asked, "Did Teeglin draw this? Why is it on my desk?"

The dwarf shook his head, a wide smile appearing on his face. "That, Max, is a thank you note from the child of the goblin you set free."

"Drig?" Max took another look at the drawing, noticing that one of the figures standing near the one with the crown was clutching a crude square that had to represent the goblin's box of meat.

"Indeed. I must admit, Max... when you first brought those goblins to the city, I had serious misgivings. But I find as time goes on, I'm growing a bit... fond of the little rascals."

"They'll do that to you." Max grinned back at Redmane. "I think Regin feels the same. He told me himself to treat them well." He looked around. "We need to get this framed and find a place to hang it. Maybe in the throne room, where people will see it and ask about it. This drawing, and the trial, will become a part of the history of this kingdom."

"I'll see to it personally." Redmane agreed.

They broke for lunch, having handled nearly everything on the desk, and Redmane left Max to his own devices. He found none of his party in the dining hall, and wondered where they were, until he remembered he'd sent Dalia and Smitty to recruit the Blooded. With Dylan's whereabouts unknown, Max decided to check out something that had been in the back of his mind.

Checking his inventory to ensure he had some food and water, he left a note for Redmane on his way out of the palace. A quick trip through the portal, and he was standing in the outpost portal room.

The day Regin had showed him the portal, he'd noted that there were several possible destinations already programmed into the pedestal. Since then he'd been pretty constantly distracted, and hadn't come back to explore those options. But now that he had his kingdom running reasonably well, Max figured to spend the rest of the day finding out what other cities or destinations he might have access to.

Using his key stone, he accessed the pedestals's interface. There was the same list he'd seen that first day. He could connect to the Stormhaven, Darkholm, and now the temple was included in the list. Beyond that there were three other names on the list, none of which meant anything to him. Max cursed quietly at himself for not thinking to bring along Redmane or one of his advisors, someone who might recognize the names of these places, and give him at least some basic information. Instead he impulsive trip left him flying blind.

He decided to keep it simple, and choose the first location on the list. The portal location was called *Skytop*, and that was it. Max chose that one and activated the portal. The instant it opened, Max gasped in awe. The view through the portal showed him an endless series of snowcapped mountain ranges stretching as far as his elven eye could see. Stepping carefully through the portal, he found himself on a stone veranda with a low stone wall. He quickly turned to confirm there was a pedestal on this side of the portal, then looked up, his mouth wide open.

The veranda he stood upon was a small extension of a mammoth stone keep. Its towers rose ten stories above Max, its thick and imposing walls dusted with snow and ice. The small windows he could see were clouded over with ice as well. Stepping toward the boundary knee wall of the veranda, he discovered that he was perched halfway up the face of the castle itself. The view downward was a sheer stone wall that ended in a field of jagged boulders scattered on the steep mountain slope.

Max ears picked up no sounds other the howling wind and his own footsteps crunching in the snow. Turning back toward the wall, he located a single door that led into the castle. Walking slowly up to the door with his hands open and empty, he watched the windows above, expecting a cry of alarm or an arrow speeding his direction. Reaching the door, he rapped on it with his knuckles, the sound creating an echo around him. When after a full minute there was no response, he used the side of his fist to pound much harder upon the door, calling out as he did so. "Hellooo? Anyone at home?"

A moment later the door opened, and a shaggy figure gazed out at Max. It stood maybe ten feet tall, and was covered from head to toe in bright white fur, with bright red eyes and two horns that curled outward from its forehead, reaching back over its skull. Max took a step back, his hand on his sword hilt as he Identified the creature.

> **Caretaker Brombis**
> **Yeti**
> **Level: ??**
> **Health: ??**

Another being whose level was too high for Max to be able to see. Max cleared his throat when the yeti simply stared at him, making no aggressive moves. When he felt he could speak without his voice squeaking, he said, "Hello, my name is Maximilian Storm."

The yeti's eyes unfocused, clearly peering at Max's information for a moment. "Ah, yes." The creature's voice was surprisingly smooth and sonorous. "Regin mentioned that he had given you access to Skytop's portal. I am Brombis, caretaker of the castle. It is a pleasure to meet you, King Maximilian Storm of Stormhaven." The yeti bowed its head slightly, not breaking eye contact with Max.

302

It didn't need to, as even with its head bowed it was looking down at him.

"Nice to meet you as well, caretaker." Max relaxed, removing his hand from his weapon.

"I would invite you inside to warm up, but I am afraid that is not possible at this time. I apologize for the inconvenience. When Regin informed me that you would be coming, he also gave me a message to deliver, should this particular situation arise." The yeti took a deep breath, then shouted at Max in a perfect imitation of Regin's voice. "Max! Go away! Yer not strong enough to ta make use o' Skytop yet! Come back when ye reach level thirty or so, and bring yer people with ye!"

Max took a step back at the unexpected volume of the message. As both yeti and chimera collected themselves, Max chuckled. "That was Regin alright. I guess he didn't expect me to come exploring so soon."

"Indeed." Brombis replied, smoothing the slightly ruffled hair on his chest. "My instruction were to deliver that message if you arrived at any level lower than thirty. And... if I may make a small suggestion?"

"Of course." Max smiled up at the imposing figure of the caretaker.

"When you return, bring food. Lots of food. The pantries in the kitchen are dwindling. And it's a long way down the mountain to find more around here. Were it not for the portal, one might starve here." Brombis looked left, then right, as if to ensure no one was eavesdropping. "Just

303

between you and me, I heard Regin mutter something about portal to Deepcrag, and watching you deal with the lich. I think he expected you would have done that before arriving here."

Max recognized the name as the last one on the list of approved portals. "I see. Thank you very much, caretaker Brombis." Max reached into his bag and grabbed a dozen kabobs, and the same number of pastries. "Please accept this gift for your kindness."

The yeti's nose was already twitching, and it quickly reached out its two massive hands, palms up, and accepted the gifts. Either of those hands could easily wrap all the way around Max's head, and the two piles of gifts looked tiny in comparison.

"Thank you, King Maximilian. These smell quite tasty. I shall treasure them." The bowed its head again, slightly lower this time, then stepped back and kicked the door closed in Max's face.

Shaking his head, Max walked back to the portal and returned to the outpost. The moment the portal closed, he opened the menu again and selected Deepcrag. The portal opened again, but this time showed nothing but darkness on the other side. Max could make out a stone floor and walls in the darkness, but nothing else.

"Just a bit of recon, to see if this really is where the lich is. And whether it's the same lich that tricked Nogroz." Max wasn't foolish enough to try and take on a creature of legend by himself. But if he could get some intel before he brought his party back and risked their lives, well he had to try.

Stepping through the portal he blinked a few times, adjusting to the nearly complete darkness. The portal behind him provided a faint light for about ten seconds, then disappeared. Max found himself alone in an empty stone room, clearly carved from the surrounding stone. The floor was smooth, and the walls were straight, if a little rough. The ceiling was set about fifteen feet above the floor, allowing Max to stand upright comfortably.

The only exit from the room was a single open doorway, which Max had to duck his head to pass through. He immediately noticed that there was no dust on the floor of the corridor outside, suggesting that someone was maintaining it. The hallway stretched out in front of him for maybe thirty paces before it terminated in an intersection with a perpendicular corridor.

With no other options other than to return through the portal, which Max was not yet ready to do, he advanced down the corridor. Just to be safe, he activated his natural stonetalon fade ability, then cast the *Fade* spell he'd bought from Josephine on top of that. He hoped the combination of the two, along with the darkness of the unlit passageways, would help to hide him from any predators or other foes he might encounter.

Max reached the end of the first hall with no trouble, pausing to listen for a full minute before sticking his head out far enough to see around the corner. The next hall was clear in both directions, to his left coming to a dead end at another door about twenty feet away, and stretching beyond the range of his darksight as it rose upslope to the right. Hearing both Dylan and Smitty in his mind telling him to always go left, he grinned to himself and moved quietly toward the door. Unlike in the forests on the surface, Max had finally learned to move stealthily on bare stone.

When he reached the door, he carefully leaned in and put his ear against it, listening for any sound on the other side. Hearing nothing, he stepped to the side of the doorway and reached for the handle. When he tried it the first time, it didn't budge. Max looked at the rust on the handle, and decided to try a little muscle. Levering it downward, he forced it until something inside broke, and giving the door a good shove, he peeked around the frame as the door hinges squealed. The door swung open maybe halfway, and stopped, the hinges unwilling to give farther without more effort.

The room beyond remained quiet, and Max stepped through the doorway. He immediately checked behind the door for any lurkers, his door-kicking training second nature by now. Then he systematically scanned the room for any threats as he shouldered the door the rest of the way open. One of the hinges popped, and the door listed slightly, but cooperated.

He found himself in what he guessed was a guard post. There were a dozen wooden bed frames, sized for beings of human or elven proportions, in two rows near the back. A dark wooden chest sat at the foot of each bed, each of them with a padlock and hasp securing it. Between

Max and the beds were three round tables with four chairs each, a couple of benches, a worktable with another much larger chest underneath it, and three weapons racks mounted to the walls on either side of the door he'd just entered.

"Makes sense." He whispered to himself, walking to the nearest rack. "There should be at least a delaying force guarding a portal, in case of unwelcome company. And maybe it was their job to collect tolls as folks came through?" Max was suddenly more interested in the contents of the chests. Based on the locks, it didn't look as if whomever was stationed here took the time to pack before leaving. The weapons racks were mostly empty as well, with just four long spears with common steel tips, and a single wooden longbow with a rotted string.

Max took a moment to close the door, as he was planning to make some noise. The hinges squealed, but didn't fail any worse as he closed it, then leaned his halberd against the door so that it would fall if anyone tried to enter, giving him some warning.

Next he approached the chest underneath the worktable. There was evident that there had been some candles and parchment atop the table, but they had long since rotted into scraps. Bending to get a grip on the handles at either end of the large chest, Max dragged it out into the open. "Heavy." He grunted as he got it moving. He took that as a good sign.

Max took a moment to scan the tabletop, then the walls near the door, looking for a key ring. "No such luck"

He shook his head when he found nothing. Taking a smithing hammer from his inventory, he took careful aim at the padlock, and swung. The metallic clang that rang out through the room made him jump, despite knowing it was coming. He looked around guiltily, waiting and listening for a reaction. When nothing happened, he took a second swing, this time breaking the padlock open.

He quickly removed the lock and flipped open the hasp, then paused as he was about to open the lid.

"If this were a game, this thing would totally shoot poison or something in my face when I open it." Looking around, he went back and grabbed his halberd. Standing as far away as he could and still reach the chest, he held the weapon in one hand and used the tip of the end spike to push the chest's lid open, holding his breath as he did so. Between the length of his own arm and the length of the halberd, he was nearly nine feet away from the box, but he was being as cautious as possible. He was also glad none of his party were here to see this.

With a little extra effort, he managed to get the lid all the way open. Nothing exploded, no gas was visible, and the chest didn't spout teeth and charge at him. Placing the halberd back against the door as he exhaled, he walked over and knelt next to the chest.

Inside was a jumble of brown leather bags, atop which sat a large book. Max lifted the book carefully, worried that it would disintegrate in his hands. The chest must have preserved its contents, because the book was solid and undamaged. Opening it to a random page, he saw two columns on each page. The first, on the left, featured writing he couldn't read in a long list of entries. The second column was clearly numbers. "Must be a log book for people coming through the portal? And the numbers are what they paid? A toll, or maybe a tax?" he mumbled to himself, flipping a few pages and finding more of the same.

Setting the book on the floor, he lifted one of the sacks, which jingled encouragingly. It was heavy, weighing several pounds, and when he stood and dumped it out onto the table, a hundred or so odd-looking square silver coins tumbled out. They were thick, and much heavier than the silver coins he was used to seeing in this world. Each one featured a face in profile, but Max couldn't determine a race based on the crude etching. Grabbing another bag, and another, he found many more of the same. Max began taking the bags out by the armful until he had emptied the chest. When he was done, the table was covered in a few thousand of the same silver squares, as well as a hundred or more round gold coins, and a few dozen platinum.   There were also a few bags that held rubies and diamonds, most of them very small stones, or just chips.

"Dylan and Smitty are gonna be so jealous." Max grinned to himself as he swept his storage ring over the table, sucking all the coins into his inventory. A quick check showed him he'd just picked up three thousand eight hundred of the silvers, one hundred thirty gold, and twenty nine platinum coins. He didn't know the value of the silver squares, but he was excited to find out.

As an afterthought, Max tossed all the empty leather bags back into the chest, closed it, and stuffed that into his inventory as well. He briefly considered breaking open the dozen chests at the foot of each bed, but decided to keep exploring. He could always hit them on his way out. The back of his neck was itching, and he had the feeling he didn't have a lot of time left.

Grabbing his halberd, he opened the squeaky door, stepped through, and closed it behind him. After a short pause to listen for any approaching problems, he reactivated his fade ability and headed down the long corridor. For nearly a hundred yards it was just plain stone walls and floor, no intersections or doorways. The floor sloped upward, and Max found himself wishing Dalia were with him. Her dwarven sense of direction might have been able to tell him how deep underground he was.

Finally the corridor opened up into a cavern. It was huge, similar in size to the one in which Stormhaven and its mushroom forest resided. The ceiling soared high overhead, and the far wall was farther away than Max could shoot an arrow, even with his steel bow. In front of Max the floor leveled out for maybe twenty feet, then descended down a long, gradual ramp. At the bottom of that ramp was a road that led to a stone bridge over a wide crevasse. Beyond that bridge was a walled town, smaller than Stormhaven, but not by much. Max studied the buildings and streets that he could see from his elevated position, but saw no movement. There were no lights, not so unusual in the underground.

"This must be Deepcrag." Max whispered to himself. After a few more minutes of observation, he started down the ramp. On either side of the road there were fallen stalactites and boulder-sized chunks of the ceiling scattered about. As he passed one, he heard a skittering sound, and a rat-like chittering, but no movement. He switched out his halberd for his bow, and nocked an arrow just in case.

He paused atop the bridge, looking over the edge into the crevasse below. As far as he could see, it was just jagged walls and empty air. The bottom was nowhere in sight. On a whim, Max produced one of his empty alchemy vials. Using his arrowhead to prick his finger, he squeezed some blood into the vial until his finger healed. Then he stuffed a small scrap of cloth inside, shook it to soak the cloth with his blood, and cast Spark on it. The moment he cast, he let go of the vial. It caught fire as it fell, and he watched the burning improvised flare fall, and fall, and fall until it was just a tiny speck of light.

Skill level up! Your Alchemy skill has increased by +1!

Ignoring the notification, Max continued across the bridge and walked up to the open town gates. Pausing to look around carefully, he strained his elven ears looking for any sound at all. There was no wind in the cavern, no sound except a slow dripping of water somewhere off to his left, and his own breathing.

Max ventured forward through the gates, examining each building as he advanced toward a central square. The buildings were all made of stone, and as Max looked closer, he saw no sharp corners or mortar, as if the buildings were shaped from stone instead of constructed. The windows, those that weren't shuttered, open to the street, with no glass. Max stepped closer to one on his right, peering through a window to see rotted wood furniture and rusted metal pots, pans, and eating utensils.

Moving along, Max entered the square. In the very center was a fountain, topped with an ebony statue of a humanoid male with a slender but muscular build, long hair, and a sharp nose. Taking one of the silver squares from his inventory, Max held it up in front of the statue. "Could be the same face, I guess." Max mumbled to himself.

The moment he spoke, he heard a shuffling sound to his right, Spinning in that direction, he focused on a two-story building with wide windows. The shuffling sound repeated, and Max raised his bow. Before he could identify a target, a low groaning sound echoed from inside a building behind. He spun again, then again when he heard the clatter of metal against stone back toward the gate.

Gritting his teeth, Max turned back toward the first sound, just in time to see a shuffling creature emerge through the door. He fired an arrow into its chest even as he cast *Identify*.

> **Undead drone**
> **Level 15**
> **Health: 1,650/1,700**

His arrow had struck the thing squarely in the chest, and only taken fifty points of health! Taking a deep breath to avoid panicking, Max reminding himself that undead needed to be killed with head shots, decapitation, or fire. Drawing another arrow, he put it into the approaching zombie's face. This time it went down, and didn't move again.

Spinning toward where he'd heard the groaning, Max froze. Half a dozen of the undead had emerged from that building, and dozens more were shuffling out of the buildings around the square. Others had exited the buildings he'd passed on the way in, and the street was becoming crowded with them. Undead were slowly but surely shuffling into the square from every direction.

Max found himself surrounded.

Chapter 16

Cursing to himself, Max put his back to the fountain and fired several arrows into the faces of the nearest undead. They were a mix of races, some looking human, others were dwarves, a few elves, but he was too busy trying to kill them to observe them all. Like the one he'd already killed, they were levels fifteen to twenty five, for the most part.

Lowering his bow for a moment, he cast *Zap!* at one of the undead to his left. The lightning slammed into the head of that zombie, then transferred to the three nearest shufflers, making them all seize up and smoke as their bodies fried. All of them dropped to the ground, lifeless.

Still, the hundred or more other undead were slowly but surely closing in. He didn't have time to kill them individually, or four at a time, even if he had the mana to do so. Already several were working their way around the fountain behind him, reaching out with skeletal fingers, the flesh worn away and the bone tips sharpened into claws.

Max was drawing his battle axe and preparing to try and rush through them, when they all came to a sudden halt. Raised hands were lowered, and all eye sockets focused on him. As one, they opened their mouths, and a long, agonized moaning poured forth. After a moment, it began to form into words.

"Ooooooooaaaaaa yooouuuu tresssspassss." Max's spine tingled, and he resisted the urge to shudder. This was without question the creepiest thing he'd ever experienced.

"Yoooouuu will come wiiiith usssss. The maaasssster awaitsss." The undead hive mind each raised a single arm and pointed toward an inner gate at the opposite end of the market from where Max had entered.

"Walk deeper into an undead slumber party? I don't think so. I mean, the smell alone…" Max shook his head, focusing on the nearest zombie as he spoke.

The entire crowd let out a growling howl and turned from the gate back toward him. Both arms up again, they began to close on him from every direction. "Folloooowwww, or dieeee."

"Yeah, no." Max focused on the spot at the top of the ramp where he'd entered the cavern, and cast *Jump*. In a flash, he found himself standing up there, wobbling slightly, looking into the long corridor that sloped down toward the portal room and guard barracks. A quick look over his shoulder showed the mob in the square shuffling around, searching for him. He turned to jog up the tunnel, when his ears picked up more moaning.

As he gazed through the darkness, bodies shuffled toward him down the tunnel. Packed tightly, they filled the space from wall to wall, bumping into each other as they advanced.

"Shit." Max cursed loudly. "Where did they even come from? This is why you never split the party. I shouldn't have come down here alone." He turned and looked back down the ramp, which was still clear for the moment, though the instant the undead in the tunnel had spotted him, those in the square had all turned and began to head his direction. Whatever mind was controlling them, it was determined to drive him into the inner keep.

Max knew he couldn't defeat them all, even with his speed advantage. But with his escape route cut off, he figured his best bet was to give them what they wanted.

Sort of.

If he could find whomever was controlling the mob and kill them, he might have a chance. Without the overmind forcing them to act as one, the undead might begin to wander about, or even fight each other, and give him a chance to take them down individually. Or even just avoid them.

The square had cleared now, all of the shufflers having moved toward the ramp. The undead were emerging from the tunnel behind him, and advancing out of the town gate toward the bridge. That gave Max an idea. He jogged down the ramp, eyeing the advancing horde as he went, trying to get the timing right. He slowed to a walk, then actually stopped and rested for a few moments, letting his mana recharge as he watched the undead come for him. The bottleneck at the gate had caused them to bunch up a bit, which was good for him. When they reached the bridge, they clustered up a little tighter.

"Perfect." Max rushed the last twenty yards or so, drawing his halberd and holding it horizontally in front of him with both hands. Picking up speed, he crashed into the horde as they were nearing his end of the bridge, using his momentum and body weight to shove the bodies aside with his weapon. The tactic worked, several of the corpses were pushed over the edge of the bridge to fall silently into the crevasse. Max changed his direction, pushing as hard as he could, and sent several more over the opposite side.

He took some hits doing this, sharp fingers and even teeth cutting at his arms, penetrating the leather bracers he wore. Max worried that bites or scratches might turn him into an undead as well, like it did in most of the movies. But he kept pushing, alternating between one direction and the other, moving forward across the bridge at a forty five degree angle each time, shoving the crowd in front of him like he was herding livestock. Dozens of the creatures fell to their doom, and still more pressed at him.

When the group from the tunnel began to catch up from behind, Max decided it was time to go. Choosing one of the single story buildings near the square, Max focused on the roof and cast *Jump* again. The zombies fell into the space he'd just left behind, stumbling over each other.

Not wasting any time, Max hopped down off the roof and sprinted across the square. Not seeing any new corpses emerging from the inner gate, he ran through and turned around. As he'd hoped, the ironwood gates were mostly intact, their dwarven steel bindings only slightly rusted. He quickly pulled and pushed both doors closed, then slid across the four inch thick steel bar that served as the lock. The metal squealed in protest, but it slid through its brackets without too much trouble.

317

"There, now you guys just wait outside while I deal with your master." Max turned toward the keep and advanced across a small courtyard. He kept a wary eye on every door and window in view, waiting for more undead to emerge at any second. As he approached the door of the donjon, he equipped both axe and sword. He was about to move into tighter spaces, where his halberd would be less effective.

Stepping through the door, Max found an empty entry hall, maybe twenty feet wide and thirty deep. Toward the back the floor was scattered with rubble around a gaping hole. It looked as if something had exploded upward from below. Something about the size of an elephant, based on the hole. He advanced slowly, scanning the room and the corridor beyond as he drew closer to the hole.

Finding nothing, Max sighed. "This is gonna suck, I just know it." He stepped to the edge of the hole, and looked down. Instead of the straight drop that he expected, there was a sort of ramp rising up from below. He could see where whatever had dug the tunnel had burst through three lower levels of the keep on its way up to the main level. Max could see bent and broken cell doors, collapsed walls, and scattered bones.

Shaking his head, he stepped down onto the ramp. The tunnel, once it cleared the dungeon levels, was circular, maybe ten feet in diameter. There was a sort of melted look to the walls and floor, almost as if something had burned its way through.

Following the tunnel downward, Max became more and more nervous. Anything powerful enough to tunnel through solid rock with such ease was going to be able to eat him for lunch. Twice he halted, considering a retreat. He could wait until all the undead were pressed against the gate above, then teleport himself past them and haul ass back to the portal.

But that was assuming there weren't more of them waiting farther up the tunnel.

Plus, this whole thing screamed *quest* to him. He'd basically been told to come here by Regin himself, and the mention of the lich by the caretaker, combined with his quest to find the heart of his mountain... Max had to go on.

The odd tunnel continued downward, curving occasionally and seemingly at random. Here and there the walls were broken when the borer crossed a natural tunnel or chamber. Max paused each time, looking and listening for any signs of life. He'd learned from Dalia that most areas in the underground were home to life of one type or another. From simple moss and plants to large predators that required whole platoons of soldiers to take down. He had a feeling he was following one such predator straight to its lair.

"Step into my parlor, said the... giant... stone-eating monster thing to the tasty little chimera." Max whispered to himself. When he'd actually said stone-eating out loud, his mind conjured up an image of the giant sand worms from one of his favorite books. Looking at the roundness of the tunnel, and the hardened liquidlike

319

surface, his sphincter puckered. "Oh, great. Didn't need that image in my head."

Red appeared on his shoulder. "I feel this would be a good time to remind ya... next time ya find a cross tunnel or chamber, take a good look. Secure it in that undersized brain o' yours, so that if a giant wormy things starts chasin' ya, you can teleport to a safe spot out of its way."

"Thanks, Red. I think." Max appreciated the advice, not so much the snark.

"Happy to help!" She grinned at him. "As funny as it might be to watch, I'd not like to have ya digested by a beastie."

Continuing downward, Max pulled out one of the square silvers. "Does this look familiar to you?"

"Nope. We fae are not fond o' silver. Tend to avoid it when possible. Same with iron... really any metal other than gold. And if ya remember, I arrived in this world the same time you did. Been everywhere you've been, seen what you've seen, and no more. So how would I know about some really old silver coins ya found a couple hours ago?"

"Alright, alright. Just thought I'd ask. That's kind of what you're here for, isn't it?" Max grumped at her, putting the coin back in his inventory. "Can you at least tell me what race that statue in the fountain was?"

"Looked human to me." Red shrugged. "But again, beyond that I can't help ya."

Max pulled out the log book from the chest and held it open for her to see. "How about this? Can you read this writing?"

Red looked down from his shoulder, then leaned a bit closer. "Oh, aye! It be a list o' names and payment amounts. Some o' the names look like persons, others are company names, I'd guess. Like that one there says Stonewalker Mercenary Guild, and this other one says Nogroz Merchants Association. Oh!" She covered her mouth. "Nogroz! That might be a clue. Maybe this place traded with them before the whole turning-to-evil thing happened?"

"Let's hope so. That might get us closer to finding his tomb." Max agreed. The conversation had distracted him enough that he almost missed the side tunnel he was passing. Red cleared her throat and jerked her head toward the opening. "Oh, right. Thanks Red."

Max stepped into the side tunnel, taking a long look around. It was more of a wide crack in the stone that ran about twenty yards before narrowing significantly. Across the worm tunnel, it continued on a good bit farther. Not the ideal location to retreat to, as there was only one way out. "This'll work until we find a better one." Max finished his inspection of the area, memorizing as many details as he could, then stepped back into the tunnel and continued to follow it.

Twenty minutes later, he reached its end. A large cavern with a low ceiling, maybe fifteen feet high, that spread out through a series of arches and short tunnels that all seemed to be interconnected. Like a giant ant farm, only built horizontally. Toward the far end of the cavern the rock glowed with a pulsing reddish orange light. Max couldn't see the source from where he was, but assumed that was where he needed to go. Standing where he was, he focused for a moment on his immediate surroundings. This location was much better than the crack he'd memorized before. Besides, he didn't think that location was still within range.

The next thing he did was try to memorize the layout of the cavern, and trace himself the most direct possible path through the maze. After focusing for nearly a minute, he was able to view a rough map of the cavern by zooming in his interface map. It was all in grey, as he'd only observed the room, not walked through it. Zooming back out, he saw the tunnel he'd just followed, crossed occasionally by side tunnels he'd observed or poked his head into. Zooming out even further, he saw the town and the bridge.

"Red, is there any way to add scale to this map? Like, to help me see how far away that other safe zone was?"

"Hmm… there might be. I'll look into it." Red tapped her chin with one finger. "I can see how that would be helpful."

Max nodded once, taking a deep breath, then drew his sword and stepped forward. He walked slowly, his Fade ability activated, keeping his head on a swivel as he tried to trace his chosen path through the cavern. He ducked under an arch here, turned left through a short tunnel there, then doubled back, sure that he'd gone the wrong way.

Fifteen minutes later, he began to see the orange glow from before. It was just around the bend ahead, through a smaller version of the worm tunnel he'd been in earlier. Max's pulse rate quickened as he continued forward, crouched down now, though he wasn't sure why. His grip tight on Storm Reaver's handle, he peered around the corner, and his shoulders slumped slightly.

The glow was emanating from a small pit in the floor, in which magma boiled and bubbled quietly. Another, larger pit sat a stone's throw away. Shaking his head, his stress level dropping slightly, Max carefully stepped around the first pit, walking toward the second. The need to avoid fire was always there in the back of his mind.

Just as he was passing by the larger pool, a voice echoed through an arch ahead of him. "Very clever, using my own gates to lock out my minions."

Max froze, his eyes searching everywhere.

"Come, come, chimera. I have watched you through my minions' eyes since you arrived through the portal. Had I wanted you dead, you'd have been added to my army already. I so rarely get to speak to the living these days. Enter my temple and sit a while. It's just ahead of you."

As if to prove its point, the ceiling above Max's head began to shift. Hundreds of small undead spiders moved just enough so that Max would notice them, then settled back down. They blended perfectly into the stone around them.

Max gritted his teeth and focused his mind, trying not to be creeped out. Thinking about how many zombie spiders he must have walked underneath since arriving in Deepcrag was not going to help him. His spine itched like something was crawling up his back, and he shivered. Ignoring the sensation, he stepped forward through the arch, having to duck down as he did so.

The temple wasn't what he'd expected. It was a small, natural chamber, the floor covered in stalagmites and scattered magma pools. The ceiling was low, and dozens of stalactites hanging down made it seem even lower than it was. The room was filled with shadows cast by the stone formations above and below. To his left, a set of roughly cut stone steps led up to a dais with an altar straight out of horror movies. A flat obsidian table was littered with skulls, shattered bones, wicked looking blades that were stained with long-dried blood.

"Welcome, chimera." The lich stood atop the dais, next to the altar. Max guessed its body had originally been that of an elf, with long white hair and sharply pointed ears. But the undead body was so emaciated that every rib showed clearly through the thin skin of its torso under a badly tattered robe that was little more than scraps. Its arms were long and thin, just bone, muscle, and skin, ending in oversized hands with sharp claws. Its head was basically a mummified skull still covered in leathery skin, its cheeks sunken deeply, withered gums and sharp yellowed teeth exposed. Only its crimson colored eyes held any life as it stared at him. "Please, be at ease. We will doubtlessly attempt to kill one another at some point, but for now, I wish to talk."

Max stepped farther into the room, putting his back to the wall to one side of the entrance. He thought he heard slight movement in the shadows, but his darksight was having trouble adjusting to the difference between the magma-lit and shadowed areas of the temple.

"Are you the lich who tricked Nogroz into surrendering his soul?"

"Nogroz?" The lich tilted its head to one side, thinking. "Ah, yes. The dwarf king. So long ago!" its eyes blazed. "Are you a historian? Come to get the true story of the origin of the grey dwarves?" the lich clapped its hands together as if excited.

"Of a sort…" Max replied. "I am Maximilian Storm, King of Stormhaven, formerly known as Nogroz. I killed the grey dwarf king Agnor and took his throne. And yes, I am curious about the history."

"Ah, yes. I saw the gods' notification about you." The lich stared at him a moment longer, eyes still glowing. "A chimera, a king, and a Battleborne as well! Wonderful!" The lich's smile revealed even more of its sharp teeth. It was not a reassuring gesture for Max.

"What can you tell me about the ritual involving the heart of the mountain?" Max leaned back against the wall, trying to relax his body and slow his heart rate a bit. He needed to conserve his energy in the event of an attack.

"Well, let me see. When I found the dwarf king, I had only recently become a lich myself. I had lived a long life as a necromancer, but my living body was growing old. I bound my soul to a phylactery and ended my mortal existence, being reborn as a lich, immortal as long as there are souls for me to drain!" It rubbed its hands together, staring greedily at Max.

"Nogroz had a heart corrupted by greed. He was jealous of his dwarf cousins, who had larger cities, larger clans, more power. His was a simple trading town, only valued for its location in relation to others. A safe place to stop and refresh oneself between destinations. He grew the city from a trade outpost into a small kingdom through sheer determination and guile. A discreet theft and murder of a merchant here and there, the proceeds going directly into his pockets. He had been a thief before taking over the town, and he used the thieves' guild to do his dirty work. For a share of the spoils, of course, and his protection."

Max nodded, the attacks by the thieves guild and the missing treasury starting to make more sense to him. If the guild had ties to the throne, and maintained them through all these centuries… his thoughts were interrupted as the lich continued.

"It was a simple thing to hide my identity from him, to whisper into his ear of greater power and wealth. I assisted him in his conquest of this place, or rather of Deepcrag above. It was another trade outpost, similar in size to Nogroz. His thieves crept into the city and poisoned everyone, a slow and painful death that allowed me to harvest unbelievable power for myself. I fed off their delicious pain and sorrow, then captured their souls to create the minions you met earlier. I also gained nearly twenty levels in one night, and was awarded several new skills."

Max growled deep in his chest. Some base part of himself was longing to rip the lich's head from its shoulders. The lich, oblivious as it relived its memories, continued on.

"Those few thieves that managed to escape me reported my actions to Nogroz, revealing my true nature. He was furious! But when I told him that a similar ritual, using the heart of the mountain as its power source, could grant him near immortality, he calmed down. When I presented him with the wealth of the entire town of Deepcrag, I was forgiven. It enabled him to expand his own city considerably. As well as to sell the various recently vacated and undamaged properties in the town to allied merchants, profiting handsomely. It wasn't long before he journeyed to the mountain's core and secured the heart for our ritual. The fool believed every lie I fed him."

"So you used the ritual to steal his soul." Max accused. "And to twist the souls of his people, creating the grey dwarves."

The lich threw its head back and laughed, a deep and throaty sound. "I did, and I did not. You give me too much credit, Battleborne. I did plan to steal his soul, and to transfer my own soul into the heart of the mountain in the process. The power in that stone…" the lich shook its head. "But I had no intentions toward his people. At least, not at that time. When the ritual began, and the dwarf king realized that I had tricked him yet again, he fought me. That one possessed an iron will, and he resisted the ritual. Our battle of wills lasted quite some time, and the power drain was immense, both of us drawing from the stone. When the power within the heart of the mountain faded, I used the power I'd gathered from the citizens of Deepcrag, and he figured out how to do the same to his own people. He drew from them, but he was untrained, and enraged, and cared not for their welfare. When I finally defeated him, he had taken something… vital from all of them, and given back something unhealthy from within himself."

Max tried to imagine being willing to sacrifice hundreds or thousands of his own people to preserve his life. He'd killed that many in his career, either personally, or by calling down artillery or air strikes. A few had even been civilians. He'd regretted it each time, had needed counseling afterward more than once, but they had been enemies, and he was a soldier following orders. What Nogroz had done… Max shook his head. "And after you defeated him?"

"We had held the ritual within his keep, in a secret chamber he'd built deep in the stone of the mountain. When his people felt what he did, they followed the magic straight to us, stormed the keep, and trapped me inside. I held them off for some time, claiming many more souls as I fought. But eventually they overwhelmed me and destroyed my body." The lich struck a pose and gestured toward its current form. "It was nearly five thousand years before a group of elven adventurers seeking treasure located my phylactery. The one who snatched up my crystal was weak-minded. I managed to manipulate him into killing one of his comrades, and took control of this body."

"Five thousand years inside a crystal?" Max whispered to himself.

Having elven hearing to go with its elven body, the lich heard him. "Yes, it was… unpleasant, to say the least. I went quite insane!" the lich giggled, covering its mouth with its hands in an odd gesture for such a creature.

Max changed the subject. "What of the stone? The heart of the mountain?"

"Bah! Who cares? It was all but useless, drained of power, before I was killed. Likely the newly twisted dwarves thought it nothing more than a bit of rubble. The chamber took some damage during our battle…"

"And where exactly was this chamber?" Max asked the question that might allow him to complete the quest.

"As I said, it was cut into the stone of the mountain, much deeper than the rest of his palace, which was still being cut into the stone at that time. Those dwarves, they are an industrious lot, and talented. They had shapers that

329

could liquify stone and reshape it to their will. I remember watching them create the skylights in one of their great halls before I died. In… Darkholm, I think. They shaped these tunnels that ran at angles up to the surface, the interiors so smooth that they reflected the sunlight all the way down through the skylights in the hall. One of them even figured out how to place the openings so that the sunbeams in the hall shifted from east to west as the day progressed. Pure genius!" The lich paused. "Where was I?"

"The location of the ritual chamber." Max growled impatiently.

"Ah, yes! Well, I suppose I could give you exact directions. Tell you where to find the hidden door that would lead you to it. But I'm afraid the information would do you no good. I've enjoyed our chat, chimera, but I have delayed you long enough. My minions have unlocked the gate up above, and the horde has nearly arrived. There is no escape for you." The lich held out one hand, palm facing up, and a green flame appeared just above it. "It has been a long time since any sentients have ventured into Deepcrag, and I'm told that the soul of a Battleborne contains great power. I shall feed on you for days before I claim your soul. I apologize in advance, Maximilian. I'm afraid it will be quite painful for you."

As the lich spoke, four undead elves emerged from the shadows around the chamber. They moved faster than the shamblers upstairs, but not as fast as live elves would have. "Meet the adventurers who were kind enough to set me free! They are quite strong, but they will not hurt you any more than necessary. Resistance is futile. If you cooperate, the process will be less painful for you."

Max used *Identify* on the first undead he saw.

Undead Acolyte
Elite
Level 30
Health: 4,000/4,000

He was so focused on his interface that he nearly missed the lich's throwing motion that sent the green flame flying toward his chest. Max dodged to the left, nearly crashing into one of the acolytes, which grabbed at his sword arm. Its claws dug into his forearm, easily penetrating the leather bracer, and tugged at him with surprising strength for a scrawny undead elf.

"Oh, no you don't!" Max growled as he grabbed it by the neck with his free hand and dug in with his own claws. Twisting his body around, he slammed the creature into the wall. When that seemed to have no effect, he lifted it off the ground and brought it down atop one of the stalagmites, the point penetrating its back, then bursting through its chest as it sank farther onto the stone. Max left it there, struggling like a bug on its back, not having time to finish it before the others reached him. As he turned back toward the lich, another green fireball struck him in the chest, the flash momentarily blinding him. He swung his sword blindly in front of him, feeling it impact something. Taking a step back, he blinked rapidly and shook his head, swinging again to keep attackers at bay, trying not to panic at the idea of being hit by fire with open wounds on his arm. When his vision cleared, a one- armed acolyte was reaching for his face, its other arm laying on the stone floor behind it. Max ducked down, the clawed hand barely scratching his face, then lunged upward with his sword, driving it in under the monster's chin. The sword's tip exited through the top of its skull, and the acolyte went lifeless. Max ripped the sword free, shattering the skull from the inside.

The other two acolytes had closed, and Max saw the lich forming yet another green fireball. He stepped to one side, putting an acolyte between him and the lich, then kicked it as hard as he could in the chest. The undead elf stumbled backward, managing to scratch the outside of Max's thigh as it fell, attempting to take hold of his foot, but failing. Its back heel hit the stone steps, and it fell at the lich's feet, freeing up its line of sight. The lich wasted no time, flinging the sickly green fire at Max's face.

Max managed to dodge, but the action put him right into the arms of the fourth acolyte. It wrapped its arms around Max, pinning his arms to his sides. Lifting him off his feet, it began to walk toward the lich and the other acolyte, which was getting to its feet, unharmed. Max tried slamming his head backward, crushing the acolyte's nose, but it had no effect. He strained to raise his arms, but again to no avail. Having no other choice, he waited for the acolyte by the stairs to get to its feet, then focused on the altar behind it.

"*Boom!*" Max cast the spell directly on the stone altar. A moment later it shattered, shards of stone, bone, and metal implements exploding outward. The lich was knocked off its feet, and the acolyte in front of Max was badly shredded. Max took several hits as well, the undead shield not working as well as he'd hoped. His health bar dropped to sixty percent, and his troll regeneration kicked into overdrive to heal the multiple cuts on his right leg, arm, and face.

The explosion had the added effect of stunning the lich, interrupting its control over the acolytes. The one holding Max, mostly undamaged from the blast, loosened its hold slightly, allowing his feet to touch the ground. That was enough for Max. With a roar, he bent forward at the waist, lifting the acolyte behind him off its feet. Bending his knees, he tucked his head and rolled forward, using the extra weight on his back to his advantage. As he curled further into the roll, the acolyte's head struck the stone floor, and Max heard the snapping of bone. Its arms relaxed, and Max simply fell to his side, not able to complete the forward roll over top of its body. He quickly scrambled to his feet and stabbed down into the thing's skull, to be sure it was dead.

Stepping toward the lich, which was just getting back on its feet but with its back to Max, he took a second to decapitate the shredded acolyte laying on the steps before advancing on the lich. The creature was descending the steps at the back of the dais, heading for a doorway that had previously been obscured by the altar. Max cast *Jump* on himself, appearing between the lich and its escape route, turning around to face it as quickly as he could, leading with his sword as he spun. The blade cut deeply into the lich's ribs, and stayed there. Max channeled *Zap!* through his hands into the sword, the lightning energy passing through the mithril blade directly into the lich's body.

As it seized up, its eyes blazing with insane hatred, Max let go of the sword. Retrieving his axe from his inventory, he swung overhead with both hands, driving the weapon down through the lich's skull, shattering it. The light in its eyes blinked out, and Max leveled up.

Red appeared on his shoulder, shouting, "Behind you, Max. Follow the magic!"

"What magic? Max spun around, seeing nothing.

"Shit! Ya can't see it? Through that door. Run!"

Not understanding, but trusting in Red, Max did as he was told. Leaving his axe and sword stuck in the lich's corpse, he dashed toward the same door the lich was trying to reach. As he went, Red explained. "There's a thread o' magic runnin' from the corpse back this direction. There was a pulse the moment ye killed it, and now the thread's gettin' thin. Run!"

Max picked up his speed, moving down a narrow corridor. When he reached an intersection, Red shouted "Left!" and he obeyed. "Through that wall!" Red pointed straight ahead at the wall at the end of the corridor. Not seeing any doors, Max produced his war hammer and struck the stone at a run. The hammer passed right thru the wall with no resistance, causing Max to lose his balance and stumble forward through the wall himself, falling to his hands and knees on the other side.

"There!" Red still stood on his shoulder, not bothered in the least by the fall. Max looked up from his position on the ground, still unable to see the magic. He did, however, see a flash of green in a stone set upon a shelf on the far wall of the small room he found himself in. "D'ya see?" Red pointed again, frantically looking from Max to the stone and back.

"I saw it flash." Max got to his feet, brushing the dust off his hands. One advantage of killing ancient undead, there were no messy splashes of blood. Max took a quick look around the room to make sure nothing was about to attack him. The room was maybe ten paces deep, five wide, filled with chests and crates. The back wall was all shelves, and the stone that had flashed was set on one at about waist height for Max. Crossing the room, he reached for the stone. It was about the size of his fist, an oddly shaped crystal with dozens of facets. Clearly not shaped by anyone, it pulsed faintly with the same green light as the lich's fire magic.

The moment Max picked it up, notifications flashed across his vision. They disappeared a second later, and Red mumbled, "Hold on, let me sort this." She chuckled to herself as she worked, then nodded. "Okay, here ya go."

Epic Quest Complete: Hard Hearted, Part I!
You have located and retrieved the Heart of the Mountain!
Reward: 1,000 gold; 1,000,000 experience; Access to epic quest Hard Hearted Part II.
Quest Modified! Hard Hearted, Part I (A): *You have retrieved the crystal heart of your kingdom's mountain.*

However, the lich has used the stone to store his immortal soul. With the stone thus corrupted, it can not be used to restore the mountain's power. You must remove the lich's corruption without destroying the stone.
Reward: 1,000,000 Experience; 500 gold, access to epic quest Hard Hearted Part II.

"That lying piece of shite!" Red floated down to poke a finger at the stone. "You'll not get away with this!" she shouted at the lich inside. Looking up at Max, she put her hands on her hips and tossed her head, sending her red locks back over one shoulder. "You'll not let him get away with this, right?"

"No, we'll find a way to kill him without destroying the stone, Red. Are you okay? You seem to be taking this a little personal."

The leprechaun crossed her arms, scowling down at the stone in Max's palm. Her voice was cold as ice as she replied, "After what that other arsebag did to Dalia's family, killed Battleaxe, and almost killed you, I want this one to die slow and painful."

Max chuckled, wanting to hug the little guide. "I agree one hundred percent. Can you hear that, lich? We'll find a way to kill you, I promise you that!" He started a bit when a golden light encase him and Red both. It seemed the gods had taken note of that particular promise.

"You're not done yet." Red smirked at him. Another notification popped up.

*Congratulations! You have captured the settlement
known as Deepcrag!
Would you like to claim this settlement?   Yes/No*

"What?" Max looked confusedly at Red. He'd been expecting to evade and escape, or have to fight his way out of the cavern past the horde of undead.

"When ya killed the lich, ya killed all his minions. And got experience for every single one o' them. That's why ya leveled."

"Awesome." Max mentally clicked yes to accept ownership of the town. This time there were no dwarven allies to take exception, or demand a share. As soon as he was done, he took another look around the room. "So, do you think this is Agnor's missing treasury?"

Red shook her head. "Look at the dust on those crates. This has been here a long time."

"So, maybe it was Nogroz's treasury?" Max ventured, walking to the nearest chest. "What're the odds the damned lich put traps on these?"

"If it's true that the lich was killed after the ritual, then it's unlikely he was able to steal the treasury. More likely this was stolen from the town above, and he lied to Nogroz about how much treasure there was. Or this is loot from the travelers the lich and his horde have killed. Or both." Red looked toward the illusory wall. "Go loot the lich's corpse. There might be keys to these chests." Max nodded his agreement, and proceeded to do exactly that.

He walked through the illusion wall, back to where the lich had fallen. He retrieved his axe and sword, cleaning their blades on what was left of the lich's robe. When he looked at his loot notifications, he smiled. There was a storage ring, which he immediately accessed. Not as hefty as the one he'd taken from the previous lich, this one had two hundred and fifty slots. Fifty of which were empty. He thought about wanting keys, and a metal key ring appeared in his hands. Hanging from it were a score of keys of different lengths and shapes.

Heading back to the treasury room, Max was about to try and find the key for the first chest he saw. He was eyeing the lock and his key ring, when Red suggested, "Maybe wait a bit? Take all of this back to Stormhaven, get someone with some stealth skills to check the chests? Just because you have the key doesn't mean there won't be magical traps as well. That lich was a devious bastard."

"Good plan, Red. Thanks. Time to do a little housekeeping, too." Max looked into the newly acquired storage ring, taking out items he was sure he had no use for. Body parts, a black staff that had a health-draining curse on it, various nasty bits that he didn't even want to touch. Dumping it all in a corner, he began storing the unopened chests and crates in the ring one at a time, each one taking up a single slot. When the big pieces were gone, and only the items on the shelves remained, Max pulled out the other lich's five hundred slot ring. He did the same purge, dumping the items that made him feel queasy, the necromancer's crafting ingredients, etc.

When he had a significant pile in the corner, he and Red began to *Examine* the items on the shelves, checking each just long enough to make sure their description didn't include a curse. When it was all collected, he cast *Jump* back to the cavern entrance, then again to the crack of a side tunnel he had memorized. From there, he jogged back through the tunnel into the keep, teleported himself back to the top of the ramp, then ran all the way back to the guard's quarters near the portal. A quick look inside at the chests still there, and he decided to leave them for another time. One thing new caught his eye. At the back of the room, where a faded tapestry had been hanging, it now lay on the floor, badly trampled. Behind where it had hung, a door stood open.

Mas shook his head. "Damn. That must be where the extra zombies came from. That's how they got behind me. Red, remind me when we get back, I need to visit Josephine and see if she has a spell that'll let me detect hidden doors, buried treasure, that kind of thing. Or maybe even to see magic, like you did with the lich."

"Will do, big fella." Red nodded, then disappeared. Max walked back to the portal room, and adjusted the interface to authorize the portal to connect to the outpost, the temple, and Stormhaven city. He didn't have the right to authorize the Darkholm portal, but that was okay.

A moment later, he stepped into the courtyard of his keep, and went looking for Redmane.

Chapter 17

Max spent the next two days waiting for his party to regroup. He sat down with Redmane as soon as he'd gotten home, and began to share the story of his explorations. The dwarf's eyes widened when he mentioned Skytop, and Max paused.

"You've heard of the place?"

"Aye, most dwarves have. It's said to be Regin's original home when he were a mere mortal, before he ascended. As ancient as the mountains that protect it." The old dwarf chuckled when something occurred to him. "It were said to be like ye plan this place to be, a place that welcomed all races. O'course, this would have been long before some o' the younger races, like humans, even walked this world. Regin's been the god o' craftin' fer a thousand dwarven generations or more."

Max went on with his story, and again the chamberlain reacted when he mentioned Deepcrag. Max just raised an eyebrow.

"Deepcrag's an abandoned trade settlement, on an old route no one uses anymore. It's said the entire population disappeared overnight, taken by a lich. There was a goblin city a day's walk from there, and a gnome settlement as well. Both were wiped out long ago, both events a mystery. After that, new routes were established, and none but glory seeking adventurers tread that path."

340

"Heh." Max grinned at the dwarf. "I might be able to help fill in some information there." He went on to tell of his encounter with the undead, his meeting and battle with the lich, and the history lesson he'd received. "Keep in mind, the lich lied through his teeth about several things, so I don't know how accurate the rest of his story was."

Max let Redmane absorb that information for a bit, the dwarf even pulling out pen and parchment to make some notes. When he finally looked up, Max said, "I think it's about time you showed me our palace treasury."

Suspicious of the sudden right turn in the conversation, Redmane nonetheless simply nodded, getting up from his desk and leading Max down a wide stairwell, then a narrower stairwell, and through a maze of corridors. Producing a ridiculously oversized key the length of his forearm, the dwarf unlocked a massive metal vault door, then pulled it open. Inside was a large room, maybe fifty feet deep, three of the walls lined with shelves. All of which were empty, as was the rest of the room.

"You weren't kidding when you said they cleaned it out." Max shook his head. Redmane cleared his throat, then pointed around the corner of the doorway. Max stuck his head inside, seeing a small shelving unit just inside the door. On it were several stacks and trays of coins. "The funds you instructed me to remove from the bank and deposit in the treasury." Redmane informed him.

Max snorted. The few thousand gold that had looked like significant wealth just a few weeks ago now seemed pitifully insignificant in the empty room. "Let's see about filling this place back up a bit." He stepped into the room and began removing chests and crates from the lich's storage ring, placing them neatly in line in the middle of the room. As he did so, he told Redmane about looting the lich's stash, and their concern about traps or curses. "Can you find someone with the proper abilities to make sure all of these are safe before we open them?"

"Ha! Indeed I can, Max." Redmane watched as item after item appeared. When he was done with the big pieces, Max switched rings and began unloading the items from the lich's shelves onto one of the side wall shelving units. He kept the gold he'd received as quest rewards for his personal use, but deposited the gold and platinum he'd taken from the guards' chest on the shelf next to the cash from the bank.

"One last thing…" Max removed the empty chest from his inventory, then poured the heavy square silver coins into it. "Any idea where these are from, or what they're worth?"

Laughing, Redmane bent down and picked up one of the silvers. He hefted in his palm checking its weight, then *Examined* it. Finally he bit the metal, then nodded his head. "It be pure silver, right enough. Heavy as five o' the silver coins we use. If yer askin' me where they came from, I've no idea. But give me a few days, and I'll ask around. Might be one o' the merchants knows, or one o' the historians in Darkholm."

"There are thirty eight hundred of those things in the chest." Max did a little math in his head. "At five silver each, that's nineteen hundred gold worth of silver."

Redmane nodded. "Aye, based on weight alone. Though it may be that they have additional value as collector's items. We'll see soon enough." The dwarf pocketed the coin he held, and the two of them left the vault, Redmane carefully closing and locking it behind them. He offered the key to Max. "I've a second key, if ye want it."

"Max shook his head." Nope. If I get killed and looted, I don't want someone to be able to sneak in here and empty the treasury. Which reminds me." He pulled the lich's key ring from his inventory and handed it to Redmane. "I have no idea which key opens what, but I'm sure whomever you bring in can figure it out."

As they walked back to Redmane's office, Max told him about the quest to cleanse the lich's soul from the Heart of the Mountain, producing the crystal as he did so. Redmane carefully took the stone in his hands, gazing at it reverently. "It be a worthy quest, and it'd be my honor to help ye."

Max instantly pulled up the quest and shared it with Redmane. "Maybe you can help us figure out how to remove him without damaging the stone?"

"I'll have old Puckerface here first thing in the mornin', and we'll begin searchin' fer a way. Would ye mind if I share the quest with him? Epic quests be rare for us oldsters that don't go adventurin' anymore."

343

"If it'll encourage him to help without emptying my supply of Firebelly's, then go right ahead!" Max grinned at his chamberlain. Thinking about the dwarven mage, Max stopped and looked around. Every twenty feet or so, there was a light glowing softly on the corridor walls. Max had been in the keep for over an hour, and hadn't even noticed! "The lights are done?"

"Aye, finished this morning. As well as some o' the extra protections we discussed." Redmane paused, then cleared his throat again. "On second thought, it might be a day or two before Puckerface be sober enough to assist with the quest... I paid him the agreed upon bottles before he left."

*****

While he waited for Dalia and Smitty to return, Max did some more alchemy work and smithing, alternating between the two, working at each for six hours at a time. He and Redmane spent a few hours each morning going through issues, but Max noticed that the piles were steadily getting smaller. Redmane said it was because precedents and procedures were being established, and his advisors were getting adjusted to the way Max wanted things done. Fewer issues needed to be sent up the chain for his review.

On the second day since his return from Deepcrag, two interesting things happened. First, a small party of merchants requested an audience with Max. When Redmane brought them into the throne room, where Max had just settled down to receive them, he was pleased to see that the group represented several races. Their leader was a dark elf, as was another of the group. There were two gnomes, one a female, a kobold, a lady dwarf, and the first human Max could remember seeing on this world!"

The entire group bowed deeply at the waist when they'd reached some invisible line in front of the throne. Max, always uncomfortable with formality, said "Welcome to Stormhaven! It makes me happy to see such a diverse group. What was it you wished to speak with me about?"

The group all straightened up, several of them smiling up at Max. The leader spoke with a surprisingly deep and pleasing voice. "My name is Indoril, Majesty. My associates and I represent the Greystone Conglomerate, a newly formed merchant's association. We've recently been informed that your majesty has claimed the abandoned settlement of Deepcrag." He paused for a moment, and Max nodded for him to continue.

"We came here to Stormhaven just a week ago, after news of your open city reached us. Our plan had been to purchase a guild hall here in your city, and potentially a warehouse too, once we had confirmed that your majesty truly embraced all races."

"Except grey dwarves." Max interrupted before he could stop himself.

"Yes, of course." The elf grinned at him. "However, now that we have heard news of Deepcrag, we would request permission to purchase facilities there, as well. My great grandfather once operated a branch of our family business there, and I would like to return, now that the… danger lurking below the town has been removed."

Max raised an eyebrow. "One danger has been removed, certainly. Though I traveled through a tunnel that looked like it was made by a giant stone-eating worm of some kind. It burst right up into the entry hall of the palace. I didn't run across the creature, so there's a chance it's still … *worming* its way around the area." He grinned inwardly at his own pun, which all the others pretended not to notice. Except Redmane, who rolled his eyes.

"That is a danger we are quite capable of dealing with, Majesty."

"And you're aware that the entire trade route that used to pass through Deepcrag has been abandoned as well?" Max leaned forward a bit, interested in the answer.

"We are, Majesty. We hope to be able to correct that, in time. Until then, the portal would keep us connected to our trade partners, and allow us to provision ourselves."

Max's mind spun, his instincts telling him he was missing something important. He understood their interest in a rapidly growing city like Stormhaven, but why set up shop in an abandoned settlement on a defunct trade route? Acutely aware of everyone staring at him, he shook his head.

"You'll have to forgive me, ladies and gentlemen. As I'm sure you're aware, I'm very new to this position of king. I'm a soldier by profession, and not at all familiar with the business of trade. It seems… odd to me, your interest in Deepcrag." He paused to look at his chamberlain, who was rocking slightly on the balls of his feet, hands clasped behind his back. "Chamberlain Redmane, what am I missing here?"

Surprised, Redmane approached and spoke quietly. "Perhaps you would like to discuss this in private, Majesty?"

Max shook his head, giving the dwarf a wink. "It's okay, I'm sure these fine merchants won't mind observing as you teach me a lesson." He grinned at the group, who were looking uncomfortable.

Redmane nodded. "It is true the trade route has long gone unused. This was due not only to the demise of all the Deepcrag residents, but also the sudden disappearance of the inhabitants of two other nearby settlements, Majesty."

The light bulb went off in Max's brain. "Two unclaimed, and potentially loot-filled settlements. Which would bring great wealth to those who got there first and claimed them, giving them the rights to sell off the properties at a one hundred percent profit."

The merchants looked even more uncomfortable, except for the human, who was grinning. "You understand perfectly, King Max!" his reply surprised and mortified his companions.

"Chamberlain Redmane, how long would it take to travel to Deepcrag, or these other settlements, without using our portal?"

Attempting to suppress a grin under his beard, the dwarf answered, "If I remember correctly, the next nearest portal to that area would be... nine days' walk from Deepcrag. A few days more or less to the other two."

This time it was Max who was surprised. He'd imagined the town to be much closer to Stormhaven. To get a better idea of the scale, he asked, "And how would one get to that portal? Also, how long would it take to walk from here?"

"The only portal I know of that might still connect to that area, other than yer own, is the one in the former human city now occupied by An'zalor, Majesty. Deepcrag were a mainly human settlement when it was destroyed, one filled with outcasts and guarded by prisoners workin' off their debts to the human king. As fer walkin from here... me best guess would be four weeks."

From the look on the merchant's faces, they had made a similar calculation.

"I see. That is valuable information indeed. Thank you." Max looked at the spokesman for a moment, considering. "I have no objection to merchants earning an honest profit. And I see no problem with you wanting to be first to the prize, so to speak. Though I would have appreciated you being more forthright with your true intentions." The elf winced at that.

"The way I see it, you very badly need permission to use my portal at Deepcrag to help you build your new empire. And while I'm not opposed to assisting you, I have a brand new kingdom of my own to grow. That takes resources, my friends. A lot of resources."

The elf bowed his head slightly, acknowledging Max's insinuation, while the gnomes' faces showed absolute dismay. Max could practically hear the wailing inside their heads at the potential lost profits.

Taking the hint, the elf turned briefly to his companions, all of whom nodded. The gnomes last of all, and with sad looks on their faces. "Majesty, we would gladly assist you in your expansion efforts. To begin with, we would offer you the sum of ten thousand gold for the deed to my grandfather's old residence, which we would use, at least temporarily, as our guild house. And another five thousand gold for a moderately sized warehouse. We would also be stationing a score of guards to protect our interests there, whom we would happily loan to your majesty if the need to defend the city arose."

Max caught Redmane winking at him, still trying to suppress a smile.

"That seems a generous offer, though I remind you, I know little of these things. When you've presented your full offer, I'll want to discuss it with a few of my advisors."

"Of course, Majesty." The dark elf bowed his head, before continuing. "As for the two nearby settlements. We would happily enter into favorable trade and taxation agreements that would assist Stormhaven in its development of Deepcrag. And of course, just as it was in the past, we would pay a tariff on any goods transported through the Deepcrag portal."

Max shook his head, not needing to see the frown on Redmane's face. "That sounds lovely, but you offer only what I would receive from everyone else seeking to use the portal. Give me a reason, my new friends, not to take my own people through that portal this afternoon and claim those other settlements before you could walk a tenth of the way there. Or to seek more favorable terms with another merchant group."

Several of the merchants gasped at his bluntness, and the human was visibly sweating. The dark elf spokesman retained a poker face, seeming cool and collected.

An hour later, the merchants exited the throne room, heads shaking, but smiling. Max, with Redmane's assistance, had reached a tentative agreement with them. He had promised to give them his final answer in two days, after consulting with his full staff of councilors.

The basic terms of the agreement were that Max would provide them access to the area via his portal, and not allow any others access for a period of one week. They would pay him his fifteen thousand gold for the residence and warehouse, and station thirty guards at Deepcrag. In addition, they would cover the salaries of one hundred of Max's guards for a period of two years, payable on the first of each month. Failure to pay would result in loss of portal access.

Max would also receive the rights to twenty percent of the real estate in each of the other two settlements, to be held as embassies, or sold to buyers of his choice, but only after a year's time, to give the merchants time to profit from the other properties. Max was fine with this, as they would be doing all the work to recruit residents, and hopefully raising the property values with each sale. One of his representatives, along with fifty soldiers, would accompany the merchants to both settlements and have first choice of the properties, excepting the main keeps themselves. Max had been tempted to insist on taking the keeps, but decided he didn't want the responsibility for defending the residents.

In addition to the property holdings, Max would receive ten percent of the taxes collected for each settlement, and ten percent of the sales proceeds from the remainder of the real estate. This included any properties that changed hands more than once. Both the taxes and the sales proceeds would be paid to Stormhaven for a period of fifty years, and the properties he held would be his in perpetuity. Each of the merchants would be required to enter into an agreement sworn before the gods, and be responsible for enforcing it. Meaning any slight of hand or misreporting relative to the taxes collected, or real estate sales price, would have severe negative repercussions for them. They would also enter into a non-aggression agreement that covered the same fifty year period.

The second thing that happened that day, in fact within an hour of his discussion with the merchants, was that an assassin from the assassin's guild showed up at the palace. Even more interesting, when that assassin was brought before Max in his study, it turned out to be none other than Nessa!

"Majesty, this be the one who can safely open yer boxes." Redmane began to introduce her, but Max held up a hand and smiled. "Nessa, it's good to see you again. But I have to ask... the assassin's guild?"

Nessa shrugged. "My master was not pleased with the treasure I brought from the temple. She refused to consider the quest completed and grant me the rewards I was due. Not wanting to let my particular skills go to waste, or work as a clerk or barmaid, I had limited choices available to me. Had I gone out and... liberated valuables on my own, the thieves' guild would have hunted me down. So I joined the assassin's guild on a probationary basis. This job is my first test."

"I see. Makes total sense." Max grinned at the panthera. "How attached are you to the idea of joining that guild?"

"Not very." She shrugged. "I do not look forward to the idea of killing strangers for money, or being killed in the attempt. But it is the only way I can make use of my skills without looking over my shoulder every day."

"What if I were to offer you the opportunity to live here, and adventure with me and my party. We worked well together, I think. You'd be eligible to receive an equal share of the loot, of course. And if you swear an oath not to liberate items from me or mine, you can live here in the palace when we're not running around exploring."

352

Nessa stared at him for a long moment, her cat eyes impossible to read. "That would be... acceptable. Though, I must complete this contract for the guild, and you must pay them for my services, as agreed."

"Of course." Max looked at Redmane. "Are we going to piss off the assassins' guild by stealing her?"

Redmane shook his head. "She is not officially a member. As long as we pay them for this job, and maybe a little extra, there should be no repercussions. No guild is anxious to anger a king, Max. And certainly not over a low level probationary recruit. No offense, lass."

"None taken." Nessa actually smiled at the old dwarf.

"Then it's agreed!" Max got up and joined them as Redmane led them down to the treasury vault. "I found all of these in the lair of a very, very old and crafty lich." Max warned Nessa. "We looted some keys, but we suspect there might be magical traps as well. If you don't feel up to this job, there's no shame in declining it. I'm in no rush to get to whatever's inside, we can wait for a higher level person..."

Nessa glared at Max, and though he couldn't be sure, he thought maybe the claws at the ends of her fingers lengthened slightly. "I am perfectly capable of disarming a few traps!" She snapped at him. Hearing her own tone, she sighed. "I apologize, your majesty. I am... sensitive at being denied the improved skills that should have been my quest reward." She took a few deep breaths as they approached the vault door. "If I see something I'm not absolutely sure of, I will back away and leave it for another."

"Fair enough!" Max agreed as they arrived. Before Redmane opened the vault, he made Nessa take an oath not to steal anything from, or reveal to anyone what she saw inside, the vault. When it was done, the dwarf opened it up, and Nessa went to work. Redmane handed her the key ring, and they both stood at the entrance to observe as she did her thing. Redmane whispered to Max to be ready to help him close the massive door quickly if Nessa set off a trap that released poison gas or some similar danger.

It took her nearly four hours to inspect locks, locate keys, check for traps, and open all the chests and crates. As it turned out, none of the chests, and only two of the crates, held traps. Both of which Nessa handily disarmed. One featured poisoned darts, another a capsule of gaseous acid.

Max noticed that she looked away immediately after opening each one, quickly moving on to the next. When she was done, and got up to leave the vault, he asked her, "Don't you want to see what's inside?"

"I've sworn an oath not to reveal what I see in there. If I do not see, I do not risk breaking that oath, either accidentally or under duress." She smiled up at him. "Also, I will be less tempted to break in here later to steal it all."

"Ha! Fair enough." Max motioned for Redmane to follow her out, then stepped out himself and closed the door. "We can check it out later. For now, let's get you paid and back to the guild to turn in your quest, or work order, or whatever. As soon as you're back here, we'll get you set up in some quarters. The others should be back anytime now, and I'll fill you in on what's been happening when I tell them."

"Thank you, Majesty." Nessa bowed her head. They walked her back to the portal, and Redmane activated it for her.

As he turned around, Redmane cleared his throat. "So, I take it you've met miss Nessa before?"

Max froze midstep, turning back to the dwarf. "Did we not tell you she was with us when we claimed the temple?"

"You did not, Max." the dwarf's tone was half amused, half scolding.

"Oh, well let me tell you the story while we go through the stacks on my desk."

*****

Lagrass awoke in his makeshift bed in the same tavern basement where he'd first awakened in this new world. After killing the rats that attacked him, barely surviving the fight, he'd stumbled upstairs in his canvas diaper, torn and bleeding, and run into the innkeeper. After some initial yelling, and a little help from the increased *Charisma* that Loki had gifted him, he'd struck a bargain with the woman. He could sleep in the cellar, and would receive one meal per day, if he continued to eliminate the rats down there. She even gave him a repeatable quest; for

355

every ten rat tails he turned in, he'd get some experience and a bonus meal. That quest had helped him reach level two, and put enough food in his belly that he didn't starve. After the second quest turn-in, she handed him an old kitchen knife to help with his extermination mission.

He had stolen some clothes and linens from laundry lines in various places, enabling him to walk the city without turning too many heads. He'd pushed three crates together in a back corner of the cellar, behind a stack of barrels, and laid out the stolen blankets as a sort of bedroll. Except for the one he rolled up to use as a pillow.

When he tired of killing rats, Lagrass began to prowl the streets and alleys at night. He kept his dull kitchen knife tucked up in his sleeve, and a smile on his face for everyone he met. His first big opportunity came around midnight of his sixth day, when he turned into an alley and found a bruiser of a man who was throttling a beggar boy of about fourteen years of age. Two of the boy's younger friends were trying futilely to loosen the man's grip, both of them shouting.

"I'll teach ya to hold out on me, you little thief!" The man growled, lifting the boy by his neck and shaking him. "Now, turn over what you've hidden, and I'll let you live."

Lagrass wasted no time, dropping the knife from his sleeve into his palm and gripping the hilt tightly as he walked up behind the man. With no warning, he plunged the blade into his lower back, aiming for a kidney. The man screamed in pain and dropped the boy, but Lagrass barely noticed. He yanked loose the knife and plunged it in again and again, as rapidly as he could.

Though he'd worked a desk when he died on Earth, he'd started as a soldier just like the rest of the mercenaries in his unit. He knew how to kill quietly and efficiently, and he knew how to make it as painful as possible.

Critical Hit! Striking a distracted opponent in the back! +50% damage!

Critical Hit! Striking a distracted opponent in a vital organ! +50% damage!

Lagrass ignored the notifications, and the horrified stares of the three boys, as he continued to plunge the blade into the already dead man's body. In his mind, he saw the faces of Blake and Storm, mocking him and laughing at his current circumstances.

Finally, a shout from a guard patrol broke him out of his trance, and he looked down to see the bloody mess he created. He quickly touched the mutilated corpse with his free hand to loot it, then dashed away. The terrified boys stood frozen until the guards arrived, and Lagrass heard them say to the guards. "Dolby there was killing Aaron, choking him and smashin his head against the wall. That fella saved him, stabbed Dolby in the back. But then he... just kept stabbing." The last thing Lagrass heard before he got out of earshot was the sound of someone puking.

That had been why he'd been running from the guards. They'd hunted him for an hour before he managed to evade them and get over the city's outer wall. He'd stumbled the short distance to the river and dunked himself in the cold water, washing away the blood and bits of Dolby that covered him. Then he'd crawled under a thick shrub on the riverbank and shivered himself to sleep.

In the morning, when the sun had dried and warmed him a bit, he'd walked downriver a ways, then hitched a ride on a farmer's wagon. He'd given the farmer one of the silver coins he'd looted from Dolby to let him ride along into the city. Lagrass was sweating by the time they reached the gate, worried that the guards might already have his description. But the gatekeepers barely glanced at him, just greeted the farmer by name and waved him through.

As soon as he was back inside the city, he leapt off the wagon and made his way via back alleys and side streets to his cellar shelter. This was his second day hiding in the cellar, eighth day on-world. He'd only left the cellar to go up to the kitchen and scarf down his daily meal, and ask the innkeeper if anyone had been by asking for him. No stranger to customers of questionable morals, she quickly realized he was wanted by the guards. After extorting another of Dolby's silver coins from him, she promised to keep his whereabouts to herself, and to send his meals down to him if he preferred not to show his face. She didn't even mention the announcement of a reward on his head.

Tired of being closed in, Lagrass decided to venture out into the night. He'd attained level three after murdering Dolby, and increased his knife skill by two points. After

358

quickly taking care of three more rats that dared intrude upon his domain, he made his way upstairs and out the back door of the kitchen. He wasn't three steps down the alley when the innkeeper stuck her head out and shouted, "Here! Guards! He's here!"

Lagrass cursed to himself, already hearing running footsteps ahead of him at the end of the alley. He quickly turned and dashed back toward the kitchen door, which the innkeeper attempted to slam in his face. He was faster, lashing out with his blade, stabbing the woman just under her sternum, angling the blade up into her heart. He shoved her lifeless body aside, looting it even as she fell, then slammed and bolted the door behind him. Rushing through the kitchen, bloody blade still in hand, he burst into the common room and out the front door, the shouts of staff, customers, and guards following him as he ran. His heart pounded, sweat dripping from his nose as he dashed down one alley after another. He saw a sewer grate and tried to pull it free so he could hide in the tunnels, but he didn't have the strength to move it. He had to abandon the effort when he heard the shouts of guards nearby, coordinating their search pattern. The guards were all much higher level than he was, stronger and faster, with the stamina to run all day. Lagrass was a noob, weak and slow, and already tiring fast.

He stumbled over a passed out drunk in the next alley, cursing as he skinned his hands on the cobblestones, a minus five in red drifting across his vision. Angry, he equipped his knife and stabbed the unconscious man through the heart, receiving another critical hit notification, an instant kill, and reaching level four. He quickly looted the drunk, then pulled off his ratty jacket to cover the blood stains on his shirt from stabbing the innkeeper. After a quick look at the man's boots, he took those too. They were too big for him, but he could stuff some cloth in the toes. Where he was going, it was better than being barefoot.

Another thirty minutes of dodging the guards, and he reached the outer wall. Several homes were built right up against the inner face of the wall, a tactical mistake as far as Lagrass was concerned, but one he was grateful for. He used an empty crate to boost himself up to the roof of a warehouse, and from there went up and over the wall. One of the guards stationed fifty paces down the parapet spotted him, and shouted. But Lagrass was already gone, dropping the twenty feet and rolling when he hit, then dashing off toward the river. Wasting no time, he dove into the water and began swimming as fast as he could downstream.

Five minutes later, as he was getting tired, guards on horseback and carrying torches came galloping down the riverbank. Lagrass took several deep breaths, filling his lungs with oxygen, then ducked down under the water and relaxed, letting the river's current move him. He stayed under as long as he could, nearly a minute, then surfaced just long enough for another breath. He kept at this for an hour, until he no longer saw the light of torches through the water. Surfacing for good, he rolled over onto his back and simply floated downstream until the sky began to lighten.

Chapter 18

When Dalia and Smitty finally returned, they
brought bad news. The Blooded were still not yet ready to
become citizens of Stormhaven. They were willing to
enter into an alliance, and establish trade, which Max
supposed was a good start. Picklet had returned with
Dalia, the two of them not even trying anymore to hide the
blossoming relationship between them.

As it turned out, Dylan had been in Stormhaven the
entire time, learning from the minotaur enchanter as he help
him set up shop. Though Max certainly could have used
his help at Deepcrag, he considered the ogre's time well
spent on learning to enchant.

"Has he made any progress on the project I gave
him?" Max purposely didn't state out loud what it was, and
Dylan took the hint. "A little. He's working to combine
some other enchantments that he's already used, and it
involves a lot of trial and error." The ogre shrugged. "He
estimates it'll be a few more weeks, at least."

Max didn't complain. If it was something that was
easy to do, someone surely would have done it by now.
Besides, he could wait. The plan was to work on finding a
way to cleanse the heart of the mountain stone, which Max
expected would involve a lot of research, and waiting
around.

Still, since everyone was back home, he gathered
his party, including Nessa, Redmane, and Spellslinger, in

his informal meeting room. They sat around a long table with refreshments set in the center, drinking and nibbling on sandwiches as Max relayed his entire adventures through the portals. Redmane had administered an oath to Nessa the day before, as soon as she returned through the portal. She'd leveled up, and learned a few assassin skills for completing her contract. Max was surprised when Redmane had included a statement in her oath that ensured she had sworn no contradictory oaths to the two guilds she'd worked with. It hadn't occurred to him that she might be a plant from one or the other, and the fact that he'd missed it bothered him.

He amused himself by watching the faces of his friends as he revealed some of the more exciting details. Of all of them, only Redmane had heard it all, and of course Red had experienced it with him. She kept quiet, sitting atop a pile of sandwiches as Max spoke, still invisible to Nessa, Redmane, and old Puckerface.

As Max reached the part where he killed the lich and retrieved the stone, Dylan laughed aloud. "I was wondering why I got a quest completion and leveled up all of a sudden. I was carrying a stack of materials for Erdun, nearly stumbled and dropped them all." Smitty and Dalia nodded, having had similar experiences. Though Dalia didn't share it, she'd been about to kiss Picklet when she leveled up. It caused some confusion, and a little awkwardness.

When he'd finished the story with Nessa unlocking all the boxes before they left the vault, Smitty jumped to his feet. "Whaaat? Are you kidding me? Chests and crates full of loot, and you just left without checking? That's... you... you're not human, boss!" Dylan nodded his head, emphatically agreeing. "We need to go down there *right now!*"

Smitty was headed for the door, and Dylan was getting to his feet, when Max called them back. "Hold on, hold on. We'll head down there next. But we've got some things to discuss." First, Max invited them all to a party and shared the new quest with all of them that didn't have it. It was faster than sharing it individually. Then he looked at Redmane and Spellslinger. "Any thoughts yet on how we cleanse the stone?"

Spellslinger shook his head, answering first. "Not yet. Our tried and true method fer banishing a lich from a stone be to simply smash it with a hammer. Simple, effective, but not helpful for yer purposes."

"I doubt it would work in any case." Redmane added. "The Heart o' the Mountain be no simple crystal. It were formed under the weight of a mountain, imbued with the ancient power o' the earth, and possesses the strength o' the mountain herself. No simple hammer bash would even scratch it."

"Right. Smashing is off the list. Thanks for that." Max's voice dripped sarcasm.

Redmane continued. "I met with Ironhand, and he's ordered his scholars to do a quiet search o' the library. He also summoned the Grand Master Enchanter, Master Crystalsinger, from his cousin's city. It'll take another day or so for him to arrive."

363

Dylan piped up. "I'll ask Master Erdun, on the off chance he has an idea. I won't share the information about the gem being the heart of the mountain, just that we want to banish the lich without damaging its crystal."

Max looked around the table, but nobody else had anything to offer. "Alright, it sounds like this might take a while. Which I suppose is what you'd expect of an epic quest line. If it were too easy, it wouldn't be epic, would it?" He thumped the table. "So while we wait, let's make the most of our time here in the city. Dylan, I suggest you go back and help Erdun, continue to learn all you can. Dalia, your father and I have been crafting health potions like crazy. If you'd like to help? He can fill you in on the details. Nessa, there's supposed to be a hidden door somewhere here in the keep that leads to a ritual room. At least, if we believe the lich. I'd like you to see if you can locate it? And, Smitty... didn't you mention something on the trip here with Gr'tok and his people about marrying that lady orc you brought with you? I think it's about time we made that happen." He grinned at his corporal, expecting him to cringe.

Instead, Smitty surprised him. "Great idea, boss! You can marry us, and we'll have a party!"

Slightly disappointed, but happy for his friend, Max smiled. "Okay you guys figure out the details, and tell me where and when. In the meantime, unless anyone has anything else...?" When nobody spoke, he continued. "I suppose we should go check out the treasury before Smitty or Dylan's head explodes."

It turned out that the lich had been quite the packrat. There were bags and piles of coins, from copper to platinum, and another couple thousand of the heavy square silvers. Redmane and Spellslinger transferred them to the shelving with the coins from the banks as they found them, the chamberlain keeping an accurate accounting as they did so.

One of the larger chests had turned out to be a chest of holding, with one thousand storage slots. Max felt like jumping for joy, until Redmane informed him that it was mostly empty. Only a quarter of the slots were filled, and it was all weapons and armor. None of it matched any of the other pieces, and they surmised it was gear looted from adventurers that had fallen into the same trap that Max had. The good news was that it would let them arm another hundred or so soldiers, and provide at least a piece or two of armor for each. That combined with more gear found in other chests that was more uniform, likely belonging to the Deepcrag guard force, and their armory was going to receive quite a boost.

There were a few high quality weapons, rare and epic, that the party members claimed for themselves. Nessa claimed a black leather belt filled with throwing knives that looked like it had been crafted with her in mind. All sixteen daggers were enchanted to cause a bleed effect that was stackable with each hit.

Spellslinger claimed a gnarled wood staff that fit his personality perfectly. It had a plain looking blue crystal mounted at its top that initially seemed to be of little value, just +4 to *Wisdom*. But upon seeing it, the old dwarf mage cackled happily. "The crystal be a mana storage crystal. It'll hold five thousand mana!"

Redmane took a golden quill and ink set that offered an *Intelligence* boost of +5 just for having it sit on his desk. In addition, the inkwell magically refilled itself, and the quill always remained perfectly sharpened.

Dylan discovered a pair of elven boots that reformed to fit his giant feet when he claimed them. They added +10 to agility, and reduced his weight by half. They were meant to help an elven ranger dance through the tree branches, but for the massive ogre, they were a true blessing. "With these, I can walk faster and not get tired!" Max thought it would make things easier on whatever mount they eventually found for the ogre, but kept that to himself.

Dalia found an epic quality healing wand that contained ten charges of a light magic spell that would heal one thousand points instantly. While the potions they were making could heal more, they were slower to use, and slower to act. The wand might save a life in a critical moment. She also found a leather helm with raven's wings on the sides above the ears, which had no bonus attributes, but that she quite liked.

Smitty claimed a quiver full of metal arrows much like the ones that Max had purchased from Fitchstone. The metal not only accepted his archer's skill enchantments more easily, but actually amplified the effects by twenty percent. There was also a bow that matched the quiver, but it wasn't as nice as Smitty's Bow of Shootyness that was crafted by Regin. Still, he stuck it in his inventory as a backup, just in case.

Max hadn't planned to claim anything for himself, happy with the gear that Regin had crafted or upgraded for him. Until Dalia removed an item from one of the last crates that he couldn't resist. It was a pair of enchanted bracers that would go a long way toward easing his mind regarding one particular issue.

Bracers of Dire Winter
Item Quality: Rare
Attributes: +50 Armor, Wisdom +10, Intelligence +5

Enchantment: Frost Cone
When activated by wearer, these braces will each produce a cone of ice crystals that will reach up to twenty feet. This spell can be channeled at a cost of 20mps per bracer.
In addition, the wearer receives a forty percent resistance to fire and fire magic.

Max beamed at the dwarfess after he'd read the description. "Forty percent fire resistance? Yes, please!" He removed his bracers and replaced them on the spot, holding them up for everyone to admire. They seemed to glow faintly with a blue-ish white light.

As they were finishing up, Teeglin came running into the vault. "Master Redmane! There's a problem in the kitchen! The chef told me…" Her voice drifted off as she took in the piles of money and loot. "Wow!"

"What did the chef tell you, lass?" Redmane nudged her.

"What? Oh, one of the barrels of pork sprung a leak, and the meat went bad. He said to ask you to order more…" She drifted off again, her gaze fixed on a nearby belt with a sheathed dagger. It was a simple weapon with small *Agility* and *Dexterity* bonuses. Max picked it up and handed it to her. "In case m'lady needs to help defend the castle."

"For me?" The little dworc's bottom lip trembled. "Thank you King Max!" She hugged the belt and weapon tightly to her chest. Dylan cleared his throat, and handed her a medallion he'd been eyeing for himself. It offered +10 to *Constitution*, which would bring a nice health boost to the little girl.

"Here, this will help to protect you while you protect us."

The girl leapt up into Dylans arms, surprising him so that he barely managed to catch her. Throwing her own arms around his neck, she gave him a kiss on the cheek. "If I wasn't going to marry King Max when I get bigger, I would choose YOU!"

Blushing, the ogre gave her a gentle squeeze before setting her down. She thanked them both again and rushed from the room even faster than she'd entered, already feeling the *Agility* boost.

Smitty snorted. "Who knew? The way to a young lady's heart is jewelry and knock-knock jokes!"

"Shut it, greeny." Dylan retorted, still blushing. "Aren't you about to get married? Maybe you should find something in this pile for your girl?"

"Oh, right." Smitty was suddenly serious. "Good idea. Is that okay, boss?"

Max kept his face blank, barely looking at the corporal's face. "I'll just deduct it from your pay."

Smitty balked for a second, hunching his head down between his shoulders as he calculated the likely value of something in this treasure pile. The others watched him, waiting...

"Hey, what pay? Are we supposed to be getting paid for this?" He looked up at Max, who burst out laughing. The others joined in, including Smitty himself. "Good one, boss."

*****

The party spent a full week going about the business of improving their skills, assisting the citizens of Stormhaven, or in Smitty's case, getting married. Max presided over the ceremony, which consisted of a few quick vows and a pronouncement. There was a big party, during which Dylan got drunk and showed off more of his dance moves. Picklet, not realizing how bad they were, joined in and did his best to imitate the ogre, which encouraged several drunken dwarves and orcs to join in. Seeing that he had a crowd, Dylan started teaching them the electric slide, even getting Dalia, Teeglin, Smitty and his new bride in on the action. Which was about the time Max snuck away to get some sleep.

Max, Dalia, and her father completed the thousand health potions, with the two younger alchemists leveling up their skills several times. Max also had a couple more lessons from Oakstone, learning the finer points of forging with steel. By the end of the week, Dylan, Smitty, Dalia, and Max all had their dragonscale chest pieces delivered. They featured a jaw-dropping +500 armor, plus ten percent resistances to all elemental magic. The pieces were lightweight and flexible, and though Dalia was very complimentary of the work, she declined hers in favor of Regin's gift, as Steelbender had predicted. Instead, the old smith refitted it for Nessa, who was thrilled by the magical gear.

Steelbender also presented an awestruck Smitty with his sword, a mithril-edged blade like Max's with +10 Agility, +10 Endurance, and an enchantment called *Creep* that let him move in absolute silence, at half his normal speed. Thrilled with the name as much as the effect, Smitty tried to hug the smith, who nearly punched him in the gut when he approached. They settled on a firm handshake, and Smitty's declaration of undying gratitude.

Despite all efforts, none of them had found a viable way to cleanse the lich's soul from the stone. Max asked Redmane and Spellslinger to continue their efforts while he took the party out for some additional exploring and leveling. His plan was to take the portal to Deepcrag, check on how things were going there, then visit the other two settlements to see what holdings he'd ended up with.

While they were out, they could battle whatever denizens of the underground they encountered.

The afternoon before they planned to leave, Max visited the bakery just outside the inner gate. The baker's nephew had set up his shop, which had become among the most popular spots in the city. He'd hired a young orc and two goblins to help him increase production, and still was often sold out by mid-afternoon each day.

Max was happily cleaning out the remaining inventory, when the bell on the shop's door rang behind him. He turned to see a gnome with strawberry red hair entering the shop. "I'm sorry, but I'm afraid I've just cleaned out the inventory." Max apologized, then held out a couple of apple cinnamon pastries. "Here, these are for your trouble. I'm sure he'll have more for you first thing in the morning."

The gnome silently accepted the gifts, then looked up at Max, tilting his head way back in order to meet his eyes. "Maximilian Storm? The Chimera King?"

Max nodded. "And you are?" Max used *Identify* on the gnome and saw the name "Undertall", which made him smirk, but didn't sound familiar.

The gnome took a step back, spreading his arms wide, and grinning just as widely. "What? You don't recognize your old buddy? Wolf three, reporting for duty!" The gnome came to attention and snapped a sharp salute.

Max blinked in confusion for a second, then his jaw dropped. "Blake? Blake! Holy shit am I glad to see you!"

Max dropped to one knee and shook the gnome's hand, then pulled him in for a bro hug.

"Easy there, boss! Don't crush me!" the corporal complained. Max let him go immediately, sitting down right in the middle of the baker's shop to be closer to eye level with Blake.

"A gnome?" Max chuckled. On Earth, Blake had been one of the largest humans Max had ever met. At six foot six and two hundred eighty pounds of wide shoulders and pure muscle, they often joked that the man could flip an APC if it pissed him off.

Blake shrugged. "What can I say? I usually played a tank or bard with the fellas. It just sort of seemed natural, yaknow?" Max did know. He'd heard the corporal pretending to sing some nonsense bard spells during their games. Even one where he attempted to seduce a dragon. And Blake often sang at night when they were outside the wire. He had a voice that could have made him a lot of money as a singer.

"But when I died, and they let me choose my new body... the gnome just called to me. And I'm a squishy caster, too!" He grinned at Max. "Level twenty already. I spawned in a gnome city that was under attack by grey dwarves. The battle lasted for weeks, and I ran fetch quests, crafted, and took low level mage guild quests inside the city until I was strong enough to stand on the walls and fight. We repelled attack after attack, and I had a quest for each one. Talk about power leveling!"

"Awesome!" Max fist-bumped the gnome, his tiny fist barely the size of Max's thumb. "How'd you find me here?"

"I went to the palace, and the dwarf with the white hair told me to try this bakery." Blake deadpanned.

"Har har." Max shook his head. "How did you find Stormhaven?"

"Wasn't that hard. I saw the notification when you became king. The gnome city has a portal, but they charge friggin fifty gold to use it, unless you're on city or guild business. I did a bunch of quests that paid me a few silvers here and there, and raised my rep with the guild, but it was taking forever to earn gold. Finally I saw a quest on the board at the mages' guild for apprentices willing to work to recharge the mage lights in Stormhaven. It's considered a shit job, and apparently nobody wanted it. But I snatched it up, and the guild paid for me to take the portals here."

Max couldn't help but smile. One of those unintended consequences of his Sovereign class that Red had mentioned. He'd made the decision to hire the guild to light up his city in order to make things better for his people, and that choice had brought him one of his closest friends. Wolf three had been with Max when they had both served their country, and made the transition to being private soldiers with him.

"I tried to carry you out after you got hit." Max said, preparing to apologize for getting Blake killed. "Dylan and I were running you to the rear, and you took a round in the back. Then a mortar took out Dylan and I a few seconds later. I'm sorry, man."

The gnome's eyes became fierce. "You saved me, boss. I did take a round to the back, but my back plate mostly stopped it. And you protected me from the mortar round, though my legs got torn up a bit. When I woke up, the medics were workin' on me, and there wasn't much left of you, or anybody else." He paused and took a deep breath.

"They medivac'd me out. I lost a lot of blood, and was in pretty bad shape. My arm was toast, and the round to my helmet rung my bell pretty good. But the moment we landed at base camp, I ditched the medics long enough to put a few rounds into that asshat Lagrass." His face was grim. "He totally set us up for that ambush. I saw it on his face. Before I shot it off."

"Hell yeah!" Max pumped a fist in the air. "One of my biggest regrets has been not being able to make him pay for that. Our whole unit, wiped out…" Max shook his head. "So, what? Did they put you in front of a firing squad? How are you here?"

"Nah, it took all I had to get to that shitstain's office and put him down. After that I just blacked out. The next thing I know I'm doing the whole reincarnation or Valhalla thing."

"Well I'm damn glad you chose to come here, corporal! And I've got some good news. Dylan and Smitty are here, too! Wait till you see them." Max got to his feet. "In fact, let's go find them right now! We were about to leave to do some exploring and grinding in the morning. You want to join us?"

"Hell yes!" Blake grinned, following Max out of the shop and through the inner gate. The moment they reached the courtyard, Max tilted his head up and roared, "Corporal Dylan! Corporal Smithfield! Report!"

Blake chuckled as they waited, watching the doors of the palace. His eyes widened when Smitty came sprinting out, half dressed, struggling to pull on pants as he moved. Max smacked his forehead and looked down at Blake. "Shit, I forgot. Smitty's a newlywed, still on his honeymoon."

Blake's mouth dropped open when Dylan came charging out in his massive ogre form. He came to a thundering stop in front of Max, shield and axe in hand, looking around. "What's wrong, boss? We under attack?"

Blake shook his head. "Sheesh. You slip into a gnome body and nobody recognizes their long lost brother war dog!"

Both corporals froze, looking down at the gnome. Max chuckled as he watched them struggle to identify him. "Gentlemen, Wolf three has rejoined the pack!"

"Holy shit! Blake!" Dylan reached down and scooped up the gnome, tossing him into the air like a toddler. "Damn man, look at you!"

Smitty, smiling widely, was more circumspect. "Dude. A gnome? Your whole body is now smaller than your pecker was on Earth!"

"Heh." Blake laughed, despite being tossed upward again by the ogre. "Biggunz? That's classic, my man!" When Dylan caught him and was about to throw him again, he added, "Dylan if you throw me again I'm gonna piss all over you."

The ogre halted mid-throw, then gently set Blake on his feet. Sounding slightly hurt, he said "Sorry, man. I was just really glad you're here."

Blake walked over and patted the ogre on the knee, which was as high as he could reach. "I know, big fella. I feel the same. Been hoping more than just Max chose to be here."

"Okay, enough lollygagging around here wasting time!" Smitty pointed in the general direction of the tavern. "We've got some drinkin' and catching up to do!"

Dylan looked down at Blake, holding out is hands as if to a child. "Wanna ride on my shoulder?"

"I will cut you." Blake backed away. A blade appeared in his hand as if from nowhere.

"Cool! How'd you do that? Do it again!" Smitty began walking backwards, watching.

Blake made the knife disappear, then reappear. "It's a spell I learned, called *Conjured Blade*. I can make it appear out of thin air, anywhere within ten feet of me." The knife disappeared, then reappeared an inch from Dylan's nose, making the ogre go cross-eyed. A moment later it disappeared again, and reappeared behind him, poking him in the butt.

"Okay, okay! I get it. You can walk. Sheesh." Dylan grinned at the little gnome. "Small stature, big temper."

"And don't you forget it!" Blake recalled the knife and followed Smitty out the gate.

Chapter 19

Morning came way to early for the Battleborne among Max's party. They had left the tavern late, the proprietor keeping it open past normal closing time for the king and his friends. They had stumbled back into the palace, Blake riding atop Dylan's shoulder, and fallen asleep on the floor in Max's study. The thick carpet was more comfortable than a lot of places they'd all slept. Even Max had managed to get drunk, despite his genetic gifts.

They were awakened by the door slamming open, and a bright, cheerful Teeglin rushing into the room. "King Max! Knock knock!"

"What?" Max shook his head, his mind and his tongue both fuzzy.

"Nooo! You're supposed to say, 'who's there?' after I say knock knock!"

"Who?" Max stared at the little girl.

Teeglin looked at Dylan, who was sitting with his eyes closed, taking deep breaths. "Dylan, did you not teach King Max about knock knock jokes?" This caused all four soldiers to chuckle.

Max took a deep breath. "Okay, sorry Teeglin. Just woke up, and I wasn't ready. Try again."

"Knock knock!"

"Who's there?"

"It's me! Teeglin!" The little girl clapped her hands and hopped once in excitement.

Max opened his mouth, then shut it again. He was trying to decide if he'd missed something, when Smitty swooped in. "That was a very good try, little princess. But we need to work on our knock knocks a little bit." He picked her up and carried her out of the room, quietly trying to explain where she went wrong.

Max exhaled, collapsing back onto the carpet. "I thought for a minute there she outsmarted me."

This got a snort from Blake, and a groan from Dylan. Red appeared on his chest, and asked, "Did she not do it right? These knock knock things seem complicated."

Dylan and Max howled with laughter, holding their heads as Blake hopped to his feet, pointing at Red. "Who's that?"

"Oh, shit. Blake, meet Red. She's a leprechaun, and soulbound to me as my guide. Nobody but us and Dalia can see her, so please don't react to her shenanigans in public. Which reminds me, I suppose we should let Nessa know about you, too. And Redmane."

"What about Redmane?" The dwarf asked, walking into the room and frowning over his king lounging on the floor.

"Redmane. Uhm, there's somebody we'd like you to meet. Her name is Red, and she's a leprechaun. She's been with me from day one, as my guide here on this world, and has been invisible to everyone but us

Battleborne. With my recent level increases, she can now make herself visible to a select few. I'd appreciate it if you'd keep her existence a secret."

Red appeared in the air a couple feet in front of Redmane, who leaned back for a moment, then smiled. "That actually explains a lot, Max. My fellow councilors and I, along with the guard captains, were wondering if you were fully sane. You've been seen quite a bit talking quietly to yourself, or staring off at odd directions and appearing to be listening to something."

"Ha!" Dylan managed to get to his feet, if a bit unsteadily. "I can attest that Max is definitely not quite sane."

"I second that." Blake added. "And always nice to meet a fellow redhead, Red." He grinned at her.

Redmane looked at Max's condition, then those of the others. "I take it ye celebrated the arrival o' corporal Blake last night?"

"We did." Max grinned. "Please extend my apologies to the tavern owner, whose name I can't seem to recall right now. We kept him up past his bedtime, and I probably forgot to pay him."

"Do you still intend to travel to Deepcrag today?" Redmane's voice was full of judgement. After all, dwarves could drink all night, then hop up and fight all day with no sleep.

"We do." Max nodded his head, then regretted it. "Possibly a little later than we originally planned. Could you... escort Blake down to the treasury and help him pick out some useful gear? I'm going to go wash my face, possibly throw up."

"As you wish, sire." Again, more judgement. Max tried to detect whether his chamberlain was just messing with him, but simply didn't have the brainpower right then.

An hour later the party was assembled in front of the portal. Dalia and Nessa had been ready and waiting impatiently at their original appointed time. Max completely threw Blake under the buss. "My apologies ladies, another of my corporals showed up last night, and I'm afraid he's a bit of a drinker. Wasn't fit for polite company until just now." He winked at the two ladies, grinning shamelessly.

Blake bowed to them, a little unsteady as he straightened up. "I'm Blake, nice to meet you both. Max told me all about you last night, though he was pretty drunk, so I'm not sure any of it was true."

Dalia snorted. "Ha! If ye managed to get Max drunk, I think we'll get along just fine." Nessa merely nodded her head in acknowledgement of the greeting.

Introductions made, Max moved to the portal and dialed up Deepcrag. They all passed through the portal, Teeglin and Redmane waving at the them as it closed.

Max led them to the guard room, and was pleased to see that the merchants hadn't looted the dozen chests there. He pointed them out to Nessa, who quickly unlocked them one after another, leaving Smitty and the others to open them.

The loot was disappointing. There were a few silver coins, even fewer gold. Lots of personal items like clothes, carved figurines, belt knives, and the like. Nothing worth carrying away. They left the items where they were, closing but not locking the trunks. Anyone desperate enough to take those items was welcome to them. They briefly explored the room behind the hidden door, but it was nothing but a storage room filled with broken crates shattered glass.

Max then led them down the long corridor to Deepcrag. Here they found some signs of life. Twenty guards were either patrolling or resting at two locations. The dark elf had apparently found his family's old home and claimed it, a large three story home with a small courtyard behind a wall with a pedestrian gate. And they'd claimed a medium sized warehouse near the outer wall, just as they'd promised. Dylan took a moment to question one of the guards, who informed them that the main group was currently in the gnome settlement.

They explored the city a bit, walking the empty streets, sticking their noses into doorways here and there. The fact that it had last been a human-run settlement meant that they could read what few signs still remained on the buildings. After an hour of touring, they made their way into the inner keep, and the palace. They all exclaimed over the size of the hole in the entry floor, then spread out to explore the rest of the castle. Like every other building, the palace had been fully looted long ago. The rooms were empty, the walls bare.

While they explored, Redmane had organized and sent through the portal a force of fifty guards, mostly orc volunteers. There was some tension from the merchant guards when the orcs marched across the bridge, but they quickly figured things out. Max greeted them at the palace doors, and invited them in. "For now, you'll all stay here at the palace. I'd like at least three guards on this hole at all times." He pointed at the floor. "If whatever made this comes back, don't try to fight it. Just shout really loud to warn everyone, and get out of the way."

This earned him some laughter from the guards, one of whom was Lo'tang from the arena. "Lo'tang, I'm glad to see you again. Are you leading this bunch?"

"I am, King Max." Max was glad to hear he'd dropped the chimera king title. "And I have a few questions."

"Shoot." Max replied, then when he saw the confused looks on the orcs faces, he amended it to "Go ahead."

"How long will we be here?"

"Well, a week or so, at least. I'm planning to build this place up just like Stormhaven, but it will take time to recruit new residents. Especially since I haven't yet filled my capitol city." Max paused. "Of course, any of you who'd like to settle here are welcome to do so."

"Could we bring our families if we settle here?"

"Lo'tang, do you believe I would force you to separate from your family for more than a short tour of duty?"

"No, King Max. But it is best to ask, rather than assume." Max couldn't argue with that.

"Your families are welcome to join you wherever you choose to settle. If you decide to bring them here, and see a house or apartment that you like, I happen to know the landlord." He winked at Lo'tang.

"Thank you, King Max. What are our orders?"

"Close the gates, defend this place against any hostile visitors. If you need them the merchant guards are required to help you fight. If you can't hold, send a runner back through the portal. And if absolutely necessary, you can retreat down this hole and find a place to wait for us to find you."

"We brought two weeks' rations, will that be enough?" Lo'tang patted his belt pouch, which was a storage device.

"We'll be back in a week, maybe a little more. If you begin to run low on supplies, send someone to Stormhaven for more. In fact…" Max pulled out a sheet of parchment and a quill set. Sitting on a step, he wrote a quick note to Redmane. "We might as well start bringing through volunteers and supplies." He looked up at Dalia. "Give me your portal key, please?"

"Not necessary, King Max. Redmane gave me this. It works only between this portal and Stormhaven." Lo'tang held up a portal key.

"Ah, good." Max handed him the note. "Send someone back with this. Keep an eye on things here. If the merchant guards misbehave, straighten them out. Same goes for any new residents who show up." Max looked at the imposing orc warriors around him. "Any of you who wish to send messages to your families, send them with the runner. They can be forwarded on to wherever they are. I've requested some cots and other basic furniture, but until it arrives I'm afraid you'll have to sleep on the floors."

His business in Deepcrag handled, Max led the others out of the city. They headed in the direction of the gnome settlement. The merchant's guard had pointed them in the right direction, a tunnel exiting the main cavern to the north. The group set off at a jog, not wanting to take a whole day reaching their destination. With his new boots, Dylan was surprisingly able to keep the pace for quite a while before his endurance flagged. Likewise, Blake surprised everyone, his tiny gnomish legs pumping away under his robe. Even with stops every half hour for their less agile party members to catch their breath and recover, they made very good time.

Once in the tunnel they were able to follow the tracks of several wagons that the merchants had brought along. Nessa took one sniff of a pile of boar droppings they encountered, and declared the merchant caravan to be three days ahead of them. Max was hoping to catch them before they finished their business in the town and returned.

Though the caravan ahead of them had clearly faced some battles, as evidenced by the dried blood spatter they occasionally encountered, Max and his party only ran into two fights. The first was a large rock spider the size of an Earth SUV, which they came upon as it fed on a freshly killed kobold.

> *Rock Spider*
> *Level 30*
> *Health: 3,200/3,500*

Blake had taken the first action, not even slowing down as he cast a flame spell at the spider. Instead of a fireball, there was a sort of lightning bolt made of fire that descended from the tunnel ceiling onto the spider's back. All the tiny hairs on its body caught fire, and the creature screeched as it turned to retreat. Rock spiders were ambush predators, and not prone to stand and fight when wounded. Arrows from both Max and Smitty slammed into its side, disappearing completely into its body.

Dylan activated an ability and rushed forward, slamming into the spider and knocking it off balance. Two knives flashed from Nessa's hands, each one slamming into a leg joint on the two closest legs. The limbs went limp below those joints, and the spider staggered. A chop from Dylan's axe, and a third leg was severed.

Blake, giggling madly in his little gnome voice, waved his hands in an intricate pattern that took three seconds to complete. When he was done, a blade of air shot past to Dylan's right, not quite severing a leg, but knocking two of them aside so that the spider's body slammed into the floor.

Without making a sound, Nessa leapt up onto the smoking spider's back and produced two long daggers from sheaths on her hips. Raising them over her head, she slammed them into the joint between the spider's head and abdomen segments. The screeching came to an abrupt halt, and the legs stopped flailing. Of the group members, only Blake leveled up. They looted the corpse, Dalia and Smitty harvested the tasty meat, and they moved on.

Max let them walk this time, figuring they'd made up enough ground that they'd arrive at the gnome town late in the afternoon. He caught up to Blake, who was walking with Dalia in the middle of the pack. "Nice work back there. It'll be handy to have more offensive magic."

"Thanks, boss. I learned a lot from the guild between the battles. And the grey dwarves just threw themselves at us like they were suicidal. All of my combat spells are level five or higher already. That *Fire Strike* spell is level ten."

"Yeah, about that." Max looked sideways at the little caster. "I may not have mentioned this last night, but my troll heritage makes my blood susceptible to fire."

"What?" Blake looked up at him.

"He's basically a walking, talking, napalm grenade." Smitty helpfully offered. "If you cut him and light him on fire… boom!"

"Oh, shit. That would have been a good bit of intel to have, boss." Blake scolded.

"Yeah, I was distracted. So, the fire spell is awesome, just be a little careful if I'm all up close and stabby with the bad guys, right?"

"Roger that, boss. And… if it helps, I have a water spell, too. In case, you know, you catch fire. Maybe I can't hose you down before you explode."

Both Dylan and Smitty snorted at that. Dylan covered his mouth and coughed to disguise the word "Phrasing!", making Smitty chuckle.

Blake shook his head. "Damn, I missed you idiots."

Max asked, "What was that hand motion you did before you hit the spider's legs?"

"Oh, that." Blake looked at his feet for a moment. "That's the way the guild taught me to cast spells. Some require hand motions, some a keyword or incantation. It's a real pain in the ass." He paused, then looked up. "I've figured out that once I've leveled the spell up a bit, when it's solidified in my mind, I can skip all that. Like my *Fire Strike* spell. I used to have to say '*Heat of the sun, burn my foes, Fire Strike!*' which was too slow, and frankly corny. Now I just think it, and it happens."

"Aye, the guild be very formal in its instruction. Ye really don't need any o' that to cast yer spells, as ye've discovered. At most, a trigger word is required, like with Max's explodey spell. The whole show just be how them

388

snooty guild mages impress those without magic, and justify their fees fer teachin' ye."

As they walked, Red made an appearance on Max's shoulder. Remembering that he'd wanted to make introductions, he called to Nessa. He gave her the same short speech he'd given Redmane, then Red revealed herself. In typically Nessa-like manner, the panthera simply nodded her head at Red, said, "Nice to meet you, Red." and resumed walking as if meeting a leprechaun was an everyday thing.

Their second encounter came an hour later, when they followed the wagon tracks into a massive cavern with a waterfall on one end and a pond near the center. Standing at the edge of the pond with its head down so that it could drink, was a giant lizard. Its skin was so black it shone with a sort of multicolor sheen in the light from Dalia's globe, which floated ahead of the group. About twenty feet long from nose to tail, it had short but powerful looking legs. Max cast *Examine* on it, then whistled when its stats came up. "Huge health pool at level twenty."

"The thing is the size of a bus." Dylan added, admiration in his voice.

Pteradon
Level 20
Health: 6,000/6,000

"Almost big enough for Dylan to ride." Blake added. The entire group turned toward him, staring. "What? What did I say?"

Max turned to Dalia. "You're a druid. Can we tame this thing and make it so Dylan can ride it?"

"It be possible to tame wild creatures, aye." Dalia looked at the lizard, doubt on her face. "It ain't my specialty, though. If it be aggressive, that makes it more likely to resist. Also, me spell only makes it more open to accepting a bond. I can't force it."

"How does one bond something like that?" Dylan asked, glancing back at the lizard.

"Well, in this case, I'd cast me spell, then you would have to approach it. Give it some food, sweet talk it…"

"Gaze into its eyes…" Blake grinned at the ogre.

"Aye, that'll help too." Dalia agreed, not realizing he'd been joking.

"Is there anything we can do to help with the bond?"

"Pteradon's be no laughing matter." Dalia warned. "This be the first one I've seen meself, but our miners and scouts run into them from time to time. Usually they be much bigger and older. They consider us food, and have no sense of self preservation like that spider. They'll fight to the death, and them jaws can crunch a fully armored dwarf into paste."

"So… this is just a baby one?" Smitty asked, taking in the size of the thing and shaking his head.

"Not a baby, no. More like… a youngster. Like Teeglin."

"You can name it Princess!" Smitty clapped the ogre on the back.

"Anyway…" Dalia glowered at the orc. "It might help me spell be more effective if it be weakened, stunned, or even unconscious. That way its natural resistance will be lower."

Blake nodded. "We've had games like this. Burn it down till its health is low, then tame it. We can totally do this!"

"Burn it down?" Dylan gasped. "Don't you hurt my baby!" he turned toward the lizard, taking several steps forward. "I'll handle this. Dalia, stay behind me. When I stun it, you cast your spell. If it doesn't work, then we'll do some damage and try again." He stared meaningfully at Blake. "As little damage as possible. Don't go burning it or slicing off parts!"

"This is so cool!" Smitty rubbed his hands together. "Dylan is totally getting his own Godzilla mount!"

Ignoring him, Dylan jogged forward, the others a dozen paces or so behind him. The noise of the party alerted the lizard, and it turned to face them, opening its mouth wide enough to swallow all but Dylan whole, and roared. Max and the others hesitated, the sound having some kind of debuff. But Dylan shook it off and charged forward. As soon as he was within range, Max cast

Confuse on the beast, and it hit just a couple seconds before Dylan shot forward and slammed his shield into its nose.

Dalia cast her spell as Dylan stood there, shield at the ready. He'd switched his off-hand weapon from his axe to a hammer, hoping to bonk the monster on the head and knock it out instead of cutting into it.

The combo of the stun, Max's spell, and Dalia's seemed to work. The lizards legs went weak, and it fell onto its belly. Its eyes were unfocused, and it wasn't lunging at the ogre right in front of its nose.

"Here, man! Feed it!" Smitty tossed the entire supply of rock spider meat he'd just harvested to his friend. Dylan gathered it up and set it directly in front of the lizard's mouth. He took a step back as he saw its eyes begin to focus, and began talking to it as he looked it in the eye.

"Gooood Princess. I brought you some meat. There you go, help yourself. I'm sorry about the sore nose, but I needed to get your attention. I'm Dylan, and we're gonna be best buddies. That's it, sniff the tasty rock spider. It's all yours, munch it right down. Much tastier than grisly ogre meat…"

Max clamped a hand over Smitty's mouth, as he could see the orc fighting to restrain himself. He didn't want a stray taunting comment to break the spell."

The lizard sniffed at the meat, then looked at Dylan. A moment later its tongue shot out faster than Max could follow, and the meat disappeared. It sniffed again, this time at Dylan. The entire party froze. If that tongue shot out again, the lizard's jaws could crunch their tank before any of them could do a thing.

"Nice Princess. That meat was tasty, right? You're welcome. How bout you and I be friends?" He stared into the lizards eyes, just three steps from its maw.

Smitty struggled in Max's grip, overcome by the urge to say something. He gave Max a pleading look, doing his best puppydog eyes.

Max tightened up and shook his head at the orc. He almost missed it when the tongue shot out again, straight at Dylan. But instead of grabbing him, it just lightly brushed his chest. Surprised, Dylan stopped speaking for a moment, and the lizard began to pull its head back.

"No, no... don't go, Princess. You just surprised me is all." Dylan slowly reached out his empty right hand, still speaking softly as if talking to a frightened horse. The lizard's head went back to resting on the floor, and it stared at the ogre.

All of a sudden Dylan went silent. His body went rigid, one hand just inches from the lizard's snout. The lizard's eyes unfocused again, and its tongue slipped out slightly to one side. The party held its breath as the two of them remained still for half a minute.

The lizard blinked, and Dylan exhaled. Its tongue shot out again, this time touching Dylan's hand, then it pushed its nose forward to nudge him in the chest. Not knowing its own strength, it knocked the ogre on his butt.

Max and the others stepped forward, and the moment Max removed his hand, Smitty cut loose. "Dude! I didn't mean you should *actually* name her Princess!"

"Princess is a he, and shut up! I could feel I needed to name him to bond him, and your stupid idea was the first thing that popped into my head." Dylan spoke quietly, stroking the lizard's head. Sensing his new master's hostility, it shot Smitty a threatening look, causing the orc to stop walking.

"Hey, uh… no offense, Princess. Good doggy! Lizard. Whatever." Smitty held both hands up while Dylan patted the lizard's head reassuringly.

"It'd be a good idea to feed it again soon, and every few hours for the next lil while, just to reinforce the bond." Dalia advised. She handed over some of the rock spider meat she'd harvested. "Give him a bit now, then more later."

"Open up, Princess." The ogre tank cooed at his giant carnivorous pet. The lizard obligingly opened its maw, and Dylan dropped some meat on its tongue. After swallowing the morsel, it made a rumbling sound deep in its chest and nudged Dylan again. More gently this time.

As Dylan cuddled with Princess, Blake's smile stretched from ear to ear. "Damn, I love this world. I mean… nothing like this could ever happen back home. Dylan and Dalia just tamed a four ton lizard."

"And named him Princess." Smitty snickered.

Dalia chuckled. "Ye think that's funny now, wait till he's twice as big." This got everyone, including Dylan, laughing.

"Ha!" Blake snorted. "Imagine our boy here riding through a town, shouting, 'Princess, no! Don't eat the nice people!' while the townspeople flee in terror."

"If they're mean to Princess, I'll totally let him eat them." Dylan huffed, causing more laughter.

"Alright, let's move on. I want to get to the settlement ASAP. Dylan, do you think Princess will let you ride?" The moment he said the words, he knew it was a mistake. Smitty nearly fell over laughing.

Dylan ignored the orc, and rubbed the lizard's head. "What do you say, Princess? Are you ready to be my trusty mount?" When the lizard didn't reply in any way, Dylan took it as assent. He walked back along the massive neck to where one of its forelegs was curled up. Stepping carefully, he climbed up onto its back, throwing a leg over as he sat down just in front of its front shoulders.

"Okay, Princess, go!" He kicked gently with his heals, just as he would with a horse. The lizard literally leapt forward, soaring thirty feet before touching the ground. Dylan rolled backward off its back, hitting the ground hard and cussing. Princess immediately turned around, rushing back to poke Dylan with its nose, emitting a sort of high keening like a dog's whine. This time even the stoic Nessa joined in the laughter. Red's giggling and pretending to roll on the ground only made the rest of them laugh harder.

"It's okay, buddy." Dylan patted the lizard's nose. "We'll work on that. Maybe figure out some kind of saddle for you."

Dylan remounted, and convinced the lizard to move at a walk, which was a fast-walk or jogging pace for the rest of the party. Smitty led the way, looking back over his shoulder occasionally as if worried that Princess might eat him.

With the increased pace, they reached the former gnome settlement in just a few more hours. More of the merchant's guards greeted them at the gate, extremely wary of Princess. When Max identified himself, they bowed their heads, opened the gates wide, and sent a runner into the city. A short time later, the dark elf leader of the merchant group and one of Max's merchant councilors, a dwarf named Enoch, met them in the first market square they reached.

They too looked nervously at Princess, until Dylan dismounted and led him over to one side of the square.

"Welcome to Greystone City, Majesty!" The elf greeted him warmly, bowing his head. "That's… quite an interesting pet your friend has."

"Yeah, his name is Princess." Max grinned.

"The pet, or your friend?" the elf asked, confused. Behind Max, Smitty guffawed.

"The lizard. It's a long story. How are things going here?"

"Splendid! The city is larger than we expected, and we have high hopes. We've set up our guild headquarters within the inner keep, as agreed..." The merchant paused as if expecting Max to argue. Max simply nodded for him to continue. "We've had our scouts map the entire area inside the walls, and Counselor Enoch here has been touring the city. We were just about to identify which properties he wishes to claim on your behalf."

"Excellent. I hope at least one of the buildings is a warehouse?" Max nodded toward Princess. "I don't think he's going to fit in a standard stable."

"Indeed." Enoch chuckled. "I think you'll be pleased, Majesty. In the goblin city, I'm afraid most o' the buildings be unusable, built to a smaller than normal scale. So I simply claimed a quadrant equal to one fifth o' the total area. We'll likely be needin' to demolish and rebuild over time."

Max looked around at the buildings along the square. "That doesn't seem to be the case here."

"Aye, Majesty. We were discussin' that ourselves. Records from that time be rare, and we dunno whether some other race originally built this place, or the gnomes just built to accommodate visitors. It were a trading settlement, after all."

"That's fortunate for all of us." Max smiled at the elf. "If you don't mind, I'd like to spend some time with Enoch and review his choices before we finalize them. Can we meet in the morning and let you know?"

397

"Of course, Majesty. In the meantime, the palace is bare, but we've fully furnished and stocked a nearby inn, if you'd like to rest there this evening?"

"That would be wonderful, thank you." Max appreciated the gesture. "Shall we say, eight bells?"

"As you wish, Majesty." The elf bowed again and took his leave.

Enoch grinned at Max. "This be quite a deal ye made, Max. Wait till ye see what I found!"

"Lead the way, Enoch. I find this all very exciting. It's like a treasure hunt and Christmas morning all wrapped into one!"

Not understanding the reference, the dwarf merely nodded and led them deeper into the city, with Dylan and Princess bringing up the rear.

Chapter 20

The group followed Enoch through the empty city, which was laid out in a roughly circular shape, if the one drawing the circle was drunk, their hands unsteady. It sat in the center of the cavern, which seemed like a bad idea to Max. It would be hard to defend the wall from attacks for the full three hundred and sixty degrees. It would have been better to construct it up against one of the cavern walls, like Stormhaven and Deepcrag were.

The main gates, through which they had entered, were on the south side of the city. Enoch led them east from the main street, which led straight across several intersections and through two market squares to the inner keep, set against the northern wall. As they walked, Enoch described the city.

"I've walked most o' the area over the last two days. The best I can figure, the city be about a half mile across from wall to wall, with a few variances here and there." Max did some quick math in his head. If the city was a circle, and had a half mile diameter, or a quarter mile radius, that was about thirteen hundred and twenty feet. Square that and multiply by pi... He shook his head. He was out of practice. Stopping and holding up a finger, he closed his eyes and took a deep breath. This should be easy math for him. He was constantly calculating more complicated things like mortar or artillery target projections, and this grade school geometry should have come natural to him.

After a long moment of calculation, he came up with it. The total area inside the wall would be roughly one hundred and twenty five acres. It occurred to him that they might not even have acres on this world. Though, if they used miles… "Enoch, by my calculation, the city is about one hundred twenty five acres, yes?"

"Correct, Max!" Enoch sounded impressed. "You did that calculation just now? It took me a full minute with pen and ink."

"Part of my training." was all Max said. "So our portion would be about twenty five acres. And based on how much space the inner keep is taking up, I'm guessing that's something close to a third of the balance of the city?"

"Slightly more than a third, yes. Though the area I've mapped out be just under twenty five acres."

Max nodded. "Maybe we can round it out by claiming a random strategic spot all by itself. Have that be our secret bat cave, or something."

"Bat cave, Max?"

"Uh, hideout. Safe house? Maybe a place where we can set up a shop or something, and use it to observe what's happening outside our section of the city?"

"Ah, I see. Not a bad idea. We could actually claim two or three spots like that in different quarters. I'll sell it to the merchants as me young king bein' eccentric, pickin' buildings that looked attractive to him."

"There you go." Max grinned at him. "One near the palace entry, if our section doesn't already have a view of that. Another near the main gate, since we seem to be walking a good distance away from it. I'll leave the selection up to you, but I recommend choosing something that will see a lot of traffic, and where alert eyes and ears can learn things. Like, a livery stable near the gate? Or a tavern, or an emporium that sells a wide range of goods."

"Very clever." The dwarf nodded. "I would go with a trade broker's warehouse. When caravans begin to pass through again, they'll stop in to see about pickin' up cargo, or guards, or contracts, as well as information about where they might sell their own cargo."

"Now you're speaking my language." Max nodded. "But won't the merchants object? It would seem like they'd want that job."

"Oh, there will be a dozen or more brokers in the city once it be up and runnin'." Enoch assured him. A moment later he stopped and waved his hand. "This'd be the edge o' your territory."

Max looked around. They stood at the intersection of two roads, one wide enough for three wagons, the other barely wide enough for two. The wider road ran from the wall inward toward the keep like the spoke of a wheel. The buildings on the side that Enoch indicated were nothing special, a bunch of squat one-story housing and small storefronts. Max didn't see the attraction.

Enoch saw the doubtful look on his face, and explained. "Imagine all along this side o' the street, we demolish these buildings and construct a wall. From the outer wall almost all the way to the keep." He brought out a parchment with a rough diagram of the city, one large pie wedge marked it bolder lines. Pointing to the intersection where they stood, he said, "We can create a city within the city. Sovereign territory of Stormhaven, accessible only with permission, if ye like. Able to be shut off and defended if ye gets grumpy with the merchants, or the city begins to fall to attack."

Max was intrigued. He looked at the drawing more carefully. "Alright, I like the concept. But why this particular section of the city?"

"Ah, for that, we'll need to go downstairs." The dwarf led him down two more streets, deeper into what would be their territory. Stopping in front of a plain looking two story building, Enoch said, "I were passin' down this street, not much interested in the area. There be a more practical section on the other side o' the city, with a park, what was obviously a very large inn, a fancy house that you could have made yer home. But I happened to glance up and see this." He pointed to the building's front door. Max and the others stared at it, not comprehending.

"There be dwarven runes above the door." Enoch supplied, stepping closer. "Ancient runes, so old I can't even read 'em. Well, mostly." He pointed to one particular rune near the center. "That one be familiar enough, and it means *door*."

"So... a rune that says door, above a door?" Smitty raised an eyebrow at the dwarf.

"Ha! Right, it struck me as funny as well. But it got me curious enough to check inside." The dwarf entered the building, then walked through a front room and into what looked like a kitchen area in the back. There was a stone stairway leading downward, and the group followed him down. All but Dylan, who didn't want to leave Princess alone outside.

Down in the cellar, Dalia pushed her ever present light globe out to the center of the room. They were in a nondescript cellar, maybe thirty paces square. Enoch walked across toward the back wall. "I been a merchant most o' me life. Haven't worked the stone in a mine since I was a wee lad, some two hundred years ago. But I still be a dwarf, and the stone still speaks to me blood." He placed his hand on the wall, and it lit up. Dwarven runes formed an arch about ten feet high, eight feet wide. After a moment, the wall within the arch simply disappeared. Beyond it was a small room, then a ramp leading downward.

Dalia gasped. "The old magic?"

"Aye, lass. That be me own thinkin' as well. I can't pretend to know much about it, it were a subject that bored me in school. But if this be part o' the lost magic..."

Dalia turned to Max. "Max! Ye must protect this! If this be what it seems, Ironhand would give ye half o' Darkholm for its secrets." She paused and grinned. "Old Puckerface would buy ye an entire cellar o' Firebelly's fer the chance to study it."

"Damn." Max whistled. "What exactly is it?"

Dalia shook her head. "There be a legend that we dwarves once possessed powerful magic. Harnessed the power o' the earth to do wondrous things. The spells were based on runes, and Runemasters were the most respected among our people. Elevated even over Master Smiths."

Enoch nodded. "Some were said to be able to move through time, or cause great ships to float through the air. The school where they trained up the young ones was said to be a floating town that traveled the remote lands, never stayin' in one place fer long, accessible only by portal, or flyin' mounts."

"We still have magic, o' course, as ye seen. But what we can do now be a small fraction o' what the Runemasters could do." Her face fell as she continued. "There was a war, and the clans fought amongst themselves. The kings o' each clan bade their Runemasters to create more and more powerful weapons to use against their cousins. Blood ran through the mountains, and whole forests were laid waste. Dwarvenkind, once one o' the most numerous and powerful o' the races, was reduced to a mere fraction of what it had been. Entire clans were wiped out, wee ones slaughtered to prevent them from polluting other bloodlines." Dalia sniffed, and her voice caught.

Enoch took over. "It were a shameful thing. Some say our kings were under a compulsion o' some kind. We may never know what caused it, or why so many set aside their honor and committed such despicable acts. What we do know is that the Runemasters could no' stand their shame. It were them that pulled down entire mountains with their magic, killin' thousands o' their own people in a day. They left their kings and clans behind, takin' all knowledge of their magic with 'em."

Max looked at the still glowing runes of the archway. "So if these runes are part of that old magic... what's to stop the same thing from happening again? If I were to allow Ironhand's scholars or mages to study this, what's to stop them from using it against other clans to consolidate power?"

Dalia's eyes went wide and her mouth dropped open. Enoch growled and balled his fists, taking a step closer to Max, his face contorted in anger. "Ye'll not say such a thing about me king again, or I'll make ye bleed despite me oath!"

Dalia quickly stepped in front of the other dwarf, looking up at Max. "Max, that were a grave insult. The great war be our people's deepest shame. King Ironhand would sooner cut off his own legs than attack one o' his cousins."

Max was conflicted. He wanted to apologize for his thoughtless words. Ironhand and the other dwarves had all acted honorably toward him from his first day in their city. Even when he practically stole Agnor's crown and city from them. But kings did not apologize, especially for asking necessary questions.

He sighed. "I am sorry, Enoch, Dalia. I meant no insult. I'm just trying to figure out how dangerous this magic might be."

Both dwarves relaxed, and Enoch bowed his head. "I be sorry as well, Max." He turned toward the arch. "Like any tool, this magic could be used fer great benefit, as well as great evil." He paused, looking at Max. "I'll make no mention o' this to King Ironhand until ye tell me to."

"Thank you Enoch." Max looked at the ramp. "What's down there?"

"Dunno. I dared not pass beyond the arch. I were alone, and wasn't sure it would open from the other side once I passed through. Didn't want to be trapped wherever that leads."

"Good thinking." Max thought back to his recent solo adventure through the portals, and how foolish it had been to go alone. The elder dwarf had shown wisdom in his restraint, though Max could tell he was itching to know what was beyond the arch. "Alright, let's explore. First things first. How did you activate it? Is it just by touch?"

"Aye, ye touch this rune here. It be the same one as above the door outside."

"Okay, turn it off. I want to test something."

Enoch did as he was told, placing his hand on the rune. The wall in front of them flashed back into existence, and the runes faded. When the glow was gone, Max could barely make out the faintest scratches in the stone where the runes had been, and only because he knew they were there.

Reaching out, he placed his hand on the same rune. Nothing happened. "Is there a timer? A cooldown?" He asked the dwarves. "Maybe only dwarves can activate it?"

In answer, Dalia stepped forward and placed her hand on the rune. It instantly glowed again, the arch forming and the wall disappearing. She deactivated it again and removed her hand.

"So, maybe it takes dwarven blood to trigger the rune." Max mused aloud. "Or, earth magic? Smitty, Nessa, please try to activate it."

Both the orc and the panthera tried their luck, to no avail.

"Alright, for now let's assume this is a dwarves only exclusive club. Now let's address Enoch's concern about the other side. Dalia, please activate the arch and step through. See if you can close it from the other side. If you can, we'll wait one minute for you to open it again. If you don't, Enoch will open it from this side.

Nodding her agreement, Dalia opened and stepped through the portal. She looked around for a moment, then reached to touch the wall on the other side. The arch disappeared, and the wall remained solid for about ten seconds before opening back up again. Dalia smiled and waved from the other side.

"Alright, does that ease your concerns, Enoch?"

"Aye, let's go see what's down there!" The dwarf grinned, already moving toward the arch.

"Smitty, run upstairs and let Dylan know where we're going. Tell him no one enters this building, no matter what."

"Roger that, boss." The orc sprinted across the cellar and up the stairs, already yelling for Dylan. He returned a minute later, chuckling. "Dylan parked Princess right in front of the door. I don't think we need to worry about company."

"Heh. Okay good, let's go." Max stepped through and joined Dalia and Enoch on the other side. He immediately noticed it was a good deal cooler on that side. Once the others were through, Dalia closed the arch, and Nessa led the way down the ramp. She moved slowly, scanning for traps as she descended the gradual slope. The ramp was roughly eight feet wide, the same as the arch, and the floor and walls were impossibly smooth. Nessa found no traps as they descended, curving in a wide spiral to their left almost like a parking garage ramp, and before long they were in a natural cavern that Enoch informed them was a hundred feet below the cellar they'd started in.

Max was pretty sure they hadn't walked that far down the mildly sloped ramp. "How did we get so deep? If I had to guess, we've only walked downward about a quarter of that. Two or three stories, maybe."

Enoch nodded. "Aye, that first step were a big one. The runes didn't just open the wall. When we stepped through, we teleported nearly straight down at the same time." Max looked at Dalia, who nodded in confirmation.

Not for the first time, Max wished he'd inherited that dwarven sense of location and direction.

The cavern ahead of them wasn't that large, but it was packed with things to see! Across the back of the cavern was a row of six crude statues, each standing fifteen feet tall, with shoulders at least six feet wide, and arms that hung nearly to the ground. Max thought they might be depictions of rock trolls, or some other kind of underground beast. In front of them were several rows of long, low stone buildings with narrow slots for windows. Off to their left was a small waterfall that fell into a man-made, or probably dwarf-made cistern with low walls that were raised up maybe three feet above the floor level. A gate in the wall sat open, allowing the water to fall into a deep stream bed that was cut across the floor, to disappear through another gate set directly into the cavern's wall. Smitty spotted it about the same time as Max.

"If you closed that gate, this place would flood pretty quickly."

Enoch shook his head, pointing to another gate in the wall about forty five degrees to the right of the first, and a closed gate that could be seen set into the side of the stream bed's wall. "It be a diverter. Aye, ye could close that open gate and flood this place all the way up to the portal. Or ye could open them other gates n divert the water in that direction." He pointed to the open gate. "That one leads under the city, me guess is that it feeds the wells. If ye closed it, and opened the others, ye could send the water off away from the city, causin' everyone above to get a mite thirsty."

"Why would you want to deprive your own city of water?" Nessa asked.

Max answered first. "This is a fallback position. If the city were attacked and overrun, whomever constructed this could retreat down here, divert the water, and wait for the enemy to get thirsty enough to leave." He looked around the cavern. "My guess is there's another exit down here somewhere, one that would let them escape completely, or rally and attack their enemies from behind. Maybe disrupt any supply caravans bringing water."

"Aye, that be me own thinkin' as well. Especially with these big baddies here to help em fight!" Enoch pointed toward the back wall. Max followed his finger, scanning the area for any movement.

It took a moment, but he realized the dwarf was pointing to the statues. He focused on one, then whistled when *Examine* kicked in. "Those things are…" He didn't know how to finish his thought.

Battle Golem
Level 45
Health: 100,000/100,000

"Way better tanks than our sweet young ogre." Smitty finished for him. "A hundred thousand health? Imagine that thing stomping through the streets above, just shrugging off hits as it crushed buildings and punted grey dwarf warriors a hundred yards." Smitty paused, looking at

410

Max, and a grin spread across his face. "Never let Dylan get control of these bad boys. If he starts teaching 'em dance moves, they could shake the place to the ground!"

Ignoring his corporal, Max began to walk the rest of the way down the ramp onto the cavern floor. As he passed the nearest of the buildings, he glanced through the open door. The first thing he noticed was that the wall, and the stone door, were both nearly two feet thick. The window slots were placed about six feet apart, and were cross-shaped, with vertical and horizontal openings. This would give a defender on the inside with a crossbow a wider field of fire. A quick check confirmed that the buildings facing each other on his left and right had staggered door and window locations, making the space he was standing in a kill zone with very few, if any, safe spots. It made his spine itch to stroll through there, a flashback of mortar rounds causing him to stumble slightly before he recovered.

Leading the group past the buildings, Max stepped up closer to one of the golems. His pulse quickened, and he felt a twinge of fear as he looked up at its bulk. Each of its stone hands could easily engulf and crush him. Its feet were the size of bumper cars, large enough to crush two or three frontline tanks, if they were stupid enough to try and hold their position. Everything about this monster screamed power and danger.

Enoch stepped up next to him, grinning like a madman. "With these, ye could flatten the orc city in an hour."

Max agreed, but that brought up a concern. There were innocent civilians in that city. "How do you control them?"

"I dunno." The dwarf shook his head, leaning backward to stare up at the golem's face. "That secret be lost with the rest o' their magic." He raised a hand as if to touch its foot, then paused. "Ye mind?"

"Go right ahead. Just don't piss it off." Max nodded.

Enoch set his hand tentatively on the golem's foot, ready to yank it back if it moved. Max saw it was shaking slightly, and he didn't blame the dwarf one bit. A moment later, the dwarf closed his eyes, then smiled and withdrew his hand. "It give'd me the option to claim this place. I did not presume, as this be your property."

Max reached forward and touched the foot as well, but nothing happened. "Nope. Just like the arch. I must not have the right blood."

"Lemme try." Dalia stepped forward, much more sure of herself since the other two hadn't been harmed. She placed her hand on the foot and closed her eyes. A moment later, Max got a notification.

Congratulations! You have taken ownership of Guild Outpost 42!
You now have access to all facility resources, and can assign control to others.
This includes operational control of doors, gates, portals, and battle golems.

Warning! As you are not a registered Guild Officer, a
notification of transfer
has been sent to Guild Headquarters.

"Oh, no." Red muttered from atop Max's shoulder, causing all but Enoch to look her way. "If the Guild still exists, ya might have just made a powerful enemy, Max."

Impatient, Enoch watched Dalia, his foot tapping on the stone. When she in turn looked up at Max, her face gone white with fear, Enoch asked, "What? What happened?"

"I… I claimed this place in Max's name." Dalia whispered.

Max read the notification aloud to everyone, and Enoch actually took a few steps backward, looking from the golems to the exit ramp back to the arch, as if considering making a run for it. Unwittingly mimicking Red, he said, "Oh, no."

Max was barely listening, as he'd noticed something the others hadn't, yet. The eyes of all six golems had just lit up, glowing a pulsing red. A moment later, the others couldn't help but notice as well.

With a grinding of stone on stone, the heads of all six golems shifted to focus on Max.

Chapter 21

Lagrass crawled out from under a large fir tree, where he had taken refuge for the night. His bed had been uncomfortable, a hundred tiny dead needles poking at him anytime he moved. He'd had to run without grabbing his blankets, or any of the items he'd kept in the cellar. All he owned now was his knife, which he'd used to kill the woman who loaned it to him, his clothes, the coins and items he'd looted from his victims.

Once he'd pulled himself out of the river onto a wide flat boulder, he hadn't dared to light a fire, fearing that the guards might be close enough to spot the smoke. The rock was warm from the sun overhead, so he'd sat there checking his loot and inventory as his clothes dried.

It wasn't much. He had ten slots of storage, nine of which were filled. There was his kitchen knife, a smaller belt knife in a sheath, a ratty leather jerkin he'd looted from the drunk, a packet of spices, a heavy skillet, and a bottle of wine from the innkeeper. He'd purchased a meat pie from a vendor before his troubles, along with a cheap water skin. And the last item was a promising looking rock he'd found on the riverbank. He thought it might be flint, which he could use with his belt knife to start a fire. If not, he could always try and sharpen it into a spear point or crude axe head.

Walking back to the riverbank, he took a moment to wash his face and hands, then decided he needed a bath. His skin felt like it was crawling after sleeping under the tree. Removing his clothes, he dunked himself in the chilly water and used sand to scrub his skin. Getting out, he filled his water skin as the breeze dried him off, then got dressed.

His clothes stained and wrinkled after two murders and two soakings in the river, Lagrass looked and felt like a beggar. The good news was that the innkeeper had been carrying ten gold coins and several silver. In all, he'd looted nearly twelve gold from his kills. Based on the prices he'd seen at the city's shops, he should be able to get a decent set of traveling clothes and a better weapon for that. Maybe more, if he negotiated hard.

He had walked for most of the day after climbing out of the water, keeping to the woods and continuing to follow the river. His hope was that he would come across a town, or a road that would lead him to one. He hadn't found either by the time the sun began to set and he took shelter under the tree.

Now it was a new day, and he continued in a new direction. Moving directly away from the river, he did his best to use the sun to keep himself going in a straight line. The canopy above was thick, but there were enough breaks that he could find the sun regularly and sight something ahead to aim for. It didn't really matter if his orientation was perfect, as he had no idea where he was going. But he felt that it was a good idea to practice.

One of the things he'd learned was that activities earned him skills, and skills helped him survive. His float down the river had earned him *Swimming*. His multiple murders had increased his *One Handed* skill several times, much as bludgeoning rats with a chair leg had granted him three points in *Blunt Weapons*. After several hours of taking sightings on the sun and adjusting his course, he earned himself the *Navigation* skill.

Lagrass was beginning to fear he'd be spending another night in the wild when he caught the scent of wood smoke. Following his nose into the wind, he quickly came upon a small cabin in a clearing. The stone chimney smoked merrily, and the glow of a candle could be seen through the only visible window, just to the right of the front door.

Wasting no time, he hurried across the clearing and called out, "Anyone home?" before knocking on the door. A muffled voice answered from inside, and he waited impatiently for someone to open the door. After what seemed like an interminably long time for such a small cabin, the door opened. Looking out at him was an old man with a badly scarred face and a long white beard.

"What do ya want!?" the man grumbled, looking Lagrass up and down, clearly not liking what he saw. "Go away!"

"Please, sir. I was hoping to purchase a meal, maybe some clothes?" Lagrass paused, thinking quickly. "I was robbed and tossed into the river, left for dead. The thieves took nearly everything I had, but I managed to hide a bit of coin..." He pulled a silver coin from his inventory and held it up for the old man.

"Bah! I can sell you a meal, easy enough. Was just about to eat, and there's enough for two. Nothing fancy, just some beans and carrots in a stew with a bit of rabbit." The old man's hand flashed out more quickly than Lagrass would have expected, seizing the silver coin and making it disappear. The door opened wider, and the old man motioned for him to come in. "Take a seat there at the table."

Lagrass sat as the old man moved to the fireplace, where a pot was hanging from a hook over the flames. He stirred it briefly as he spoke. "Got no clothes to sell you. But I got an extra blanket or two. Got a wolf hide stretched out on the rack out back that's just about cured. I was planning to trade it in town next time I go for supplies. If you have any skill in leatherworking, I could sell you the hide, too."

"I'm afraid I have no idea how to sew. But I would appreciate the blankets. And if you have a weapon of some sort you'd be willing to part with?"

The old man snorted. "Only weapon I got is old Lizzy there." He nodded toward a sword mounted on a couple of pegs above the mantle. "Got me through three wars, Lizzy did. Wouldn't part with her for any price."

Lagrass considered trying to negotiate, but didn't figure he was holding enough gold to overcome the old man's sentimental attachment to the blade. He was the same way with his service weapon back home. It was lovingly cleaned, oiled, and stored in a case under his bed. For a moment, he wondered who owned it now.

"Fair enough. You mentioned a town. How far away is that? Could you direct me there?"

"Not far, a day's walk to the west. You can follow my walking trail from here." The old man pulled the pot off the hook and set it on the table. Grabbing two bowls, he filled them both and handed one to Lagrass before taking a seat. "Eat up, before it gets cold!" He tipped the bowl up to his lips and slurped loudly.

Not seeing anything resembling a spoon, Lagrass copied the old man. The stew tasted horrible, but it filled his belly, and would give him energy to continue. By the time they were done eating, darkness had fully fallen in the forest. The old man glanced out the window and said, "It'll be another silver for the blankets. And you can sleep on the floor by the fire if you like, no charge."

Lagrass agreed, handing over another coin. The oldster disappeared into another room for a moment, and returned with two blankets that were in decent condition. There were a few thin spots in the weave, but no actual holes. Thanking the man, he spread one out on the floor, then rolled the other up to use as a pillow.

"G'night." The old man muttered as he stepped into the back room and closed the door. Lagrass heard a bolt click, and smiled to himself. He'd been surprised the old man had let him inside at all, let alone stay the night. The inhabitants of this world were much more trusting than he was used to. Either that, or his *Charisma* was working hard in his favor. As he settled into his makeshift bed, he happened to glance up at the mantle, and smiled wider when he saw that Lizzy was no longer mounted on her pegs.

418

The old man was trusting, but not an idiot.

*****

Max froze, unable to decide whether to stand his ground in the face of the giant golems, or scream like a little girl and flee. His mind was filled with a vision of six pairs of eyes shooting laser beams at him and his party.

After several seconds, when the golems didn't make any further moves, he relaxed a bit. Looking at the equally frightened dwarves, he whispered, "Could these things be controlled long distance? Like, from a guild office somewhere?"

Enoch thought about it for a second, then shook his head. "Unlikely, but again, there be much about this magic that we don't know, Max."

Smitty, also whispering, but doing so loudly enough that anyone within fifty feet could have heard him, said, "The message you read to us said that the Guild had been notified. Does that mean this place has a way of communicating? Or is it going to be like the notifications we get about quests and things."

"This one, I know." Dalia answered. "The gods will have notified the owner o' this place that Max has claimed it." She looked up guiltily at Max. "Or rather, I claimed it for him. I'm sorry, Max."

"Don't be sorry. You were trying to help." He smiled down at her, putting a comforting hand on her shoulder. "Right now, let's focus on these golems. They don't look happy to see us, but they're not attacking. Any suggestions?"

"Try a verbal command." Smitty suggested in his overloud whisper, his eyes never leaving the giants.

Max focused on the one they were standing in front of. "Golem, raise your right hand." He waited for several seconds, but nothing happened. On his shoulder, Red coughed.

"Okay, I think I got it. Been lookin' at your tabs for this place. There be one called Sentry Golems, and... well just look for yourself."

"Hang on a minute, guys." Max said for Enoch's benefit. "I'm checking something." He accessed the tab, which Red had helpfully highlighted for him with a blinking red light. Once it was open, there was a list of the six golems, and he was surprised to find that each one had a name, rather than a number. The one at the top of the list was named *Bastion*. When he focused on that name, a sublist of options appeared. The first option was *Assign control*.

Concerned that his lack of dwarven blood, or whatever triggered the ability to use the arch and other items down here, might cause him to lose control of the golem, Max assigned control to Enoch. The dwarf's eyes unfocused as he received the notification. An idea struck Max, and he closed his own eyes for a moment, working through his tabs. When he opened them again, it was just in time to see Enoch read his interface, and laugh.

"Aye, Max. I can do that." He turned to look up at the golem whose name they now knew was *Bastion*. "Golem, raise yer right hand."

Immediately, the sound of grinding stone rang out again, and the golem's arm lifted until its hand was level with its shoulder. Smitty took an involuntary step back, then looked sheepish. Max didn't blame him one bit. "Alright, lower your hand again." Enoch instructed, and the golem complied. The dwarf went through a few more basic commands, having it walk three steps forward, turn around, and walk back. When he was done, Max's quest was completed, and the dwarf actually leveled up!

"Ha! I can't even remember the last time I gained a level. Thank ye, Max."

"You're most welcome." Max had been surprised by the huge amount of experience he'd been able to assign to the quest. His best guess was that it had either represented a significant amount of danger, or the rediscovery of this ancient magic carried great significance to the world. On a whim, he assigned the same quest to Dalia and the others, minus Dylan who was still upstairs.

Dalia was able to activate a second golem, Smitty was not. Dalia's reward experience was significantly less than Enoch's, so Max figured the initial activation was what had been important to the gods. It struck him just then how easily he accepted that it was indeed a pantheon of gods watching over the world and issuing quests, experience, and such. After all, he'd met one of them face to face.

421

"Okay, Enoch, Dalia, assign your two golems to sentry duty. Station one here, one by the entrance. Instruct them that anyone entering here other than the members of this party, including Dylan and Princess, should be squashed like a bug." After a moment's consideration he said, "Actually, don't have them attack any Guild members that might show up. I don't want to start an outright war by trying to kill them if they come to reclaim their outpost."

"Good idea." Enoch nodded vigorously.

The dwarves set their golems, watching Dalia's walk slowly between the buildings to stand to one side of the entry ramp. The ground trembled under their feet with each footfall, and once again Max felt a sense of fear. When it reached its post, it once again went still as a statue. The eyes in all six golems went dark, and the cavern grew silent as a tomb.

"We'll come back and investigate more later." Max said as they walked up the ramp. "See about locating that other exit. They certainly didn't intend to bring those things up this ramp and through the house upstairs. There must be a larger, more direct exit somewhere."

Enoch cleared his throat. "Eh, Max? I'd like to ask ye a favor."

"What is it?"

"Let me run this place. Goldentongue can take over me duties at Stormhaven. Now that trade agreements be in place, and the crafters n merchants be fillin' the city, ye don't need two of us there. And I can always return to Stormhaven every few days to help, if necessary."

Max nodded. Goldentongue was the other of Max's councilors with a merchant background. He and Enoch had performed miracles together getting Stormhaven started.

Enoch wasn't done. "This be the most important thing ta happen in me lifetime. Hell, in ten lifetimes! Protectin' this place, learnin' what we can o' the rune magic here... it'd be me honor to watch over it all. I'll claim the house upstairs as me office and residence, maybe expand it a bit to make room for some staff. We'll secure the area from prying eyes, build the perimeter wall, assign a heavy guard. I'll bring in engineers n masons to get the projects goin' right away. It'll drain yer treasury a bit, but..." the dwarf hesitated.

"But what, Enoch?"

"If ye be willin' to share this secret with Ironhand and the other clan leaders, they'd flood yer treasury with all the gold ye need to protect this place. Hell, they'd buy the whole city from the Greystone group if ye asked. That be how important this is to us. I'll dedicate me life to it from this day forward."

Max was a little taken aback. He'd already been considering whether to let Ironhand know about the outpost. But he had questions. Like why, after so many thousands of years, had no other outposts been found? And could the dwarves be trusted to use the magic, assuming they could figure it out, for good rather than evil?

The one thing he didn't doubt was Enoch's sincerity. The dwarf treated the outpost as if it were holy ground, and the reverence in his voice was real. "I'll need your oath that this place and its contents remain known only to this group, until I say otherwise. I may share this with Ironhand and the others, but not before I think things through a bit."

"Ye have me solemn oath to keep yer secrets until ye order me otherwise." Enoch put hand to heart as he swore, and a bright golden light swirled around them both.

"Alright, this place is yours to run. I don't even know the name of it, do you?" Max smiled at the dwarf, who shook his head. "In any case, I charge you with securing this place. Inform the merchants of our selection, including whatever independent spy buildings you think are best. I'll bring Redmane into the loop, so he can help you move resources here to accomplish your goals. Hold on a minute."

Max closed his eyes and opened his *Sovereign* interface again. There was a *Quest Creation* tab, which he'd just found and used to give the golem quests. He took several minutes to compose a quest that covered all he wanted for this place, then issued it to Enoch and the other members of his party. The quest included a reinforcement of the secrecy requirement, and significant rewards if all the objectives were complete. It would be a good way to grant some serious experience to his friends, and Enoch could probably use the help. It wouldn't be easy to get everything done and keep the secret at the same time.

Leaving the building that housed the access point, after convincing Princess to move away from the door, Max looked around. If this outpost was as important as it seemed, and he was beginning to understand that it was, then the first thing he wanted to do was place a portal here. The ability to move supplies and troops here quickly was vital. They needed to get back to the temple as soon as possible and start Glitterspindle working on it. Get him the materials he needed, and probably a much more difficult challenge, get him focused on the job.

Max knew he could go to Ironhand, and the king would dispatch Spellslinger to create a portal immediately. But he wasn't ready to reveal his secrets yet if he could manage it on his own.

Dylan had been increasing his bond with Princess while they'd been waiting, and was able to convince the lizard to carry three passengers. With Dylan, Blake, and Dalia riding, and Enoch staying behind, the party was able to run back the way they came at a much faster pace. Smitty, Max, and Nessa all had the *Endurance* and *Agility* to run for hours, and recovered quickly during rest stops. Especially Nessa, who simply took her full panther form and trotted along. As a result, they reached Deepcrag in just six hours. Not stopping to check on Lo'tang and the others, they made straight for the portal back to Stormhaven.

There was a bit of panic when they arrived in the courtyard, but Princess remained calm, and Max and the others reassured the guards and nearby citizens that the lizard was tamed. Dylan immediately went to find someone who could help him with a harness and saddle, and maybe get some training in pet management. Smitty went to go check on his new bride, with a warning look from Max about operational security. Dalia and Nessa accompanied Max and Redmane to Max's study, where they obtained an oath of secrecy and let the old chamberlain know what they'd found.

He began to fidget as soon as they mentioned the door runes, then got up and paced when they described the arch and its gateway. By the time Max had relayed the whole story, with the ladies filling in some details, Redmane was breathing hard and wringing his hands.

"Enoch be right, Max. The entire dwarven race would help ye protect this outpost, if ye'd only ask."

Max chuckled. "I'm not ready to involve the entire dwarven race just yet. I want to find out how quickly we can place our own portal there, and whether we can protect it ourselves." He held up a hand as Redmane opened his mouth to object. "I won't put it at risk. If there's a threat, I'll shout for Ironhand and the others to come help. But for now it's safe enough, and the best way to keep it safe is for as few people to know about it as possible."

Redmane stared for a moment, his cheeks red, but then nodded. "As ye wish, Max."

"Good. Now, we need to hire some help for Enoch. All of our engineers, masons, guards and such are working at the mine, the way station, or here in the city. I don't want to pull them off of that work, so can you reach out to some trustworthy folks who can work in the gnome city for an extended time, and keep what they see to themselves? They won't know about the outpost, just our need to secure our section of the city as quickly as possible. We can blame the war on the orcs, and our fear that they might hear about an easy target and attack."

"Aye, I'll hire some o' me own clan, and swear them to secrecy." He thought about it for a moment. "We can have two hunnert bodies, engineers, stoneworkers, and stout warriors, there inside a week. This'll seriously deplete yer treasury, Max."

Max had already considered that. Despite the good fortune he'd had, there was a limit to what he could do with the money from the arena, the gold he'd found in the city bank, and the loot from Deepcrag. Merchants and crafters were settling in around Stormhaven, but it would be a while before their taxes, rent, or property purchase proceeds would amount to much. His mines were producing, but after the miners and the dwarven leaders took their share, and he paid for having the ores refined, the profit margins were less than optimal. He had the fifteen thousand gold he'd just received from the Greystone merchants, and would probably receive significant funds from the use of the Deepcrag portal as folks settled the area. But again, that wouldn't help him much in funding such a large project. He was afraid that sometime very soon he was going to have to bring in Ironhand and the others, or risk bankrupting his kingdom.

His thoughts turned to Glitterspindle and the need for him to start building a portal pedestal. "Redmane, how much could we sell a portal pedestal for? Assuming we can get the metal gnome to start building them."

"Maybe fifteen thousand gold." The dwarf replied.

"That's it? The merchants paid me that much for access to the Deepcrag portal, a manor and a warehouse. Why doesn't every settlement have one?"

Redmane shook his head. "That be a lot o' gold, Max. They likely cleaned out their entire fund to pay ye, gambling that the investment would pay off. They stand to make a hundred times that, but only if their gamble is successful. Look at it this way. If ye had to run this city on its taxes alone, no vault full o' found money, no big winnings in the tournament, just what the city earns day to day, could ye scrape together fifteen thousand gold fer a portal?"

Max slumped back in his chair. "I could not. At least, not for a while. I did give instructions to start a fund for that on day one though. How much is in that fund now?"

"One hundred eighty gold." Redmane grinned at him. "Not bad, considerin'. And keep in mind that most settlements or cities don't have hundreds o' guards on loan from their allies, or the naturally low crime rate of a dwarven city, or oathsworn citizens dedicated to helpin build up the city. There be crimes, fires, attacks from outside, attacks from inside… a thousand lil things that drain yer average settlement's treasury." He paused, holding up a finger. "Speakin' o the treasury, since I'm reachin' out to me clan, there be a young lass who'd make ye a fine treasurer."

"Right. I'm sorry, Master Redmane, I've been slacking when it comes to finding one. You've been pulling double duty all this time. I'd be happy to meet with this young dwarfess. Is she related to you?"

"Aye, the granddaughter of a cousin once removed, I think. Her name be Matilda Hammerfist, and she's been workin' at her da's accounting firm for… forty years or so. If ye get along, she'll be able to serve ye for a century or two."

Max blinked for a moment, having to remind himself that a hundred year old dwarf, or dwarfess, was still considered young among their people, who often lived between two and three centuries.

And that he himself might live for thousands of years. Talk about needing to plan for the long run.

"Alright, with the portal at Deepcrag, and the opportunities there, can we raise some more income selling properties to merchants?"

"Aye, but ye'll be competing with them Greystones for recruits. They'll be lookin to fill their own cities. The competition could drive down the prices."

"Right. No point in that. We'll figure something else out." Max mumbled, mostly to himself.

"What about the kobolds?" Nessa's voice was hesitant, barely more than a whisper.

"The kobolds?" Both dwarves and Max repeated in unison.

"I have spoken to a few of them here in the city, and they offered me gold for fresh meat."

Max got excited. "Fitchstone told me when I sold him my grey dwarf loot that first night that the kobolds spend gold and gems like water!" A moment later he was less excited. "But they've been chowing down on grey dwarf stew. Why would they be after more meat?"

Nessa wrinkled up her nose. "Apparently grey dwarf does not taste very good. They are eating them out of a sense of revenge more than anything. They crave more palatable meat."

"And apparently drink, too." Redmane grinned. "If the speed at which they cleaned out yer wine cellar be any indication."

"Okay, let's send a message out to the orc and minotaur hunters at the mine and way station. We need every bit of game they can get for us in the next three days. We'll pay them whatever the going rate is for the meat, then charge the kobolds... more? How much more can we get away with and not anger them?"

Redmane shrugged. "I'll leave that to Goldentongue."

"Thank you, Nessa." Max smiled at her. "That was a wonderful idea. Every little bit helps. Maybe we can sell them the next shipment of mead from the Blooded, as well. Something new for them, so we can charge more."

"Might be worth yer while to have a few scouts search around Deepcrag. If there be kobolds there, it'd be an untapped market. They might have piles o' gold…" Dalia winked at him.

"That too! Wonderful!" Max was grateful for his friends' input. "We'll need to get to them before the other merchants do."

Just then, Teeglin came bursting into the office. "King Max! A messenger! He says its urgent!"

Max got to his feet as she motioned for the messenger to enter. It was an orc warrior, and he was breathing hard. He took a knee and bowed his head before speaking. "King Max! Lo'tang sent me. Deepcrag is under attack. A force of several hundred hobgoblins and trolls are marching toward the city from the direction of the goblin settlement. I ran to the portal as fast as I could, but they will have arrived at the city gates by now." The moment the message was delivered, Max got accompanying notifications.

The kingdom of Stormhaven is under attack!
Quest Accepted: Defend Deepcrag!
An invading army has attacked your Deepcrag settlement.
Gather your forces and defend your territory!
Reward: Variable
This is a mandatory quest, and cannot be declined.

Redmane was dashing out the door, already yelling for the general. Max patted the soldier on the shoulder. "Thank you. Rest for a few minutes, get something to eat.

We'll be heading back there as soon as we can gather some troops!"

"Thank you, sire." The orc trotted off toward the barracks and mess hall.

"Dalia, can you go load up on healing potions from the lab, just in case? I want every warrior to be carrying two, at least. One of the good ones, and a common one."

"Aye, I'll be ready in ten minutes." She got up and hurried off.

Nessa was on her feet as well. "If you'll send me through the portal now, I can do some scouting for you."

"Thank you, let's do that." Max took off at a jog, the panthera right behind him. He sent her through the portal, then turned to see the general mustering troops. The alarm bells were ringing, and the place looked like a freshly kicked anthill. A moment later a runner asked Max to open the portal to the temple, so that he could retrieve some troops from the mine. Max did as requested, not sure he liked the idea of weakening those locations, but trusting in the general to know his strengths and weaknesses. While he waited, he opened his interface and figured out how to share the quest with everyone, all his citizens and the troops on loan to him.

In ten minutes, a force of two hundred orcs, dwarves, and kobolds were assembled in the courtyard, all armed and armored and ready to fight. Behind them stood Smitty, Dylan, Dalia, Erdun the old minotaur enchanter, and half a dozen other minotaurs carrying hefty axes, two-handed swords, and steel bows much like Max's own. When Max waved them over, the elder bowed his head slightly. "It would be our honor to fight alongside you, King Maximilian."

"It would be my honor to have you." Max nodded with respect to the large warriors. Each was between eight and ten feet tall, with bulging muscles and fierce eyes. The tips of their horns glistened as if recently sharpened and oiled. Each wore a chainmail shirt and leather pants with steel bars sewn into them along the thighs and shins for protection. Max decided he wouldn't want to face any one of them in melee combat.

A whistle blew, and the portal opened. The moment it did, the troops began to surge through, led by Rockbreaker. The general stood to one side, hollering at the warriors as they passed him, both encouraging them and threatening them against failure. "Ye lads and lasses go whup them puny hobs and bring me their heads! Don't ye dare come back dead!"

The moment they were all through, the minotaurs chased after them, followed closely by Max and his party.

Chapter 22

The entire force hit the ground running on the
Deepcrag side of the portal. Rockbreaker led the
Stormhaven force at a fast jog, allowing for everyone to
move quickly toward the battle, but conserve their stamina.
Even warriors with high *Endurance* and the natural strength
of dwarves or orcs could get tired running in armor, and
they needed to be able to fight when they arrived.

Max and his party sprinted to the front of the
column as soon as they got near the end of the tunnel.
While Rockbreaker was an excellent captain, who had
showed himself to be a worthy leader in the battle with the
greys, Max and his corporals had a whole other
understanding of battle tactics. Their wars had evolved
well beyond the swords and spears, bows and arrows of
Earth's medieval times.

When they reached the ramp that led down to the
bridge, Max pointed. "If we can, we should draw them to
us, fight them at the bridge. That choke point will negate
their numbers advantage, and bunch them up for us to kill."
He spoke for a bit longer with Rockbreaker and his party,
watching the battle at the gates.

The hobgoblins hadn't prepared for a siege of a
walled city. They were massed near the gates, the trolls at
the front pounding with massive stone clubs, trying to bash
through. The defenders, both Lo'tang's troops and the
merchant guards, were firing down at them with bows and
crossbows, or simply tossing down heavy rocks upon their

heads. While scores of the hobgoblins were down, either wounded or dead, the trolls just shook off the injuries. The full-blooded monsters had an even higher regeneration rate than Max.

Max made sure his people were in place, moving forward toward the bridge, making as little noise as possible, before he took off on his part of the mission. He had the simplest job of the bunch...

Go piss off an army of hobgoblins and trolls.

He ran down the ramp and across the bridge, not making any particular effort to be quiet, but not making a lot of noise, either. In his hand he held an unfortunate sacrifice, a bottle of Firebelly's with a burning cloth fuse. As he approached the back of the hobgoblin horde, he flung the bottle over the heads of the hobgoblins, straight into the gates that the trolls were busy pounding. There was a hush from the hobs as the flame passed over their heads, several of them turning to see where it had come from. Max took a deep breath and roared, joined a second later by all two hundred plus of the troops behind him, and Princess. A few seconds after that, the defenders atop the wall joined in as well.

As one, all of the enemy turned to face the new threat approaching the bridge. They saw Max standing just twenty or so yards behind them, then the bottle struck. It never reached the gate, instead shattering against the raised club of a troll. The liquid splashed over the troll holding that club, as well as half a dozen of his brethren, and the flames began to spread. To help things along, Max focused on the club, and shouted, *"Boom!"*

The stone weapon, six feet long and weighing at least a hundred pounds, shattered. Stone chips and chunks embedded themselves in every living thing within twenty feet, drawing blood from the trolls even as the flames from the Firebelly's Molotov cocktail spread. The troll holding the club dropped dead, its arm, shoulder, and head mostly gone. The others roared in fear and pain, trampling the hobs in their panic. One of the trolls nearest the dead one knocked the corpse into the pool of flaming alcohol at their feet, and a moment later that corpse exploded as well, raining flaming bits of troll meat in a wide circle. Hobs and trolls alike were knocked down or killed by the explosion, and three flaming trolls bulldozed their way through their allies, fleeing the flames. They exploded one by one, the last having almost reached the outer edge of the confused and terrified hobgoblin horde.

Shocked by the unexpected effectiveness of his attack, Max stood and watched for a moment longer than he should have. Several of the hobs had started toward him before the fire even started, and they were now within a few steps of him.

The hobgoblins were larger than their goblin cousins, about four feet tall on average, and slightly bulkier. Dalia had explained to Max and his corporals as they jogged toward Deepcrag that it was believed hobgoblins were the result of interbreeding between orcs and goblins. The trolls, by comparison, were closer to Dylan's size, averaging ten feet tall and bulky, built much like the outpost golems. Wide shoulders, long arms, thick bodies, they made natural tanks.

Not wanting to get stuck in a melee with hundreds of hobgoblins, Max focused on a spot atop the wall next to Lo'tang and cast *Jump*. His body disappeared just as the lead hobgoblin jabbed a spear at his belly.

Now atop the wall, Max turned to look down at the destruction he'd caused.

Of the twenty or so trolls that had been pounding on the gate, only six remained standing. The others had either been killed by the explosions, or caught fire and exploded themselves. Those still on their feet had mowed down scores of hobgoblins, while their exploding cousins had killed a hundred more, and wounded about the same number. A few of the little monsters rolled about on the stone, flaming troll bits stuck to their skin, screaming in pain. The archers atop the wall were quickly picking them off, though they were getting hard to see. An unfortunate side effect of the explosions was that the gates were damaged, and aflame.

Lo'tang looked down upon the decimated horde and shook his head. "Damn. King Max, that was... effective."

"Heh." Max patted him on the shoulder. "Way more than I expected. I had planned for them to be scared away by the fire. But when the club got all soaked, I improvised."

The two of them watched as their reinforcements reached the bridge, the dwarves having moved to the front to form a shield wall. The orcs and minotaurs, as well as Smitty and Dalia, raised bows and crossbows while Blake prepared to cast some offensive magic.

Most of the remaining horde charged toward the bridge, three hundred at least, all of them wanting to get far from the flaming gates and exploding trolls. Some few scattered in terror, dropping their weapons and running back the way they'd come, toward the goblin settlement. Some of those charging toward the dwarves seemed to have second thoughts and began to slow. Not wanting them to escape, Max cast *Boom!* on two of the rearmost, causing one's head and the other's chest to explode. Then he cast *Zap!* into a cluster of three others, stunning them so that they fell on their faces, their bodies locked up and appearing to be dead. This motivated the rest to keep going.

All except for one clever hobgoblin, who turned and took a knee, raising a crossbow and aiming at Max. A wicked looking barbed bolt flew upward, striking his neck. The force knocked him backward off the wall, blood spurting from an artery as he fell. When his back struck the stone twenty feet below, the air that was forced from him propelled a fountain of blood into the air. He felt his ribs crack, and he nearly lost consciousness when his head struck the stone a fraction of a second later.

Max's ears rang, and he couldn't seem to take a breath. He could hear a voice he thought was Lo'tang's shouting, but couldn't make out the words over the ringing. His vision was blurry, and fear gripped him. Closing his eyes, he tried to focus on casting a heal, but couldn't manage it. Something deep in his consciousness laughed at him, calling to mind the grey dwarves he'd shot and knocked off the walls of Nogroz. The same had just happened to him.

He felt a tug at his throat, and a flash of pain, then his mouth filled with a warm liquid he assumed was his own blood. But the pain receded quickly, and Max felt the familiar sensation of a healing potion working through him. Keeping his eyes closed, he found that his throat had cleared enough for him to take a much needed breath. Then another. After the third deep breath, he managed to cast a heal on himself. He thought it odd that Dalia hadn't healed him, then remembered that she was on the other side of the wall, across the bridge. *Never split the party* he thought to himself.

Opening his eyes, he found Lo'tang looking down at him, holding an empty potion vial. "King Max! Can you hear me?" the orc looked alarmed. Unable to speak yet, Max raised a hand and patted the orc's arm. He continued to lay there, casting another heal on himself as he waited for his throat, ribs, and skull to mend fully. When he was mostly pain-free, he held up a hand, which the orc grabbed and pulled him up. Looking down at the stone, he saw an alarmingly large, roughly Max-shaped pool of blood. His own chest was covered in it as well, and when he reached behind his head, he found his hair sticky, fresh blood covering his hand when he pulled it away. No wonder Lo'tang had looked so concerned.

Back on his feet, Max looked around. The gate was partially open, and fully engulfed in flame. Several guards were tossing buckets of water at it, without much success. Max wished Blake were there with his water spell, but again he'd left his friends in the rear. His plan had been to frighten and aggro the enemy, then race back to the bridge with them following.

"Even the best battle plans don't survive first contact with the enemy." He muttered aloud, causing the orc next to him to nod in agreement. "Let's get back to the top of the wall."

Lo'tang led Max to a nearby stair and they climbed to the top, Max moving slowly, his balance still a little shaky after the blow to the brain. When he looked out from atop the wall, he saw that the hobgoblins had engaged with his people. The dwarves had formed up their shield wall two rows deep at the far end of the bridge, and the hobs were savagely throwing themselves at, and occasionally over, the tanks. Any hobgoblin that cleared the wall was instantly mobbed by three or four kobolds, who mercilessly massacred them. The orcs fired arrows and bolts from the two flanks, the hobs packed so tightly that the archers couldn't miss. Max saw one of the minotaurs pull a long spear from his inventory and hurl it over the dwarves' heads into the horde. It blasted through three of the hobgoblins before stopping halfway through the chest of a fourth.

Blake's *Fire Strike* spell crackled through the darkness and struck the center of the bridge, the impact scattering hobs, causing half a dozen to be pushed over the sides of the bridge to fall into the crevasse. The fire spell also frightened the remaining trolls, who had been advancing through the horde toward the dwarves. They moved more quickly, fleeing the fire behind them, and more hobs were crumpled.

Max feared for the dwarves as the trolls approached. The massive creatures made the frontline warriors look tiny by comparison. The dwarves, for their part, began to chant, their shields locked together. Fortunately for them, the trolls didn't coordinate and hit their lines all at once. With each impact, the tanks in front of the troll were pushed back a step or two, but those behind helped reinforce them. All six trolls were stopped, but not defeated. They began to rain down blows from their massive fists or clubs. The second row of tanks raised their shields over their comrades' heads, and a blue glow emanated from the entire double row of shields. Fists and weapons bounced off, and the trolls roared in frustration.

Just then Max noticed the minotaurs running forward. A shout from Rockbreaker cleared their path, and the defenders on the wall cheered as the brutes drew sword and axe. Easily able to reach over their dwarven comrades, they chopped and sliced at the trolls. Erdun's axe beheaded one of them, a surprised look on the monster's face as it rolled under the shield wall. Another troll lost an arm at the shoulder, and another had its skull split by a massive two-handed sword. Troll blood sprayed the front lines of both friend and foe, and Max prayed that Blake had noticed the explosions at the gate, and wouldn't cast another fire spell.

Used to being able to relay real-time orders via comms, Max found himself shouting, "Hold fire! Hold fire!" and cursing the lack of radios on this world. He watched the battle dreading the explosion that Blake's spell could cause, blasting dwarves along with hobgoblins.

It never came. The remaining trolls roared in challenge, bashing at the dwarven shields or reaching over top to take aim at minotaur warriors. The minotaurs happily obliged, their blood boiling in battle rage, calling for the dwarves to step aside so they could get at their enemies. Having no such order from Rockbreaker, the dwarves held their positions, forcing the taller combatants to fight at arm's length. While the brutes swung at each other, the front line tanks stabbed and hacked at the trolls' legs, draining them of small amounts of blood before the wounds healed. Over time, the blood loss slowed the trolls, and the minotaurs got more and more clean hits. A hand removed here, a deep cut to the neck there. Max nearly jumped off the wall and ran to help when the blue glow of the shield wall faded, and two dwarves were crushed under troll blows. Lo'tang held him back, shouting, "You can't help them!"

As the melee fighters wore down the trolls, the archers mowed down the hobgoblins. Max guessed there were at least a hundred of them, every shot wounding a target, if not killing them. In minutes, there was but one troll standing, and less than a hundred hobgoblins.

"Push open the gate!" Max ordered, seeing what was coming. "Everyone get down there, now!"

He leapt off the wall, his stone-hard bones absorbing the impact as the soldiers behind him scrambled down. Trotting toward the bridge, he didn't wait to see how many followed him out of the city. The diminished hobgoblin force was soon going to realize it was doomed, and attempt a retreat. Max didn't want them to. The more afraid the local monsters were of Deepcrag, the happier he'd be. Let the only reports they hear be from the terrified few that fled.

Drawing his bow, he put an arrow through the back of the nearest hobgoblin, then another, then another, only slowing to a walk as he fired. He heard the clomp of heavy boots on stone behind him, and smiled. Lo'tang had managed to push past the burning gate and join him with his forces.

Stowing his bow, he drew Storm Reaver, and raised it high. Looking over his shoulder, he saw eighty warriors, faces grim, ready to fight. "The troll is mine." He growled loudly enough for everyone to hear. "As for the rest, slaughter them all!"

The orcs roared in approval, weapons thrust in the air. A moment later, their army across the bridge joined them, the dwarves shouting in unison, taking a step forward and shoving the hobgoblins back across the length of their line. One of the minotaurs went insane with bloodlust, taking a running leap over top of the dwarves and swinging his massive axe at the last remaining troll. The weapon chopped through its upper arm, the blade lodging between ribs and getting stuck there. As the nearly senseless minotaur tried to free its blade, half a dozen hobs chopped at his legs and back, creating small wounds with each blow.

The troll turned and used its remaining hand to grab the minotaur by his neck, throttling him even as it crushed his windpipe. Still, the brave warrior grabbed at the trolls face, pushing a thumb into each eye, blinding it before he went limp and died. The enraged troll tossed the body, knocking down several dwarves, then began to thrash around blindly. Max dashed forward, then cast *Jump* to a clear spot near the troll. The moment he arrived, he was smashed in the face with a blindly flung forearm, knocked off his feet, and very nearly over the edge of the bridge. The troll, feeling the solid contact, roared in his general direction and stepped forward.

Max cast a heal on himself, then cast *Drain* on the troll, channeling it as he quietly got to his feet. Raising his sword, he waited for the beast to take another swing, then cleanly removed its remaining arm at the elbow. The monster charged toward him, head first, and Max simply stepped to one side and thrust his sword's point forward. It pushed through the troll's cheek, driving its jaw open and slicing away teeth as it penetrated deep into the creature's brain.

Breathing hard, Max turned back toward the city to find that both sides of his forces had charged, slaughtering the remaining hobs in a chaotic melee free-for-all. Even as he stepped toward them, the last of the enemy fell, and his troops met in the middle, shaking hands and patting shoulders in congratulations. From somewhere above the bridge, a small voice shouted, "Gnomes rule!"

Max spent the next ten minutes helping Dalia heal the wounded. Their casualties had been light, thankfully.

Of the nearly three hundred total fighters in Max's force, there were six dead orcs, three dead dwarves, and three dead kobolds, and two dead elven guards from the merchant force, in addition to the heroic minotaur. All of the wounded were fully recovered thanks to healing potions, and Dalia and Max's spells.

"Lo'tang, Rockbreaker, I want at least one tenth of our forces to be able to heal." Max told them after receiving their reports. "I don't care whether that means you recruit healers, or teach our warriors how to heal, or some combination of both. Ideally it would be more like one third, but I'll settle for one tenth, for now."

Both saluted with fist to chest, and Lo'tang bowed his head. Rockbreaker knew better, and just grinned at Max.

"Alright, Lo'tang, take your troops back into Deepcrag. Get that fire extinguished. Rockbreaker, leave a dozen of yours here to bolster his forces, and head home. Take our fallen with you for a proper burial. Loot the corpses first, and split it all between the troops. The families of the fallen will also get a payment from the kingdom treasury. Tell Redmane to send some people to repair the gate immediately. Or…" He looked at the burning ironwood. "I guess, replace the gate."

Max looked at the members of his group. "I need to go to the temple and convince Glitterspindle to make us some portal pedestals right away. You guys can come along, or head back to Stormhaven and do your own thing."

"Back to the temple sounds good." Dylan, who had spent most of the battle trying to control Princess, replied. "I want to take Princess hunting. He's hungry."

Nessa, ever pragmatic, nodded toward the bridge and asked, "Does he enjoy hobgoblin meat?"

"Good idea!" Dylan led the lizard toward the bridge, where they waited for the bodies to be looted.

Dalia volunteered, "I'll wait here for them, and take them through the portal when Princess is full. We'll join you at the temple."

"Boss, before we go, what was that radio thing you did back there?" Blake asked. "Also, hold on. You're a hot mess, boss. This might be a little cold." Blake waved his hands and several buckets worth of water plunged down on Max from above, washing most of the blood from him. Blake was right, it was cold.

"What radio thing?" Max spluttered, forcing himself not to cuss at his corporal for his dubious help.

"During the battle. Right after the minotaurs got all slicey dicey on the trolls. I heard you like, inside my head, telling me to hold fire."

Max froze.

"You mean, you heard me yelling from atop the wall?"

"Over the sounds of the fighting, the trolls and minotaurs roaring at each other? No, boss, it was your voice inside my head. Not even like it would sound through an earpiece, like our old comms. It was... I wanna say telepathy, but that's not right. It was literally like your voice echoing inside my skull."

"Red?" Max's pulse was up again, and he found himself crossing his fingers as he looked for his guide. She had disappeared before the battle, not a fan of the blood and gore.

"I'm checking, Max." She looked him up and down from atop Blake's head, the gnome looking upward and slightly cross-eyed at hearing her voice from above. "At least yer learnin' to wash up a bit after a fight." She pretended to sniff at him, then made a disgusted face.

"Very funny." Max mumbled, looking around to make sure no one was observing too closely. "What did Blake hear?"

"Sounds like party chat to me, boss." Smitty volunteered. "Though I didn't know that was a thing here."

"Party chat?" Nessa asked, her head tilted to one side like a curious cat.

"It's when members of a party can speak to each other without speaking out loud, so only other party members can hear it. Kind of like a magic link that allows you to hear each other's voices in your head."

"I've never heard of such a thing." Nessa looked from Smitty to Blake, then Max. "But I can see how it would be very useful. Especially when operating in stealth. I would be able to sneak into an enemy stronghold and report what I see as I see it. It would prevent me from having to sneak back out again, and in the event I was captured or killed, you would still have the information."

Smitty nodded. "It's good for coordinating attacks from multiple directions at the same time, or at staggered intervals. Or calling for a change in plans during a fight, or a retreat."

"Or in my case," Blake added, "Max was making sure I didn't cast a fire spell on those wounded trolls and blow up our dwarves and other allies. Not that it was necessary, I'm not a total noob." He winked at Smitty.

Max barely heard the conversation, his focus on Red as she moved a tiny finger in the air, making poking and swiping motions, clearly manipulating her interface, or Max's. He wasn't sure how her access to his info worked.

"Ah, here it is!" She clapped her hands together. As she did, Max got several notifications. "Ya should have read these sooner." She admonished him. Max had received several notifications when the final hobgoblin had perished or fled the area, but he'd been too concerned about healing to read them. With a wave of her hand, they popped up again.

Quest Complete: Defend Stormhaven!
Congratulations!
You have successfully defended against an invasion of your territory.
In addition, you defeated an enemy force more than twice the size of your own,
with minimal losses among your own forces.

Reward: 1,350,000 experience; Class level increase! +1 to Sovereign Class.
Morale boost! The morale of your citizenry is boosted by 5%.
Production boost! Due to the morale increase, your citizens are 2% more productive.
This includes crafters, farmers, miners, and citizen fertility.
Title earned: Foe Hammer!
For single-handedly destroying 25% of the enemy force, you have earned the title Foe Hammer.
Additional 500,000 experience awarded.
Reputation with hobgoblin and troll races is now: Feared.

Max blinked several times. When Smitty asked what he was seeing, he read them the notifications. The orc snorted at the title. "Should have been more like *Murder Hobo*."

Red wasn't done. Another notification popped up, completely distracting Max.

Congratulations! New magic discovered!
By combining a desperate need for a specific action, your intimate knowledge of how it should work, your indomitable will, and your desire to protect your citizens through the use of this action, the gods have granted you the right to use, name, and teach, a newly created magic.
Reward: Experience: 1,500,000; +5 Intelligence; +5 Wisdom;
What would you like to name this spell?

Max nearly leapt for joy as he read the words. He quickly named the spell *Party Chat*, and another notification popped up.

You have created the new magic spell Party Chat.
*This is a spell in the **Mental** magic school. As its creator, you have the*
ability to teach this spell to anyone with sufficient ability to use it.
Party Chat allows all members of a party, numbering up to twenty,
to speak directly to each other privately, without non-party members hearing.
Range limit: 2 miles. Mana cost: 20mp initial cast; 1mp/minute to maintain.

Rather than read the announcement aloud to his friends, he simply cast Party Chat, and shouted, "We have party chat!". He felt bad a moment later when they all winced at the shout ringing in their brains. "Sorry."

*****

Lagrass was awakened by the rattle of metal as the old man placed the pot back on the hanger and swung it over the fire. He sat up, rubbing his eyes, feeling the aches and pains from sleeping on the floor.

"Breakfast is on the house. It's only gruel with a bit of honey." The old man grumped at him as he set a small pot of honey on the table. "Or if you'd prefer, you can walk to town in time to get bacon and eggs and such at the tavern."

"I appreciate it. Smells good." Lagrass got to his feet and rolled up the blankets into a single bundle. The old man handed him two lengths of leather cord to tie it up.

"Don't mention it. Be just a minute or three till it's ready." He moved to grab a couple of bowls from a cupboard.

"Is there anything I can do to help you here before I leave?" Lagrass asked, looking out the window at the dawning day. The sun was still well below the tree canopy.

"Nah. Though, I may walk with you into town. I was planning to go soon enough, anyway. Might as well have some company. The woods are pretty tame, but you never know." He glanced at the mantle, and Lagrass followed his gaze, noticing that Lizzy was back in her place.

"Not that a low level weakling like me could be of much help, but I too would welcome the company." Lagrass bowed his head. The old man moved to the fire bending to stir the gruel in the pot with a wooden spoon. As he straightened up, he grunted in pain, Lagrass' kitchen knife sliding into his back and through his liver. One hand tried to reach for Lizzy, but Lagrass quickly stabbed two more times, then spun him around and drove the knife up under his beard and into his brain.

Leveling up again, Lagrass took a minute to drag the body out of the small cabin and a short distance into the trees out back. Returning, he pulled the pot of now thick and half-burnt gruel off the fire. Spooning some into a bowl, he poured a liberal dose of honey over it, and ate a leisurely breakfast as he checked his notifications and assigned attribute points.

Breakfast finished, he spent an hour searching the small cabin for anything valuable. He'd grabbed the wolf hide on his way back inside, and taken Lizzy and her scabbard down from her place above the mantle. She was now belted around his waist, and he felt stronger and more secure with her there. When he looted the old man, he got his silver back, plus a few copper coins. He found a small box under the head of the mattress in the bedroom, but it only contained a letter and a lock of grey hair. There was a clean shirt, which he promptly traded for his bloodstained one. The only other thing of value that he found was a ring that looked to be made of silver. When he put it on, he discovered that it was a storage ring with twenty five slots. It contained a frying pan, a canteen, thirty feet of rope, and a large oiled tarp that could be used to create a shelter in a pinch.

Sticking the few useful items he found into his inventory, Lagrass left the cabin and followed the trail the old man had described, heading for the town, and hopefully a good meal.

Chapter 23

Max buried his face in his hands, shaking his head as he did so. Talking to Glitterspindle was like talking to a five year old schizophrenic genius on a sugar high. The little metal gnome never stopped moving, and refused to focus on any topic for more than a few seconds. Already, the flood of dwarven and gnomish engineers that had crowded the temple hoping to learn from the mechamage had mostly given up in exasperation. Only a die-hard few had been motivated enough to hang in there. They were treated like disciples, ordered around by the brain in the glass, given menial jobs seemingly at a whim.

"For the last time, Glitterspindle. I need to know how quickly you can build me at least three portal pedestals." Max had asked this question half a dozen times already, and each time the gnome began to answer, he got sidetracked talking about materials, tweaking the spell formulae, or what color Max wanted the pedestals to be.

Glitterspindle halted mid-step, his tiny metal body freezing in place. "A month, at least!" the little gnome shouted, its high-pitched voice grating on Max's ears. He resumed his hustle over to a control panel on one wall, already forgetting they were having a conversation.

"A month? Why a month? Spellslinger built me one for Stormhaven overnight!"

"He most certainly did not!" Glitterspindle turned on Max, momentarily forsaking the control panel. "He may have *programmed* a pedestal in a single night, but he did not create one from scratch!"

Max paused with his mouth open, halting the annoyed reply that was about to gush forth. He tilted his head, considering. "What do you mean by programmed?"

"Spatial magic is very exacting, stupid orc! One must know one's place in the universe exactly, and know the same about every portal one wishes to connect to. In addition, one must take into consideration gravity, the world's rotation speed, and a hundred other factors when one decides to rip a hole in reality that others can pass safely through! The math involved..." the little metal head shook back and forth, grinding slightly. "Oh! I need some oil. Minions! Where are those stupid little orcs when I need them?"

"Glitterspindle!" Max shouted. "What about the math involved?"

"What? Oh! Do you have any oil on you, perchance?" the construct's head moved back and forth again. "No, how unfortunate. The math involved is beyond the capacity of most minds. And if one does not get the calculations exactly correct... poof!"

"Poof?" Max sighed.

"My guess is it'd be more like boom!" Red said from his shoulder.

"Implosion, explosions, being sucked into a merciless vortex that dumps your highly compressed body into a formless void for all eternity... just a few of the consequences of sloppy math." Glitterspindle looked at Max, raised one eyebrow, and cackled like a madman. "Even I, a true Master, have killed myself at least once, that I can remember!" the gnome tapped its chin, the metal finger making a *tink* sound with each impact. "Or rather, I killed the minion dressed up as me. Yes, yes. Always better to send a minion through to start with. Can't put my incredible brain at risk, oh no! But in case it works, it must be the spitting image of me that arrives at the other end, mustn't it? Best thing for building my reputation!"

Max pictured hapless gnome acolytes trudging up to a newly constructed pedestal, dressed like Glitterspindle as they risked their lives as test pilots. Only to explode, implode, or perish in other painful and spectacular ways.

"Alright, so Spellslinger used an already constructed pedestal, and just programmed it to work in Stormhaven, and to connect to the other portals. I understand. Now we're making progress. If it'll take a month to make three pedestals, how bout just one?"

"A month! I can build three as quickly as one, assuming I have all the materials, and some assistance. Creating a part from scratch is time consuming. Duplicating the finished part is much quicker."

Max almost felt like he was making progress now. "Alright, what can I do to help? Can you teach me some teleportation magic so that I can assist you in your work? What materials do you need?"

"I gave you the list!" the gnome barked at him, its eyes glowing briefly. "Just triple the quantities! Once I

455

have the materials, I will build you new portal pedestals as fast as anyone can!"

"We're working on gathering those materials. The merchants will send them here as quickly as possible. In the meantime…"

"Yes…?" The gnome arched an eyebrow on its surprisingly versatile metal face. "Oh! The teaching. Yes, I can teach you. Spatial magic can be painful, though. Are you sure?"

"I already have a spell that teleports me short distances…"

"Well then! This will be slightly less painful for you. Follow me." Glitterspindle walked to a blank wall and placed a metal hand on a spot about two feet above the floor. Max was only half surprised to see a section of the wall, a short section, slide to one side. The gnome walked through, motioning for Max to follow. He had to bend deeply at the waist to fit through the door, then remain that way as the tiny room beyond also had a low ceiling. It turned out the room was an elevator car, and they dropped quickly after the gnome pressed the bottommost button.

When the car stopped, the gnome strode into a wide expanse with high ceilings that allowed Max to straighten back up, which he was grateful for. He followed the fast-moving little metal monstrosity through stacks of crates and around piles of gadgets. A moment later they passed through another door as Glitterspindle said, "There's a scroll that will help you with the basic principles. Faster for you to read than for me to try to teach them to you…"

Max was no longer listening, as the room they stepped into appeared to be lined along both walls with... portal pedestals. He stopped walking and stared at one until his *Examine* skill kicked in.

Portal Pedestal
Unprogrammed
Item Quality: Epic

Max looked from one pedestal to the next, then switched sides and began counting the ones on the opposite side of the room. Clearing his throat, he called out. "Uhhh, Master Glitterspindle, could you come back here a moment?"

The gnome pivoted on one metal foot without losing a step, turning back toward Max and continuing to talk about the scroll as he approached. When he got to within a few feet of Max, he stopped both the walking and the talking. He leaned way back and tilted his head to look up at Max. "Yes?"

Max tried his best to remain calm. "This appears to be a room full of portal pedestals."

Glitterspindle rotated his head left, then right. "It does, indeed. Okay, let's go! That scroll is just in the next room, in my junk trunk."

"Wait. Glitterspindle, if you have all of these here already, why will it take you a month to get me three of them? Why can't I just take three of these?"

The tiny metal monster clenched both of its fists, its eyes flashing a deep red. "Stupid orc! You did not ask me if I had three portal pedestals! You asked me how long it would take me to create three new ones!"

Max gritted his teeth, quietly wondering if he was strong enough to squeeze the construct's metal neck until its head popped off. He'd give the head to Redmane to use as a paperweight. Or maybe to Teeglin, as a toy. He relaxed a little, imagining the conversations the child and the insane gnome might have.

"Why did you not tell me you had a supply already constructed?" Max tried to keep his tone patient and calm.

"Of course I have a supply! What did you think I did to pass the time all these years? Write my autobiography? Why do you think I was out of materials for the three new portals you want built? Because I used them all, building *these*!" he indicated the rows of devices. "No one ever came to purchase them, so I stored them down here. Really starting to clutter up the place."

Max bit his lip. He jammed the claw on one thumb into the palm of his other hand, focusing on the pain to help calm himself. After several deep breaths, during which the gnome disappeared into the next room, Max called out. "How about if I just grab three or four of these?"

The little mechamage's voice echoed out of the doorway. "Found it! Here's the beginner scroll for minions!" He walked back into the room carrying a scroll high over his head in victory. "What? Oh, sure. Take all the pedestals you want!" He waved the scroll at Max.

"Read this, then come find me. I'll teach you some more. If I'm not too busy making you those three new pedestals!" He cackled, handing over the scroll.

"But now I don't need..." Max paused mid-sentence, thinking. He could simply take the pedestals and end this whole infuriating conversation right then and there. "Thank you, Master Glitterspindle. I will study this and return for a lesson." He took the scroll, then walked over to one side of the room and touched four of the pedestals, each one going into a separate slot in his inventory.

When he turned around, the gnome was back on the elevator, and the doors were closing. It gave him a friendly wave just before they clanked shut, and Max was left stranded in the room. Lucky for him, he had party chat available now, or he might have been forgotten and left for dead down there.

"Smitty, when the little shit gets there, would you please send him back down here to get me?"

"Sure thing, boss!" Max could almost hear the grin on the orc's face. Hanging his head in resignation, Max decided to just take the finished portals as a win, and get out of the temple as quickly as possible.

Which turned out to be nearly an hour, as the gnome didn't return to where Smitty was, and the rest of the party had to search the temple for him.

*****

Max and the others returned to Stormhaven, where there was quite a bit of activity. Redmane's clansmen were already arriving, along with needed materials, and were preparing the first convoy through Deepcrag to the gnome settlement. He quickly informed his chamberlain that he had four pedestals in his possession, and wanted to place one of them in the gnome city as quickly as possible.

"If yer willin' to bring Spellslinger in on yer secret, he can install it quickly enough." the old dwarf offered.

Not seeing any other way, Max agreed. "This is going to cost me more bottles, isn't it?"

Redmane shook his head. "Nah. Give him the same quest ye gived me, the one to secure the outpost, it'll be payment enough." He shrugged. "Besides, none would be more motivated to learn the rune magic than a dwarven mage like himself."

Max handed over one of the pedestals. "Then please call him here, get an oath of secrecy from him, share the quest, and send him along with this first caravan. Make them wait for him if necessary. The delay will be more than worth it if we can just send everyone straight there. But this portal remains a secret." Max warned. "Your clansmen who'll be using it will need to keep quiet."

"They've already sworn, Max." Redmane's tone of voice let it be known that Max was on the verge of insulting his clan's honor.

"Perfect. Thank you, Master Redmane." Max backed off. "When the time comes, we'll put another portal at the goblin settlement. And I'm considering putting one at the way station."

Redmane shook his head. "That'd be a waste o' resources, Max. Ye got one at the temple already, only six miles away. The way they be buildin' up that settlement, they can hold against the entire orc army for several hours, at least. More than enough time fer our reinforcements to arrive."

Resisting the urge to tell the dwarf that they had access to dozens of pedestals, Max just nodded. For all he knew, the insane gnome would start passing them out like candy now, and Max would only have the four he'd already taken. Which, he had to admit, was more than ample reward for the time spent clearing the temple. That line of thought got him itching to run back there and grab a dozen more.

"Please have Enoch place that portal someplace aboveground and well inside our planned walls. Maybe put it in a market square we can surround with additional walls? What am I saying? He'll know what to do." Max shook his head. He was trying to micromanage too many things. It was why he had limited himself to running just a squad in the private sector, instead of a larger force. He liked being hands-on, managing his small elite group.

"I'm going to go work at the forge for a while, clear my head, and keep from poking my nose in where it's not needed." Max waved to a chuckling Redmane and walked away.

*****

461

Dylan stepped into Erdun's shop and looked around. The elder minotaur called out from the back, "Is that you, Dylan?"

"Yes sir!" Dylan walked toward the back room where the enchanter did most of his work, and where Dylan had been learning all he could about enchanting.

"Found a place to house your lizard?" Erdun asked, the phrasing causing Dylan to chuckle to himself.

"I did, at least temporarily. He's out in the mushroom forest outside the gate, hunting critters. I warned the farmers to keep clear of the place for a day or two, so there are no accidents."

"In that case, I have something for you." the minotaur held up a carved figurine as Dylan entered the room. It was carved from onyx, or maybe obsidian, and was a nearly perfect representation of Princess.

"Wow! It looks so much like him. Thank you, Master Erdun. But how did you have time to carve this?"

"It isn't carved, it's shaped. I had one of the dwarves that was with us at Deepcrag create it for me. Then I enchanted it for you." He placed the figurine in Dylan's open palm. "Hold this in contact with his skin and yours, and activate the enchantment. It will allow you to dismiss and summon your pet at will, storing his essence within the likeness. Keep it safe, my friend, for if it breaks while his essence is contained within, he will be lost to you."

Dylan stroked the lizard figurine's back with one finger. "That's... amazing! Thank you so much!" He looked up at the elder. "But you shouldn't have taken so much time away from Max's project."

"Bah! It's a simple enchantment, known to any novice worth his or her salt. A matter of minutes to complete. I'm surprised no one mentioned this option to you before."

Dylan rolled his eyes. "They've been having too much fun teasing me about Princess and watching me try to wrangle him. It's getting easier now, as we spend time together. I can feel our bond growing stronger."

Erdun nodded. "I had a bonded companion when I was young. A grindler named Ogtor. In the years we spent together, we developed an exceptional bond."

"What's a grindler?" Dylan asked.

"Ha! I suppose they'd be rare around here. They live mostly in the frozen mountain ranges where I was born. Picture a massive, shaggy round head with a tooth-filled mouth large enough to swallow a goblin whole. Add four stumpy legs and a short tail, that's a grindler. They don't move very quickly, most often just rolling in the direction they want to go. But they are fierce and fearless in battle. I found him in a cave, wounded from a battle with a rock troll. He had a broken leg, cracked skull, and was missing several teeth from biting the troll. He was also quite sick from eating troll meat. I took pity on him and healed him, and we were companions for twenty years."

"I'd have to be pretty hungry to try and eat a rock troll." Dylan grinned at the minotaur.

"He was starving, too wounded to hunt. I think he held out as long as he could."

"Well, thank you again." Dylan held up the figurine briefly before stowing it in his inventory. "I have something for you, as well." He pulled a pouch containing five hundred gold coins from his inventory." This is from Max, for the family of the fallen minotaur. He apologizes that it isn't more, but the kingdom is not very wealthy yet."

"There is no need." Erdun tried to push the pouch away. "We live a warrior's life, and expect to die in battle. It is the death we seek. His children are fully grown, with children of their own, and his wife is a skilled crafter. They can look after themselves."

"I'm glad to hear that, but please take this anyway. It would make Max feel bad if you refused."

"Very well." Erdun accepted the pouch and bowed his head. "Please thank King Max on behalf of the family. Also, I think I may have what he's looking for in another week or so."

"Yes, about that. If you wouldn't mind stopping by the palace, Max has something he wants to share with you that I think might help your project along. He sort of accidentally discovered this spell called *Party Chat...*" Dylan went on to explain the magic, and Erdun was on his feet and headed out of the shop before the ogre was even done speaking.

They found Max at the forge, where he set down the hammer he was using, leaving the dagger blade he'd been working on to cool on the anvil.

"Master Erdun, I wanted to offer my condolences, and my sincere thanks. Your warrior fought bravely, and died a hero."

"Thank you, King Max. It is what we all desire. To die in honorable battle." The enchanter paused for a moment, then his eagerness got the best of him. "Dylan tells me you have created a new spell."

"Ah, yes. It was sort of an accident. I really, really wanted to be able to talk to Blake, to keep him from killing more of our people, and was thinking about a system similar to what you've been working on. It seems the gods took my knowledge of how it should work, and granted me the spell. I can teach it to you, if you'd like."

Erdun hesitated. "A new spell is a rare thing, King Max. A spell as useful as what Dylan describes is invaluable. Were you to sell it to the Mages' Guild, they would shower you in gold. I have nothing of equal value to exchange with you."

Max shook his head. "If you can figure out the enchantment I've asked for, that's more than payment enough. *Party Chat* is useful, but at a limited range. The ability to communicate instantly with all my outposts and settlements has more value to me than I can describe."

"Then I will accept this magic." Erdun bowed his head. "And hope that it will indeed help with research on your enchantment."

Max placed a hand on the minotaur's head, because that's what everyone who had taught him a spell had done. "I have to warn you, I've never taught a spell before. I'm not sure how…"

Erdun's voice was calm and even. "Simply focus on the spell, then on your desire to share it with me."

Max did as the elder instructed, closing his eyes to remove distractions. There was a feeling of warmth, and a tingling in his hand, and seconds later he knew the transfer had been successful.

Erdun's eyes widened, and he bared his teeth in the minotaur version of a smile. "Ah, I see! Yes, quite useful, this magic. I believe you are right that it will simplify my enchantment. And allow greater numbers of connections. Where before I might have managed half a dozen connected items, I believe I might see how we can make twenty." He snorted, a loud bull snort of laughter. "I was not exaggerating when I say the Mages' Guild would pay dearly for this. In gold, in magic spells, whatever you might need. If I were you I would contact them immediately."

"Thank you, Master Erdun. I'll consider it. I could use some funds for… another project we're working on. And the kingdom's treasury could always use a boost. Which reminds me, anything you need for your research, just let Dylan or Redmane know, and we'll find a way to get it."

"I believe I have all I need, thank you." Erdun bowed his head again and departed. Dylan gave Max a thumbs-up and left right behind the enchanter, on his way to bind Princess and the lizard figurine.

Max looked at the cooling roughly shaped blade on the anvil, his attempt at a dwarven steel dagger. With a sigh of regret he grabbed it with his tongs and set it atop the scrap pile. As much as he wanted to relax and practice his skills, the promise of much needed income took priority. Putting away his tools, he went to go find Redmane to find out how to get in touch with the Mages' Guild. A last look at the half-finished dagger reminded him of something. He quickly checked his inventory, then smiled.

*****

Max sat in the small dining hall, having breakfast with Smitty and Birona, his new bride, who refused to look up at Max, blushing whenever he spoke to her. Initially it had been endearing, but now it was getting awkward, and Max mostly focused on Smitty.

"Meeting with the Mages' guild this morning." He said between mouthfuls of scrambled eggs. The eggs from the local birds tasted different than the chicken eggs they were used to, but were still delicious. And bacon was good no matter which animal it came from. Except maybe turkey bacon.

"You sure you want to do that, boss?" Smitty asked. "Right now, it's one hell of a tactical advantage for us in fights. You teach the spell to them, before you know it, everyone will have it."

"I considered that. Redmane and I discussed it at length yesterday. I think our need for cash right now overrides the loss of that advantage. Besides, so far I'm the only one who can teach the spell. It'll take whatever mage they send to learn it a while to level up the skill enough to teach it to others. And I'm not giving them exclusive rights to the spell, so I can sell it to Ironhand and a few others before they do." Max winked at the two orcs, causing Birona to blush again. "And I won't be selling the guild Erdun's enchantment. That's way more valuable. I'm going to make him rich, creating these items for me to sell to our allies."

"You're going to change the way this whole world works, boss."

Max nodded, chewing thoughtfully. "I'm starting to think that's why I was sent here. At first, when Red began saying I was sent here for a reason, I figured it was to overthrow some big bad evil. But I've not heard of any such thing in the time we've been here. So maybe I'm just here, *we're* just here… to make things better."

"That'd be nice." Smitty hugged his wife with one arm. "I hope you're right."

Teeglin came bounding into the room a moment later, followed by Redmane and a tall light elf mage in deep blue robes. The mage carried a walking staff with a glowing green crystal mounted on the top.

Excited, Teeglin practically shouted, "King Maximilian Storm, may I present Archmagus Eldilon of the Mages' Guild!"

Everyone in the room smiled at her enthusiasm as Max got to his feet and the elf bowed his head slightly. "Welcome, Archmagus, and thank you for coming. Please, have a seat and join us for breakfast." Max indicated the several empty seats at the table. "This is Smitty and his new wife, Birona."

The elf smiled at the two orcs, making his staff disappear as he took a seat across from Max, Redmane settling next to him.

"I must admit, I was surprised to hear that the Archmagus himself was coming here. I would have expected just one of the local mages stationed here to maintain the lights."

The elf paused in dishing up some food, and looked up at Max. "Well, it seems one of the most promising mages we sent here for that purpose has abandoned his post to go adventuring with you, Majesty." His lips twitched in a small smile. "But no, a spell of this value must be learned by one of our elite, so that they may quickly level up the skill and distribute it. Also, I am a Battlemage, and a spell of this nature is of particular interest to me."

Max nodded. "The battlefield uses are many and varied. I've been a soldier most of my life, and had access to something similar... where I'm from."

This time the elf actually laughed. "Ha! You need not fear, King Maximilian. I know what you are, and where you're from." His eyes flickered around the table, unsure of who was aware of Max's status as Battleborne. "I had an informative chat with your corporal Blake when he first joined us."

Recognizing where the conversation was headed, Smitty got up to clear the room. "Well, lots to do today! It was a pleasure meeting you, Archmagus. Birona, we need to see to... that, thing we talked about." He practically pulled his confused wife from her chair. "Teeglin, we'll need your help too. Come with us." Max gave him a look of thanks as he nearly dragged the two ladies from the dining hall.

"Your men are well trained, and clearly loyal." the elf observed. "I must say, I have never heard of an instance where four Battleborne gathered together in one place. Or even more than one working together. In the past, they have either battled each other, or avoided contact."

"If you're willing, I'd like to talk with you about that. The history of Battleborne in this world, who they were, what they did. I'm still trying to figure out why we were sent here. There wouldn't happen to be a rising dark power gathering strength somewhere, would there?"

"Heh. Not that I'm aware of, King Maximilian. And our guild has eyes and ears in most major nations and cities." Max tried not to smile as Redmane cleared his throat at that statement. He found himself very glad that the dwarf hadn't let the guild light up his palace. "And of course I'd be happy to share whatever information we have on Battleborne. Consider it a gift, in celebration of your new office."

"Thank you, Archmagus. I'm sure that on this world, much as on my own, knowledge is power."

"Speaking of which, I would like to invite you and the other Battleborne to visit our academy. I think our instructors could teach you a great deal of useful magic."

Max caught a look from Redmane, and nodded. The negotiations had begun. "I would love to visit there, and am eager to learn from your esteemed mages. However, I'm afraid that must wait a bit, as I've got a rapidly expanding kingdom to build and strengthen. I'm afraid it will be some time before I can leave for any extended period." He smiled at the elf, being careful not to bare his fangs. "What we truly need more than anything right now is to build up our treasury. We've got guards and soldiers to pay, construction costs mounting, and an ever increasing number of mouths to feed."

"Yes, I have heard rumors about the reclaiming of Deepcrag and its portal, as well as your interests in the goblin and gnome settlements. The Greystone merchants are announcing far and wide that they're recruiting new residents, and opening up a long lost trade route."

"Word travels fast." Max sighed, pretending disappointment in a supposed secret revealed. "I suppose that was inevitable."

"We can certainly assist with your expansion efforts, Majesty." the elf began.

Max held up a hand. "Please, just call me Max, at least in informal settings like this. I don't pretend to know the social hierarchy of this world yet, but I figure your position as Archmagus has got to be on the same level as a small-time king."

"Not quite, but I shall honor your request, Max. And please call me Eldilon." He bowed his head slightly. "In any case, in exchange for teaching me this new magic of yours, we are prepared to offer you sixty thousand gold." He set a heavy sack full of platinum coins on the table. "In addition, you and your party will be welcomed at our academy at your convenience, where our instructors will teach you all they can over the course of two weeks."

Max raised an eyebrow. That was a tempting offer. But there were a few other things he had discussed with Redmane that he wanted from the mages. "The funds will come in handy, thank you. And again I appreciate the offer of an education. However, I would like to add a few items, if you're willing to listen?"

"Of course, Max." the elf smiled.

"First, something for you. If you so desire, I will allow you to set up branch offices in Deepcrag and the gnome settlement, whatever the Greystone folks end up naming it. Much like our deal here in this city, I would ask that your mages light both settlements, and maintain them for a period of ten years. All of my kingdom will be open to all races, many of whom don't see well in the dark."

"That is acceptable." The elf smiled as he nodded. Light elves were one of the races without natural darkvision.

"If you have anyone who can speak and read the grey dwarf language, or maybe even ancient dwarven runes, I would appreciate the opportunity to hire them to go through some things we recovered here in the city. Part of what we found was an inscriptionist shop full of what we hope is spell scrolls and books. There might be additional new spells there."

"It is doubtful that the greys had magic we are unaware of, but I shall determine whether we have someone with those abilities." The elf kept a neutral face, but Max saw the flash in his eyes at the mention of potential new magic. They'd have to watch whomever he sent very carefully.

"The last item is healing magic. I would ask that you station… half a dozen healers with varying types of healing magic here in Stormhaven's guild branch, and that they make themselves available over the next three months to teach that magic to as many of my people as possible. Where I'm from, the most valuable members of any military force are its medics."

The elf scowled briefly at this, his eyebrows knitting together. "Our mages are normally paid a premium to instruct others outside the academy."

"I know you understand the value of the magic I have to teach you, Eldilon. I also know that you and your guild will make small mountains of gold teaching *Party Chat* in all the nations and cities you mentioned before…" His grin was only slightly wicked.

"Ha! You are correct, Max. Very well. If that is your last condition, I believe we have an agreement."

"I believe we do!" Max held out a hand, and the elf shook it. His grip was surprisingly strong for an elf, and Max wondered if it was magically enhanced, or whether battlemages invested in *Strength*. A silver light engulfed them both, and the agreement was official.

"Please, take your time and finish your breakfast." Max offered as Redmane politely scooped up the bag of platinum coins. "These are especially tasty. Though, I suppose they're just what you're used to, being from this world."

Taking a bite, Eldilon nodded. "They are quite good. My compliments to your chef."

Chapter 24

Lagrass left the village of Hunter's Reach at a dead run, looking over his shoulder as he dodged trees and avoided tripping over shrubs. A hundred yards or so behind him, six torches flickered in a rough line, his pursuers spreading out as they gave chase.

He'd entered the village nearly a week earlier, following the path from the old man's house. Once he spotted the smoke from several chimneys, he stowed the stolen sword in his inventory, not wanting it to be recognized.

His first stop was the tavern, a larger building than he'd expected for a village of maybe thirty structures. Stepping inside, he took a seat at a sturdily built table in the common room. A young lady in a plain linen dress appeared almost immediately. "What can I get for you, stranger?"

"I'd like some breakfast, please, pretty lady. Whatever you have." He gave her his brightest smile, his god-given *Charisma* working its charm. She blushed slightly before rushing off to the kitchen.

Surveying the room, he found it mostly empty. There were twenty tables, but only three were occupied. It was late morning, and he supposed most of the village was off doing their daily work. Two old timers sat near the back wall playing something similar to checkers, sipping at drinks and not speaking at all. A pair a men in leather gear with bows over their shoulders were finishing up a meal, speaking too quietly for him to overhear. The last table was a single woman with a ledger and several papers spread out on the table in front of her.

The girl returned with two plates, and upon seeing him looking at the woman, offered. "That's my mum. She owns this place." She set the plates on the table, then gave a small curtsy. "What would ye like to drink?"

"Ale, I suppose?" he gave her another smile. "And when your mother is through with her work, I'd like to speak with her about renting a room for a night or two."

"Oh, I can help you with that!" She smiled. "Our best room is one silver per night, and that includes two meals per day, as well as laundry service."

"That sounds wonderful." He placed two silver and several copper coins on the table. "Can we consider this my first meal for the day?"

"Of course! I'll bring you a key and your ale in a moment." She scooped the coins off the table and walked over to her mother, who glanced at Lagrass and smiled. She made a quick entry into her book and pocketed the silver coins. Her daughter had kept the coppers.

He quite enjoyed his meal. The old man had been right. There were plump sausages, cooked just right, and this world's version of pancakes. They were a bit oaty, but still tasty with liberal honey and fruit sprinkled on top. After breakfast he took some time to explore the village. All the locals stared at him as if outsiders were a rare sighting, but he just shrugged it off, telling himself there was no way they could know he had killed the old man. He was slightly concerned that word from the city guards about the price on his head might have reached the village, but so far no one had seemed aggressive or afraid of him.

He made a quick stop at a general store, the only one in town. Taking out the wolf hide, he used his charm to negotiate the best price he could, which turned out to be three silvers. He left the store quickly, promising to return and purchase some supplies before he left town.

Next he stopped at the blacksmith's shop, where the smith's apprentice, who was also his daughter, sharpened both his belt knife and his kitchen knife for the price of three coppers. While he waited, he perused the items available in the shop, eyeing a knife that practically called to him. It was shaped similar to a bowie knife, with a long thick blade. Its handle was wrapped in leather, the curved butt thick and strong. When the young lady returned with his sharpened blades, he asked how much the knife was.

"That old thing? It belonged to a hunter who traded it for a better skinning knife. We can let you have it for... five silver."

"I'll give you four, if it includes the sheath." He held out four silver coins plus the coppers he owed for sharpening services. She quickly took the coins, which told him that he'd offered too much, and handed him the blade and sheath. He stowed all three blades in his inventory, thanked her, and left.

The village included a stable, an alchemist's shop, a bakery, leather goods shop, a town hall that doubled as the mayor's residence, a small lumber mill that included a carpenter's shop, and the rest were small homes made of stone and wood. A small creek ran behind the mayor's house, and there was a community water well in the central open area, not quite a square.

For the next few days, Lagrass observed the villagers at their work. Every day several of them took their wash to the creek, gossiping amiably as they worked. The carpenter employed three lumberjacks and two mill workers who cut and processed the lumber while he worked at creating furniture, wagon wheels, and other items in his shop.

The two hunters who'd been at breakfast with him on the first day were locals as well, though they were out in the forest more than not. The game they brought in was quickly sold, the meat to the innkeeper, the hides to the leatherworker.

The smells from the bakery that woke him his second morning had him following his nose there right after breakfast, and he found he could buy a large cookie or a small apple tart for a copper each. The place became a daily stop for him.

Extending his stay, he prepaid for five more days, earning him a genuine smile from the innkeeper's daughter, who flirted with him at every meal. He considered taking advantage of what she offered, but did not yet know how much trouble that might get him into.

On his third night in the village, the hunters returned. He bought them a couple rounds of ale, and asked whether one of them would be willing to teach him how to shoot a bow. They agreed, for the sum of two silvers, to help him reach at least level two in Archery. The following morning Max went back to the general store and purchased the most inexpensive bow available, as well as a quiver, two extra strings, and twenty arrows. He also traded his oversized boots plus a few coins for better boots that actually fit him. They had thick leathers soles that supported his feet nicely as he followed the hunters to an area cleared by the lumberjacks. They tacked a rumpled parchment with a crude bunny silhouette drawn on it to a tall stump, and got to work.

His first several shots missed completely, the arrows flying high and wide. Unlike Max, Lagrass had never had any archery experience on Earth. But after an hour, and several trips to locate and retrieve his arrows, he began to hit the target. When he hit it three times in a row, they called it a day, and the hunters left him to walk back to the village while they went to work.

The following day, another lesson had him striking the now tattered bunny five times out of six, and his skill had actually leveled up to three. He thanked the hunters as they moved off into the forest, then returned to the inn, where he continued to observe the villagers as a plan formed in his head. He identified two of the town drunks and bought them several rounds at his table, pumping them for information on the local residents. They gossiped happily as he refilled their mugs time and again. Flirting with the waitress garnered him some interesting tidbits as well, including that the Mayor was canoodling with the baker's wife while the baker was tending to his early morning baking.

In many of the games that Lagrass had played, your character started in a village much like this one. If you played your cards right, befriended the locals, completed enough quests, you could actually take over the town. He could learn some crafting skills here, maybe do some chore quests to earn a few coins and experience in the process. The gold he'd looted would last him for months if he was careful with his spending.

His fifth night in the village, his plans very nearly went wrong. He'd snuck out of the inn and behind the stable late that night, and was using Lizzy to try and teach himself the sword skill. He slashed and hacked at imaginary enemies, hoping he was getting the forms right, adjusting his feet for better balance, leaning forward or backward as he stabbed and swung.

"Hey, ain't that Lizzy? Old Maldin's blade?" A voice from behind him almost made him drop the sword in surprise. He turned to find one of the two drunks he'd befriended, one hand holding himself unsteadily up against the barn as he pissed on the wall while looking over his shoulder at Lagrass. "I'd recognize that beauty anywhere. How'd you get her? Don't tell me that old hermit sold ya his beloved blade!"

Thinking quickly, Lagrass turned and smiled sadly at the drunk, walking slowly toward him. "Maldin? Was that his name? I found him dead in front of his cabin on my way here. I'd gotten lost in the woods, and the sound of squawking drew me to his clearing, where I found several birds picking at his corpse. I chased them away and buried him, then I'm afraid I helped myself to his sword. I didn't think he'd care, being deceased." He stopped a couple steps from the drunk, shaking his head as he repeated the sad smile. "I didn't realize he was known to the folks here, or I would have mentioned it. Did he have family here in the village?"

"What? No, no. No family anywhere. His wife n children were all killed during the last border war. That's why he moved way out here." The drunk gazed at the sword, clearly jealous that Lagrass had gotten it instead of him. "You... mind if I hold it for a moment?"

"Certainly!" Lagrass smiled at the drunk, placing one hand on his shoulder. With his other hand, he ran the man through, the sword slicing easily through his body, the point sticking into the wall behind him.

"No!" the man tried to yell, but it came out more as a cough. Lagrass withdrew the blade, stepping back to avoid most of the splatter as he did so. A second stab penetrated the man's heart, and he went limp, falling silently into the grass. He looted the corpse, getting a single copper coin and a storage belt that had twenty slots, then quickly wiped the blade on the man's sleeve before returning it to his inventory. He tried to lift the corpse, but didn't have the strength, so he dragged the dead man by his feet over to the creek, and dumped him in. He washed his hands and did a quick inspection of his clothes as the body slowly drifted downstream.

When he was reasonably sure the body would keep going far enough not to be found, he returned to the inn, walking casually in through the front door and taking a seat at the bar. His heart pounding, sure that every time someone looked his way they would point and shout, "Murderer!" he ordered a couple drinks from the bartender and did his best to calm down. After finishing his second drink and buying a few for the two old men at the bar, he made a show of stretching and yawning, then retiring to his room for the night.

Before going to sleep, he checked the dead drunk's storage. The only item inside was a half-empty bottle of spirits that smelled like licorice and burned its way down his gullet when he took a swig. The shot actually calmed him, and he was eventually able to drift off to sleep.

Much to his good fortune, there were three strangers in the common room at breakfast. Unsavory looking travelers bristling with weapons, they barely spoke other than to order food or drink. Mumbled speculation among the locals ranged from them being highwaymen who robbed poor travelers, to agents of the king on a secret mission. That latter option had Lagrass avoiding them as much as possible without being obvious.

That afternoon, one of the stable boys came bursting into the common room, shouting about blood. He'd been doing his chores and spotted a blood trail in the grass, leading to the creek. Half of the village congregated behind the stables, inspecting the grass and following the trail to the creek one or two at a time, as if its course might change. Lagrass joined them, making a point of acting as amazed and afraid as the others, cursing himself for not thinking about the blood that leaked from the wounds.

When the gawking was over, and a couple of men were sent downstream, he went back to the common room with the others. Most of the village had gathered there now, and it didn't take long for them to notice the absence of his victim, who never ventured far from the tavern.

Lagrass felt a brief period of hope as one of the villagers suggested maybe the drunk had simply fallen and cracked his head, then stumbled into the creek. That there was no foul play at all. His hopes were dashed, however, when one of the hunters pointed out the blood wasn't in droplets, as it would have been if he were walking, and that there were clear drag marks.

Things got rowdier when the men returned with the body, which had gotten stuck on a branch hanging low to the water about a mile downstream. The clear stab marks left no doubt that the man was murdered. As the crowd began to get louder, fear and suspicion mixing with alcohol, Lagrass made his move. Standing just behind one of the quieter citizens, he whispered, "It had to be those three bandits." Even as the man began to turn around, Lagrass ducked down and moved to the side, disappearing into the crowd. He did this half a dozen more times, speaking just loudly enough for one or two villagers to hear him before moving on as quickly as possible.

Taking a spot at the end of the bar nearest the kitchen door, he waited and listened. He detected the words highwaymen and bandits here and there, then heard someone shout it outright. "It was the three strangers! Had to be!"

The three strangers in question, who were sitting and drinking at a table near the center of the room, got to their feet. "We had nothing to do with this." The largest of them, clearly their leader, spoke loudly but calmly.

His goal accomplished, Lagrass left the bar and was headed toward the kitchen to ask for a snack when he heard something that made him pause. "We are Rangers, the king's scouts, on a mission for his Majesty. Several of you saw us arrive this morning, and this man has been dead since long before that!"

Lagrass cringed as the angry muttering died down, and several in the crowd began to nod in agreement. Instead of heading to the kitchen, he climbed the stairs and took refuge in his room. Sitting on the bed, he began to panic. Not only was he likely to become a suspect, as the only other stranger in town, but the scout had said they were there on the king's business. Was that business hunting the fugitive murderer from the city? If so, how good was their description of him? As far as he knew, the only one who had seen him clearly was the innkeeper, and she was dead.

He slept fitfully that night, only after emptying the bottle of spirits he'd liberated from the drunk. The next morning he went downstairs to breakfast, only to find the village preparing for a memorial service. The three rangers were sitting at their same table, and the leader glanced at Lagrass briefly, then nodded his head and looked away. Feeling slightly more secure, he took a seat and ordered breakfast. On a whim, he stopped at the bar on his way out to speak to the bartender.

"The other day, when I was drinking with the deceased," He began.

"Bart. His name was Bart." The bartender, a burly man with a scar on his forehead growled at him.

"Yes, thank you. Where I'm from we don't speak the name of the deceased until after they have been interred. It's an old tradition, as silly as it may seem." Lagrass cleared his throat. "In any case, he shared with me a taste of a spirit I've not had before. It was quite good, and he said it was a favorite of his, so I thought I might purchase a bottle to place at his grave?"

Softening up some, the bartender nodded and reached under the bar. "Horrible stuff, but Bart did seem to like it. Mostly because it was all he could ever afford." He handed the bottle to Lagrass. "Five coppers."

He passed a silver across the bar and thanked the man, turning to leave. As he was stepping through the door, the bartender mumbled to himself. "Odd custom..." then a bit louder, he called out, "Where is it that you're from?"

Lagrass continued out the door without pausing, pretending not to hear, and hoping the rangers hadn't heard either. Concerned about answering that question if asked again, he stopped in at the general store. When the shopkeeper greeted him, he said, "As promised, I'm stopping in before I leave. I plan to head out in the morning, first thing. Don't like the idea of a murderer creeping around at night."

"I don't blame you." The shopkeeper nodded. "We haven't had a killing here since the Deghan brothers had it out in the middle of the road and stabbed each other to death."

"Goodness." Lagrass feigned a low level fear response. "This place is more dangerous that it looks. I think the sooner I leave, the better. I was thinking of heading west, but I don't know what lies in that direction?"

The shopkeeper obliged, scratching his head. "Several small villages, for the next hundred miles or so, then the river city of Portis. Beyond that is the orc lands, and the sea. And, of course, beyond the sea is the elven lands. Don't want to go that far, humans aren't treated all that well there."

"Thank you, that's a big help. I'd like a few things to take with me on my journey. Do you have a proper tent?" He went on to give the shopkeeper a list of basic survival items. When the man began to look at him oddly, he explained. "I was set upon by thieves about a day's walk from here. They took nearly everything I had, and… oh!" He put a hand over his mouth. "Do you suppose they are the same brutes that committed the murder here? There were three of them…"

He did his best to reinforce that idea in the shopkeeper's head as they continued to discuss the items he needed. When he was all done, he asked, "What about storage items? I have this bag, but I could use a little extra space." He didn't mention the belt he'd looted from Bart.

"I have a ring here that'll hold twenty items. But it costs five gold."

"Ah, too rich for my blood." Lagrass decided the extra storage wasn't worth such a large chunk of his remaining funds. "If you'll round up the other items, I'll stop by to collect them in the morning on my way out." He handed the shopkeeper two gold, and got a few silvers in return.

"I'll load it all into this pack." The shopkeeper held up an oiled leather backpack. "Free of charge. Comes in handy if you run out of storage in your bag."

"Thank you, sir! Most kind of you!" he flashed his brightest smile at the man. "It has been a pleasure doing business with you."

Stopping at the alchemist's shop for the first time, he chatted amicably with her as she presented him with a selection of potions. An elderly woman, she moved slowly and carefully as she produced her wares and set them on the counter. The most expensive were health potions that restored a thousand points each. He passed on those, as his total health at the moment was only just over three hundred. She produced some lesser potions that would restore two hundred points, and that only cost three silver each. He took all six that she had in stock. He also bought a couple poison cures, two mana potions in case he ever found himself casting spells, and a vial of acid that she said came in handy for removing leeches. "Just a tiny drop on their back, and they'll drop right off before the acid gets to your own skin." She assured him.

He handed over the coin, making the vials disappear into his storage. As he was heading out, she called him back. "I'm always in need of ingredients for my potions. If you find yourself in the forest and spot useful plants, I'll pay you for them. Either in coin or in trade. I'm getting a little old to be traipsing through the forest."

He sighed. This was exactly what he'd been hoping for. The kind of quest one gets in starter villages that lets you earn coin, learn a trade, and increase your reputation. Though he now planned to flee the village before either the rangers nabbed him, or he was accused of murdering Bart, he saw an opportunity he couldn't pass up.

"I'd be happy to help, but I'm afraid I don't know anything about plants or ingredients. Can you tell me what you're looking for, and how to identify it?"

"Such a kind young man. Of course I can. Come, lean over the counter where I can reach you…"

He left the shop five minutes later with a veritable encyclopedia of knowledge of plants and other alchemical ingredients, where to look for them, and the proper way to harvest them. As well as a quest to bring ten each of three herbs back to the old alchemist. He had no intention of returning and completing the quest, but it would have looked suspicious had he not accepted it.

He attended the funeral service, standing quietly near the back and mostly staring at his feet. When it was over, there was a pot luck meal served in the main area around the well, and he mingled enough to be seen, nodding in sympathy as people spoke about his victim, mostly telling stories of his drunken shenanigans. As soon as others began to drift away, he returned to the inn. Stopping to see the bartender, who was already getting a crowd streaming in, he asked for another bottle of the licorice spirits for himself. He'd made a display of leaving the first one upon the grave, taking a moment to publicly grieve for the man.

With his new full bottle, he retired to his room and drank quietly, waiting for the sounds of the wake downstairs to fade away.

A few hours after midnight, he grabbed the matches and candle in his room, and crept downstairs. The kitchen was empty, the staff having just cleaned up and gone to bed. He opened the back door as quietly as he could, then closed it behind him. Walking as stealthily as he could over to the stables, he stepped inside and looked around. He expected to find the stable boy who had raised the alarm sleeping in one of the stalls, or a tack room. After a quick check revealed no kid, he lit a match and tossed it onto a bale of hay. Leaving out the back of the barn, he moved through the darkness as quickly as he could. When he got to his destination, he crouched down against the wall and waited.

In just a minute or so, the first call went out. "Fire! The stable is on fire!"

Shouts echoed through the village, and people burst from their homes and shops, many only half dressed as they ran toward the well with buckets in hand. Lagrass watched as they formed a line and began to pass full buckets from the well to the fire.

Taking advantage of the distraction, he slipped in the open door of the general store. He'd seen the shopkeeper in the bucket line, so he was reasonably sure he was safe. The man hadn't mentioned any family during their earlier chat.

The first thing he saw was his pack sitting on the end of the counter, waiting for him to pick it up in the morning. He grabbed it, and holding his breath, tried to stow it in his inventory. He was now wearing Bart's belt, and the pack easily slipped inside, taking only one slot despite being filled with a dozen items.

Next he walked behind the counter and grabbed the cash box, not bothering to open it before shoving it into his storage as well. He'd surveyed the shop during his last visit, and quickly grabbed several items that looked valuable, including the storage ring that sat in a small cloth bag on a shelf behind the counter. Placing the ring on his finger, he was about to grab a few more items when a voice behind him shouted, "Thief!"

Lagrass turned to see a middle-aged woman in a nightgown who had just emerged through a curtain that hung in the doorway of a back room. Without thinking, he unsheathed the knife he'd bought from the blacksmith's shop and stabbed the woman in the chest. His first strike perforated her gut, causing her to groan in pain. Another quick stab up under the sternum, and she was dead. He quickly looted her, then dragged her back through the curtain and dropped her on the floor of a small living area. Seeing the back door he'd been hoping for, he burst out into the night.

His next stop was the alchemist's shop, where he hoped to grab a few dozen of the expensive potions. But when he tried the door, it was locked. Worse, someone spotted him trying to get in, and shouted. Since her shop faced the well, everyone in the fire line looked up to see his suspicious activity. As one they began to point and shout.

Out of time, Lagrass took off around the corner of the shop and charged into the forest.

And that was where he found himself now. A small mob of angry villagers chasing him with weapons drawn and torches held high. He used every bit of his training to evade them, changed his direction often, hiding as they passed by and then doubling back for a short while, then hopping into the creek and wading downstream a ways.

Eventually the voices faded along with the torch light. Still, he kept moving through the rest of the night and the following day. He assumed the three rangers would be tracking him now, and needed to put as much distance between them as possible.

Nearly exhausted as the sun fell below the canopy, he stumbled across a wide hole in the ground, angled in like a burrow, only larger than any burrow he'd ever seen. "Might be a bear den." he mumbled to himself, barely able to keep his eyes open. Not seeing any recent tracks or freshly disturbed dirt around the opening, he shrugged and lowered himself to the ground. Crawling headfirst, his still bloody knife in his right hand, he entered the hole.

When he was maybe six feet inside, it came to an abrupt end. It stank like moldy bear ass, and the dirt was suspiciously muddy, but he didn't care. There was just enough room to curl up, which he did, hugging his knees to his chest. Still gripping his knife, he was asleep in less than five minutes.

He awoke to the sound of voices, and a barking dog. Panic filled him for a moment until he realized where he was. Curled up in a bear den, his eyes and nose running from the stench, his entire left side wet from laying in the mud. Though he couldn't actually see the den's opening from his position, morning sunlight streamed in through the hole and provided enough light for him to see. He was considering wiggling his way out and making a run for it, when the barking grew dramatically louder. A voice shouted, "He came this way!" and at least two other voices answered.

A moment later he held his breath as a shadow passed over the hole. He could hear the sound of a dog snuffling. A moment later there was a yelp, and the sound faded, along with the sound of steps crunching sticks and leaves. The awful bear stench that was now thoroughly soaked into his clothes had masked his own scent, and scared away the hunting dog as well.

Relaxing a bit, he settled down for a long wait. He produced his canteen from storage and swished water around in his mouth, washing away some of the taste before spitting it out and taking a drink. He was hungry, and there was some jerky in the pack the shopkeeper had prepared for him, but he just couldn't bring himself to eat anything while down in the hole.

Lagrass remained where he was for the remainder of the day and night, falling asleep again in the wee hours of the morning.

Chapter 25

It took three days to arrange for Spellslinger to join
the first caravan to the goblin settlement, get him there, and
have him set up the portal. Max met him in Stormhaven
before they left, and he and Redmane sat in his office with
the old wizard while Max explained what had happened,
and what he wanted. Old Puckerface lived up to his name
when he produced a bottle and took a long swig, his face
puckering up and making both Redmane and Max grin.

"Damn, boy. Ye don't do anything in half
measures, do ye?"

"Oh, that's not all." Max shared the quest with him,
then invited them both to join his party. The wizard shot
him a quizzical look, but accepted. The moment he did,
Max spoke through party chat. *"Hey folks, say hi to
Spellslinger and Redmane."*

"Wizard dude!" Smitty's voice was first, and Max
enjoyed the look on Spellslinger's face. First his eyes
darted around the room, looking for Smitty. When he
realized the voices were in his head, his eyes widened, and
he gaped at Max.

"Master Spellslinger, welcome." Dalia's calm voice
was next, followed by Dylan, Nessa, and Blake.

"It's a new magic I sort of invented. Or maybe
discovered is a better word? I'm not sure. Anyway, I'm
going to teach you the spell. While you're gone, make
good use of it. Practice it and level it up. I'm going to

Darkholm to teach it to Ironhand, for a fee." He winked at the mage.

"Ha! Be sure n charge him proper, lad! This be a right useful skill." A moment later, Max had taught a spell for the second time in his life. Spellslinger took a moment to review its limits, then shook his head. "Two miles. Ye know most battles don't be spread out so wide. Ye could bring all yer captains into a party, then control the movements o' yer companies instantly, all across the field."

"Yep." Max nodded. "There are any number of ways this will give you an advantage. But like I said, level up the skill as fast as you can. I've sold it to the Mages' Guild, and they'll be looking to sell it around the world. You now have a slight time advantage over everyone else."

"Thank ye, lad." The old dwarf actually bowed his head slightly. "Fer the spell, the quest, and yer trust in me. Ye do me a great honor."

"It is my honor to call you friend, you old grump." Max produced a bottle of his best Firebelly's vintage and held it up. "Shall we have a quick toast to your safe and successful journey?" Redmane produced glasses, and between them they finished the bottle in short order.

As he was getting up to join the caravan at the portal, Spellslinger hesitated. "Max, may I... visit the outpost?"

"Of course. You've taken a quest to protect it, and the magic it holds. If you can in some way help us rediscover the rune magic, well..." Max paused and created another quest, sharing it through their whole party. Spellslinger chuckled. "When you get to the outpost, share that with Enoch. I'm told you old farts don't get much of a chance to level up anymore."

"Impudent welp!" the old mage grinned at Max, thumping him on the back. "I'll see that yer property be properly protected. When ye get there, ye'll find so many protective spells the place will practically glow!"

*****

Max stood in the palace courtyard with Redmane and the rest of his party as the portal opened. Enoch and Spellslinger stepped through, wide grins on their faces. Behind them stood an honor guard of twenty dwarven warriors of Redmane's clan.

"Welcome, King Maximilian, to yer new stronghold. Them merchants have decided to name the city Dara Seans, which translates from the old tongue to *second chance*." Enoch waved them through the portal.

On the other side, Max found construction already underway. The small buildings along the border street were mostly demolished, and an earth mage was busily raising a section of wall in their place. Max was fascinated. The fifty foot wide stone section rose slowly, about a foot per minute, and the outer surface was smooth as glass. Max stood off to one side of the portal, watching the mage work as a second caravan of workers and supplies passed through the portal behind him. As soon as they were through, the empty wagons from the first caravan returned to Stormhaven to reload.

When the mage was through, he sat down on a nearby stone to rest. The section he had just raised joined seamlessly with a previous section. It stood twenty feet high, and about three feet thick. Enoch moved to stand next to him. "This be just the first stage, to secure the perimeter. Over the next few weeks, we'll thicken the wall, make it wide enough to man the top, place weapons, and a few surprises. There be three more earth mages on the way, then the work will move faster."

"It's amazing." Max was truly impressed by both the speed and quality of the work. He saw the dwarf mage drinking a mana potion, and walked over to him. Handing over three of the mana potions Dalia had made from their highest grade Brightwood ingredients, he said, "These are the most powerful we can provide. Use them sparingly, but use them. We'll send more as soon as we can."

The dwarf *Examined* the potion, then blinked rapidly several times. "King Max, this be… there be no need fer this. This potion restores two thousand mana. That's double me own mana pool! Ye can sell this to top tier mages fer thirty gold a piece. The common potions be good nuff fer me."

"Just take small sips, then." Max patted the dwarf on the shoulder. "Only the best for those protecting my kingdom and my people." Max looked down at the dwarf. "Maybe save one of them for your next battle, just in case."

"Aye, thank ye, Majesty." The mage bowed, then took a small sip of the potion before immediately getting up and beginning to raise the next section. "We'll make ye a proper wall, sure enough!"

Max followed Enoch deeper into his territory to the outpost location. A banner had been hung over the runes above the outside door. "Very clever." Max smirked at the dwarf.

"Heh. I had to improvise. Made a tracing o' the runes, and we'll cover them better in the coming days." He led them inside and downstairs. When they entered the outpost arch and began to walk down the ramp, Spellslinger took over. "I found the second exit, we think. There be another archway behind the golems, but we dared not activate it. Fer all we know, it could connect directly to another outpost, or their headquarters."

"Good thinking. If there are living Runemasters out there, we don't want to push our luck." Max agreed.

Dylan whistled as they entered the cavern, not having seen it the first time. "Damn. Those golems really are... badass." He stood next to Bastion, who was on sentry duty at the door, looking up. "Yeah, I wouldn't want to face off against one of those."

Spellslinger grinned. "They be enchanted in more ways than one. They give off a fear aura, even to allies. We think it be so that friendly fighters don't get too close and get stomped accidentally."

"Makes good sense." Blake agreed. "Nothing worse than friendly fire incidents." All the Battleborne were silent for a moment.

Enoch cleared his throat. "We uhm… found a cache of weapons when we searched the buildings, enough to equip two hundred fighters. There be six chests of holding, each with a thousand item storage capacity. Two were filled with battle rations like I never see'd before. One held a thousand books, but all the ones we checked were written in the ancient runes. Another, normal chest be filled with them square silver coins." Enoch held one out for Max to see. It looked the same as the others he'd found. "There be a chest full o' furniture, tables, chairs, cots, and the like. We took some out and set up housing for a hundred down here, and I used a bit upstairs as well."

"That'll save us some money." Max complimented the dwarf. "Might as well use it. I assume they stored it all in there to preserve it?"

"Aye, this place was well and truly packed away, Max. It's as if they built it, then abandoned it, leavin' it fer emergencies."

"Well, let's hope we never need to use it for one. But I approve of making it ready, just in case. Master Spellslinger, can I assume that you'll be remaining here for a while?"

"Aye, lad. A good long while. This be a dream come true for me." the old dwarf stared hard at Max. "Ye should consider lettin' me king in on this secret, Maximilian."

Max cringed inwardly, a reflex from his childhood, when his parents only used his full name if he was in trouble. Which he was, a lot. "I have been considering it, believe me. But would Ironhand be content to keep the secret to himself? Or would he want to send dozens, or hundreds of people here to help? How long can a secret such as this remain secret when that many people know about it?"

He could see he wasn't convincing the dwarves, who had unshakable faith in the honor and oaths of their brethren.

"Let me put it this way. On my world we don't have magic. We have science, and technology. When one nation develops a new weapon, or a new device that improves their defense, other nations immediately begin killing, bribing, and stealing to obtain it. The best way to prevent this is to keep the secret tightly held for as long as possible."

"I understand, lad." Spellslinger's voice was quiet. "But we do have magic here. Me king will swear an oath, the same as we did. An oath he'll not break without yer permission. As fer helping, that can be done more quietly than ye think. We dwarves be experts at secret projects. Traps, escape tunnels, hidden rooms, all be built without an extra soul knowin' about 'em."

Enoch piped up. "Most o' the help ye need is fer the work up top, Max. The walls, the buildings, getting merchants, crafters and workers to fill up the space, turn this place into a workin' settlement. Thousands o' residents willin' to defend this place with their lives, none of 'em even aware o' what be hidden below."

Spellslinger nodded. "I placed the portal where it can be seen from the outer wall. Meaning the Greystones likely already know about it. That be our excuse for our own wall, and all the protections we'll be adding. It seems ye be a greedy king who wants to charge every merchant and mouse who passes thru yer portal." He grinned.

Enoch looked uncomfortable. "The elf in charge o' the merchants wants to speak with ye at yer earliest convenience, Max. Me guess is that he's worried this new portal is yer attempt at cheating them in yer deal. They paid dearly for property in Deepcrag cuz that's where the portal be. Since ye placed the portal here…"

"They think I've done an end run around them, somehow." Max nodded. "Send a runner to invite them here. Have you picked a place for me to stay while I'm here?"

"Aye, there be a manor house not far from the portal square. Nothin' fancy, but we can enlarge it over time, clear some o' the surrounding buildings, put a wall around it." Enoch set off walking, the entire group following. It turned out the chosen manor was only a few blocks from the outpost entry in addition to being a short walk from the portal. Max approved of the location.

The manor itself was three stories tall, set back from the street about fifty feet. To one side was a pair of small shops with storefront windows, void of glass. On the other side was a row of two story homes. Enoch led them inside, and Max found that the place had already been furnished, if roughly. There was a dining room with a long table and eight chairs, an office set up behind that with a crude, bulky looking desk. Enoch shrugged. "It were the only one sized ta fit ye, Max."

There was a formal sitting room, currently furnished with four chairs and a low table arranged in front of a fireplace. "Upstairs be a large master suite, and four other bedrooms. There be a smaller house out back with four servants quarters and its own kitchen."

"This will do nicely, thank you Enoch." Max had never lived in such luxurious quarters on Earth. The best he'd had was when he'd blown a month's pay on a suite in a Vegas hotel where he'd spent a wild week with a cute redheaded lieutenant from communications.

They waited an hour or so for the dark elf merchant and his gnome companions to show up. Max met them in the dining room, as it had the most chairs. Enoch and Spellslinger joined Max, and after the merchants bowed properly, they all took seats.

"Welcome to our humble abode. I understand you wished to speak to me?" Max smiled politely at the merchants.

"Yes, Majesty. Specifically regarding the portal you've added here in your sector of the city."

"You're curious as to whether I'd planned that all along, and possibly dealt with you in bad faith. But can't figure out how to suggest such a thing without offending me?"

The elf's face grew tight, and Max chuckled.

"Don't worry, I'm not offended. The truth is I had no intention of placing a portal here. However, a few things have changed since we arrived at this place. You may have heard that Deepcrag was attacked?" He waited for the merchants to nod. "Well, it seems that your earlier foray into the goblin settlement angered a nearby hobgoblin and troll community. They sent a large force to follow you, and ran into Deepcrag on the way. Had we not had the portal there, your forces and mine would likely have been massacred, the settlement lost to us. Then that same army might have continued on to this place and done the same to you and yours. Do you disagree?"

Looking glum, all three merchants shook their heads. The dark elf replied, "We sent a pair of scouts to the goblin settlement after we heard of the attack. They just returned via teleport scroll. The settlement is crawling with hobgoblins, and there is no sign of the guards we left behind, other than some torn armor, and blood."

Max had suspected as much. "I'm sorry to hear that. But that just reinforces our need for a strong defense." He took a deep breath. "The other thing that happened was that I obtained the portal pedestal unexpectedly. The need was there, and the solution seemed obvious. As for its placement, do you object to Stormhaven maintaining control over its own portal?"

Again the merchants shook their heads.

"The good news for you is that we can reach an agreement for you to make use of our portal under specific circumstances. Like the need for reinforcements in case of an attack. Let me be clear, this portal will not be for public use. Merchants seeking to do business in Dara Seans, who are not citizens of Stormhaven, will still need to use the portal in Deepcrag, or travel by caravan from somewhere else. I'm installing this portal mainly for defensive purposes, and for growing my sector of the city. And while our merchants and crafters may do business outside the walls, access to Stormhaven territory will be severely limited. I believe Enoch has established a few locations outside the walls where your people and ours will be able to conduct business freely amongst themselves, and any traveling traders." He watched their faces as he spoke.

"This leaves the main access to this trade route in Deepcrag, which maintains the value of your investment there. It gives you the security of knowing that you can draw reinforcements from your other settlements, or mine, quickly enough to defend this place. That should make it easier for you to convince new settlers to take up residence here. And to discourage any other bands of monsters from attacking. I don't care if you publicize the existence of the portal, as long as you make it clear it's not available to your clients or residents."

The dark elf opened his mouth, then closed it again. He looked at the gnomes, who both nodded their heads slightly. "We find your explanation entirely reasonable, Majesty. And while we'd obviously prefer more access to your portal here, your reticence is understandable. Please know that we plan to install a portal of our own, once the city is generating sufficient income." He paused to think for a moment, his gaze focused on his hands, which lay flat on the table. "What will you charge us should we need to bring in reinforcements?"

"Nothing. I would not hold you hostage in such a situation. And, if it becomes necessary, should the main gates fall during an attack, we would shelter your people within our walls as needed. That will give those who can't reach your inner keep a safe harbor. This is my city too, and it's in my best interests to make sure it is stable and well defended. I could have taken prisoners in the battle at Deepcrag, but I ordered the entire enemy force massacred, minus those who escaped early in the battle. We need to show we have the strength to put down any challengers, and the willingness to do so without mercy." He smiled widely at them, baring his fangs. "I am, after all, the mighty and terrible Chimera King!"

"We are grateful for your willingness to help grow and defend our city." The dark elf bowed his head. "And thank you for reassuring us as to your intentions. Having such defensive measures available will indeed help us to encourage new settlers."

"And raise the real estate values!" One of the gnomes grinned at Max.

"Ha! Let us hope so." Max looked at all three merchants, one at a time. "Was there anything else you wished to discuss? With myself, or with Enoch, while we're all here?"

"No, Majesty, I do not believe there is."

"Then I have just one more thing for you before you go." Max spoke as they began to rise from their chairs. All three sat back down, looking curious. "I have struck a bargain with the Mages' Guild. In return for a property in which to establish a branch location here and in Deepcrag, they will be providing and maintaining lights for my public areas. That means the areas around your Deepcrag locations will be lit free of charge for you. Since they will have their people here already, you might reach out to them and make a deal for them to install and maintain lights in the balance of Dara Sean at a deep discount." He waited for their response, which was mixed. To sweeten the pot, and promote goodwill, he added, "You may even tell them that I have approved the use of my portal by their people free of charge as part of your bargain. I would rather not have the smoke from torches filling the air in this cavern if we can avoid it. They can offer the mages stationed here the ability to travel home and visit family or see to business interests without paying portal fees, at least on our end."

The second gnome nodded. "An incentive for decent mages to accept the posting. It's a job most of their kind consider beneath them. But if we offer sufficient wages, and they can travel freely back and forth…"

"The information and the offer are both greatly appreciated, Majesty." The first gnome finished for his partner.

Spellbinder, always thinking ahead, thumped the table, surprising the merchants. "As a representative o'

King Ironhand, a friend and ally o' King Max here, I'll be makin' sure yer front gates are no' so easy to break down. We'll put on some strengthening and magic resistance spells that'll keep most monster hordes at bay." He looked at the dark elf. "Assuming ye don't object."

"No, of course not, Master Spellslinger. Thank you."

With the merchants mollified and on their way out of the sector, Enoch led Max's group, minus Spellslinger, who went back to work, on a tour of the rest of the Stormhaven sector of the city. It turned out to be a more significant area than it had looked like on the map. There were scores of buildings along multiple streets, and Max thought it might be larger than Stormhaven City itself. He was going to need to focus even more on recruiting.

The tour completed, and Enoch properly congratulated for his efforts, Max returned to Stormhaven, where he picked up Redmane, and the two of them stepped through the portal to Darkholm to seek an audience with Ironhand.

*****

Lagrass left his hole, having spent another uncomfortable night in the foul-smelling mud. Crawling out, the daylight streaming in from outside showed him something that very nearly made him vomit. The mud he'd been laying in… wasn't mud. It was accumulated bear feces and urine, mixed with shed hair, twigs, and dirt.

507

He desperately searched his map for the nearest creek or stream that he had crossed, and located one about a quarter mile back the way he'd come. Jogging through the forest, he gagged and choked, wanting to strip down right there and abandon his clothes, but he didn't dare. Besides risking being caught in the open, he didn't want to leave evidence of his location laying around. Also, ditching the clothes wouldn't get him clean. He felt a desperate need to scrub himself until his skin peeled off.

Finding the creek, he plunged right in, submerging himself in the cool water. He rubbed his hands together until they were reasonably clean of the filth, then began with his face and hair. He eventually stripped his soiled clothes off and used the sand near the bank to scrub them clean. One of the things he'd asked the shopkeeper for was soap, and he used most of the bar trying to scrub away the bear juice from himself, his clothes, and his boots over the next hour. No matter how hard he worked at it, how often he nearly drowned himself dunking his head in the water, he couldn't seem to get the stench from his nose.

Finally leaving the water, he stowed the wet clothes in his inventory, and removed a replacement set from his pack. Nervous that the villagers or the rangers were still hunting him, he tried to formulate a plan.

He'd fled roughly north from the village. Which meant he couldn't head south back toward that danger. His pursuers had followed him in a northerly direction this far, and he assumed had continued in that direction. And he'd told the shopkeeper that he planned to head west, so it definitely wasn't safe to go that way. This left him only one option. Quickly checking his map, he turned eastward and began to walk.

The forest remained unchanged for most of the day, and Lagrass had no real way to measure how far he'd gone. Thanks to his interface map, he could maintain a roughly eastward trajectory, and he hoped to eventually encounter another village. Or at least a road that might take him somewhere. His plan to take over a starter village was still foremost in his mind, behind not getting caught by anyone hunting him. Maybe if he walked far enough, long enough, he could find a place that was outside this kingdom, where he could start from scratch.

As the sun began to set, dark came more quickly than Lagrass thought it should. The reason for that quickly became apparent as lightning flickered in the sky. A moment later, the sound of thunder rolled across the forest canopy. Though it was early, he began to search for a protected spot to make camp. He now had a real tent, but would prefer a cave or similar hiding spot that wouldn't be so visible to hunters who might happen by.

The rain burst forth in a deluge, the sounds of millions of drops hitting leaves roaring around him. The trees swayed in the sudden winds, opening holes in the canopy for the heavy raindrops to soak him to the bone.

"I hate this world. I'm constantly wet." He complained to himself as he trudged along. It was difficult to see more than thirty feet or so in any direction, between the rain and the deepening darkness. The creaking of tree limbs and shifting shadows from the lightning flashes had him practically jumping out of his skin. He felt like a prey animal surrounded by predators he couldn't see.

Eventually he spotted a rock overhang at the base of a hill. It wasn't a cave, but it was mostly protected from the weather. He stepped in under it and immediately began gathering kindling and firewood. Ten minutes later he had a small fire burning, and had removed his wet clothes. After setting up his tent, he used several sticks to create small frames, across which hung both sets of wet clothes so that they could dry. He produced a few pieces of jerky and his bottle of licorice spirits, and saw to his next most immediate need; hunger.

Sitting with his back to the stone wall as he ate, he pulled the shopkeeper's cash box from his inventory. Before now, he'd been too tired and stressed to take time to go through his loot. The box contained eighteen gold, thirty silver, and fifty copper coins, as well as a single platinum coin. "I'm rich!" he whisper-shouted to himself, adding all the cash to his inventory. There was also a small stack of folded papers in the bottom of the box. Opening them he found that they were all IOUs from villagers to the shopkeeper. One of them was from Bart, for six silver and change. "What a schmuck." Lagrass mumbled. "Giving credit to people who'll never be able to pay it back." He tossed the notes into the fire, then checked the box for any other contents before sliding it back into his inventory.

His loot from the dead woman in the shop was six silver coins, a silver inlaid hairbrush, which she'd been holding in her hand when he killed her, and a silver hairpin with a small ruby stone shaped like a teardrop. "Should be able to sell these for a good bit." He mumbled, putting it away.

When he went back and checked his notifications, he received a shock. There was the small bit of experience gained from killing the woman in the shop, who was only level five. But there was another kill listed, with even less experience awarded. The name of the person didn't register at first, and Lagrass did his best to think back. Did he attack someone without realizing it? He shook it off, and finished his meal before adding a few more sticks to the fire and crawling into his tent. He was just drifting off to sleep when his brain made the connection and he recognized the name. It was the boy who had discovered the blood trail. The stable boy. From the stable he'd burned down.

Lagrass felt a bit of guilt. Had the boy been asleep in one of the stalls and Lagrass just hadn't seen him? Or had he run inside after the fire started and choked on the smoke? There had been a few horses in the stable, but they'd obviously escaped, because he got no kill notifications for them.

He decided it couldn't have been his fault, that the boy must have chosen to run into the burning barn, absolving Lagrass of any responsibility. "It was his own fault." He mumbled to himself as he lay down on his blanket. "What fool runs into a burning building? It was his own fault."

Lagrass repeated that to himself over and over until he fell asleep.

Chapter 26

Max and Redmane walked into the meeting room behind Max's favorite valet. The dwarf was seriously helpful, and Max was considering trying to steal him away from Ironhand. The dwarf king was waiting for them, calling out happily to them as they entered.

"Max! Redmane, you old battleboar, good to see ye!" He smiled and indicated for them to sit. Max noted that a chimera-sized chair had been placed for him, angled away from the table so he had plenty of leg room.

"Thank you, highness." Max didn't bow his head, as he'd been coached not to do so. Still he respected this king and wanted to show it.

"Ye requested a private meeting, and that in itself be unusual enough ta make me curious. Be there a problem? A new foe ye need help with?"

Max grinned. "Always problems, and we beat the last new foe easily. Still have the same old foe in the orcs, but that's not why we're here. I actually have a secret I want to tell you, and something I want to sell you."

"Oh ho! A negotiation! Well, let's save that bit fer last, so ye can tell me whatever ye have to say without cryin' over the deal we make!"

"Heh. Alright, I know your time is valuable, so I'll skip right to the point. Underneath the land I've claimed in the abandoned gnome settlement now known as Dara

Seans, there is an old Runemaster's outpost. With a working portal from the surface, and half a dozen working giant golem sentries." He watched Ironhand's mouth drop open, his face turn red, and decided to mess with him. "I'll show it to you, but I want a hundred thousand gold first."

"What??" the king roared, getting to his feet! "Max! That be... no! I'll give ye fifty thousand, and no more! And yer a damned thief fer askin it! I thought ye were me friend, Max..." He trailed off as he noticed the grins on Redmane's and Max's faces. "Bah! Ye be messin with me!"

"Only about the gold. Of course I wouldn't charge you to see it. But the rest is true." Max watched as a very suspicious Ironhand, raised an inquisitive eyebrow at Redmane.

The chamberlain nodded. "On me own honor, it all be true."

The dwarf king sat down, letting out a long slow exhale as he gathered his thoughts. "Ye be a nasty trickster, damned oversized, sharp-toothed half-beastie! Nearly drove me to a conniption!" He shook his head, a slight smile escaping his control. "Well played. Now, tell me from the beginning."

Max and Redmane together told him the story. Max shared the two relevant quests with Ironhand, effectively recruiting him into helping protect and study the outpost.

"Ye'll have whatever ye need, down to me last gold coin, if necessary. Max, this be our history, our pride, and

our greatest shame. If we can regain the rune magic…"
Ironhand drifted off, imagining the possibilities. "Thank ye
for sharing this with me." The experienced and savvy king
had instantly grasped the ramifications of Max sharing the
knowledge.

Congratulations! Reputation increase!
Your reputation with the entire dwarven race is now:
Respected!
Your reputation with the dwarves of Darkholm is now:
Revered!

"Thank you, Ironhand." Max tried using the king's
name, but it felt awkward. "I would appreciate you
keeping this to yourself, at least for a while. You're
welcome to visit, of course. But the fewer people who
know about this, the better."

"Ye have me solemn oath." Ironhand put hand to
heart, and golden light surrounded them both as a sound
like tiny bells tinkling could be heard. An oath between
kings was no small thing in the gods' eyes. "What can I do
to help?"

"Well, to start with, building up and securing that
sector of the city is expensive. So I figured you could give
me a small mountain of gold!" Max winked at Redmane,
who was watching Ironhand with some amusement.

"Done!" Ironhand didn't hesitate.

"Wait, wait. I was kidding again, I don't want a
hand-out. Look, the other reason I came here was actually

to sell you something. Something of value, worth the gold I need to complete construction around the outpost. Accept my invitation." Max sent Ironhand a party invite, which the king accepted. Max was getting a little tired of going through this process, but it was important.

"Can you hear me?" He sent through *Party Chat.*

"O' course I can hear ye!" Ironhand shouted out loud. "Yer right here in-"

Ironhand's mouth clicked shut when he heard Redmane answer without moving his lips. *"Loud and clear, sire."*

Max continued, his own lips not moving either. *"This is a new spell I sort of accidently created. It allows up to twenty party members to hear each other, to speak without speaking aloud. It works for a distance of up to two miles. Go ahead, try it. Just think about answering me, but don't speak aloud."*

"Can ye hear me?" Ironhand's voice was tentative. When both his guests smiled, he shouted, *"Ye can hear me!"* causing both of them to wince and grab their heads. Out loud, he said "Sorry."

"This is what I've come here to sell you. I am currently the only master of this ability, and can teach it to you and a few of your leaders, for a price. I've already sold it to the Archmagus of the Mages' Guild, but it will take him some time to level up the ability to the point where he can teach it to others." Max spoke aloud.

Ironhand thumped a fist on the table. "Ye sell'd it to them wand-wavers first?!" He glowered at Max, who took it in stride. He could already tell Ironhand was just trying to get back at him.

"No offense, but you dwarves are a bunch of shield-bashing, hammer-swinging brutes without much talent for magic. Though I hope to rectify that with the rune magic soon. In any case, it would take one of you years to level the ability up to where you could teach it!"

Ironhand eyed him askance for a moment, then burst out laughing. "Aye, that be true enough. Mages be rare among our people. I'm glad ye came to me with this when ye did, Max. It'll take a year or more before this spreads across the continent. Even longer for others to learn to use it effectively. By then we'll have all our elders and commanders used to it. What did ye charge the damned elf for it?"

"Much more than I'll charge you, my friend." Max smiled, getting one in return from the king. "They'll use it to make a pile of money, so I charged them sixty thousand gold and some favors."

Ironhand whistled. "That be a significant amount, Max. Ye be improvin' yer negotiation skills."

"Let's test that theory." Max leaned toward the dwarf. "I'll teach you the spell, along with… let's say twenty of your commanders or elders or whomever you select. In return you'll pay me one thousand gold per head, to help me offset the costs of protecting the outpost."

Ironhand gave him a considering look. "Each one o' them can speak to twenty others?"

"Yes. Here's how you do it. Let's say the greys attack again. You create a party with twenty of your commanders' seconds, who don't need to know the spell if they're in your party. The commanders themselves each create a party with twenty of their captains, sergeants, or quartermasters, or whomever they need to speak to. They get real-time reports from their twenty, and they relay the vital bits to their seconds, who relay it to you instantly. And not only can you hear it, but all the seconds can hear each other, so they can coordinate among themselves without your input. So you get nearly instantaneous information from nearly four hundred sources across the entire battlefront, and the ability to immediately relay detailed orders, which will help you to better wage your war."

"Damn." Ironhand reviewed the math in his head for a moment, stunned by the possibilities. But he quickly recovered. "Five hundred per head!"

Redmane snorted, and winked at Max, who quickly agreed. "Ten thousand gold it is!"

"Bah, that's what ye came here wantin' ta get, ain't it? Yer no fun, Max!" the king reached out a hand, and Max shook it.

"I can always use more, of course. But friends don't take advantage of each other." Besides, I need to save my energy to talk you out of immediately sending hundreds of dwarves to Dara Seans to help with the outpost."

*****

Max stopped at his favorite market square after leaving Ironhand a few hours later. The king had worked hard at pushing Max to accept a multi-clan dwarven migration into his sector of the city. In the end they'd agreed on three more mages to help with construction, a few dozen crafters, a hundred extra guards, and their families if they wanted to bring them along. None of them would be given even a hint of the outpost's existence. Any who wanted to become citizens of Stormhaven could do so with no hard feelings. At one point, just to throw off Ironhand during one of his more excitable moments, Max actually did try to steal the old valet.

His first stop was Fitchstone's emporium, to visit with the old merchant and try to recruit him one more time. They talked about the revival of the old trade route, and the possibility of finding an unknown kobold tribe in the wilds that they could milk for gold and gems. That last part caused a gleam in the old dwarf's eyes, but he still refused to move.

Their next stop was the meat on a stick vendor, whom Max also tried to recruit while he bought out the dwarf's entire inventory, as well as some more spices. Again, he failed. So he made his final stop, at Josephine's shop.

She greeted him with a bright smile as he stepped through the door, then gave Redmane a lesser, but still friendly, smile. To Max, she said, "Why, King Max. Do you need a chaperone to visit me these days? Are you afraid I'd take advantage of you right here in my shop?"

Max actually blushed. "Well I wasn't, but now I might be, just a little." He replied as he approached the counter. As before, she stepped up onto the counter and grabbed Max's face to pull him in for a kiss. When she let him go, she winked at Redmane, who was laughing aloud.

"Are you prepared for the dinner you promised me?" She purred at him.

"Actually, yes I am." He pulled out a kabob and offered it to her with a smile. When he saw the hurt look on her face, he put it away. "I was just teasing. We have a really good chef now, and actual furniture, and everything. When would you like to honor me with your presence, m'lady?"

"Oooh! Sweet-talking me? I like it." She grinned. "How about three days from now? A girl needs a little time to prepare."

Max heard Redmane, who had drifted away to inspect some books, mumble to himself. "I be thinkin Max might need a lil preparin' too." Unfortunately, gnomes could hear nearly as well as elves. Josephine giggled, causing Max to blush again.

"While you're here, can I interest you in some of my wares?" She leaned over to poke Max in the belly, exposing some cleavage in the process. Redmane snorted.

"Yes please." Max grinned at her, letting her take it any way she wanted.

Half an hour later, after they exited the store to head to Firebelly's, Redmane grinned up at Max. "Oh, I like her. She'll keep ye on yer toes."

"She had me so flustered, I don't even know what I paid for those spells." Max shook his head in resignation.

"More than ye could have, but not too much. She was more interested in pokin' at ye, and wantin ye to do some pokin at her, than takin' yer gold." He made a vaguely vulgar hand gesture.

"Oh hush!" Max thought the chamberlain was having way too much fun at his expense.

They were at Firebelly's, submitting another significant order, when they both got another notification.

The kingdom of Stormhaven is under attack!
Quest Accepted: Defend the temple!
An invading army has attacked your temple.
Gather your forces and defend your territory!
Reward: Variable
This is a mandatory quest, and cannot be declined.

Max was already running for the portal, Redmane doing his best to keep up. Max didn't wait, the old dwarf could take care of himself. When he got to the portal, it was already connected to another dwarven city, but the mage running it saw Max coming, and shut it down. Max growled, "Stormhaven is under attack" and the dwarf just nodded. Redmane caught up as the portal opened, and both of them ran through. The moment it was closed, Max turned around and opened the portal to the temple while Redmane began shouting orders. The quest was shared around to the citizens, and they began mustering. There was no sign of anyone on the temple side of the portal.

Max didn't wait. Speaking calmly into party chat, he called his group together. "Portal. Now." It turned out not to be necessary, as Dylan, Smitty, and Nessa were already jogging into the courtyard. Dalia emerged a moment later from the direction of the alchemy lab, Picklet running beside her. They passed General Lightfoot, who had taken over from Redmane and was commanding the troops that were gathered. Blake came running through the gate from the city side, and Smitty grinned at him. "Your robe is on backwards. What, or who, were you up to?"

Blake just winked at him and followed Max through the portal.

The portal room at the heart of the temple was empty, no Glitterspindle or any of his so-called acolytes. Max's elven ears picked up the sound of shouting, and they activated the door that led them outside. As soon as they were all out, Smitty closed the door behind them. When one looked from the outside, all you could see was the pyramid, no sign of the door.

Max followed his ears out to the wide paved area behind the main temple building. There he found thirty or so dwarves formed up in a small square, shields locked. Glitterspindle and four gnomes stood inside the formation, the mechamage riding his spider construct, both its weapons turrets out and taking aim. The gnomes with him carried small crossbows. At their feet lay two dwarves and a gnome, all of whom looked dead.

"Stupid orcs! I'll blast you all into oblivion!" Glitterspindle was screaming, his glass brain pan crackling with angry red lightning, his eyes glowing.

Despite the mechamage's words, it wasn't orcs that were attacking the dwarven formation. The enemy was well back from the shield wall, firing crossbow bolts and casting spells of lightning, fire, and a spell Max hadn't seen before that ripped up sections of the paving stone and flung it in chunks at the dwarves.

It was gnomes.

Max could see maybe a hundred of them, mostly hiding in the dense shrubbery that surrounded the temple's paved area. They were dressed in an odd assortment of armor that was so laden with gears and spikes and misplaced steel plates that it looked ridiculous.

"Don't worry, Mechamage! We're here to save you from these brutes!" A gnome riding a mechanical cat shouted before casting a lightning spell at the dwarves, whose shields absorbed the magic.

Max walked up behind the dwarven formation and held his arms out wide, Storm Reaver in his right hand, his massive two-handed axe in the left. Tilting his head back, he took a deep breath and roared at the gnomes. The sounds caused the little fellas to pause and cringe a bit, and even a few of the dwarves twitched in surprise and turned their heads.

Having everyone's attention, Max bared his fangs at the gnome on the cat, their presumed leader. "Why have you attacked my temple?

"It's our temple! And he's our mechamage!" the feisty gnome shouted back, raising a fist and shaking it at Max. "You stole them both, and are holding a gnome hostage! You'll pay for that insult!" The gnome cast another bolt of electricity, this time at Max, who was an easy target standing tall above the shield wall.

Max just stood there and let the spell hit him. The bolt struck square in his chest, spreading across his armor and stinging quite a bit. It took about two hundred points off his health bar, and locked up his muscles for a few seconds. When he could move again, he shouted, "We are holding no one hostage. Glitterspindle agreed to become one of my citizens, and I claimed this temple as part of my kingdom. A kingdom allied with the dwarven nations on this continent. A kingdom which you have invaded, and whose king you just tried to murder!"

The moment he was done speaking, he focused on the gnome leader's cat mount and shouted, "*Boom!*" A second later the cat exploded, shredding the offending gnome and several others nearby. The gnome leader's corpse flew into the air, landing with a messy wet splat about halfway to the dwarven formation.

"Who's next?" Max roared, stalking forward around the shield square. Smitty, Dalia, Picklet, and Blake followed behind, Nessa having disappeared shortly after they arrived. Dylan moved far to one side and summoned Princess, whose roar froze about half the gnome force in fear. Taking advantage of that situation, Max shouted, "Princess is hungry! Who wants to be lizard lunch?"

Several crossbows fired, and half a dozen bolts peppered Max, the impacts surprisingly hard for such tiny weapons. Two penetrated his chest armor, one in his gut, the other his shoulder. Another hit his forehead, tearing a nasty gash in his skin, but not penetrating his skull. Blood began to run down his face. One took him in the left arm, the one holding the axe, and the others struck his right leg. At least the same number had missed him altogether, one striking Dalia behind him, another hitting Blake, who cussed loud and long.

Max felt heals from Dalia, but didn't bother removing the bolts. Instead he roared again and charged forward, casting *Zap!* into a dense section of gnomes, who all went down twitching and smoking inside their armor. He cast *Boom!* on another gnome with particularly ornate armor, which turned into shrapnel two seconds later and mowed down a dozen nearby gnomes.

Behind Max, the dwarves roared along with him, and broke formation, charging forward behind their shields.

Smitty started firing arrows, which blasted completely through any of the little gnomes they hit. Blake, angry over being shot, called down *Flame Strike* again and again, frying two or three gnomes with each hit.

There was a series of sickening crunches when the dwarves activated some sort of shield rush ability, shooting past Max and impacting the gnomes, whose bodies crunched inside their armor. Gnomes screamed in pain as the dwarves hacked or smashed them into oblivion.

Max halted, lowering his weapons. Despite their actions, he felt bad hurting the little gnomes. Picklet had no such issue, charging past Max and removing the head of a crossbow wielding gnome who had just fired at him.

The little bastards had guts, Max had to give them that. Despite seeing their comrades massacred, not one of them ran. They held their ground and fought until they were cut down, or fried by Blake. A few more dwarves fell to lucky crossbow shots or a spell here and there, but Dalia and Max healed them instantly.

When Nessa emerged between the final two standing gnomes and eviscerated one of them, Max shouted, "Nessa! Hold!" She paused with one of her daggers to the last gnome's throat, looking curiously at Max. "I want to speak to one of them. I think he's the last one alive."

Nodding, she used her free hand to disarm the very frightened gnome while keeping the blade to his neck. She easily manhandled the three foot tall warrior, pushing him toward Max, who was yanking tiny crossbow bolts out of his flesh one at a time, growling with each pull.

"What's your name, gnome?" He bared his teeth, thinking about biting the gnome in the face, his *Intimidation* ability causing the little guy to wet himself.

"B-Bert. Bertlegard." the gnome stammered, trying to take a step back, but bumping into Nessa's legs. He looked nervously left and right as Dylan, Smitty, Picklet, and a few dozen angry dwarves closed in around him. "Don't kill me."

"Where are you from, Bert? Who sent you here?"

"We… we came from the capital. The gnome capital, Steamwhistle Gorge. I… don't know who sent us! We just followed our section leader, Tinripper!" he looked around for a moment, then pointed to the wet blob that had been the cat rider. "He said you had taken the great Mechamage Glitterspindle prisoner, and we were to rescue him and retake the temple of our ancestors." The gnome sniffed, clearly doing his best not to cry.

Max waved his hand at the gathered warriors. "Relax. Step back a bit. He's no threat to anyone at the moment." The dwarves did as he ordered, moving back several steps and stowing their shields and weapons. Several went to see to their dead, while others went to loot the gnome corpses.

As soon as the ring of dwarves broke up, Glitterspindle came charging in, still aboard his spider bot. "Stupid little orc! Why did you attack? You killed one of

527

my acolytes, and a couple of other stupid orcs!" He looked back at the dead dwarves and gnome.

The gnome warrior, seeing Glitterspindle, dropped to one knee and bowed his head. "We came to rescue you, great Mechamage! You are a legend among our people! When we heard you still lived, and were being held prisoner…"

"Prisoner? Hah! None could hold me if I didn't allow it! This big stupid orc is my friend!" Glitterspindle's shoulder weapons both focused on the kneeling gnome and fired, killing him instantly.

"No!" Max shouted, but it was already done. "Shit. Why did you do that?"

Glitterspindle turned to look up at him. "They killed one of my minions. Now I will have to begin training another one. Big waste of my time! He deserved it!"

Shaking his head, Max said, "He was an unarmed prisoner, Glitterspindle. We don't kill prisoners once they've surrendered. At least, not without a trial. Am I understood?"

"Fine, big stupid orc." The little metal body shrugged its shoulders. "No more to kill, anyway." He turned away from Max toward the pile of bodies and watched, fascinated, as Dylan let Princess munch on several that had already been looted. He peeled their armor off first, then tossed the tiny bodies to the lizard, who caught them mid-air and gulped them down with just a crunch or two. One of the gnome acolytes lost his breakfast all over Smitty's boots.

"Oh, damn, man. Really? That's nasty. What the hell did you eat?" Smitty tried to wipe a boot on the gnome's robe, but missed as he quickly retreated. Blake hit Smitty's feet with a water spell, mostly washing away the nastiness. "Thanks, brother."

"Had no choice, self-preservation. I'm downwind of you." Blake winked at him.

Right then a gnome that Dylan had just tossed into the air woke up and screamed for a brief moment before Princess grabbed it and finished it off with a crunch. "Oh, shit." Dylan covered his face with his hands, "I thought he was dead." That was apparently the last of the gnomes, and they all received experience for completing the defense quest. It was enough to level up Max, and most of the others got a level or two.

"Shake it off, corporal." Max moved to put a hand on the ogre's shoulder. "Axe or teeth, he was dead either way. He went quickly." Dylan just nodded, looking at his feet. Max understood. Killing the little gnomes felt a bit like killing kids, something a soldier never wanted to do. He told himself they were fully grown adults of their race, and had killed some of his people first. It didn't help all that much.

"Nessa, Smitty, take a dozen dwarves and make sure there are no other gnomes lurking about out there. If you find any, capture them if possible. I have more questions." He shot Glitterspindle a look, then turned away

529

as Nessa morphed into her cat form and dashed off, nose to the ground. Smitty organized the dwarves and followed.

Not feeling much like talking to the insane metal gnome, Max walked back into the temple. He found the trigger for the door in the pyramid, and entered the control room. From there he took the elevator down and grabbed six more portal pedestals before heading back up. While he waited for the scouts to return, he sat on the floor with his back to a wall and pulled up his interface. It had been three levels since he assigned his points.

Not in the mood to spend a lot of time on it, he simply put four into *Wisdom* and four into *Intelligence*, the final point going into *Dexterity* in hopes that it would help with his smithing. His three levels meant three more automatic points in *Strength* and *Constitution* as well, bumping his health pool up to three thousand. He considered adding more to *Constitution* with his next few levels, but if he were truly going to fight from the back ranks more often, he probably didn't need it. One point with every level would keep him healthy enough. He'd also picked up significant attribute bumps from discovering a new spell, from Storm Reaver, and the bracers. The combination put both his *Wisdom* and *Intelligence* up over sixty! Which boosted his mana pool by more than fifty percent, up to sixteen hundred. And he'd picked up five points of *Luck* from Lisbane's blessing.

After some time spent reviewing his information, Max finalized his choices and leaned his head back against the wall, closing his eyes to rest while he waited.

Maximilian Storm	Health: 3,00/3,00
Race: Chimera; Level 23	Mana: 1,600/1,600
Battleborne, Sovereign	180,000/4,000,000
Endurance: 25 (35)	Intelligence: 42 (62)
Strength: 41	Wisdom: 42 (67)
Constitution: 48	Dexterity: 16 (17)
Agility: 24 (30)	Luck: 16 (28)

Chapter 27

Lagrass walked for nearly a week through the forest. On the second day he found a road, but was too frightened of being discovered to use it. So he walked parallel to it through the forest, heading roughly northeast. Anytime he heard horses or travelers on the road, he took cover and froze until they were well past him. On the fifth day, as he moved closer to the road just to make sure he hadn't lost it, he spotted a tall stone marker. Checking carefully in both directions, he got close to it. It was painted two different colors, one on each side as you approached from either direction. Clearly a boundary marker of some kind, Lagrass hoped it meant he'd entered a new kingdom. One where they wouldn't care if he was wanted somewhere else.

Sticking to the woods, he continued his slow trek through the forest. When it began to grow dark, he would either find a convenient cave or fir tree, or set up his tent and sleep in that. He never dared make a fire so close the road. Though he was far enough from it that he doubted anyone would see the light, he had no control over which way the smoke drifted.

As he walked, Lagrass spotted and harvested a ton of plants he identified through the knowledge the alchemist had given him. While he had no interest in alchemy, he hoped to be able to sell them in the next village.

Except the next village turned out to be a town. He was just beginning his seventh day since emerging from the bear den when he reached the crest of a hill and found himself staring down at a walled town placed at the intersection of two roads. There were gates at all four sides, with wagons, riders, and pedestrians moving in and out of them. Hundreds of buildings sat inside the walls, with a twin-towered keep of some sort set into the center. From that distance he couldn't make out any designs on the pennants mounted above the nearest gate. He'd have to ask around when he got down there, and as he descended he realized he'd never even asked the name of the kingdom he'd fled.

It took nearly until dark to enter the gate. By the time he walked down the hill, there was a line of carts and wagons waiting to get in. Guards were inspecting each one and charging the owners a tariff based on what they found. Lagrass saw that the guards were clearly overcharging, some of the coin they took going into their pockets before they rest went into a strongbox on a table by the gate. People grimaced, but paid the fees without protest.

When it came time for him to enter, a surly guard approached him. "State your name, and your business."

"My name is Lagrass, and I have no real business. Just traveling, and thought I'd stop here for a night or two, get some good meals in me."

"Not carrying any goods to sell or trade?" the guard looked at his storage belt with a raised eyebrow.

Not wanting to risk trouble, Lagrass produced one of the plants he'd picked. "I did gather a few herbs on my way here, was hoping to sell them to an alchemist, assuming you have one here?"

The guard snorted. "We have a half dozen, maybe more. And selling goods within the walls requires a vendor chit. That'll be three silver." The guard held out a hand, and Lagrass deposited the coins. The guard didn't even try to hide it when he slid one into a breast pocket and the other two into the coin box. "Be on yer way!"

Lagrass trudged through the gate, noting the heavy iron portcullis that loomed above him as he passed through. He'd seen no river close by from up on the hill, and the walls were surrounded by a half-mile wide open plain. He also noted that a perimeter street ran along the inside of the wall, leaving a sheer twenty foot climb for anyone attempting to get over it. If he found himself having to escape this place, he was going to need to do it before they could lock down the gates, or he'd never make it out alive.

Following the road into the town proper, he quickly found a tavern not three blocks in. Stepping inside, he looked around the common room. It was about half full of diners and drinkers, with a bard singing softly on a raised stage in one corner. The place looked clean enough, so he took a seat where he could see the door but wasn't facing it, and ordered a meal and a drink. For a few hours he sat and observed the customers who came and went. There must have been a shift change, because the guards he'd seen at the gate came in and got rowdy, buying drinks for everyone with their graft from the so-called tariffs. He saw the one who'd spoken to him take note of his presence, then turn his back and ignored Lagrass for the balance of his time there. Tipping the waitress ten coppers, he got up and walked outside. Moving deeper into the town, he took a few side streets at random, exploring.

When he ran across a much quieter tavern with three stories, he stepped inside. A quick inquiry to the bartender, and an innkeeper came over to rent him a room. The place was much nicer than the one he'd stayed at in Hunter's Reach, but surprisingly, the rate was nearly the same. Still one silver per night, but it only included one meal, and laundry was extra. Lagrass figured it was due to the level of competition in town, versus the village having just the one inn. He paid for three nights, and retired to his room, where he had the first comfortable night's sleep since he fled the village.

The following morning he ate his complimentary breakfast, a delicious meal of fried eggs on thick toast, bacon, a fruit very similar to strawberries mixed with cream, and dark ale so thick he could have floated one of the strawberries in it without it sinking at all.

On his way out of the inn, he asked the waitress where he might find an alchemist. She gave him quick directions that involved street names he didn't know, but he followed the general direction she had pointed, and found it in less than thirty minutes. A middle-aged man was just unlocking the front door as Lagrass approached. "Good morning." He smiled at his first potential customer of the day.

"Good morning!" Lagrass turned on the charm. "I was wondering if you might be interested in having someone gather herbs for you? I've acquired a bit of knowledge of herbs and how to harvest them over the years…" He didn't offer to sell what he had right away, hoping to instead gain a quest that would earn him some experience.

"I'm always looking for a good supplier." The alchemist nodded. "But I warn you, I won't accept damaged or improperly harvested goods. Come inside and let's see what you know." Once inside the shop, the alchemist set a book on his counter and opened it. "Flip through here, and show me which herbs and plants you recognize."

Lagrass stepped up and leaned over the book, surprised to find that he knew most of the plants in the drawings on sight, in addition to at least one recipe they might be used for. In the case of the more common plants, several recipes.

Not wanting to actually have to go out and pick plants, he pretended to be ignorant of all but those he had in his inventory. He'd picked dozens of plants, but only five of them did he see in any real quantity. He pointed out those five, and looked hopefully up at the alchemist.

"This first flower here, angel's wort, how do you pick it?"

"Oh no, sir. You don't pick it. You gently remove the dirt around it in a circular motion until the roots are exposed, then slide your hand underneath and lift it free of the earth."

"And this one? Dibbleberries?"

"Well, those you do pick. But only when they're the exact color you see here. Any lighter or darker, and they're all but useless. The berries on each bush ripen at different times, so that one doesn't strip the entire bush of its fruit in one visit." He indicated his storage belt. "I do have the storage space to keep them fresh until I return."

"Alright, fair enough. You seem to know these few, at least. And they're useful ingredients. I'll tell you what, you get me two pounds of the berries, a dozen angel's wort..." By the time Lagrass left the shop five minutes later he had five quests to deliver quantities of the items he already had in his inventory. He was a bit short on the berries, but rather than go gather more, he'd simply purchase what he needed from another alchemist. The money he would earn from the quests wasn't his main concern. He needed experience to level up as quickly as possible.

He spent some time in a nearby market square, where he found a leather goods vendor that showed him a leather vest with short sleeves, a backup set of comfortable boots, and leather pants with two pockets on each leg, all for a single gold coin. The price had started at one and half, but Lagrass had charmed the merchant into a discount. As soon as he paid and received the goods, he got a notification that his *Barter* skill had increased by one.

A hungry week in the woods with nothing but jerky to eat had taught him an important lesson. He immediately purchased some cuts of meat from a butcher, some seasonings from a street vendor, and filled an inventory slot with this world's version of oranges. They smelled so good that he stood right there at the farmer's cart and ate one. It was juicy and sweet and slightly tangy, better than any orange he'd had on Earth.

After asking the farmer for directions to another alchemist, Lagrass went to that shop and purchased the berries he needed. He also sold all the plants and herbs he didn't need for the other alchemist's quest for a quite satisfactory two gold and five silver.

He decided as he walked back to his inn that the town was too big for him to try and take over. He'd stay for a few days, maybe a week, fatten himself up a bit, get some better supplies, see about taking on a few quests, then maybe hitch a ride to a village more his size. He might even buy himself a horse with the looted gold he had accumulated, though he'd never ridden one in his old life.

A scuffle in an alley caught his attention as he passed by. Two men had cornered a young woman, one of them with a hand over her mouth to keep her quiet, and they clearly had bad intentions. Even as Lagrass stepped closer, one of them ripped her dress at the shoulder. Drawing his hunting knife, he moved in quickly and stabbed the larger of the two men in the back. He angled the knife so that it slide between his ribs, scraping bone on the way in, and punctured a lung. Quickly ripping it back out, he stabbed again, lower this time, right through the man's kidney.

His victim let out a gasp and lost his grip on the girl, his chest heaving as he drew in a breath to scream. Lagrass let him go, moving aside and grabbing the other man from behind. He threw his weight backward, lifting the man off his feet as he fell, slamming him headfirst onto the cobblestones. He'd been hoping the move would break the man's neck, but no such luck. It did stun him long enough for two things to happen. The girl, her mouth now uncovered, screamed. And Lagrass had time to get to his feet and stomp on the man's neck, hearing it snap. He repeated the motion once more as people come running from the street.

Stowing his knife, he backed away from the girl and raised his hands to calm her. Placing his back against the alley's opposite wall, as far from her as he could get, he asked, "Are you alright, Miss? It looked like you were in pretty serious trouble there." He flashed her his most sympathetic smile, keeping his hands where she could see them.

Several people ran up, seeing the girl's tattered dress and the blood, then Lagrass standing there with bloodstains on his hands. Two men made to grab him, and he didn't resist, as he saw a squad of guards running toward them. The last thing he needed was this town's guards after him as well.

Just as the two man grabbed ahold of his arms, the guard with the most stripes on his arm shouted, "What's going on here!"

The girl, starting to cry now that she realized she was safe, pointed to the two men on the ground. "These two men, they grabbed me and pulled me in here. That one said horrible things to me, that they were going to sell me after they tested my wares, and he ripped my dress." She paused, a sob overtaking her as she remembered.

The guard took her hand and patted it. "Take your time, miss."

She nodded and took a few deep breaths. "The next thing I knew, that man there had pulled them off of me. There's blood all over him, I... I think he killed them."

"I did kill them." Lagrass stepped forward, the two men holding him having relaxed. "They were hurting the young lady."

The guard that Lagrass assumed was a sergeant took a long look at the wounds on the first man. "You stabbed this one in the back."

"There were two of them, only one of me, and the only weapon I have is my knife. I needed to be sure one was down before I took on the other."

"Why didn't you call for the guards?" One of his temporary captors asked, giving Lagrass a suspicious look.

"Again, two of them, one of me, and things with the girl were getting ugly fast. Should I have shouted and risked them running off with her?"

The man shook his head, and mouthed a quiet "Nooo..."

"Alright, you'll come with us. The magistrate will decide whether this was justified." He looked from Lagrass to the girl. "I'm sorry miss, but you'll need to come along as well, to bear witness. Can I send one of my men to your home to notify your family?" He produced a cloak from his inventory and placed it over her shoulders. She immediately gathered it in front of herself to cover her torn dress.

As they marched out of the alley and up the street, the sergeant looked Lagrass up and down for a moment. "I don't think you have to worry. From the girl's testimony, you acted to save her. You might have been a little… enthusiastic, but it was two against one. And those two are known to us. There might even be a reward on their heads. I'll check for you when we get to the courthouse."

For the first time, Lagrass started to panic. If the courthouse was where they kept the information on fugitives, like wanted posters at a police station back home, would there be a poster or a notice on him? He looked around carefully, pretending a casual interest in the shops as he considered possible escape routes. "This is my first time in this town. It's quite lovely." he chatted to the sergeant. His hands were unbound, a courtesy for saving the girl and cooperating. Up ahead there was a dark alley. He could knock over the sergeant and make a run for it, maybe outrun the guards and make his way to the…

He stopped right there. He was far from the gates, and one whistle blast from the guards would ensure those gates would be closed long before he got there. There was no way he could escape and evade the guards until the gates reopened in the morning. No, he would have to take his chances at the courthouse.

It took twenty minutes or so to reach their destination. A massive stone building two stories tall and a full block wide. Lagrass noticed a row of small windows at ground level, all of them with bars on them. "Am I going to have to wait long for my trial?" He asked, pointing at the windows. "I don't enjoy small dark places." He thought back to the bear den, and gave an honest shudder.

"There be a magistrate on duty that'll hear the basic facts o' the case. If he decides there's cause to charge you, you'll be held for a day or two while evidence is gathered and reports prepared. You'll be provided a barrister to represent you if you go to trial."

Just as they climbed the steps to the massive double front doors, a wagon arrived with the girl's family. Her parents rushed to gather her into a hug, her mother already crying, which caused the girl to begin crying again.

The guards herded them all into a waiting area, where they spent less than ten minutes before being escorted into a courtroom. It was empty except for the magistrate who sat at a wide table in the front of the room. As they filed in, Lagrass was told to take a seat in the front row of pews. The sergeant sat next to him and mumbled. "Behave yourself. Speak when spoken to. Answer truthfully. The magistrates can detect lies."

"Thank you." Lagrass whispered back even as his mind screamed "Oh, shit!"

The magistrate banged a round stone on a flat stone pad, and waited impatiently for everyone to take their seats and get quiet. "Sergeant, what is the case you bring me?"

"This man killed two men who were attacking this young lady in an alley near the fourth market square, magistrate. We were patrolling the street a block or so away when we heard some shouting. Advancing at a run, we encountered this man, whose name is Lagrass, standing over the two dead men with blood on his hands. Upon further investigation, I learned that he acted to save the young lady. He has admitted to killing the two men, both of whom I must inform the magistrate are wanted by the guards for several crimes against the crown. He has not resisted arrest, and has cooperated fully."

The magistrate listened intently to the report, then nodded once. Turning toward the girl, he said, "Young lady, would you tell us in your own words what happened?"

She stood up nervously, the cloak falling away to reveal her torn and dirty dress. Tears streamed down her face as she related what happened. The magistrates face softened as he listened, and gently nudged her regarding a few details. Watching his face, Lagrass would have bet all the gold in his bag that the man had daughters.

The magistrate thanked her after asking a few questions, took note of her name and address, and allowed her parents to take her home. Turning to Lagrass, he said, "Let's hear your version."

"I was walking back to my inn after doing some shopping, and I heard a scuffle in the alley. When I walked closer, I saw two man roughing up the young lady. One of them had a hand over her mouth to keep her from screaming, and was saying... unseemly things to her. The other was pawing at her, and even as I drew close, he ripped her dress." He paused and took a deep breath, then let it out in a sigh as he shook his head. "I did the only thing I could, magistrate. I ran up behind them and stabbed the first man, taking him out of the fight so that I could deal with the second. I'm not a hero, and I didn't like my odds, but I couldn't allow them to hurt her."

"And you didn't simply alert the guards because..."

"As I told the sergeant here, it didn't look like she had much time. Had I given them warning, they might have dealt with me and absconded down the alley with her before the guards ever arrived. I'm afraid I didn't do a whole lot of thinking, sir. I acted in the best way I know how."

"How did you deal with the second man?"

"I broke his neck after we grappled a bit." Lagrass did his best to look innocent. "At the time I wasn't sure that the first man was down for good, and feared he would attack me from behind. I couldn't see him, or hear anything over the young lady's screams. So I did what I had to do."

"Sergeant, does this fit with what you observed at the scene?"

"It does, magistrate. This man's story coincides with the girl's, both at the time, and here in your courtroom. I believe he acted in good faith, and did the town a service in the process. I recommend he be freed without charges, and that he be paid the rewards posted for the dead men."

The magistrate stared at Lagrass for half a minute. Finally, he raised the stone ball in one hand. "I agree with your recommendations, sergeant. Mister Lagrass is cleared of all charges, and is hereby awarded the aforementioned reward monies, with the crown's thanks." The ball slammed down, and the case was over.

Relieved, but still dreading a potential wanted poster incident, Lagrass followed the sergeant out to the main lobby, then down another hall. He was tempted to just tell him to forget the reward, but thought it might seem suspicious. Especially since he didn't know how large it might be. Suspicion was the last thing he wanted to arouse right then.

Down the hall they entered a small room with a single desk. The sergeant told the clerk who Lagrass had killed, confirmed that the magistrate had approved the rewards to be paid, then signed half a dozen papers. The clerk produced a sack of coins, and gave Lagrass a paper he couldn't read to sign. He scribbled his name, was handed the bag, and escorted out.

When they reached the main exit doors, the sergeant paused. "I noticed you didn't read the receipt before you signed it. Can you read?" When Lagrass shook his head, the sergeant signed. "It said you were paid ten gold for one, twenty for the other."

"Wow! Thirty gold?" Lagrass made his eyes go wide and stared at the sergeant in false wonder. "I've never had ten gold to my name, let alone thirty!"

"Yes, well, don't go around advertising it." The sergeant looked over his shoulder. "There are those about who would relieve you of it, as you've already seen today."

Lagrass pulled five gold coins from the bag and offered them to the sergeant. "Please, take this, as my thanks. For assisting me with the magistrate. You didn't have to make those recommendations."

The sergeant refused the coin, pushing it back toward him. "I appreciate the gesture, but I was just doing my job. And we're not allowed to accept gifts..." He paused and looked around before continuing more quietly. "Especially here in a public building."

"Ah, of course. I was just going to return to my inn, the Golden Orchid. Should I happen to see you there, I'd be happy to buy you a drink or three to express my gratitude." He put the coins into the bag, then the bag into his inventory. The sergeant gave him a wink and departed, the rest of his squad waiting for him outside.

Wanting to get out of the limelight as quickly as possible, Lagrass exited the building and walked down the very center of each street, following his map back the way he had come with the guards until he reached his inn.

Returning to his room, he sat on the bed and just breathed long, slow breaths for a while. Maybe staying in the town wasn't such a good idea.

He took some time to review his notifications, and assigned all his attribute points to *Strength* and *Endurance*. The guards in this town were even higher level than in the starter city, and he wasn't going to get caught out of shape if he had to fight or run again.

After an hour or so of trying to calm himself, he went downstairs to the common room. He ordered a meal of meat stew and warm rolls, and a bottle of his favorite spirits. He had just finished eating when the sergeant appeared. Waving at the barkeep, he moved to sit opposite Lagrass, who immediately offered to buy the man a meal. He called the waitress over and the sergeant ordered, and Lagrass asked her to bring an extra glass. The moment it arrived, he poured some of the alcohol. "I'm told this is not very good compared to some others, but I find I quite like it. We can get you something else, if you prefer." As he spoke, he placed five gold coins on the table near the sergeant's hand. A second later, it was gone.

"This will do just fine. I kind of enjoy it myself." He took up the glass and downed the shot in one gulp, pounding his chest as it burned its way through him. Max poured him another, and this time he only sipped at it.

"Thank you again, sergeant. I believe without your help I might have visited those small dark cells."

"As I said, just doing my job." The sergeant replied as his food arrived. The table was mostly quiet for the next several minutes as he wolfed down his own bowl of stew. When he was done, he wiped his face with a napkin, and got up. "Gotta get back to work, they only give us twenty minutes to eat. Good luck to you, Lagrass." He nodded his head and departed.

Not wanting to be cooped up in his room alone with his thoughts, Lagrass paid for the meals and the drinks, stowed the remainder of the bottle in his inventory, and headed out of the inn.

He'd only gone two blocks when he spotted a pair of guards following him. Two blocks later, he noticed another pair up ahead staring at him. Not at all comfortable with this development, he turned onto a side street and walked into the first shop door he saw.

It turned out to be bookstore. Embarassed, he turned to leave, but a female voice called out to him. "What can I help you with, sir?"

Turning, he found a lovely young woman with long chestnut hair smiling at him. Blushing, he stammered. "I'm... I'm afraid I walked into the wrong shop. I don't know how to read."

Still smiling, she asked, "Would you like to learn? I have a primer here somewhere..." She turned her back to him for a moment, bending over to grab something from a low shelf. When she turned back, he tried his best to focus on her face. "Here it is. If you study this, it will teach you the basics of reading. After that, it's just a matter of practice."

He gave her a sincere smile, stepping forward. "Thank you so much. How much do I owe you?"

"Three silver." She replied, her eyes meeting his. "For the man who stepped into the wrong shop."

He gladly paid her, thanked her, and left the store. Two of the guards were waiting just outside, making him jump a bit in surprise when he noticed them.

"Mister Lagrass? I'm private Colin. The sergeant asked us to watch over you for a day or two. Them two you killed, they had friends, and we're to keep them from repaying you in kind."

Lagrass looked at the two guards with their serious expressions, then back to the street he'd been on before, where the other two were waiting.

"Uhm, thank you, private Colin. I appreciate the goodwill." He handed them each a gold coin, then gave Colin two more for their partners on the corner. He held up the newly purchased book. "I think I'll just return to the inn for the rest of the day. Got some studying to do."

"Probably safer that way. They'll not bother you inside the inn." The private nodded for him to proceed, and they followed him at about a half block distance. The other two, seeing him coming, faded into the crowded street.

Chapter 28

Max sat at a table in one of the stone buildings inside the outpost. Around the table with him were Redmane, Ironhand, Spellslinger, Enoch, the corporals, Dalia, and Nessa. They'd brought Ironhand to give him a tour, and the king had openly wept at seeing the place, then laughed when watching the golems move and react to instructions.

Now they were discussing the best way to move forward. There were a lot of unanswered questions, and challenges to be addressed.

"Redmane, Ironhand, the mages you've provided have worked wonders on the city above. In the last week they've finished construction on our entire perimeter wall, then gone back and widened and improved it so that we effectively have an elevated road with small fortified emplacements every five hundred paces or so."

Enoch grinned. "That ain't all. There be a dozen underground strongholds scattered about the city now. Each one with a water supply, and room fer three hundred souls to take shelter if needed. By the end o' next week, each one will have a hidden tunnel that all connect to a larger one that leads out o' the city."

"And yer dwarven steel gates will be ready about the same time." Ironhand added. "Me gift to a promising young king. There'll have to be a celebration when it's installed, so it do no' seem suspicious."

"I'm always up for a good party." Max smiled. "We'll be sure and have enough food and ale for the crowd."

"It might help ye to recruit more crafters n such, as well." Enoch suggested. "The more rumors o' this place get spread about, the easier it will be."

"The Greystones have been recruiting like their lives depend on it, which maybe they do, if they sunk their whole nest egg into this trade route." Max thought about it for a moment. "Might be better to ease off on our own recruiting a bit. As long as we have sufficient residents to keep this place running, feed everybody, provide at least a basic level of goods… it might be better to let them build up first. It'll make them happy, ease the tensions between us, and make our sector more attractive in the end."

"There be a great opportunity here." Redmane pulled out a large scroll and unrolled it across the table, using one of the heavy square silvers to hold down each corner. It turned out to be a map of the underground region, with Deepcrag at its center, and Dara Seans marked with a gold star to one side. The goblin settlement was shown too, with a red X over it. "Beyond the trade route, there be wilds around the settlements that ain't been explored in centuries. There could be mines out there, for example, that ye could claim and operate, or sell to a mining consortium."

Ironhand put his finger over the star. "And if we can figure out the rune magic, this place will become the center of a rebirth o' the dwarven race!"

Max shook his head. "Assuming we haven't pissed off the Runemaster's Guild, and they don't come through that portal over there and wipe us all out." He motioned over his shoulder in the direction of the portal Spellslinger had found. "At some point, we're going to need to activate that, and find out where it goes. It's better to stumble into a fight than to sit with our head in the sand and get ambushed when we're not expecting it. I'd rather fight on someone else's turf. We can always retreat back here and destroy the portal, if necessary."

"Don't ye even think it!" Spellslinger was on his feet, thumping the table with his fist. "Ye put one tiny scratch on one o' them runes, I'll carve out yer heart n feed it to Princess meself!"

"Easy, old goat." Ironhand placed a hand on the mage's shoulder. "Max meant no harm. It be a sound tactic, to retreat and cut off the enemy's access. We'd not do such a thing unless the need were desperate." He sighed. "Reclaiming the rune magic be vital to our people, but we'll accomplish nothin' if we're all dead."

"I agree." A voice from the doorway surprised them all. This was a secret meeting in a secret location, and guests were not expected. A moment later, Dalia gasped and practically fell out of her chair, kneeling.

"Lord Regin." She bowed her head, followed immediately by all the other dwarves, including Ironhand, Smitty, and Nessa. Dylan looked confused for a moment, but copied the others.

Max, knowing Regin detested such displays, still took a knee for the sake of the dwarves, and bowed his head. "Welcome, Regin, to our not-so-secret bat cave."

"Ha!" the god of crafting winked at Max. "Get up, all of ye! Take yer seats." He waved a hand and a gilded chair appeared at the end of the table opposite Max. He hopped up into the chair and smiled at the dwarves who hesitantly took their seats as ordered.

"I've only a few minutes, can't leave that little goblin thief alone for long, so stop yer nonsense and pay attention." He looked around the table, everyone seeming to calm as his gaze met theirs. "Max, ye have done well, lad. Growin' yer kingdom, protectin' yer people, provin' yerself in the eyes o' yer allies like Ironhand here, as well as the gods. But these be just the first steps in a long journey. Don't ye give up, or falter along the way. Many lives will depend on it."

Max felt a tingle as he absorbed the words. He wasn't at all sure that he liked it.

"Ironhand, ye support Max in his efforts, yer cousins, too. He'll bring ye the reward ye seek, in time." The dwarf king bowed his head almost to the point it would touch the table.

"Ye three other Battleborne, and the rest… ye be the bulwark, the eyes and ears, the healing hands, weapons, and wisdom, that'll help carry Max to his destiny. Yer loyalty be without question, and ye'll accomplish great things if ye watch each other's backs."

All three soldiers nodded at the divine dwarf, accepting his words as fact. Dalia, Redmane, Enoch and Spellslinger looked as if they'd prostrate themselves on the floor again, while Nessa remained stoic, as usual.

"Ye need to know that there still be Runemasters in the world, though they be greatly reduced from what they once were. They're no enemy to you, Max, and ye need not fear them. In fact, they could use yer help. Ye won't be the only ones seekin' their knowledge and power, and others have much less honorable intentions. The time has not yet come for ye to step through that portal, but it will, soon enough. Get stronger, gather allies, prepare yourselves as best ye can."

Regin nodded at Max, about to take his leave, when something caught his eye. "Ha!" He reached out and scooped up one of the square silver coins off a corner of the map. "Where'd ye find these?"

"Some in Deepcrag, some here." Max replied. "You know something about them?"

"I should…" Regin held up the coin and pointed at it. "That be me own face right there."

Max's eyes widened, as did those of the rest of the companions. *"That's you?"*

"Aye, from back when I first ascended. Fer a while, I ruled a kingdom like yerself and Ironhand, though one so vast it'd be hard fer ye to comprehend. It were a time of great prosperity, if I do say so meself. Crafters were honored, wars were rare, and me people were mostly content." He sighed. "When I ascended into the pantheon upon me death, some crafters created these tribute coins. Each one was meant to be a prayer, an offering of thanks brought to the temple, or payment for the priests to perform healing. They were never meant to be currency fer trade."

Regin scratched at his beard for a moment. "Someone who came here when this place were active must have discovered one o' me old temples n looted the coins… did ye find many?"

"Thousands." Max confirmed, and an idea struck him. "Regin, would you object if we revived the custom? You've been a tremendous influence in my life since I arrived here, and maybe this is a way I can thank you. We'll build you a temple here, and in each of my settlements, and distribute these coins as rewards for quest completions, acts of heroism or kindness… and the people can bring them to your temple as they did in the past. To ask for healing, or a blessing, or simply to say thank you."

Ironhand nodded. "Darkholm will have a new temple as well."

Regin stood, his back straight and his chest puffed out. "I'd be honored." His voice was rough, and Max thought his eyes looked a bit watery. With a flick of his thumb, he tossed the coin into the air. They all watched it fly down the length of the table, where Max caught it. When they looked back toward Regin, he was gone.

Sensing an opportunity that Max couldn't argue with, Ironhand grinned. "Max! I'll need a thousand o' them coins to distribute among me own people. And considerin' their purpose, and the fact that they feature the face o' Regin himself, I'll be payin ye twenty gold a piece." He held up a hand when Max started to argue. "Now, don't be tryin' to deny the good citizens of Darkholm the right to commune with one o' their gods! I'll hear no argument. You can spare a thousand o' them coins and still have plenty left fer yer own folk!"

Redmane laughed aloud, as did Enoch. "Let it go, Max. He's got ye this time." The chamberlain winked at Ironhand. "And twenty thousand gold would be a nice boost to our treasury."

Max sighed, and nodded once. It wasn't technically a handout, as the dwarves took their religion very seriously. And he was sure Ironhand would put the coins to good use. Plus the story of where the coins were found might motivate more settlers to join him. It was a win for everyone, and he only had to swallow his pride just a little.

"You have a deal." He shook hands with the dwarf king as a golden light surrounded them both.

Congratulations! Your Sovereign Class level has increased by +1!

By setting aside your pride and accepting an offer that significantly benefits the
citizens of two kingdoms, you have earned the next level in your Sovereign Class.
Morale boost! *The morale of your citizenry is boosted by 5%.*
Production boost! *Due to the morale increase, your citizens are 2% more productive.*

This includes crafters, farmers, miners, and citizen fertility.
Your Diplomacy skill has increased by +1!

Red appeared on the table, standing in the middle of the map and clapping her hands. "Well done, your Majesty." Her tone held almost no sarcasm at all."

Distracted, Max replied, "Thank you, Red. That means a lot coming from you." When her eyes widened, and she looked around the table, Max realized he'd spoken out loud. There were those at the table who didn't know about Red. He supposed it was time they did.

"Uh, Red, go ahead and become visible to everyone here. For those of you who haven't met her yet... this is my soul-bonded guide, Red..."

*****

Lagrass spent a few more days in the town, his escort of guards present in the background anytime he left the inn. It wasn't always the same guards, but there were always four of them, and they kept their distance. On the second day, as he unobtrusively observed their movements, it occurred to him that they weren't so much there for his protection. They were too far away to help if someone tried to stab him in the back, for example.

"I'm bait." The epiphany struck him. He couldn't help but chuckle to himself. The guards weren't kidding

557

about the dead men's friends. They were hoping the criminals might take a shot at revenge, or at stealing the reward money, and they could swoop in to make more arrests.

That realization, combined with his growing concern over being recognized and arrested for his various murders, motivated Lagrass to hit the road. He visited the alchemist to turn in his quest on the third day, that being a plausible amount of time for him to have gone out and gathered the items in the forest. That earned him enough experience to bring him up to level nine, almost to ten. Instead of gold, he accepted some healing and mana potions, and his first spell.

It was a simple light magic healing spell that, at level one, granted him fifty points of health over ten seconds. "This will help with all the little bumps and scrapes one gets while crawling around in the forest after herbs. Use the spell as often as you can to level it up." The shopkeeper had advised. "At level ten, it can heal for as many as a thousand points."

Lagrass tried casting it on himself, and a pleasantly warm tingle passed through his body. Motivated by how cool and useful the spell was, he asked where he might learn more. The alchemist told him that normally one would go to the Mages' Guild, but there wasn't a branch in town. There was an inscriptionist in town, but his scrolls and spellbooks cost more gold than Lagrass carried.

When the alchemist saw his look of disappointment, he asked, "What other spells do you know?"

Lagrass shrugged. "None. This was my first."

"Not even *Spark*?" the amazed man asked. "Every child is taught *Spark*, at least."

Lagrass saw another opportunity, and grabbed it. "I had no family, no one to teach me."

After thinking for a moment, the alchemist came out from behind his counter. "You seem like a good sort." He stepped over and locked the shop's front door. "I'll teach you *Spark*, and one other spell that might help you in your adventures. But you must tell no one." He stared expectantly.

"I'll never speak of it. And thank you." Lagrass put his hand over his heart. The alchemist placed a hand on his forehead, and a moment later Lagrass knew how to create fire out of thin air! Even better, he also knew how to cast *Mana Bolt*, which shot a magical arrow at a target, doing fifteen to twenty points of damage each.

"Just as with the healing spell, the more you practice, the more damage that one will do." The alchemist smiled at him, turning to unlock the door. "Now, off with you. Go practice. There are plenty of small woodland creatures just outside the wall to use as targets. And while you're out there, if you should happen to stumble across more ingredients…" He smiled as he renewed the quests that Lagrass had just turned in.

"Thank you, I will!" Lagrass practically bounded out of the shop. "Who's a badass magic casting squirrel killer? I am!" he chuckled to himself as he walked down the busy street.

He made his way to the nearest gate, noticing that his escort didn't follow him through, then out into the plains that stretched around the town's perimeter. It was mostly just tall grass, anything larger than a small shrub being dutifully hacked down by the guards to keep the kill zone free of cover.

That was okay with Lagrass, tall grass was where squirrels and bunnies romped. He stepped off the road and began to head toward the distant tree line, his left hand held up and ready to cast the spell. As he waded through the knee-high grass, he heard multiple rustlings to his left and right, but spotted nothing.

"This won't work. Too easy for them to hide." He moved a little faster, jogging to the tree line where the grass didn't grow as tall. There were clusters of brush here and there among the trees, but the ground was mostly clear. "Much better." He knew that hunters and snipers used tree stands, where they sat in an elevated position and waited for deer or other prey to stroll by. Not confident in his ability to sneak up on any woodland creatures, Lagrass decided to do the same.

He picked the nearest tree with a branch low enough for him to grab. With a leap, he pulled himself up onto the branch, then climbed two branches higher to a fork in the main trunk. Settling into that fork in reasonable comfort, he watched the ground below and waited.

It wasn't long before a black squirrel-like creature hopped into view. It stopped and sniffed a few times, its head tilting to one side as it sought out any threatening sounds. Lagrass watched as it dug at the base of a nearby tree, unearthing some moldy nuts and stuffing them into its mouth.

As soon as it was close enough to his own tree, he held out his hand and whispered, "Mana Bolt." He'd expected some recoil, but he felt nothing other than a slight tingle as a six-inch long blue projectile rushed silently from his hand. It blasted into the squirrel's side, knocking it over and leaving its body mostly ruined.

A quick check of his log told him that the bolt had done twelve points of damage, killing the unwary critter instantly.

For the next hour, Lagrass remained in the tree, firing at two more squirrels, then a large feral cat that came sniffing around at the squirrel corpses littering the ground. When he fired at the cat, it screamed in pain and leapt straight into the air, then quickly departed the area. Disappointed at the missed kill, but happy enough with is overall results, Lagrass climbed down from the tree. He quickly looted the squirrel corpses, getting just four pieces of squirrel meat total, and no hides. His spell had pretty badly mutilated the little bodies.

His spell was still level one as he walked back toward the town gates, but he figured he'd have more opportunities to use it on his journey to the next village.

Once again he planned to avoid the road and hike through the forest.

As he reached the gate, he spotted the same guard who had greeted him when he first entered the city. The man smiled and gave a half-hearted wave. "Lagrass, right? Herb vendor?"

"Heh. Lagrass, yes. But I'm no vendor. I just sold what I happened to gather on my way here."

The guard flashed a fake smile. "Well, now that you've left town and returned, your vendor token has expired. And since I assume you've been out gathering more weeds, you'll need another token. That'll be five silver." He held out a hand, the smile turning into a smirk.

"Five silver? But it was only three last time."

"Are you questioning one of the queen's guards?" The man growled at him, and a couple of other guards approached with hands on weapons. Lagrass, not wanting trouble, was reaching for the five silvers when the guard added, "Now it'll cost you five gold!"

"What?" Lagrass took a step back. "What are you talking about?"

"We heard what you did the other day, and about the reward you collected." One of the other guards commented. "It's time for you to share the wealth a bit. You heard him, five gold. Now."

"I'm not..." Lagrass trailed off. The last thing he wanted was attention from the guards, but he also could not allow himself to be robbed by every guard he came across. He thought quickly, and compromised. "I'll give you one gold. And I'll keep your little scam here to myself." He flashed his most cocksure smile at the guards.

"Ah, you shouldn't have said that." The third guard shook his head.

"Aye, that was a mistake. You should have just paid up." The first guard took a step closer to Lagrass, leaning in so that their noses nearly touched. "You just threatened a member of the guard." He growled. Before Lagrass even realized what was happening, the guard's baton struck him hard in the solar plexus, bending him over and taking his breath away.

"You won't be needing this." A guard behind him removed his storage belt. "Not where you're going."

Realizing what was about to happen, Lagrass put his hand over his mouth and pretended he was about to puke. The guards backed away as he retched, quickly transferring everything left in his personal storage into the inventory ring. Then, still bent over, he used his teeth to pull the ring from his finger and swallow it. *Let them try and steal that*! He thought to himself. He coughed a few times then straightened up.

"Where I'm going?" He didn't try to negotiate with the guards. He knew men like them. Hell, he *was* like them. They would rob him blind and likely try to kill him. He was wondering if he could outrun them as far as the woods, when the first guard answered.

"Congratulations! You've just joined the queen's army! Trash like you goes straight to the front lines as fodder. Enjoy what little time you've got left!"

Lagrass felt a blow to the back of his head, and he went down. All three guards kicked at him, dropping his health bar quickly below half. A final kick to his face, and everything went black.

*****

Max sat in his study with Redmane and Spellslinger, a disappointed look on his face. He stared at the crystal sitting on the desk in front of him.

"We be sorry, Max. No one that we can find has any idea how to remove the lich without destroying the crystal." the old mage's shoulder's slumped in defeat.

"We even asked the Archmagus." Redmane added. "There be no magic that he knows of that can pull a lich from his crystal."

Max blinked a few times, looking at his chamberlain. "What did you just say?"

"There be no magic-" Redmane stopped talking when Max began to laugh.

"Are you okay, Max?" Spellslinger leaned forward, concerned.

"I am. I am, indeed." Max shook his head. "All this time, all this effort to find some spell... it can't be that simple."

"What're ye talkin about, Max?" Spellslinger sensed the chimera was up to something, and began to grin himself.

"I need a crystal. One the lich would consider acceptable to transfer his soul."

Spellslinger produced a blocky crystal with jagged edges, about eight inches long. "It ain't pretty, but it holds a good amount o' mana."

"Are you sure you're willing to part with it?" Max asked. "You won't get it back."

"Aye, if it'll help ye clear the stone, it be worth the price."

"I don't understand, Max." Redmane looked from one of them to the other. "We just tell'd ye that there be no magic strong enough ta force the lich to transfer."

"Oh, yes there is. It's an old fashioned kind of magic! I'll show you." Max set the new crystal on the desk next to the heart of the mountain. He invited both dwarves to his party, then used chat to speak with them. *"Master Redmane, you're going to need your hammer..."*

A minute or so later, Max had removed the needed items from his inventory and set them on the desk as well. With a nod to the dwarves, he said through party chat, *"Watch this."*

Placing his hand on the sickly glowing heart of the mountain, Max spoke aloud. "I know you can hear me, lich. And you know what I want. So here's my offer.

Leave the heart of the mountain, transfer your soul into this new crystal. Do that, or I'll take the heart of the mountain and drop it into the deepest, most remote magma pool I can find. You think five thousand years trapped in your crystal was a long time? How about eternity? The stone will sink deep into the earth, surrounded by molten magma, never to be found by unwary and foolish adventurers who might set you free. Are you ready to face eternity in your own company, lich?"

Keeping his hand on the crystal, Max heard a voice in his head. *"You wouldn't dare destroy the stone! Pathetic mortal."*

"Wouldn't I? If you won't leave it, the stone is no good to me. I can't complete my quest, and I certainly can't use it, or sell it. Why would I keep it around and risk you escaping? If I can't benefit from the stone in any way, then I'll take what pleasure I can from knowing how much you'll suffer, you sick bastard."

"You're bluffing." The lich's voice sounded a little less sure of itself.

"I'm really not. I'm going to give you ten seconds to vacate the heart of the mountain. If you haven't done so by the time I reach zero, well… Master Redmane what's the biggest, deepest volcano you can think of?"

"You'll just destroy the other crystal the moment I occupy it." The lich hedged.

"I give you my word that if you occupy that other crystal, I will not destroy it." Max replied. "I'll even sweeten the pot. There are four soul crystals sitting there, can you sense them? They are the souls of elite grey dwarf guards that previously defended King Agnor. I was planning on resurrecting them to use as my own guards, but if they have any use to you…" he let his voice trail off. After a few breaths, he continued. "Alright, here we go. Enough messing around. Ten… nine… eight… seven…"

"*Wait!*" The lich's voice sounded resigned. "*Place the crystal so that it touches my stone. The transfer will take a few minutes.*"

"Then let's begin. I'm anxious for this to be over and done with." Max moved the crystals together, and sat back. When the new crystal began to bleed some of the green glow from the heart of the mountain, he winked at the dwarves. All three watched in silence as the heart's glow dimmed, and the other crystal grew brighter. After maybe five minutes, the new crystal pulsed once, and Max put his hand on it.

"*It is done.*" The lich's voice held an unmistakable sneer.

"I don't think so, lich. My quest has not completed, and I can still see some of your filthy green glow in the heart stone. If you don't comply, I have no reason to keep my promise. Can you transfer all of yourself back into the heart stone before I crush the new crystal? Let's see. Master Redmane can I borrow your hammer?"

"*No! I will complete the process. I have your word you will not destroy my new crystal?*"

"You have my word." A green light flashed around him, acknowledging his promise.

"*One moment.*" The lich growled telepathically. Max watched carefully as the very last bit of green faded from the heart stone, and notifications flashed before his eyes. Waving them away, he lifted the heart of the mountain, and used *Examine.*

Cleansed Heart of the Mountain
Item Quality: Unique; Legendary
Quest Item

That was good enough for him. He pulled his hand from the lich's new phylactery, snatched up the four soul stones, and leaned back in his chair. He'd barely settled himself when Redmane's hammer smashed down on the glowing crystal, cracking it. A second blow widened the fractures, and a third merciless blow shook the entire desk as the crystal shattered.

Taking up his own hammer, Spellslinger assisted Redmane, the two of them smashing the pieces into smaller and smaller bits, until there was nothing but dust. When they were done, Max's desk was badly damaged, but the crystal dust was a dull grey, no green glow visible anywhere. To be sure, Spellslinger quickly took out a vial and poured some kind of viscous liquid onto the desktop, then cast *Spark.* "Sorry, Max. We'll get ye a new desk." He apologized as the desktop burned brightly, the crystal dust motes popping in the heat of the flames. When he thought it was all done, the mage waved a hand and the flames went out, leaving a burnt and bubbling desktop with a completely unharmed heart stone resting on it.

All of them leveled up, another clear sign of the lich's final demise.

The two dwarves laughed, congratulating each other. Redmane looked at Max. "Old fashioned magic, indeed!"

"I just appealed to his sense of self preservation. My words had the advantage of being absolutely true. If I couldn't save the heart, I would absolutely have dropped him into a magma pool."

"And ye didn't break yer promise with the gods that ya wouldn't harm him, cuz ye let us do it!" Spellslinger beamed at Max. "Ye just might be clever enough to become a decent mage, Max."

"And a decent king." Redmane added, his face gone serious. "Now ye need to restore the mountain."

"Just one more thing on the list…" Max sighed. When the two dwarves left the room to go celebrate, Max told them he'd catch up, taking a moment to go through his notifications.

__Quest Completed: Hard Hearted Part I (A)!__
You have successfully cleansed the Heart of the Mountain of the lich's soul!
__Reward: 1,000,000 exp; 500 gold; Access to quest Hard Hearted Part II!__
__Skill Level increase! Your Deception skill has increased by +1__

Quest Granted: Hard Hearted Part II! *Return the Heart*
of the Mountain
to its chamber in the... heart of the mountain. Protect the
stone for 24 hours
as it recharges and renews its bond with the mountain.
Reward: 5,000,000 experience; Legendary item;
mountain will recover its former glory.

Max stowed the cleansed heart stone in his inventory, leaned back in his chair, and started to put his feet up on the desk. Noting the still smoking surface, he changed his mind and moved to a chair by the fireplace.

Red appeared, standing atop his knee as he settled into the chair. "Ya did it!" she beamed up at him. "You can restore your mountain, make your kingdom even stronger."

Max rolled his eyes. "And how long will that take? Mountains take millions of years to form..."

"Aye, but this mountain remembers its former greatness. It'll take a few years, but not as long as ya think, Max. The mines will begin producing better, and new ones will emerge. The water that filters down through the stone will be cleaner, and sweeter. More beasties will roam the tunnels, getting bigger and more powerful. You'll see, soon enough."

She crossed her legs and sat on his knee, changing the subject. "And well done on tricking that lich! I can't believe the solution was so simple!"

"Yeah, sometimes simple is best." Max nodded. "We've been on quite a ride since we arrived here, haven't we?" He thought back as Red nodded. "I love this new world, and it's hard to imagine how we lived without magic back on Earth."

"Or without me!" Red stuck her tongue out at him, making him chuckle.

"Or without you, my wonderful, snarky, annoying guide. What was with that last notification, anyway? You couldn't come up with better phrasing?"

Red shrugged, blushing slightly. "I was in a hurry! Should I have said restore the heart of the mountain to its place at the very center of the-"

"HA!" Max interrupted her. "Gotcha! I knew it was you composing all those snarky notifications!"

Red opened her mouth, then shut it, crossing her arms as she got to her feet. "You great big pile of stupid! O'course it was me. Who else would it be?" She scowled at him.

Max chuckled and reached out a finger as if to poke her belly. The warning look she gave him could have turned him as crispy as his desk, so he withdrew the finger. "I'm just saying, some of those were a little unnecessary." He fake-grumped at her. "But I still love ya, Red."

She stomped her foot on his knee, still scowling up at him. "Shut it! You're ugly, probably smelly, and not very smart! What I did in my previous life to deserve bein' stuck with you, I'll never know!"

Max just grinned at her. "You love me too, and you know it. Now, how about we round up the others and break open a few bottles of Firebelly's to celebrate?"

*** End Book Two ***

Acknowledgements

Thanks as always to my family for their love and support. They are my alphas, my sounding board, and the ones who aren't afraid to tell me when something sucks! And a thank you to a brand new set of beta readers. Recent divisions in our nation, combined with insidious fake news on social media, have caused more than a few rents in long term friendships, and cost me a few friends and betas. I'm grateful for those who were willing to step in.

For semi-regular updates on books, art, and just stuff going on, check out my Greystone Guild fb https://www.facebook.com/greystone.guild.7 or my website www.davewillmarth.com where you can subscribe for an eventual newsletter.

And don't forget to follow my author page on Amazon! **That way you'll get a nice friendly email when new books are released**. You can also find links to my Greystone Chronicles, Shadow Sun, and Dark Elf books there! https://www.amazon.com/Dave-Willmarth/e/B076G12KCL

PLEASE TAKE A MOMENT TO LEAVE A REVIEW!

Reviews on Amazon and Goodreads are vitally important to indie authors like me. Amazon won't help market the books until they reach a certain level of reviews. So please, take a few seconds, click on that (fifth!) star and type a few words about how much you liked the book! I would appreciate it very much. I do read the reviews, and a few of my favorites have led to friendships and even character cameos!

You can find information on lots of LitRPG/GameLit books on Ramon Mejia's LitRPG Podcast here https://www.facebook.com/litrpgpodcast/. You can find his books here. https://www.amazon.com/R.A.-Mejia/e/B01MRTVW3O

There are a few more places where you can find me, and several other genre authors, hanging out. Here are my favorite LitRPG/GameLit community facebook groups. (If you have cookies, as always, keep them away from Daniel Schinhofen).

https://www.facebook.com/groups/940262549853662/

https://www.facebook.com/groups/LitRPG.books/

https://www.facebook.com/groups/541733016223492/

Made in the USA
Las Vegas, NV
08 June 2023

73127407R00333